The Demolition
of the Century

Also by Duncan Sarkies

Two Little Boys
Stray Thoughts and Nose Bleeds

The Demolition of the Century

Duncan Sarkies

JOHN MURRAY

First published in Great Britain in 2013 by John Murray (Publishers)
An Hachette UK Company

1

A CIP catalogue record for this title is available from the British Library

Trade Paperback ISBN 978-1-84854-110-8
Ebook ISBN 978-1-84854-538-0

Typeset in Plantin by Servis Filmsetting Ltd, Stockport, Cheshire

Printed and bound by CPI Group (UK) Ltd, Croydon, CR0 4YY

John Murray policy is to use papers that are natural, renewable and
recyclable products and made from wood grown in sustainable forests.
The logging and manufacturing processes are expected to conform to the
environmental regulations of the country of origin.

John Murray (Publishers)
338 Euston Road
London NW1 3BH

www.johnmurray.co.uk

I am so lucky
to have had you
as my guiding light.

(for Doug)

Tom

Wednesday

Restocking the miniature refrigerator

9.18 a.m.

I wake up to this buzz.

A low-pitched rumble that feels like it's shaking the inside of my head, like a dentist's drill . . .

And then there's this beeping sound.

A high-pitched beep that sounds like a seagull being strangled.

And then back to the low buzz – which is piercing through my skull.

Then back up to the high beeping sound.

Back to the buzzing.

Beeping.

Buzzing.

Beeping.

These aren't musical sounds.

Everything is black.

I quickly realize that this is because my eyes are still shut. With . . . this noise in my ears . . .

Where am I?

In a torture camp?

What the hell did I do last night?

I have been able to sleep in many situations. I have slept through thunder and lightning. I have slept to the sound of a screaming baby. I have slept through the sound of a child breaking a window. I used to be a good sleeper but as I approach the age of forty I am watching my sleep gradually disappear.

I open my eyes to find out where the god-awful sound is coming from, and it is like I have just mistakenly looked into the middle of the sun – my retinas must currently be as wide as a kite because I am completely blinded by the light coming from an open refrigerator.

It's a very small refrigerator. Knee-high to a grasshopper, as my mother would say. How could something so small make *so* much racket and give off *so* much light?

I shield my eyes from the refrigerator light beam, and I see inside . . . a lot of bottles of wine.

Most of the bottles are tipped over. Some have spilled on to the floor in front of the refrigerator. The bottles make a trail all the way to my bed. There are about sixteen open bottles – big bottles and small bottles – of various types of Chardonnay, Sav Blanc, Pinot Gris, Riesling . . .

And all of them are open. Every single one.

There are chocolate wrappers too. Someone must have eaten a lot of chocolate here last night. There's a plastic wrapper with a half-eaten giant biscuit in it. I suspect someone ate half of a giant biscuit last night. Just a hunch.

The floor is cold. And hard. I've got this pain in my neck because I must have slept in a . . .

a funny position, and I'm . . .

in a bathroom.

I have to stop falling asleep in bathrooms.

I'm lying on porcelain tiles, right at the border where the tiles meet a carpet that I recognize.

Geometric patterns really went out of fashion after the 1970s, but these days it's hard to find a carpet like that. But here at the Ascot, they've kept it the same.

Hold on . . . It's coming to me . . .

I remember the whole debacle of checking in. I have a fake ID card under the name William McGinty. Unfortunately the photo looks nothing like me. I adopted the name after the whole debacle with Fire Chief. The McGinty name enabled me to have another life. Maybe not the one I wanted, but better than the alternative.

6

At least that's what I was thinking at the time. I was wrong, of course.

I remember struggling with my key card – the magnetic strip on it is faulty, I'm sure of it – and, finally, getting in here . . .

And I remember feeling such a strange sense of accomplishment, and I remember going directly to the knee-high refrigerator, and I remember seeing all that booze and I remember thinking . . .

you know, maybe I shouldn't . . .

And I remember feeling pretty good about myself for roughly three-quarters of an hour, and then I remember thinking, one miniature bottle of wine won't hurt anyone, and then . . .

Well actually, my memory fades quite badly at this point, but I've got a few clues about what might have happened . . .

Uhhhh . . . Okay.

You know, my grandmother once said a wonderful thing to me. Four words. She said, 'Use <u>and</u>, not <u>but</u>.' In other words, you could say, 'Tom's a nice man, <u>but</u> he's an alcoholic.' But I prefer people to say, 'Tom's a nice man <u>and</u> he's an alcoholic.' See the difference?

My body really doesn't want to move, but my brain overrides it and I get up quickly, and I immediately feel this enormous surge of pain in my neck. Have I sprained it?

Unsurprisingly, I'm still in last night's clothes. I'm wearing my favourite suit. I'm a vision in brown. Once upon a time brown was the new black. My pants feel damp. I take them off and I can smell the stench of last night's wine . . .

Today is a very important day. This is not the ideal way to start today.

I look at the laminated menu of the refrigerator. It has all the prices of what I have drunk and eaten, itemized quite neatly.

Yes . . .

Yes, how very expensive.

Shockingly expensive. Get this – last night I drank a 130-dollar bottle of wine. I have to question the ethics of the management at this place. What kind of person would place a 130-dollar bottle of wine in a mini-bar fridge?

Everything is expensive here! The chocolate bars I ate are four dollars each. Four dollars! For a chocolate bar! It is not a very large chocolate bar. Ten pieces of chocolate, if you're lucky.

That's forty cents per piece of chocolate.

Extortion.

It's not enough to fleece you half a weekly wage per night. They have to rub salt in the wound by throwing temptation to lonely people in the middle of the night. I can't believe that last night I drank and ate EVERYTHING in the miniature refrigerator. EVERYTHING.

My night-self would have liked that, *aesthetically*. My night-self is always putting obstacles in front of my day-self. And my day-self is always fighting fires. It's not quite Jekyll and Hyde proportions, but it does make my life more complicated than it needs to be.

I'm looking around the room and I can't seem to find any of my other things. I travel light, and I managed to get it all in one suit-case. But that suitcase isn't here. I hunt through drawers and cupboards and I look under the bed (where I find a used condom. Had nothing to do with me, I swear).

What the hell did I do with my suitcase last night?

I must've had it with me. Unless I left it on the bus . . .

I go to the telephone and I dial zero, and I get the general enquiries desk down below. 'Excuse me, I'm from room number, uh . . .'

'834, Mr McGinty,' a female voice says.

'Yeah. I had a case, which is missing. It's an old Lethalite case—'

'Lethalite?' she says.

'It's a nice case. Dark green. Has a combination lock on the front. I have a lot of my stuff in it.'

'Just a second,' she says, and she puts down her phone. A few seconds later she's back with, 'There's nothing out back. I could talk to the porter.'

'I would appreciate that. Also, when do the maids clean the rooms?'

'Eleven a.m.'

I look at my digital alarm clock: 9.40.

'Okay. Thank you for your help.'

'Glad to be of service, Mr McGinty,' she says, and the phone clicks off.

I tell you. I have no affection for William McGinty. I want to be Tom again. I will be Tom again, once I've cleared up this mess.

I pull a pencil from my pocket and on the hotel pad I add up what I owe the good people at the Ascot Hotel.

Hmm . . .

Not good news . . .

But I can halve that cost if I act quickly. I look out my window and I see there is a new convenience store across the road. Outside the street is teeming with pedestrians. Everyone is busy and the hustle and bustle has an electricity that you just can't find in the country.

It's great to be back in The City. I'm looking forward to visiting my old haunts. I'm looking forward to seeing Codfish Bay again. And I'm really looking forward to seeing Frank.

I'm in the hallway of the Ascot with three large plastic bags full of wine and chocolate. The bottles clink together noisily, making it hard for me to be inconspicuous as I sneak past the cleaners. I arrive back at my door and I swipe my plastic key to get in, but it doesn't go. What is it with me and technology today? Maybe I'm carrying excess static electricity or something.

I swipe it again, and then I see, coming down the hallway, a vision of great beauty. She has red hair, a tight crimson blouse, stockings and swagger. I play it nonchalant and I try to swipe my card like a young Robert Mitchum would, but it won't work. I try it again and in my peripheral vision I see the redhead take out her swipe card and swipe. I swipe again, and I'm starting to get a bit hot under the collar when she emerges at my shoulder and says, 'You got the strip on the wrong side.'

'Huh?'

'The magnetic strip.'

So much for Robert Mitchum.

She opens my door for me, and I say, 'Thanks, neighbour.'

'You're welcome,' she says, and she looks down at my plastic bag full of wine bottles and chocolate bars.

'Restocking, huh?'

'Something like that.'

'Big night?'

'I've had bigger.'

'I bet you have,' she says.

Now she's within touching distance I see she's a little older than I first realized. Still, I can be open-minded. She swivels her hips and heads next door.

'I'm Tom,' I yell, a little too late. She stops by her door and looks my way.

'Linda,' she says.

Wow, I lost my poise for a moment there . . .

I might have to borrow a cup of sugar from her some time.

Refilling the refrigerator is a difficult procedure. There's a lot to fit in to a small space. Reminds me of packing the car for a family holiday with Deborah and Frank. I might've boxed Frank in a bit much at times. Deborah used to insist we take half the house on holiday with us – so I'm only partially to blame for that time I hit a pothole and Deborah's jewellery box fell on his head. He was just a baby too. Oh well, he survived.

I get a lot of pleasure in refilling the 130-dollar bottle of Mount Lincoln with the cheapest wine, called Le Château du Jour which was twelve dollars. Twelve dollars is expensive for cheap wine. I remember when cheap wine was less than five dollars. The economy marches on, huh?

I realize my fridge arrangement won't look like the original layout, but I figure I'm not going to get prosecuted for 'rearranging the wine'.

Well, 'mission accomplished', as the vicar said to the nun.

I sit up on my bed and light a cigarette. I open my wallet and pull out a very important receipt.

TAX INVOICE
Northcote Tavern & Grill

2 x Porterhouse T-Bone $17.50

4 x Frogman's Pilsner $13.60

$31.10

Please add 25 cents for cheques

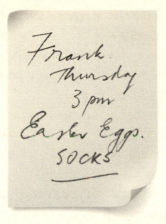

Frank.
Thursday
3 pm
Easter Eggs.
SOCKS

I wrote this message after my phone call with Deborah. My handwriting looks shaky. She often had that effect on me.

I left The City four years ago. Now I'm back, to get my old life back. Well, kind of. I'm here to pick up my son, Frank, for Easter weekend. I haven't been the best father. Things in my life got out of hand. I went a bit AWOL. I didn't do it lightly, but I regret doing it deeply.

I've been out of town in Northcote, which is about a hundred miles from here.

You know, when I got away, I thought I would straighten my head out. I had a 'farewell to booze' celebration and everything. In fact, I had several 'farewell to booze' celebrations. It didn't take long before I gave up giving up altogether.

I've always had one rule. I never phone Deborah when I'm drunk. I got into a habit of calling her at work, before I'd had my second drink. It's difficult to rekindle an old flame when she's in work mode. Still, I've portrayed myself to her as efficient, psychologically stable, on the wagon and caring. I've even tried not to be argumentative.

So what does she do? She phones me at the Northcote Tavern and Grill. It's a mean trick. She phones after ten o'clock, just to catch me at it. She's won that little victory, and I have to act as sober as possible, which is challenging, as I've been downing shots with old James Hollister, who seems to want to talk in great detail about a blockage in his intestine.

'Hello, Tom,' Deborah says.

'Hi, Debor—'

'Did you get my message, Tom?'

'Deborah, it's so lovely to hear your voice again—'

'Did you get it or not?'

Deborah has changed. Her voice sounds permanently hostile under a sassy veneer. I suspect she's doing better without me.

'I asked if you could look after Frank this Easter weekend.'

'Where are you going?'

'Can you do it? Yes or no?'

'Yes.'

'Got a pen and paper?'

I opened my wallet and grabbed my mini-golf pencil and a receipt.

'Pick him up Thursday after school. School gets out at three.'

'Jesus, Deborah. I know when school gets out—'

'What will you do with him, Tom?'

'Oh, we'll have a great weekend, Deborah. I might take him to the movies—'

'Don't give him any chocolate.'

'That's not realistic. It's Easter—'

'Okay, well just get him a small egg then.'

'I'll get him some marshmallow eggs—'

'No. Those things are even worse—'

'Gosh, Deborah. If you don't mind I'll use my discretio—'

'And no big presents. You think the size of the present makes a difference, Tom?'

'I think Frank appreciates a gesture—'

'No big present. Okay?'

Wow. Deborah's definitely enjoying the power of martyrdom.

'Okay. Tell him I'm looking forward to seeing him. Is he there?'

'Frank? He's still finishing his dinner. He says hi.'

'Oh. Okay—'

'Goodbye.'

'Happy East—' I say, but she's already hung up on me.

Four years ago

The horse with no sperm (or how I got into this mess)

My life was turned upside down by a horse.

Fire Chief was a really expensive prostitute. I'm talking Park Lane or Mayfair-type prices. Thirty thousand dollars for a piece of horse heaven. He sired many steeplechasers and many gallopers from the top shelf of trainers. Fire Chief won the Havelock Sweepstakes two years running, but his greatest prowess was in the bedroom.

Okay, so the reality is Fire Chief's sex life was a lot less romantic than that. He was probably a victim of demand outstripping supply. I've seen it happen often. I've seen exhausted stallions with painful looks on their faces, staring at what should be an ideal view – the back end of a mare, a well-demonstrated piece of prime filly – and I've seen them groan and sigh, before going about their business.

And who can blame them? This is worse sex than any human prostitute has to put up with.

There are a lot of people present for starters. A studmaster and a vet are there every step of the way, lubing anything that can be lubed.

The job gets even worse than that. You would hope that the moment of orgasm, one of the truly personal moments in animal existence, should be a special preserve. But at this exact moment Fire Chief and many like him get wiped for excess ejaculation due to an artificial insemination loophole clause in the gentlemen's agreement that all breeders adhere to.

Don't get me wrong. I'm sure there are worse ways to live on this planet. I'm just saying, as a red-blooded male, I have great sympathy for Fire Chief's plight.

In my old line of work I needed to know a lot of stuff like that. I was an insurance investigator for Thoroughbred Assurance. In The City and surrounding districts Thoroughbred has had a monopoly on gee-gees' insurance for as long as I can remember. I handled all the bloodstock cases, pretty much a three-man department: me, another investigator and our boss.

It was a good job. Mostly tedious with the occasional burst of adrenalin.

I saw a few things that would raise the eyebrow of a hardened white-collar criminal. But I never got mixed up in it.

Not until this time.

I was clearing my messages and there's one from a guy I know pretty well, Eddy Malinga. He's an equine vet just about twenty ks up-country.

'Hey, Tom. Eddy here. I had to euthanize one of Quintin Ellery's stallions, Fire Chief. He had a compound fracture in his rear meta-tarsal. He was in a lot of distress. I couldn't get a second opinion because Pete's at a wedding this weekend. We'll get the claim sorted and in to you on Monday.'

I check our mail box and, sure enough, a claim for Fire Chief is waiting for me.

I give the studmaster, Quintin Ellery, a tinkle. I hear a little something in his voice when I'm talking to him. He sounds hesitant, then almost over-rehearsed, the way he's answering the simplest questions. He seems pretty anxious for me to talk to Eddy Malinga about it.

As I'm talking to him I'm looking at the file and I see the strangest thing. The horse is insured for mortality, but not for fertility. I look to who the owner is, but it's a name I don't recognize, a Robert Valentine. Seems strange that I've never heard of him before, but a lot of people come into this industry for a short time, so . . .

I tell Quintin Ellery I'm out of town but I'll be over to pick up a couple of documents in a day or two.

16

I pack up the file and head out there straight away. I want him to think he's got more time than he does.

I arrive at an awkward moment. A mare is being mounted. She's been well drugged, this one. Her muscles are relaxed but she's so groggy I doubt she'll remember the happy conquest tomorrow.

'Excuse me. Coitus interruptus,' I say and Ellery looks at me. Good. I've caught him off guard.

'I'm Tom from Thoroughbred—'

'I'm a little busy right now,' he says.

'I've got time on my hands. You mind if I take a walk around?' I ask, really politely. He nods and as soon as I am out of sight I hear him go inside, probably to make a hasty phone call.

I'm in a barn taking photos of the blackboard that contains Fire Chief's sex life. He's been a busy boy. There are a lot of mares, about fifty or so. It looks like someone has drawn a maths book on the blackboard, and the grid contains lots of X marks and filled-in squares of different colours and red dots, which I'm pretty sure mean the mare is in foal.

I'm picturing what my board would look like. Deborah would have had a lot of X marks at the start of the relationship, and quite a few immediately after our second break-up too. But hers have tapered off. There are a few others on my board too, unfortunately.

I've got the studmaster, Quintin Ellery, inside trying to find a piece of bogus documentation I came up with on the spot: 'a Certificate of Authorization'. He'll be deep in his filing cabinet right now. I've also asked for a cup of tea, which should slow him down another five minutes.

You know, I'm curious.

I'm curious about the discrepancy of what the board says about Fire Chief's sex life, compared to what it said in the report he supplied us with.

It's good that I surprised Mr Ellery. If I'd given him any more time I think he would have covered up evidence more thoroughly. And evidence is what I'm looking for.

Quintin Ellery comes in with tea for two, and a lot of documents.

'I couldn't find the authorization certificate. I've phoned Eddy Malinga. He's coming over now.'

'Oh, great.'

I take a sip of tea. I'm taking my time. I want to see if he's twitchy.

'Fire Chief had a busy sex life,' I say, referring to the board.

'He never shirked his duty,' Ellery says drily.

'If this was my sex life I would be so pleased. So many mares. So few pregnancies . . .' I say, and he smiles, and looks down at the board.

'That's not right,' he says.

'Oh sure,' I say, going up close to the board. 'Looks like he sired a lot of foals there. But what happened over there? Did he start shooting blanks?' I ask, real polite.

'The board's incomplete. You got his record in his files.'

'Oh, of course. My mistake,' I say, and the cup of tea he's holding looks a bit shaky.

'I could show you where it all happened if you like,' he says.

He takes me past a gate, to an innocuous patch of grass near the edge of a paddock.

'This is where we found him. He was sweating pretty bad, and foaming around the nostrils. I called Eddy and he called you and we euthanized him.'

'Tranquilizer?'

'A dose of purple death.'

A couple of horses stand in the neighbouring paddock, watching our conversation.

'It was the back metatarsal. Is that right?' I ask.

'Yeah.'

'Gee. I wonder how it happened . . .' I say, and leave a nice little gap for him to fill.

18

'Could be anything,' he says. 'Could've reared.'

'Why would he rear?'

'You know, the joys of spring.'

'Oh,' I say.

I mean, that is a possibility. The joys of spring have bought the demise of many an over-enthusiastic horse. And human, too.

'Or maybe he hit a divot,' he says. He's really getting creative now.

'Maybe,' I say. 'So where is he now?'

'Huh?'

'Fire Chief,' I say, and he points to an area ten yards away, by the fence. I take out my camera and snap some photos of where Fire Chief died. Then I take a photo of where Fire Chief was buried.

At the same time I'm studying Ellery. There's nothing micro about his micro-expressions.

Next thing Eddy Malinga has arrived to join in the merriment. I doff my hat to him from a distance and he gives me a wave. Eddy is a Sri Lankan rapscallion. We go back a way. There are only a couple of horse vets in this district, so we have a professional relationship, but it's stretched a lot further than that. We've put in many a good hour together at Barney's Twist and Shout.

'Tom, how's Deborah?' Eddy asks.

'Well, you know Deborah. Her middle name is Trouble.'

'Funny that. She's got the same middle name as you,' Eddy says with a wink.

'Tell me what happened, Eddy. Where did you find him again?'

Ellery answers the question for him. 'Right here,' he says, pointing to the ground underneath us.

Eddy changes the subject skilfully. 'I don't know how it happened. It's all guesswork, Tom. We found him there, and he was unable to bear weight—'

'Sure, sure. A metatarsal fracture you say?'

'Yeah, real nasty, Tom. He was in all sorts of pain. He was sweating, his flanks were lathering, his heart rate was through the roof.'

'You couldn't get a second opinion, huh?'

'I tried, but Pete was out at a wedding. And I called you too. It would've been inhumane, Tom.'

'Yeah, okay,' I say.

I walk to the spot where they buried the horse. It's ten yards from where he said the horse had died. I look at the fence next to it for markings or scratches.

'Okay, so, you know me, Eddy,' I say, 'I can be a little slow sometimes. Why would you bury Fire Chief here, when he died over there?'

No answer.

Ellery jumps in with, 'I didn't want a hole in the middle of the paddock.'

'Oh. I see.'

I look at the ground beneath us. It is a half-centimetre higher than the surrounding ground.

I'm keeping it polite. 'So why a quick burial then? Looks like you did it without a digger.'

'Ellery had his sons here. We figured, why wait?'

I nod. I light a cigarette. I have a look at the fence post next to the grave . . .

'You know, this grave looks pretty shallow to me. There are three of us. Why don't we dig him up?'

'Now?' Ellery says. He looks to Eddy.

'It's all in the report,' Eddy says.

'Just the same, I'd like to have a look anyway,' I say.

Next thing we're all down to our shirts, digging a hole together. Understandably, I'm digging harder and faster than they are.

I have a lot of unanswered questions running through my mind. The largest one being, why would you drag a horse ten yards to bury him?

I think I have the answer. Fire Chief died right here. We're next to a fence. I'm figuring they must have tied Fire Chief to it. Fed him some anaesthetic and bashed his leg with . . .

Well, with something. There are a million weapons to choose from in this place. Take your pick.

After a good half-hour of digging, we get down to the fallen stallion. He's already started to bloat a little. His eyes have been closed. When I inspect the head there's fluid still oozing from his nostrils.

I get my camera out and I'm taking photos from every possible angle. We dig down to his hind leg. Beneath the hock it's only held on by skin.

The skin is ripped, and I look inside at the metatarsal bone and the cut is perfectly shaped.

The bone has been cut right through.

I look at Eddy. He knows I've got him.

'The joys of spring, huh?' I say to them.

I'm driving back on Herbert Road and I've got Fire Chief's metatarsal in the back seat. And in my rear vision I can see a Land Rover, driving pretty quick and kicking up a lot of dust.

The Land Rover passes me and pulls over to the side of the road. Eddy gets out of it and stands, waiting for me, so I pull over behind him.

I get out of my car and Eddy Malinga is lighting two cigarettes for us. He hands me one.

'Haven't seen you at Barney's for a while,' I say to him.

'The City is having less and less appeal to me, Tom,' he says, looking me in the eye.

'Afraid to show your face?'

'I'm not afraid,' he says. He looks at the bone in my car. 'So what do you think happened to Fire Chief?' he asks.

'I'd say Fire Chief received a pretty hefty blow to the leg.'

'That's one theory—'

'Why didn't he insure the horse for fertility?' I ask him, and his smooth small talk comes juddering to a halt.

'What? Who?'

'The owner. Robert Valentine. I never heard of the guy.'

'Fertility is expensive, Tom. People make mistakes.'

'They sure do,' I say, and he takes a long drag on his cigarette.

'Look, Tom. My livelihood depends on this guy . . .'

'Where are you going with this, Eddy?'

Eddy reaches into his pocket. He pulls out a stuffed sock. A plain black cotton sock with a gold rim at the top. I look inside.

'Jesus, Eddy—'

'There's ten thousand in there. And there are twenty more socks waiting for you. All you have to do is drop it.'

I laugh. I try to give the sock back but he won't take it.

'Don't come all choirboy with me, Tom,' he says. 'You're not exactly squeaky clean.'

'Who is Robert Valentine? It's a pseudonym, right? Is it Ellery?'

'Ellery's an idiot. And it's not me either. I'm small fry.'

'Who is he then?'

'Better you don't pry any further—'

'I WANT TO KNOW MORE,' I'm saying.

'No you don't, Tom! For your sake, the less you know the better. All you have to do is file a report and ratify the claim.'

I stare him in the eye. He returns my gaze but I can see by the way he's breathing that underneath the poker face he's shitting himself.

This is when I made the biggest mistake of my life.

'We shouldn't be seen together,' I said.

He smiled and opened the back door of my car and he took the horse bone. He took my camera too.

He got in his Land Rover and drove off, leaving a trail of dust behind him.

The whole thing took only three months to unravel. I did my part properly. I filed my reports. I turned a blind eye just like a good boy should. The claim was ratified. Robert Valentine was paid his money. I was paid my share. Everything was neatly brushed under the carpet. It was clean. Nice business.

One of Quintin Ellery's sons blew it for all of us. Apparently Ellery Junior got boozed and told a cousin, and his cousin told some other idiot, and before you know it the rumour had spread throughout Herbert Valley.

I was at Thoroughbred, up on the twenty-third floor, when I found out about it.

I remember sitting at my desk. The sun bounced off a window somewhere in The City and it shone right in my eye. A blinding harbinger.

As my retinas adjusted I heard a heated conversation coming from the next room. Harry Macmurran came out and said to me, 'He wants to see you. It's not good, Tom.'

I moved through to the office. I didn't even have to look my boss in the eye. I saw it on his desk.

Fire Chief's metatarsal.

A few weeks later, Eddy turned up outside Barney's. His arm was in a sling.

He didn't want to talk in public, so we took a stroll down the back streets.

'What happened to your arm, Eddy? Did you fall off a horse or something?'

'Robert Valentine wants his socks back,' he said to me.

'Is that a fact?' I said.

'Take this seriously, Tom.'

'Fuck you. I've lost my whole career because of you, you stupid—'

'Yeah, you could lose more than that if you don't do the right thing.'

'What? Am I being threatened? Is Robert Valentine threatening me?' I said to him.

'Jesus. You figure it out for yourself,' he said, and he walked away.

'I'm sorry about your arm,' I called out to him.

I haven't seen him since, but I often replay this moment in my mind.

I could have cut my losses and given the money back. I should have done that, in retrospect. But I wasn't exactly on an even keel. My life with Deborah was completely in the toilet at the time. My thing with the next-door neighbour had just happened, which, to be fair, was only a retaliation on my part due to Deborah's thing with Cheeky George on New Year's Eve.

Our marriage was imploding and I was struggling with Frank too. I'm not trying to justify my actions. I did what I did.

I gave Herb Lamont a sock and asked him to keep an eye on Deb and Frank from a distance. I asked him to set up an automatic payment that couldn't be traced back to me.

And I skipped town.

Wednesday

It's good to be back at Barney's Twist and Shout

10.42 a.m.

I'm at the Hayward's bus station. I figure I must have left my case on the bus yesterday. I'm approaching a man in a fluorescent yellow vest and a green cap. I think he's a bus driver.

'Excuse me, sir. I was on a bus yesterday, and I think I lost my suitcase.'

I've interrupted his cigarette break but he's good about it. He talks on a tiny cellphone to someone else as I describe the suitcase. He gets a little impatient as I describe the bus I was on. I give him details that will jog the driver's memory: – an old woman at the back of the bus had some kind of angina attack – that caused a bit of a stir when the bus arrived in town.

The bus driver asks me my name and number. I'll need a new cellphone soon, no question about it, but in the meantime I give him my false name and my contact details at the Ascot.

I thank the driver and I head off, and a police car drives past slowly. Instinctively I cross the road. I suspect I'm being overly paranoid. There are far more heinous and important crimes than the one I committed. I'm a bad excuse for a white-collar criminal. What's a few socks between friends? Quit being paranoid, Tom. The police have bigger fish to fry.

I'm sitting on a barstool against a bar that I'm very familiar with. It's opening hours at Barney's Twist and Shout, my old haunt. It's an old horse-racing pub. A racing commentary rings in my ears and Walter Nurse's voice is almost musical as he gets to the end of the race, his pitch shifting higher as the horses hit the finish line. It's a nice sound to hear in this place.

I watched more races and sank more pints and downed more shots in this place than I care to remember.

We even had our own room out the back, the VIP facility, which is pretty much where Barney would put the regulars so we wouldn't scare off the newer clientele he was trying to attract. Now it feels like a shadow of itself. They took a couple of booths down there and they replaced them with more TVs. There are a few tables dotted around. At a table by the old dartboard there are a couple of gents in their sixties. Both are small men, with rough weather-beaten faces. Both former jockeys I'd say.

I'm hoping to find some of my contacts from the various underground economies – racing one of them – but none of the usual gang is here. Where is everybody? If I wait until eleven thirty a few of them should roll in. But at the moment it's just me, the jockeys, some old coot at the other end of the bar and a barman who looks like he just graduated from kindergarten.

'You're new,' I say to the barman.

'I just started here six months ago.'

'I used to be a regular here. It's changed a bit, huh?'

'I guess so,' the guy says.

'Where's Barney?'

'Huh? Oh. Mr Mackenzie only comes in on a Friday now.'

'Okay. Well, maybe you can help me. I'm looking for a guy who was a bit of a regular here. Eddy Malinga.'

The guy looks at me blankly. 'I'm sorry, sir, I don't know an Eddy Malinga.'

A new guy comes into the bar. He's about my age, thickset, with a barrel chest and a bit of a spare tyre hanging over his belt buckle. His hair is receding and he looks like he could do with a shower. I can feel his eyes on me, so I turn to face him, eye to eye. He quickly looks away, like he got caught by his mother looking at a porno. He almost falls off his stool, such is his hurry to leave. I look outside

28

and the barrel-chested man is doing his best to imitate someone in an Olympic walking race. Strange behaviour.

I order three Aberlours and I go to the jockeys' table. 'You two gents look like men of refined taste,' I say.

'That's a hell of a way to start the day,' one of them says.

'A sip of a nip never hurt anyone,' I say.

'Who said anything about sipping?' the other jockey says, and downs his glass.

I take a liberty and sit at their table.

'I'm sorry to bother you. I'm looking for a Robert Valentine. You ever heard that name?'

Both of them shake their heads.

'What about Quintin Ellery?'

'Oh, I know that one,' the older jockey says. 'He skipped town when that whole . . . thing went down with . . . what's the name of that horse, Jimmy?'

'No idea.'

'He could be anywhere. Maybe he's gone to Hawaii.'

'Hawaii?' his friend says.

'I don't know where he is. Haven't heard his name for a while to be honest.'

'What about Eddy Malinga? He used to be a regular here. Do you guys know him?'

'The vet?' the younger one says.

'Yeah. Where is he?'

'He's dead.'

To use the phone at the phone booth I had to buy a small, expensive piece of plastic from the convenience store.

I've copied a bunch of numbers from the phone book. I've got Herb Lamont's number. He's still at the same address. I've got Barbara Malinga's, still at Eddy's address. Ellery is unsurprisingly unlisted. I even looked up the Valentines. There are four in town, but there are no Rs. I feel pretty certain Robert Valentine will be a pseudonym and won't be in any phone book, but you can never be too sure.

I push the plastic into a slot in the phone and a computer disguised as a woman speaks to me. The computer/woman says, 'It looks like you are trying to make a phone call.' And then there's this gap. I assume I'm supposed to respond in some way.

I say to the phone, 'Yes. I'm trying to make a phone call,' and she/it asks me for a password. 'I don't have one,' I say to the phone, but the phone insists, so I say, 'Peter Piper picked a peck of pickled peppers' – just to be facetious, but the voice says, 'Password is accepted,' and it repeats my password back to me, and then tells me to dial the number. I hope I won't have to say 'Peter Piper picked a peck of pickled peppers' every time I want to make a call with this stupid piece of plastic.

The phone rings. A familiar voice answers.

'Hello?'

'Is that Barbara Malinga?'

'Yes.'

'Barbara, it's me, Tom. I just heard about Eddy. I . . . I'm very . . . sorry.'

'Oh . . . th-thanks.'

I can hear her voice tremble. She must be going through hell. 'When did this happen, Barbara?' I ask her.

'Four months ago. I'm sorry – who is this?

'Tom.'

'Tom Spotswood?'

'Yeah, I've been out of town but . . . I . . . I'm surprised no one tried to get in touch with me. I would've liked . . . I'm sad to have missed the funeral. I'm sorry. I just found out. This is still a shock to me.'

Barbara picks up something in my voice.

'You okay, Tom?'

'Yeah. What about you, Barbara? Are you okay?'

'Yeah. You get used to death, you know?'

That last comment really knocks me sideways.

'What did he die of?' I ask her.

'Food poisoning.'

'Huh? What did he eat?'

'A chicken shawarma.'

'I don't even know what that is.'

'It's a type of kebab, Tom.'

'God . . . I'm so sorry, Barbara. I . . . I'd like to come around some time. Would that be all right?'

And she says that would be nice.

I admit, my motives for coming round aren't all virtuous. I have to find out who Robert Valentine is, so I need to do some snooping.

Poor Eddy.

I catch myself sighing several times after I've hung up. I could do with another drink to settle the nerves, but I don't want to put myself out of action too early. There's a lot I have to do today.

She's concreted the front lawn!

12.03 p.m.

The taxi driver is a real nice fellow. A Pakistani. 'You like cricket?' I say to him.

'Oh yes, very much. Inzamam-Ul-Haq is my second cousin.'

'No kidding. Who's he?'

'He is one of our greatest batsmen.'

'No kidding,' I say, and he smiles proudly.

I've got some lilies in my lap. Deborah's favourite flower. I feel sorry for the lily. Someone designated that it was the flower of death. That seems a very unfair way to treat a beautiful flower. It's a bit like the dove representing peace. Put two doves in a cage together and the feathers will fly, I guarantee it. Doves and lilies, huh?

I've got the lilies as a bit of a cover. I'm arriving at my house – strike that – my ex-wife's house; it's very easy to get mixed up considering I paid for the damned thing. Anyhow, I'm arriving a day early. I've taken a calculated risk that Deborah won't be home, but I've got the flowers just in case she is. Then when she catches me I have a ready-made romantic alibi. They are very beautiful, these flowers. I bet they give bumble bees a real turn-on.

The taxi driver says to me, 'They are nice flowers. They smell good.'

'There's no sweeter smell than the smell of a flower,' I say.

He pulls out a small piece of plastic.

'This is my odorizer,' he says. 'It is supposed to fill my car with a beautiful smell, but it's not the same.'

'Yeah, well maybe you should use flowers instead of your odorizer.'

'Flowers go off. The odorizer works for weeks,' he says.

I look at the odorizer, and the letters on the front say 'Morning fresh'. I take a sniff and all I can smell is chemicals.

'I don't think that's good for you,' I say to him, and he says nothing.

We approach the traffic lights that mark the boundary of the sunny suburb of Codfish Bay.

Once upon a time I thought this was a suburban nightmare. Now I've got a real nostalgic glow for the place. It's like looking at an old familiar photograph. It's so peaceful out here, and five blocks that-a-way is a beach. Not the best beach in the world, but it's a beach. Nice place for a swim if you're a jellyfish. Not so great if you're a human being.

Ah, it's nice to be back.

We pull in to my street and I still feel like I am coming home. But this is no longer my home.

'My wife left me,' I say to the taxi driver.

'Oh, I'm sorry to hear about that.'

'Don't get me wrong. I deserved it.'

'Oh, there's nothing worse than a messy divorce,' the taxi driver says, and then he says, 'Hey, are you getting out here? I got another job on the thing.'

The thing he is referring to is a computer in the taxi.

'Funny-looking machine,' I say to him, and he says, 'I know. I can't work the fucking thing.' The ride costs thirty bucks, which is a tad pricey. Still, I figure if he's one of those ones sending all his money back home he'll need a few breaks to go his way, so I flip forty bucks on the passenger seat.

I light up a roll-your-own and stare at the old house.

She's put a fence around it.

Can you believe it?

A head-high fence. If you step up on tippy toes you can almost make out the roof of the house.

It's hard to find the opening in this fence, because she's camouflaged the gate to make it look like it is a part of the fence. It's like entering a gang headquarters, except this is more *suburban* and when I get inside the fence I get a real shock . . .

'Where'd she put all the grass?' I say to my cigarette.

The whole front yard has been concreted.

It's hard to fathom. A giant fence and a concrete front yard. Deborah? It's like I don't know her. My ex-wife was formerly a woman of taste. I never knew she could stoop so low, and so quickly.

I stare at the concrete with disbelief. There used to be an apple tree over there. Why would Deborah pull down the apple tree? Maybe it got a disease or something? I admit, the apples off that tree were small and too tart to actually eat. But if you added a lot of sugar and cooked them up good we'd have a mostly edible apple crumble.

And the lawn. There used to be lawn here. I used to mow up and down here every Saturday morning. Okay, that's an exaggeration. Once every couple of months, on a Saturday morning, I'd get out the two-stroke and fire her up. Our machine was an old rust-bucket. It took a lot of pulls of the cord to get her going. I had a way with the two-stroke. You just had to talk to her good and she'd fire up, and from there, she chewed through the grass like a bloodthirsty killer. Frank used to love that. He'd throw all the freshly mown grass at me, down the neck of my jersey and everything, and revenge was swift – I'd tickle him good.

I walk up to the beautiful old front door. Thank God that hasn't changed. I knock, hoping no one will answer, but just in case I'm poised and ready with the lilies in front of me, like a defensive shield. It's hard to be angry at a guy holding flowers.

No one answers, so I open my wallet and pull out my key. As I put my key to the door I say to my cigarette, 'I bet she's changed the locks,' and sure enough . . .

So I take a step back from the 'Welcome' mat. And I applaud

her. I applaud my wife's ability to make me feel unwelcome, and I head round the back for what I really came for, which is in the basement.

It's nice to be back in the basement again, and to see a lot of familiar things. My old tools are still on the walls, but it looks like they've rusted a lot. I can't see my stuff here. I hope she hasn't thrown it out. I've got some great suits here, and a few sentimental knick-knacks. I keep old tickets to shows I liked, and I keep newspaper clippings and souvenir pebbles – anything that will remind me of something I never want to forget. You lose the souvenir – you lose the memory, it's as simple as that. Objects have memories, you know?

She hasn't got rid of the old washing machine. I know why. Too heavy to shift. I once tried shifting that by myself and I damn near gave myself a hernia.

It'll be a tight squeeze at the back reaches of the basement. This is a hell of a lot more difficult than going to the bank. Not that banks are easy any more. At least here I'll have no problems or confusions with forms. No long queues at five o'clock. No interest or bank fees deducted. No records of cash spent and cash not spent. The underground economy truly begins here.

I take off my suit jacket and pants, and I hang them outside on a tree branch where they won't get dusty. Better my underclothes get dirty than my suit, at least for as long as I've got just the one suit.

Okay, time to get dirty.

I get on all fours, and I go in.

Who knows what dust I'm inhaling. I pass a couple of spiders, but they don't concern me particularly. Spiders and I have an understanding. I like the cunning and patience of the spider. Spiders don't mind me either. We have mutual respect.

I'm losing all signs of natural light, so I flick on my cigarette lighter. The glow from the flame is enough to capture a glint directly to my left.

I get closer and I see it's the skeleton of a cat. Perhaps that's old Muffin.

Old Muffin must have come under here to die. No need to make a fuss. A nice private place to die. Not a bad way to do it. People have it wrong with cemeteries and burial grounds. We'd be better off buried under our own floorboards. Live and die in your own home.

The light goes out so I crawl towards the darkness in a straight line. I make it to Frank's old pram. I flick up a flame so I can see it a little better. Looks pretty busted. That's a shame, for a pram to live out its tour of duty underneath the house.

I used to give him some pretty wild rides in that pram. There's this dip in Clyde Street, a large drop and then a rise. Frank was one year old and I'd push as fast as I could down the hill and then up the next hill. He liked it a lot. One time I got a little overexcited. I took my hands away from the handle to give Frank a little scare. I pretended the pram was getting away from me, and Frank screamed, a really high-pitched scream. I grabbed the pram again and stopped it safely. I picked him up and gave him a hug, but he wouldn't stop screaming, so I said to him, 'Come on, Frank. Harden up!' and I put him back in the pram.

He cried all the way home. I tried everything. I even bought him a lollipop, but he threw the lollipop out of the pram.

I have to remind myself, we have a lot of good memories too, Frank and I. But the bad ones tend to stick out when you've been an absentee father.

I'm almost at my destination. I move two feet to the right and I get right up to the far wall. From here I have to shuffle up the line of the wall, on my back.

I feel grateful that I haven't put on any weight in the last four years. I don't, as a general rule, suffer from claustrophobia, but this is pushing it a little. It's a tight fit. I'm getting to the stage where my nose is touching the floorboards above. If I had a heart attack right now they wouldn't find me for months.

This last bit is the worst. The only way I can reach the bag is to turn my neck to one side, and my neck isn't as flexible as I suspect it was last time I was here. I think I could've made it a little easier for myself, but I was being extra-careful. Still, I'm cursing myself through this last bit when I arrive, finally, at a plastic bag, and I reach inside and I can feel them all there. Socks. Glorious socks.

I'm back at the main part of the basement, and it feels good to be able to stand upright again. My muscles hurt after that exercise. I count the socks. There are twenty, just like the last time I counted.

I see an old green schoolbag. The canvas is worn and the zip is sticking, but it's a good place to put twenty socks. I'm pretty much covered in dirt, so I wash up in the laundry sink. I've got nothing to dry myself off with so I have to use my shirt, and I end up back in my freshly pressed suit sans underpants, and I must say, it's quite a refreshing experience. I take the opportunity to change my socks too. The ones I've been wearing are getting sweaty so I swap them for a brand-new pair. At least they were brand-new four years ago. It's a beautiful feeling stepping into virgin socks. I refill my smelly socks with money and throw them in the schoolbag.

I can't help it. I'm a curious person. I can't just walk past this place without looking around.

I'm round the side staring through a window, at the place of many stupendous memories: the bedroom. There's a little gap in the curtain and I can see that Deborah has removed the old mahogany bed and replaced it with something new and soft. There are two packed suitcases on the bed.

I go round to Frank's room and I see a neighbour painting his roof. Not sure if he's seen me. Anyway, it's not like I'm doing anything wrong. I mean, it's my house, right? I've got a right to be here. Technically speaking.

I get to the bathroom and I see that someone has made a security breach, because there is a window left half open.

And, you know, I'm curious.

So I climb in. The ground outside is at a higher level than the house, so I have to lower myself down on to the toilet seat. My cigarette is making the manoeuvre very difficult so I leave it on the windowsill. Now I'm standing on the toilet seat. I'm taken aback by how different the bathroom looks. I mean, they say God made the earth in seven days, but my ex-wife could give God a run for his money at this rate, because I really don't recognize anything in here.

She has painted the bathroom walls pink.

'Pink?' I say to my cigarette.

The moment my foot hits the floor a smoke alarm goes off.

It makes quite a shriek. I try to stay calm. I reach up and unscrew the smoke alarm and try to find a button that will shut it off. I am unsuccessful and the din is cutting through my brain like a chainsaw. I throw the alarm on the ground and kick the thing, but it must be made of reinforced concrete, because I can't make a dent. The noise is deafening.

I act quickly. I take the alarm and I head directly to the hot-water cupboard. I wrap it in towel after towel, I squash it in under the other blankets and towels and I shut the door.

I can still hear it a little but I'm not sure if this is just an echo or if I am imagining it. I think I've successfully muffled it.

Phew.

I walk down the hallway and I'm relieved to see she's kept a few of the old things. The bookcase I built still sits in two corners of the hallway. I took a lot of pride in that. I measured it up and I bought the wood and I sawed it and sanded it and varnished it myself, and it felt great putting my books in it. Deb's thrown out all my books by the look of it. Her taste in literature has really headed downhill.

I head into the living room and I'm blown away at how much the place has changed. There's no piano, which makes me sad. I loved tinkering away on the piano. I didn't have talent but I could certainly play four songs well. The record player is gone too. That's not so surprising, although Deb did love playing my records.

Deborah loved inviting people back to our house for nightcaps. She always made sure everyone was well liquored and well fed. I loved the records, but when Deborah got a bit tipsy her coordination would suffer and she would scratch my records to smithereens. It was a small point of tension that was more than made up for by her inclusive nature. Deborah loved to dance at home, just the two of us. A slow dance or something a bit more up-tempo. I used to feel self-conscious but she'd drag me up and dance with me in front of all my friends, and once I'd had a few I could shake, rattle and roll like I was born with rubber limbs.

The old oak table has gone too. I'd read the newspaper at the table and she'd sit next to me and steal the crossword, and – back when we were close – she'd take my hand as we both did our separate reading and she'd grip tight like a vice until my fingers went numb. Deborah sure knew how to make a man feel loved, and I loved her for it.

I'm in Frank's room.

I'm sitting on his bed, staring at the wall. Deborah has stripped away his old racing car wallpaper. He loved that wallpaper. He loved staring at the cars; the Lamborghini was his favourite. I told him off a few times for peeling it. Like a cat sharpening his claws, Frank was a born fidgeter and the wallpaper bore the brunt.

'Dad?'

Frank's voice comes ringing in my ears. I look at the bed and he's not there but I hear him just the same.

'How did the world start?' he asks me, and I'm transported back four years and I'm tucking him in.

I hear myself reply 'Gee Frank, that's a big question. Is this going to be a religious conversation or a science one?'

'I don't believe in God.'

'I'm not too sure on God myself. Have you heard of the big bang theory?'

'The what?'

'They think that once the whole universe was smaller than your fingernail. Even smaller. You can't imagine how small they thought the universe was. You see, scientists have figured out the whole universe is expanding.'

'How do they know?'

'I don't know. Telescopes I guess, and because the universe is getting bigger they figure that means it must've started out really small.'

'It's funny', Frank says, 'because sometimes I think, What if we're really little and there's bigger people out there who can only look at us through a microscope?'

'Oh yeah, now there is a very interesting thought Frank. I like how the Greek Gods work. They have lots of Gods and they all play with us like little toys, and . . . in a way it takes into account how the world doesn't make much sense, you know?'

'Yeah,' little Frank goes.

Hell, sometimes it feels like I'm talking to an adult when I'm with him. Then there's the other times, of course, when he's screaming his lungs out in public because I won't get him a chocolate bar. Then I definitely know I'm dealing with a kid.

I catch myself sighing. It's sad being back here.

I leave by the front door. I pick up the lilies at the front door and I see a big ugly terracotta pot, and I plant the lilies in there, next to the cactus.

A toy for Frank

4.15 p.m.

The City has changed so much in the last four years that I hardly recognize it. So many of my favourite old department stores have closed down and been replaced by chain stores selling worthless plastic junk. That's why I'm relieved to see that one place has barely changed. Archie Scrivener's is still going strong, thank goodness.

Archie Scrivener's is the best toy store in town by a country mile. He makes wooden toys, right here in the store. Immaculate things. Wooden cars. Wooden puppets. Wooden motorcycles. Wheelbarrows. Rotary hoes. You name it, Archie Scrivener's has a wooden version of it.

Archie has the best stack of white hair I've seen. I figure it must have gone white when he was in his twenties. I can't picture him with colour in his hair, and I've been coming here for longer than I care to remember. He's young where it counts though. He has an area where he makes toys and children can watch him doing it. He's more fun than Santa Claus. I head to the counter and he says to me, 'I'll be with you in a second. I have to chisel down this horse's nose.'

I'm here because I want to surprise Frank when I pick him up from school tomorrow. I want to get him something special. Something to say 'Your Dad's back and he's a changed man.'

I have a browse around the shop. I know there'll be something for Frank here. This place is stacked with creativity.

Archie Scrivener imports the best toys from all over. As I scan the shelves I think of all the presents I could have got Frank if I had been there at the right time. There's a lot of toys here that he's too old for now.

'I don't know what to get an eleven-year-old boy,' I say to Archie. 'He's too old for a lot of this stuff, right?'

Archie smiles and says, 'What about models? I've got ships, planes. He can build them himself.'

That's not grabbing me. Sounds like a present that is actually work in disguise.

'I've got some nice train sets back there,' Archie suggests.

'Oh, yeah. Is a train set too young for an eleven-year-old?'

'Hard to say,' Archie says, 'given that I sell a lot of these to middle-aged men.'

He takes me to a section full of Hornby train sets. The boxes are beautifully designed. I can't believe they're brand-new, because they look so old and ornate.

I'm looking at this box and it has a picture of the Night Mail train. It has a beautiful dark red locomotive and two gleaming carriages.

I ask Archie, 'Can I take a look inside this box?' and he comes over and opens it up for me, and shows me the detail in the locomotive.

I'm sold already, and I'm having trouble hiding it. I ask Archie how much and I'm unsurprised that this type of item is very expensive now. It'll cost me almost half a sock but it's worth it. Imagine Frank's face when he sees it.

The box is pretty large and Archie asks if I need a bag. I joke to him that I don't think they could make a plastic bag large enough to fit it in, and I walk out the door holding a wide box which makes it quite difficult to manoeuvre in high-density pedestrian situations. I manage to duck and weave most of the way. I accidentally bash the box into a couple of people on the way, but there's no serious harm done.

As I walk the streets I think of the time I told Frank off at the toy store. Actually it was different from a telling-off. I *humiliated* him.

I'm not proud of it. We were in front of a lot of people too. Frank was playing with a Matchbox car and he wouldn't let go of it. I said to him, 'Frank, put it down, I'm not getting you the car.'

And Frank said back to me, 'You will if I cry for long enough.'

Then I remember saying, 'No, that's not going to work this time. You think you're smarter than me? You think you can outwit me? I'm a grown-up and you're a kid. And I'm ten times as smart as you.'

And Frank just started crying. I figured that it was a genuine cry, one I'd caused rather than him *manipulating* me and so I gave in and got him the stupid toy. But he kept on crying outside the shop, even though I'd already got him the toy car. I yelled at him to 'Shut up!' but he wouldn't shut up. So I said 'Fine,' and walked off away from him.

I went my way and he went his and I only went ten steps and I knew I had to turn back.

And he was sad. Really sad.

I've been a bad father. I've got a lot of making up to do.

She's a receiver

I'm drinking in the lobby of the Ascot. I've dropped off the socks in the safe in room 834.

I must say, I'm pretty chuffed with my train set purchase. I'm on a bit of a high, and a little liquid celebration is well deserved. I'm on to my third liquid celebration when Linda from 835 tries to make it through the faulty automatic doors of the Ascot.

I rush to assist but the doors don't want to open for me. Linda finds the sensor and jumps in front of it. She wheels in a business chair and she asks, 'Can you stand there?' I stand where she tells me and the doors stay open. She goes around the corner and comes in with three more business chairs which she wheels inside. I follow her into the elevator like a loyal panting dog.

'A man and a woman and four business chairs are in an elevator,' I say to her. 'Doesn't that sounds like the start of a joke to you?'

'Yeah, sure. What's the punchline?'

'I don't do punchlines.'

'That's disappointing. Thanks for helping,' she says.

And next thing we're both in 835. I swear, I didn't mean to be in there, your honour. I was just helping her with her chairs.

'Mind if I take a seat on your merchandise?'

'Knock yourself out,' she says, her nose in the miniature refrigerator. I sit in one of her business chairs and spin around.

'So you sell these things?' I ask.

44

'No. I'm a receiver.'

'Are you a giver too?'

'Ha. I receive for a living. Outside work hours I give as good as I get.'

'What do you receive exactly?'

'When a company liquidates, I'm the friendly face who comes in and takes all your stuff. I realize it's not the most valuable public service out there, but it's a job.'

'Hey, I'm in no position to take the moral high ground. I used to work in insurance.'

She opens her miniature refrigerator and looks at the menu. 'Which wine do you recommend, Tom? Looks like you must've tried them all.'

'I only remember starting with a Riesling. The rest gets blurry. Pretty sad, huh?'

She shrugs her shoulders. 'I don't know,' she says. 'I've met a lot of messed-up sober people,' she says. She pours me a drink, and we get caught smiling in each other's direction for half a second too long.

Linda hands me a glass, gets in a chair and swivels around, using a control to make her position go up and down. Cute. We end up road-testing these business chairs pretty thoroughly. We put them through their paces, propelling ourselves around her room and combining that with some 360-degree turns and pulling various levers that make the chairs sink and tilt.

The woman is funny, I have to admit. I look at the wrinkles around her eyes. She's a little older than the type I usually go for, but she's got spunk, and I like that.

Three hours and several bottles later her miniature refrigerator is wide open and the train set is out. I have only unwrapped the locomotive, and I've done it with a lot of care. I have been careful not to put finger marks on it. Linda and I are staring at the thing and Linda says to me, 'They don't make 'em like they used to.'

'Oh, this is brand-new. Some people still make 'em like they used to.'

'Well, here's to the ones who still make 'em like they used to,' Linda says, supping from a wine glass.

The train is made of thin steel. A beautiful red and black miniature. I am assembling pieces of train track. Eight round ones join together to make a tiny circle. This train operates with a charger. I had to cut a piece of plastic to unwrap it, but I don't think Frank will notice. We're waiting for the locomotive to charge. I'm excited. I feel like a kid again.

I'm staring at the bottom of a bottle, and Linda asks me if we want to start another.

'Nah. I don't want to be hung over tomorrow,' I say.

'Me neither,' she says. 'Shall we have it anyway?'

I nod and she goes to the fridge. 'Avoid the expensive one,' I say.

'Which one's that?'

'Mount Lincoln.'

She grabs the mini-bar menu and selects the cheapest. She unscrews the top, and refills my glass.

'Jesus,' she says, handing it to me.

'Tastes like horse tranquilizer,' I say.

'Oh, you've tried horse tranquilizer?'

'As a matter of fact I have. Just a small amount. I was curious. It just made me a bit drowsy.'

'The worst thing I ever tried was my mother's rum when I was six years old,' Linda says. 'I had a whole glass of it. I didn't know it was supposed to be drunk with a chaser. It tasted horrible but I made myself do it.'

'You must have had a fun day.'

'Yeah, I had a hard time hiding it at the dinner table. I got the hiccups and everyone at the table tried scaring me for the rest of the meal.'

We both have a giggle over that one. Linda starts unwrapping the wrapping paper. Using a flannel I take the train off the charger, flick a switch and I place it on the track and it goes around and around a couple of times before the charge runs out.

'It's a beautiful thing,' she says to me. 'Your boy will be really excited.'

She has the wrapping paper out and I repackage the train set as carefully as I can. I'm so excited about giving it to him. I cut strips of Sellotape and I hang them off an ergonomic chair while Linda does a beautiful job on an awkward-shaped package. 'He'll be pleased to see you when you turn up with this,' she says, and she catches a look on my face that betrays me. 'Tom,' she says, 'why won't he be pleased to see you?'

'Oh, shall I count them on my fingers? 1. I abandoned him. 2. I'm a shitty person. 3. I've been a shitty father—'

'Oh, really? You've been a shitty father 100 per cent of the time?'

'No. We've had some great moments, me and Frank.'

I go into my wallet and I pull out the folded photograph of me and Frank on the Buffalo Boulders.

'See the cracks in those boulders? There were crabs in there. We spent hours hunting around under rocks for crabs. He was so cute. We found a dead crab and Frank wanted to take it home so we took it with us and it stank the car out. He was so excited. He was so . . .'

'Hey, Tom.' Linda puts her hand on my back. I must've got a bit misty-eyed there or something.

'I've been a bad father, Linda,' I say to her.

'It's never too late to change,' she says.

'Well, Frank will be the judge of that.'

She puts her palm against my cheek and holds it there, and I have a strong urge to kiss her. I really do, but . . .

I get to my feet and we smile to each other and I can see in her eyes that she might like me to stay, and she can probably see in my eyes that I would like to stay too. But I move towards the door anyway and she says, 'Sure you'll be able to work your magnetic strip?' and I laugh and say, 'Yes. Me and the magnetic strip are going to get on just fine tonight.' She smiles at me, and I have to use a lot of willpower to get myself out of her room.

I have a kind of permanent insomnia. I sleep for about three hours a night, generally. For another two hours there's a lot of lying in bed, and thinking, replaying the past and preparing for the future.

I've been practising what I'll say to Frank when I pick him up at school tomorrow. I'm pretty nervous about it all.

I used to love picking him up from school. In the middle of all those mothers and the total chaos of the playground; it's the law of the jungle there. And then, emerging from it, there's Frank, trying to find his way in this world. He holds my hand as we pass the kids with the giant orange lollipop. I act the goat a little as we cross the crossing. We both try not to step on any white and . . .

Oh, I loved it. He was seven then. I've missed four years of it. It won't be easy to make up for four years of being a stranger, but I will do my best.

I have to take this second chance opportunity and give it everything I've got.

I mean, I have reasons to be optimistic. I have some excellent qualities. I'm relatively charming. This isn't egotistical self-appraisal. People tell me I am, and, frankly, I agree with them. And I can start again, a new career.

And I'll just face what I have to face. I'll have a nice weekend with Frank. I'll prove to Deborah how reliable I can be now, and maybe that might rekindle something. I'll pay Robert Valentine back his socks. And once that's all square, I'll turn myself in and face what I have to face.

I mean, what's the worst thing that could happen? A year in prison? I doubt it. Not when I get Herb Lamont on the case. He's a good man and a great lawyer. He knows how to work a system, does Herb. And even if I get a month or two in the clink, it'll help me get off the drink. Whatever will happen, will happen. I've just got to face up to my actions, ditch being William McGinty and repair the name of Tom Spotswood, rebuild things with Deb and Frank, and then I can start a new life with a clean slate.

Thursday

The barrel chest and the
spare tyre

9.45 a.m.

I see Linda in the lobby and she wants to have breakfast with me. I suggest we head down to Mountain Peaks, an old regular of mine, across the road from a building that is dear to my heart.

We walk past the HGC Building and even though I've got a bad crick in my neck I feel compelled to look all the way up the building, at the top floor.

That's where I used to work. I'm contemplating sneaking in there later, but this is an ideal opportunity to get the lie of the land. I ask Linda to wait a second, and I head inside. According to the signage, Thoroughbred is no longer on the top floor. I ask an Indian man in a suit, 'Where did Thoroughbred shift to?'

'Huh?' he says.

'You work here?'

'Yeah, for about a year. I don't know about a Thoroughbred,' the guy says, apologetically.

'Thoroughbred got taken over,' a woman who comes past says.

'What do you mean?'

'You know, Providential, Prudential, Evidential, something dential. They took it over.'

'The big fish always swallow the small fish,' the Indian man says.

It gets worse. Mountain Peaks has closed down. My heart sinks when I see that Mountain Peaks has been taken over by a horrible-looking coffee chain store called Zing.

There's only one table there so Linda grabs it while I wait in the queue, but I get completely confused when they finally serve me.

'What sort of zing would you like?' a guy with too much hair gel asks me.

'Pardon?'

'What's your zing? Do you want a lasting zing or a quick shot or a no-more-headaches zing—'

'Please. Tea for two.'

'We don't do tea.'

'Coffee then. Coffee for two.'

'Uhh . . .' the meatbrain goes, like I've thrown him a really difficult request.

'You gotta choose from the menu, sir,' he says to me.

So I sigh and I look up at the menu and I get two lasting zings, two croissants and an expensive banana. He gives me a flag with a number on it.

The coffee here is terrible. I suspect I am drinking some dregs that were made yesterday and have been reheated in a microwave.

Linda wants to know more about Frank, so I tell her a few stories, like the time he scared the hell out of me on a swing bridge, and the time I let him steer the station wagon on his fourth birthday.

And that's when I see him again. The guy from Barney's. The barrel chest and the spare tyre. The receding hairline and the seven-day-old stubble. I know coincidences happen in The City, but something about him seems shifty.

'Hey, Linda. I . . . I saw this guy yesterday, and . . . he's here now, but please don't look . . . You probably think I'm paranoid but it feels like I'm being followed . . .'

'Are you pulling my leg?'

'No. That would be a fun thing to do, but no . . . I can feel a pair of eyes are looking at me.'

'I've got both eyes on you right now, so . . .'

'Peripheral. Something's happening in my peripheral vision.

He's over there, looking at me, and staying out of sight. Does that sound like crazy talk or what?'

'Oh, I don't know. We're always being watched. I always get thinking I'm on *Candid Camera*, you know, the TV programme. What does he look like?'

'He's got a barrel chest and a spare tyre. He looks half-muscle, half-fat. Like one of those shotputters. And he squints—'

'He squints?'

'Well, I think the squint is a cover-up. He looks over and the moment I see him he pretends he's looking just to the right of me, and he squints to make me think he's looking at a different depth of field. It's complicated.'

I look over at the counter menu, where he's queuing, but I stare behind, like I'm scanning the counter menu. I can see him at the bottom of my eyeball. I think he's looking my way. So I drop my eyes a little and straight away he turns, real quick, too quick, like I just gave him a close call.

'Linda, are you willing to do a little favour for me?'

'Of course.'

'I'm keen to play a little three-player game. I'll go for a walk and he'll follow me and then you can follow him.'

'Ohh, that sounds like fun. This is exciting, Tom.'

'Don't do anything silly. If you lose him, you lose him.'

'I'll be careful. I can keep my distance.'

I set off down the street, going nowhere in particular. I veer off down a well-lit alley, and the footsteps echo all around me. I stop all of a sudden and light up a cigarette. I listen for footsteps. Sure enough, I hear some footsteps slow down and come to a stop.

So I take off again. I don't want this guy to know I'm on to him. I head down the street and into a little shop, hoping he might come in too. I buy some cigarettes and I see a bunch of marshmallow Easter eggs, all individually wrapped. Frank will like those, for sure, so I buy as many as I can stuff in my pockets. As the grocer taps numbers into his till I look up at the shop's security screen. The store is fairly empty. There's an old guy at the counter, a couple of

Indian women at the refrigerator, and my guy, hiding behind a tray full of bread.

So I play another fun little game. I pretend I forgot something and I head towards the bread section. I keep my eyes well away from him, but I see him suddenly pick up a loaf of bread and take it to the grocer.

Now that's funny. I bet he had no intention of buying bread.

Anyway, while he's queuing I grab another thing. I don't need anything else. I'm just trying to look natural, so I go for a sachet of soup. An odd choice, I know, but at least powdered soup is cheap. If I'm going to buy something I don't want, it might as well be cheap.

At the counter I am careful not to lay eyes on him, but I do hear his voice.

'Thanks,' he says, and they ask him if he wants a plastic bag for his bread and he says, 'Yeah, sure,' and he leaves the shop with a loaf of bread he doesn't want.

As I exit the shop I run into Linda, who is pretty excited. 'Did you see him?' she whispers, and I say, 'Yeah. Happy Easter,' and I hand her an Easter egg, and I give the guy time to get further away from us.

Who are you?

They're pulling the old girl down

10.50 a.m.

I apologize to Linda and say I've got to go. She wants to know who my guy was and I say to her, 'He's no one. I was just being paranoid.'

As soon as she's out of sight I'm chasing my guy. To catch up with him I have to take my chances with the traffic, and I get across with only one car honking. He is leaning against a light blue truck and talking on a cellphone. He's looking back in the direction of the shop we were at. I see him get into his truck and I shift out of sight of his mirror. The traffic is busy and he's having a hard time pulling away; the invitation is too much for me. I jump on to the back of his truck as it moves into the traffic. I try the door and it flips open and I have to perform a Fosbury flop to get inside.

My body isn't quite as agile as it used to be, and I'm paying a price for my athletic manoeuvre. My eyes adjust and I see that inside the truck with me is some tarpaulin, some stone and plaster sculpture – Egyptian stuff including a gargoyle with a feisty expression on his face – and a urinal.

I don't know where I'm being taken, but I'm already planning when I'll jump out of the truck. Not too soon and not too late. But it's good to know your enemy, so I'll see where he takes me.

It's just a short trip. It feels like we've driven about five blocks and I feel the truck come to a halt. I hear another truck pull up.

I open the back door a little and look through a gap and my guy is coming right towards me, so I dive behind the urinal.

The door opens and he jumps in the truck. My face is right next to his feet.

Suddenly I hear this noise, a shrill high-pitched siren-like noise. It's his cellphone. He answers it.

I hear a male voice on the phone. 'Hi, it's Alastair Shook. You rang?'

'Hi, Alastair. I saw him,' he says.

The voice on the other end of the call is pretty faint but I can just make it out.

'Where?' the voice says.

'Zing on Collins. Then he went to a shop, on the corner of Collins and Hobs— FUCKIN THING!' he explodes.

I hear a sliding sound of tarpaulin being dragged and thrown out, and he jumps out again.

I sidle out of the truck as quietly as I can. I'm in the middle of The City somewhere, in some kind of worksite.

I get a little distance between me and the truck. I'm crouching next to a couple of pigeons. I light up a cigarette and get my bearings.

There's an old crane here with a chain attached and, resting on the ground, a big metal wrecking ball. I'm at the back of a building and there's a lot of activity here. There's a hole in the wall and people are coming and going, taking treasure from the inside, and loading it into trucks.

I sneak to the front and I get a real shock when I realize that the building they're demolishing is a movie theatre. Not just any movie theatre. It's the Century. They can't destroy the Century!

I see a figure standing on the road with a placard in hand. A young woman with beautiful brown hair. She cuts a fine figure, but a bit of a desolate one too. Her sign says, 'Honk for the Century!'

I go up to her and I say, 'They can't pull down the Century!' She hands me a flyer and says, 'Would you like to sign our petition, sir?' and I say, 'Yes! Gladly.' She hands me a clipboard and a pen.

She looks like she eats a lot of lentils. She's got fresh-looking skin and an energy that radiates off her like a spring flower. I sign her piece of paper.

'What are they replacing it with?' I say, and she says, 'I think it's going to be either high-rise apartments or a parking lot.'

'Ugh,' I say.

'This is where I work,' she says, then she corrects herself. 'Worked. Until three weeks ago. And I spent a lot of time here when I was little. My grandfather was the projectionist.'

I look at the wisps of hair that are draped across her ear, and she reminds me of Deborah somehow.

'I used to come here a lot,' I say to her. 'I took my son Frank to his first film here. It was about an Aboriginal boy who becomes best friends with a pelican. You seen that movie?'

'Before my time, I suspect.'

'Hey, watch it.'

'Sorry,' she says, all worried that she's offended me.

'Would you like to see inside?' she asks.

'I sure would,' I say.

'I'm Celia,' she says.

'Celia. Nice name. Rolls off the tongue.'

She takes my arm and pulls me past some orange cones and down a little alley.

She takes out a key and opens up a side door.

Celia and I have snuck up the stairs and we're hiding in the back row of the third-floor balcony. My guy emerges on the second-floor balcony with a bunch of guys, one of whom is having a coughing fit.

I'm staring up where the stars of the night sky used to be. Now the lights are off permanently.

'I don't know what to do,' says Celia.

'Huh?'

'It's too late to save this place. I tried phoning the council. But no one's taking my calls. No one's on my Facebook page. It feels hopeless.'

'You want to stop this from happening?'

'It's happening. I can't stop it.'

'Isn't that a bit defeatist?'

'It's realistic.'

'Hold on. You asked me to sign a petition.'

'I only have seventeen signatures,' she says.

'Oh. Okay,' I say. I'm trying to be encouraging but I'm not liking her odds.

'I've been making videos and taking photos to put on the internet,' she says.

'That's a good angle.'

'It's futile.'

'But you've got to try, right? You do what you can.'

Celia looks up at the ornate ceiling. I look up too and I imagine the lights out and the stars in the ceiling gazing down at us. And I imagine that sitting next to me is Deborah, and we're watching something Polish, and I know I should be amazed by the cinematography but all I can think about is the person sitting next to me. With my peripheral vision I watch her watch the movie. I watch the flickering lights dancing around her face. I watch her eyes which are lost in Poland somewhere. She's got her mouth open a little, and her lipstick is glowing and I really want to kiss that mouth . . .

'You okay?' Celia says to me.

'Huh?'

I wipe my eyes with my sleeve. 'Listen,' I say to her, 'you really want to hold things up for a bit? Don't bother with placards and signs. You should go for their machines.'

'What?'

'Put the machine out of action and the whole operation might be out of action for a bit. Buy yourself some time.'

'Buy myself a war, you mean,' she says. 'Like, I really care about this place, but I'm asking myself, am I willing to get arrested for it?'

'Yeah, well, that's a point. Someone wise once told me, "Don't ever fuck your future." I didn't listen of course,' I say, and she laughs at that.

'Someone wise once told me, "Don't get caught,"' she says, with a smile.

'Yeah. There's a real art to that.'

We hear some voices from the side and a gang of them appear at the opposite side of the balcony. We sneak out of view. Celia pulls out a camera. She's fumbling around with it.

'Just checking the flash isn't on,' she says.

'Smart,' I whisper.

While Celia takes some photos I keep an eye on the workers on the second floor. They are pulling out chairs. It's an assembly line type of production. One guy unbolts and then two guys grab a block of four chairs. They take it to the balcony, where they drop the chairs on some sheet that they've laid out on the ground floor. My guy is working hard too. He must be a bit of a powerlifter the way he's carrying on. I can see he's pretty strong. My guess is he's pretty low down the food chain. I still don't know how the whole hierarchy fits together but I suspect my guy works for Alastair Shook, and Alastair Shook works for Robert Valentine.

The whole thing is feeling bigger than I expected. I think maybe I should lie low until I've seen Frank. I don't want to jeopardize the weekend.

Celia finishes taking her photos and we slip out of the movie theatre.

Chicken

2.31 p.m.

I'm on the bus with a giant wrapped parcel on my lap. I'm rehearsing conversations in my head. I do it all the time. I'm rehearsing what I'll say to Frank. My imagination picks over every strain, every possibility.

I'm thinking of all the things Frank will say to me. I'll just have to stand there and take it, whatever he says. I can't justify my actions to him. All I can say to him is: That's all in the past. I'm walking a new path now.

I snap myself out of it, because the bus has just reached Codfish Bay.

As I approach Clyde Street Normal I'm thinking about how I should stand holding the big parcel. If I find a good spot outside his classroom I could sit slightly away from the other parents. Maybe I could stand by the Jungle Jim with it. Or I could wait by a water fountain, and when he comes out of his classroom I could be casually drinking from the fountain. Maybe I could go for a little comedy by the zebra crossing. Accidentally sideswipe a teacher, something like that. No – he's older now – I don't want to embarrass him.

I make it to the front gates of the school. It's a bright sunny day and there's a whole class of kids playing a game of candlestick tag. What a fun game that is, although I see a lot of cheating. Once you're a candlestick you're not supposed to move but this one kid is a slow-moving candlestick. He only moves when the teacher isn't looking. Smart kid. He'll go far. These kids are the same age as Frank. I look for a big mop of curly blond hair, but then I think what if Deborah has cut his hair real short like one of those haircuts they give to soldiers in boot camp. God, I know her taste has gone out the window but she wouldn't stoop that low, surely.

I look at the time and I'm nice and early. Some new kids in bright orange vests come out and stand at the pedestrian crossing with their lollipops. A couple of kids who must be Frank's age, and an adult – a parent probably. Hopefully I'll get to do lollipop duty with Frank one of these days. I'd really like that.

As I watch the kids I realize that I'm not the only early parent here. Down in the distance, at the other end of the tennis courts, a barrel chest . . . a balding, fat head . . .

It's him.

It's the demolition guy.

I tie my shoelaces behind a car and I watch him.

Are they following me?

Or are they threatening me?

He looks every part the hired thug. Robert Valentine can't be the wealthiest man in the world or he'd have hired someone more athletic. If Valentine is sending out the heavies he must be worried. Why am I a threat? Is there something I know that I don't know I know?

I'm curious enough to want to know more. I amble in his direction and I crouch behind a car. I watch him staring at the school grounds. He looks in his forties. He hasn't got a lot of hair at the front of his head, but a lot at the back. He obviously isn't taking care of himself in the fashion department. Must be married.

He looks twitchy. He walks down a side street, behind the dental clinic.

So I head in his direction. I must have hurt myself riding in the back of the truck because my hips feel like they've locked up a little. I suspect I've sprained something, but I shut out the discomfort and head for my target.

I make it round the bend and I find him urinating into some begonias behind the dental clinic. A nice prone position. I walk towards him and when he sees me he tries to take off, but he hasn't finished urinating so he shuffles sideways and leaves a trail of piss all over the side wall of the dental clinic. I quicken my walk and he takes off, wetting himself in the process.

'Hey,' I yell and he's moving real quick now.

I chase him, but he's quick for a big guy. He huffs and puffs his way down a side street and I follow him, and I feel this enormous shooting pain in my neck like my head is about to wrench clean off my shoulders, but now is not the time to be concerned with such matters. I chase after the guy and I must have a residual build-up of tar in my lungs because I'm wheezing, but I'm determined not to lose him this time. He's running now, and this damned giant parcel is stopping me from hitting top speed.

I round a corner and I follow him down a cul-de-sac. He gets in his truck, starts the engine and drives towards me. I stand in the middle of the narrow street and I hold my arms as wide as I can and he comes straight at me, expecting me to get out of the way but no way am I backing down for this punk, so he comes right at me, and at the last moment he swerves on to the footpath and I feel his hubcap against my left ankle. I feel it all in slow motion. I fall backwards. I instinctively twist to stop Frank's present from smashing to the asphalt, and I feel a jolt as my head slams into the ground.

His truck pulls up and he gets out and comes towards me. I try to crawl away but my body won't move fast enough. So I exaggerate the injury and I lie like I'm prone in the middle of the road. He looks at me like he broke me in two or something. I say to him, 'Hey,' and I motion for him to come closer.

'You okay?' he asks.

I stare up at his ugly fat face. 'Tell Robert Valentine I have his socks. But if he wants them he can come and face me, man to man.'

He goes to give me a hand up but I swing the toe of my foot into his groin with what feels like the last bit of energy I have. I say to him, 'I only want to talk to Robert Valentine. Not you.' I know – tough words from a guy lying on the ground – but there's a lot of bluff in this game. He looks at me with real venom in his eyes, but then he backs away as if he's scared of me, even though he's twice my size. Like a lot of tough guys, he's soft where it counts. He almost looks like he's going to cry. It's pathetic. He says, 'Fuck you, you fuckin arsehole,' and he runs away from me again and skids off in his car, leaving me lying in the middle of the road, like wounded roadkill, and I feel myself blank out.

My eyelids don't want to open.

I can hear a high-pitched electronic buzz going repeatedly, like an alarm.

I think it's a school bell.

I open my eyes and I don't know how long I've been out for. My hands are bleeding from the fall and some of the blood has made it on to my shirt. So much for looking smart for Frank.

I try to pull myself up but my body is refusing to cooperate. I use all my energy just to drag myself to the footpath. Then I shift on to my knees and I prop myself on all fours. I try to get to my feet but my body is calling for time out and I have to force myself up like a weightlifter doing the clean and jerk.

I pick up Frank's present and I hobble along the road at the speed of a snail on crutches.

I know I can walk this thing off with a little determination. I can hear children laughing and yelling in the distance. I hide the blood on my shirt by doing up my jacket button and I rehearse my excuses: I swear to God, Frank, it's not my fault. I was here early, I . . .

My muscles are screaming at me for rest but it's nothing compared to the shame I feel, so I push on, I hobble double-pace. I make it to a full stride using mind over matter. As I get closer to the school I see that my hand is still bleeding. I wipe it on a lamp post and a couple of kids in school uniform walk past and stare at me.

By the time I get to the school there are hardly any kids left. I stand by the front gate and I wait for Frank. The kids with the pedestrian lollipops have put their lollipops away and I'm thinking about where Frank is likely to be. This school has more than one gate but Frank knows to meet me at the front gate. Also, I figure if I move around in circles then he might miss me, so I stay put for a bit.

I'm having some horrible thoughts. What was the demolition guy doing outside the school? Trying to intimidate me? Have I just got Frank mixed up in this?

Who is Robert Valentine? Who would stoop this low?

I realize, of course, that the most likely explanation for Frank not being here has nothing to do with Robert Valentine. It's simple. Frank came out when the school bell rang, and he went home. Or he's waiting for me outside his class.

I head into the school. The buildings here are in a maze-like formation, and I have to keep my wits about me not to get lost. I arrive at what I think is Frank's classroom, and I look inside and see a whole lot of school desks with upside-down chairs on top of them. There's a lot of artwork on the walls. There are big letters on the blackboard that say Future Problem Solving.

Where the hell is Frank?

Stay calm, Tom. Don't jump to irrational conclusions. Keep rational.

The area is devoid of kids. I can't even find any teachers about. I walk around classroom after classroom and I see a fence close to a roof of a classroom.

I'm on the roof of the highest block now. I can see the whole school grounds but I can't see Frank. I can't see him.

'Frank!' I'm yelling. 'Frank! Where are you?'

Spud

Tuesday

An expensive date with cheap flowers

5.30 p.m.

So I'm at the shop and there's these flowers outside the window, yellow ones, so I take them to the counter and the guy tries to charge me twenty bucks for them. And I'm like, 'There's gotta be some mistake,' and the shopkeeper says, 'That's the correct price, sir.'

I go back and look at all the other flowers, looking for price tags, but none of them have price tags. The shopkeeper says, 'Those red ones are the cheapest.'

I feel a bit of guilt for buying Kimbo the cheapest flowers, so I say, 'What's second cheapest?' and he sells me these purple flowers with yellow inside them.

I feel a bit of a dork walking with the goddam flowers. I have to walk past a construction site and some guys I know jeer and give me a lot of shit.

Ha fuckin ha.

I feel shattered as I haul myself into the Dwarf, everyone's nickname for my small truck. I used to have no problems with night shift but this time round it's proving a real killer. I'm finding it hard to sleep at home at the moment. Kimbo makes a point of being real noisy. I wish I was in bed right now, but no. At the moment I'm trying to sleep from 4 p.m. until 10 p.m., so what does she do? Organizes one of our 'dates' at 6 p.m. She has no sympathy.

She's got it into her head that we need to 'work' on our relationship. You shouldn't have to work on a relationship. That's like saying you're working on eating chocolate. It should be easy, right?

69

I'm running late. It wasn't my fault. Jim went off topic on the phone and started on about his grandson's addiction to p and I couldn't exactly just, like, say, Seeya, Jim, I gotta head off for a date with Kimbo. I mean, Jim just kinda started into it and he wouldn't stop talking and it took about twenty minutes off me. As I'm driving I'm looking at my hands and I haven't had time to wash them. Kimbo will have something to say about that, for sure.

The traffic is intensely busy in The City so I have to ride the Dwarf with two wheels on the footpath for half a block. People clear a path for me and I make it to a paraplegic park and I think, well, my hernia operation was only eight months ago. I slow down to take the park when I see a guy in a wheelchair at the crossing lights and I figure, no, for the benefit of paraplegics I'll cop a telling off by Kimbo for being late.

When I get to the restaurant Kimbo doesn't comment on how late I am. Still, I can feel by her mood that I'm going to pay for it. I say to her, 'I know. I'm late.' I hand her the flowers and she stares at them.

'It's nice of you to get me flowers, Spud, but . . . you could shell out a bit more next time, couldn't you?'

'Hey, they cost me fourteen dollars. And I got this meal coming up, which'll be, what, another fifty, sixty. What am I? Made of money?'

'Shall we just have an entrée then and go home and have some beans on toast?' she says.

'It's tempting.'

'Jesus, Spud, I was joking, okay?!'

'Oh yeah, so was I,' I say, and there's a bit of a peace and quiet while we look at our menus.

Kimbo orders the porterhouse steak, which is twenty-eight dollars, just to piss me off. I know things are tight so I'm forced to order an entrée.

'How's your squid rings?' Kimbo says to me when the food arrives, and I say, 'It's calamari,' and Kimbo laughs, saying, 'Otherwise known as squid rings.'

70

Next to our table are a twenty-year-old couple with nose piercings, and one of them, the girl, looks at us from time to time and whispers to her partner, while Kimbo and me sit and eat quietly.

'This steak's delicious. Wanna bite?' Kimbo says.

She cuts me a portion of steak and holds the fork to my mouth to feed it to me. Frankly, I find this feeding-in-public thing embarrassing. She knows it too.

I say, 'Put it on my plate,' but she just holds it in front of me, and I have to eat it off her fork in front of the couple with nose piercings.

Then the restaurant dims the lights and now Kimbo and I are in candlelight, which feels a bit weird.

I start playing with the candles, not really because I have a wax fixation, it's just I don't know what to say to her that she hasn't already heard.

We can talk about TV and things we've seen. We can talk about Kenny Rogers' plastic surgery. We can talk about work a bit but not for long without boring each other. I can't talk to her about any night I went out because that will lead to Kimbo going on a rant that I'm getting more nights out than her, which is untrue. Kimbo has been out several times in the last month and I've only been out two times – once to that fuckin boring meeting about the time-share, and once that unfortunate night with the lads, down at the steakhouse.

Kimbo says to me, 'You're really good on conversation, Spud,' and I say, 'What's the point of idle chit-chat? I know your views on everything. You know mine.'

Kimbo says, 'Make a fuckin effort, Spud,' and so I look out the window and see that it is raining so I say, 'What about this rain?' and I'm finding the whole thing a complete waste of my energy. I should be fuckin asleep right now, you know?

Kimbo says, 'Careful you don't dirty their tablecloth,' and I look at the tablecloth and there's little fingerprint marks on it. I go to the bathroom and I wash my hands and my arms and I dry them on the hand towel and I feel sorry for the next guy who tries to use it. I chuck some water in my face too, and I take my time because I'd rather be in this little room right now than out in the restaurant with her. I hate it when she's like this.

When I get back Kimbo starts up with the relationship counselling crap.

'Spud. I'd really like it if you could come up with some things to talk about. I hate being the only one who thinks of things to talk about.'

I don't know what to say. There's nothing to say so why say stuff just to fill in space? It's not my problem that she can't handle a couple of moments of peace and quiet, is it?

I eat a squid ring and I say to her, 'I don't know what to talk about. If you want to talk, say something. And I'll say something back. Don't ask me to think of fuckin . . . conversation topics or any of that shit.'

She starts eating her steak in a real sulk, like, clearly I'm the worst person in the world or something.

Driving home, I cut through the pedestrian mall because it's a good short cut, and Kimbo says to me, 'You're a real romantic, Spud.'

'No chance of a blowjob tonight, huh?'

'About as much chance of me having an orgasm with you in the same room,' she says, and the car rolls past a couple of dropkicks pashing in front of where I need to drive, so I give them a little toot and they get out the way and I have to make my way carefully between two parking meters to get back on the road again. We hit a red and say nothing for the whole time the light is on red. We take off again and Kimbo rolls up her sleeve and replaces a nicotine patch.

At home I want to have a sleep but Kimbo will spew if I make the sheets dirty and I got dust all over me. I head straight to the shower and Kimbo's there. She beat me to it. Typical. I use the time to try to call Joey but my mobile phone has got this thing where it decides to switch off whenever it feels like it. The address book is a mental minefield and I can't even read the writing – they're making it so small now. I find Joey's number and I phone him, and after a few rings he answers it and it turns off again.

Fuckin thing.

So I hold down the on button and it vibrates and then I gotta wait for it to load up and it takes a fuckin age so while I'm waiting for it I got time to see if Kimbo's done and I think, Fuck it, I'll come in anyway so she can take a hint.

'That you, Spud?' she says and I joke, 'Who else is it gonna be? You expecting company?' and she reaches out behind the shower curtain and gives me the finger.

I got nowhere to go so I sit on the toilet seat and wait there while she scrubs herself and it really makes me think back to times when we couldn't wait to get naked together. We had some really wild animal moments with each other back in the day.

'How much longer will you be?' I ask her, and she says, 'I'm washing my hair,' and I go into the next room and grab a towel and Kimbo says, 'Don't use a white one.'

I hear her turn off the shower and as she comes out I head past her and I can feel her looking at me and I just feel so . . . frustrated and also . . .

I've got a semi up and running and we could easily go somewhere with that but Kimbo seems more interested in drying herself than in paying attention to dirty old me.

I hop in the shower and I have to really scrub myself clean and Kimbo says, 'You need a face cloth?' which is really her way of saying, 'Don't touch mine,' like I got some kind of disease or something.

Christ. I wish she'd leave the room so I could breathe easy, but she turns on her hair dryer and I can hear the noise of it.

I pull a nicotine patch off my chest and stare down at the onset of a middle-aged spread. I still got muscles in my stomach, but they push out at a thin layer of fat, making me look like a fat guts. It makes me think I should stop doing weights, but I need the strength for work. Still, I suck my stomach in a little just in case Kimbo decides to turn around. She used to find me attractive, you know, back in our twenties. There was a time when I used to say to her,

'Can you please slow down,' because she was always in such a rush to have her way with me. Now we've both passed the wrong side of forty there's no sex unless she's had three bottles of Chardonnay and her body is so floppy by then that it's like trying to fuck a rubber doll.

She turns the tap on to brush her teeth and I get a hot snap and I yell, 'Hey!' and she flicks off the tap again, spits in the sink and says, 'Sorry, I forgot you were there.'

I'm lying in bed and I'm struggling to sleep when I hear a yell from the next room.

'Lucy!' Kimbo yells, and I can hear Lucy getting told off and interrogated, Kimbo-style.

'Would you like to explain this?' Kimbo's yelling.

I can't hear what Lucy is saying back, I can just hear Kimbo's booming voice on its way to full throttle. 'What? You were trying to do what? On the what?'

Next thing Kimbo opens the bedroom door and she's holding her hair straightener in one hand and the sheepskin rug her mother gave her in the other, and she's looking at me and saying, 'Look what your daughter did.' The hair straightener has white fluff all over it and a whole section of the sheepskin rug looks pretty matted, and Kimbo's glaring at me. She wants me to do something about it.

What's it got to do with me? It's her fuckin rug.

'I'm trying to sleep,' I say.

'I'm trying to raise our daughter, and it feels like I'm doing it alone—'

'What do you want me to do?'

She gives me the evil eye and I have to listen to the two of them going at it again. Jesus Christ. I don't even like that sheepskin rug.

A phone call from Alastair Shook

7.34 p.m.
I'm lying in bed, unable to sleep, and I'm trying to figure whether to go for the sleeping pill. I could get three hours' sleep out of it but I find it takes me about three No-doze at the other end of it to fire up again. So I grab a nicotine patch instead and slap that on my chest. There's a shaft of light coming in the room that I can't get rid of so I shove a pillow on my face and I just lie there, hoping sleep will come, somefuckinhow among all the chaos around me.

I've finally drifted off and I'm having this dream that I'm being lifted at the seat of my pants by a crane hook and I'm being dragged through a river with my head and my hands and my feet in the water. I have this dream all the time. I don't know why but it makes me feel better, the water cooling me down, calming me, when Kimbo's voice interrupts the dream with, 'Spud. You got a call.'

She chucks the portable phone on my bed and I say to her, 'Can't it wait?' and she says, 'His name is Alastair Shook. He says it's urgent,' and I stare at the phone and all I want is forty winks but no, everyone wants a piece of me at the moment, and I put the phone to my ear, and I say, 'Hello?'

This is the last thing I need right now. I'd be lucky if I've had an hour of sleep. I'm in our little office, kinda more Kimbo's office than mine, and this computer is a piece of junk. When you turn it on it takes about ten minutes to warm up and the internet is so slow

75

that when I try to look at an email I've got time to take a quick piss before the page loads.

Downloading the picture of Tom takes for ever. They got a little bar on the screen and it pulses like it's moving but it's just an optical illusion because if you look at the bar closely you'll see that it's not even moving a millimetre.

Eventually a message tells me it has downloaded, but I can't find the fuckin file. And really, there's better things that I could be doing. I'm hunting around for the file on the desktop. How am I supposed to guess where the fuckin thing is?

Kimbo hears me groan as I take my frustrations out on the mouse. She pokes her head in. 'You okay?' she asks.

'I just downloaded a file and I can't find it.'

She opens up a little window on the computer. 'Is this it?' she asks, pointing to a file called ga064.jpg.

'Yes,' I say and wait for her to leave the room.

I don't want to look at it, but I get stuck looking at his eyes, those scumbag eyes.

I push the print button and the printer doesn't print. I yell, 'Kimbo, why isn't it printing?' and she says, 'It's probably out of paper.' I look for the doo-dacky thingamy icon for minimizing and I can't find it and she comes in. I lean in front of the monitor and she says, 'Oh, it's a paper jam. Let me show you how to fix it,' and she fucks around with the printer and she tries to use the computer but I say to her, 'I can do it.'

'Don't be a fuckin dick. I'm trying to help,' she says, and I say to her as polite as I can muster, 'I didn't ask for your help.'

'You looking at porn?'

'No.'

'If I find out you've been looking at porn on *my* computer—'

'I haven't been looking at porn, okay? Would you fuck off please?'

I make myself some breakfast and I make my lunch. Kimbo sits at the table reading a bill and punching numbers into a calculator.

'Where's the butter?' I ask her.

She's too lost in maths to give me the answer. Instead she sighs and makes a big fuss about restarting a calculation. It takes until I've finished making my sammies before she talks again.

'We got an appointment with Brenda tomorrow.'

'When?'

'One.'

Seeing Brenda is the last thing I want to be doing tomorrow afternoon.

'Okay. I'll pick you up at ten to one then.'

'Half past twelve.'

'Okay, whatever,' I say, and I get the fuck out of Siberia and I head to Lucy's room and pop the door open.

'Hey, Loose the Goose,' I say.

Lucy opens an eye and she says to me, 'Will you be in bed when I get back from school tomorrow?'

'I don't know. Maybe,' I say, and she closes her eye and faces the other way. 'You want the door open or closed?' I ask, and she says, 'Ajar.'

'Huh?'

'Ajar. It's not a door. It's a jar,' and I can't think of the last time I heard the word ajar and she says, 'A little open. Leave it a little open,' so I leave the door a little open.

I'm in the Dwarf and I'm trying to figure out where to look first: Mountain Peak, Barney's, the HGC Building, or the house out at Codfish Bay. Alastair Shook said to look for Tom in a lot of familiar times and places, so I've written down a list of his routines for him.

As I'm driving I try to phone Alastair Shook but my mobile phone has forgotten how to do its most basic function, which is to make a phone call. It takes its usual thirty-eight seconds to turn on. When I finally dial him he says, 'Hello,' the phone switches off again, and I yell, 'Fuckin stupid piece of shit!' at it.

I reach into the glove box and give myself a quick spray of Rescue Remedy.

As I drive I start thinking about Tom, and I immediately change the subject in my mind. He's not worth thinking about.

★

I haven't been to this house for ten years. The new occupants have really changed it. For a start they've put a big fence around it. Seems everyone is a lot more security-conscious all of a sudden.

I'm gobsmacked, looking at it. They've concreted the lawn. All the grass is gone and been replaced by these ugly grey tiles. I can't believe it.

I'm a bit thrown and I feel a bit weird being here. I'd like to get this over and done with.

I got my photo of Tom in my pocket, but I know I won't need to look at it. He's burned into my head, the prick.

I knock on the door. There's no answer and I look in the front window and I can see down the hallway and I see the bookcase and I curse myself for being such an idiot and not salvaging it when I had the chance. I got a lot of other stuff though. The old oak table was worth a grand, for starters. I only got three hundred for the piano, because it was out of tune. The bed was made of mahogany but it wasn't in good nick so I had to break it up and sell the wood. Still, I got a few hundy for it.

I look in the front bedroom window. There's a couple of suitcases on the bed, with clothes scattered. Looks like the occupants are set to go away for Easter weekend.

As I'm looking in I get this thought, What if Tom's hiding in there or something?

'Tom,' I'm saying, as I walk around the outside of the house.

I feel weird walking around here. I turn around, and I head straight back to the truck.

In the truck I'm back out with the Rescue Remedy. I'm wishing I hadn't got to Stage Two on the nicotine patches too. On Stage One, I can give up easy. But by Stage Two I got a lot invested in this giving-up fantasy.

I grab a second nicotine patch and I stick it on. Just to get calm or whatever. I can't be dealing with this on top of everything. I've got a full plate at the moment. What do they expect from me? Fuck him.

Fuck him. Fuck him. Fuck him.

The last great brick building in town

10.54 p.m.

I got a bumper sticker on the back of T-Rex that says, 'It takes balls to wreck buildings', and it used to be true. Back in the day a wrecking ball was the fastest way to bring down a building. But these days, with hydraulic cranes and all, they are becoming a dying breed.

T-Rex has been good to me. We've brought down a lot of buildings together: the old bank arcade, the H.M. Wrightson's brick building, the Kodak, the old stock exchange to name a few. I got a photo album somewhere in the shed that is packed full of pictures of me and the boys bringing down sites and some of those photos are pretty faded, but in them T-Rex looks brand-spanking-new. Now she's scarred and battered and bruised.

She's pretty much become obsolete, the old girl, thanks to the new cranes that are all on wheels. The number of places she can work at are getting fewer and fewer. As a result she's getting less work and when she's not working her joints are starting to seize, like she's got arthritis. I could keep her in better condition if I greased her up in her downtime, but I haven't had the time to do that lately.

It's getting harder because she hasn't done a job for a couple of months and the writing is on the wall. But you know what? She still does a good job once she's greased up and ready to go. She can pull down a building faster than any of the new hydraulics. When I knew the Century was coming down I was real pleased, because it's a job made in heaven for T-Rex.

I'm greasing the top pulleys and I'm greasing the nipples and running the motor to see how the drum is spinning and I see one of the bushes is getting worn and when that goes I hate to think where I'll get a new one. I got my mechanic, Arthur Chapman, in town, but he's getting crankier and crankier in his old age and he doesn't have the parts any more because he sold them to a guy from the quarry, which fucked me off no end. The parts are getting harder and harder to find and so are the guys who can help you. All the old mechanics are dying and they're taking their knowledge to the grave with them.

I'm having to pump in a hell of a lot of grease just to get her to spin properly. I sit in the cab and turn her on and I can already hear the slopping. I get down underneath again and one of the pulleys is wobbling like a drunk and I have to loosen another bolt and clear out some grit just to get the ballbearing rolling again, and she runs a little better.

I leave her idling and head round to the front. The Century is a beautiful brick building. The bricks were painted black and white, but the black and the white faded a long time ago so now they are grey and cream. The main pillars look like zebra crossings, four of them running up the front. Above the bottom balcony there's an old stairwell criss-crossing the front and centre. There are big front windows, as big as doors, and up above a little frieze juts out. That's a beautiful piece of work, right there. There's two round windows either side of it. Stained-glass, beautiful little windows that Jim will take for sure. They look like little owl's eyes at the top of the building. Just above them are the giant letters, all in caps: CENTURY.

Wow. This building must have been a pride and joy to whoever put her up in the first place. I'd like to meet that man and shake his hand.

It's a while since we've brought down a building as grand as this one. Most of the old brick buildings got taken down about a decade ago but the Century survived and survived. I'm amazed she lasted this long. She's the last great brick building in town. I get a bit of a shiver of excitement. I can't wait to get stuck into her.

★

I walk round to the back of the Century. I've left all the fluoros and tools in the Dwarf. There's no trucks here, nothing. We don't want to bring attention to ourselves. The trucks will come in only at the last possible moment. I knock on a side door and Bull lets me in.

It's good to see everyone. There's a bit of food on the table there, sammies and there's some coffee. I grab a sammie and I sit down and I see Jim's put together a pretty good team. A lot of familiar faces. The men in this room musta pulled down . . . let's say roughly twenty-five buildings a year for ten years is two hundred and fifty, and that's just counting the boom period. Even when things slowed down we would all still be at fifteen a year for the next ten years. I'd estimate the guys in this room must have pulled down about four hundred buildings between us. Probably more.

Good to see Temaia here. He's a nephew of a good friend of mine. He'll be my dogman. His uncle had no fear of heights whatsoever. He could be up ten storeys and he'd be walking around as if he was on the ground. I wonder if Temaia is a chip off the old block.

Dick is cracking jokes just the way Dick always does. He'll be working in the shed. He's never short of a story, is Dick.

But I'm not feeling real social today. I see Joey and he must see I look a bit tired or whatever. He says, 'You wanna coffee, Spud?' and I say, 'Yeah, okay,' and he pours some coffee into a plastic cup and brings it over.

'Things good?' he says to me, but his eyes are saying something else. I think he knows I'm on the edge of holding it together.

'Yeah,' I say back to him. 'Things are good, things are good.'

I'm in the main circle in the Century, on the bottom floor. It's immaculate in here. They took as much care inside as they did outside when they built her. The screen has been taken down and the pillars holding the place up are works of art in their own right.

Jim sees me and comes my way.

'Spud.'

'Jim.'

81

'You want some urinals?' he asks.

It's been a standing joke for as long as I can remember that Jim has a toilet problem. If you go to his yard you'll find more than a hundred toilets sitting there. Decent quality, all of them. He's got more toilets than he can sell.

'Sure,' I say.

He winks and does a loud wolf whistle and all the troops gather round.

Jim always cracks a few jokes when he gives orders, and the boys are lapping up every word he says. He has a dry sense of humour, does Jim. Tonight Jim has hired the trucks and we're taking as much out of here as we can without raising attention. A quick, quiet job.

The team has already been here for five days so they are well under way. Now that the bigger team has arrived I can see that there's a lot more to do before we start attacking on Thursday night.

All the chairs on the bottom floor have been taken out and they're all stacked up on the stage. There's a few floorboards lifted out and a rubbish pile where those floorboards used to be.

All the easy pluck is stacked on the main floor. There's four, eight, twelve chandeliers in mint condition, wrapped in blankets in the corner. Those must be worth, say, three grand each, so there's a good thirty-six grand right there.

A stack of timber sits near the area I'm about to hit. Next to that we got piles of doors – full door frames, some big ones too with nice curves. They're piled four, eight, twelve, fourteen high by four, eight, twelve; that's 168 doors stacked here with varying values but let's say conservatively they fetch an average of two hundy per door then Jim's sitting on 32,000 plus 1,600. There's about 33,600 worth in those stacks. Jim musta wet his pants when he saw this lot.

They've already taken up about a fifth of the floorboards and that's where the real money is. It's good flooring too – six inches thick and is that rimu? If it is, then that alone will be worth a mint. Good long chunks of floorboard, five, six, seven, eight across by, say 100, 120 . . . There would be 960 floorboards on the bottom floor alone. If that's fetching thirty dollars a floorboard and we're looking at 960 by thirty; that's just under thirty grand. That's probably only a fifth of the floorboards in the building, so that's 150 grand in the floorboards alone. Jim'll be having an orgasm every time he thinks about this place.

I climb up on to the stage. They've stacked all the chairs from the bottom floor here. I look at the letters of the rows – they go up to GG which means there are twenty-six plus a, b, c, d, e, f, g, seven more so that's thirty-three rows of ten, twenty, thirty, forty chairs; thirty-three by forty is 330, 660, 990, 1,320 chairs. And that's just the bottom floor.

That's a lot of chairs. The leather in these chairs is a little worn but most of them are in pretty good nick. I sit in one and it feels comfy.

I stare up at the wall and I see a whole lot of plasterwork that Jim hasn't taken yet. This was a themed movie theatre, Arabian nights, and above me is a real ornate Egyptian-themed frieze, with carved figures of Cleopatra and a bunch of other pharoahs and shit. And next to them a whole lot of hieroglyphics that make me think of that old Indiana Jones movie. Did I watch that here?

The hieroglyphics are really cool. There's one of a tiger ready for the kill, and there's an owl, a noose and a snake. I'm thinking in America that would fetch a shitload on eBay. There could easily be twenty grands worth of plasterwork up there. I'm surprised Jim hasn't taken it out but it does look hard to get at.

I don't know how much else Jim is going to take, but I got a feeling it could be a good idea to talk to Muzz and some of the truck boys.

Wednesday

What am I gonna do with nine hundred chairs?

12.04 a.m.

I get the raised eyebrow from Jim. That means it's time for me to put the old dinosaur to work so I hop in the cab and track over to where they've kindly marked a big X for me to hit. We've coned off the area and I've got enough room to get a decent swing up and running. I gib up and aim, swing the ball to the right and back in, just soft, just getting it moving and I swing back further and hit the wall, right on target. Now I slew hard to the right and get a real good swing in and the first bang is music to my ears. It's tough brick down at the bottom of the building so I give it some more oomph and I have to swing in hard another four times before the sound gets softer and one more swing opens up the start of a hole. I start coming in faster, chipping away at the hole, and from there I attack the edges and swing in another twenty or so times and now the hole is big enough that I can see inside the building where the guys are waiting to unload. I move up the line and attack above and around the hole until it is big enough to get a truck in. T-Rex is grunting like a geriatric but no matter, she'll loosen up when I get her rolling for a few hours of sustained work. Temaia, my dogman, gives me the signal to bring the ball down and I wait for the ball to stop swinging and I track back away from the street, as far out of public view as possible.

I jump out of the machine and give her a little whack and I say, 'Good girl,' to her. It sure feels good to have the old dinosaur back in business.

★

There's no time to waste. As soon as I've cleared the area Muzz has put his truck straight in there and the boys start loading the pluck. It's a pretty precise operation. We're trying to get as much out as quietly as possible in the middle of the night. The council have asked for the big push to happen over Easter – when most people have cleared out of town – but there's always a few who hover around. The more we can get done before they see what we're up to, the better. If we can get the building unstable by Sunday we'll have done our job. It'll be tight because we can't start the true work until Thursday night.

In the meantime Jim wants me to try to hide T-Rex but it's a big ask. I lower the crane and chuck all the tarp I can find over her but it's a bit like trying to hide an erection when you've got a g-string on and your hands tied behind your back – not that I've ever had that experience. Still, I do my best. A couple of the boys, Bull and Butterfingers, help me out and we lay out some more orange cones halfway down the alley in case anyone gets curious.

As we're covering up the chairs I see across the road a protester, a young woman in her twenties, and Joey gives me a nudge because she's a bit of a fox but not in a slutty kind of way. She looks educated. She's across the road, clipboard in hand, staring at the cinema. She's on to us for sure. As I drive out of there she pulls out a video camera and starts filming. Looks like our cover is blown.

We're in the walkway between the ceiling and the roof and it smells like no one has been here for a quite a long time. There's ropes on the side which must have been used for bringing the curtains up and down. There's a little gap in the ceiling where we can see right down to the stage. The boys have tied a rope around the truss and I'm leaning down cutting a big circle of plaster with a saw. The plaster spews up white dust and it's easy to cut through.

Next thing I'm down on the stage again with a ladder while the guys lower the thing and I'm staring at the design close up. I love this Egyptian stuff. It looks like a scene of two men fighting for the same woman, who must be Cleopatra. Cleopatra looks like she's into the pharaoh dude, and next to them a guy with a sparrow's face looks a bit fucked off about the whole thing. Then again, maybe he's just fucked off because he has a sparrow's face. I shouldn't rule out that possibility.

We're lowering her down real careful. I'm steadying the rope, guiding her down with a couple of boys below ready to cover it in bubblewrap when Jim yells at me from below.

'Yeah?' I say.

'I'm only taking 420 chairs,' he says.

Straight away I've got my inner calculator up and running but Jim does the maths for me. 'There's another nine hundred down here. I need this stage collapsed as soon as possible. I want the flooring under it.'

I'm staring down at all these chairs thinking, What am I gonna do with nine hundred chairs? They've gotta be worth something but if Jim can't hold them that means he's exhausted all the usual contacts, for sure, so I might be sitting on them for a while. I haven't got a yard. I got junk all over town, in people's garages and on people's back lawns and I definitely haven't got room for nine hundred chairs, unless I can convince Arthur Chapman to take them.

'You want them?' Jim says. 'Be a pity to chuck 'em.'

As soon as smoko comes along I'm in the cab of the Dwarf, yelling at my mobile phone as it does its usual tricks. It manages to stay on long enough for me to wake up Muzz and I ask him how many trucks he can organize. He tells me one is better than zero, which is true enough. I head to the hut and ask Joey and Temaia if they want to be in on this and they say yes without blinking.

I got four hours to clear as much out as I can, and I'm struggling to think where I can put it all. I got Muzz, Joey and Temaia behind me in the big truck, and I've loaded up the Dwarf with urinals too for good measure.

I'm fumbling about with my keys outside Arthur Chapman's garage. I woulda phoned him but my stupid piece of shit mobile phone blanked out mid-call. Joey thinks I may have to delete some texts or something but I don't have time to be fucking around with all that shit right now. Any chance of not waking anyone up has vanished with Arthur's dog barking like a lunatic. I find the right key and I open her up and she's packed full of old cars with my stuff in behind.

I hear Arthur yelling at his dog and coming in my direction. He's wearing a dressing gown and some underpants that he probably bought two decades ago by the look of them. 'I tried to call you, Arthur,' I say to him, and he looks out back at my truck and says, 'Sorry, Spud. No room at the inn.' He lights a cigarette and Joey gives him a twelve-pack of beer as a pre-emptive thank-you gift.

'I need you to clear your shit outta here,' Arthur says, and I say to him, 'I got nowhere to put it,' and he smokes his cigarette and I so want to ask him for a puff it's not funny. 'Donna is giving me grief about your shit. It's gotta go,' he says.

This isn't what I need to hear. I got a truck full of chairs and nowhere to put them. The boys think it's all a bit funny which isn't helping.

'Where am I going to put a truckful of chairs?' I ask them.

'You could do with one of those *Dr Who* phone boxes,' Joey says, with a smile on his face.

Muzz has an idea where to dump them so next thing I'm following him through town, on to an off-ramp and about two k up the motorway where we come to a bridge. He swings off it and we come down to an empty traffic island under the bridge.

He gets out of his truck and says to me, 'Whaddya reckon?' and it's the best of a bad bunch of ideas and even though I know I'll regret it I agree to it. It's council land which isn't ideal but then again, at least it's Easter so I won't get grief from them for a few days. I hate double-handling and I know this is a shitty short-term solution but these chairs could be worth a lot of money. I just think, Fuck it, no one else is using this traffic island so why not me?

Something I was once told was Sometimes the reward is greater than the risk. This is definitely one of those times. I mean, what are the council going to do? A slap on the wrist and a lecture.

Muzz lifts up the back of his truck and dumps them all in one big heap, like his truck is dropping a big shit on the traffic island. I don't have time to second-guess my decisions right now so I drag some tarp out and I'm thankful there's no rain, but the wind is picking up and it's a real bitch trying to cover the load. As me and Joey try to hold it down against the wind I get this picture of Tom out walking the streets somewhere. I refuse to let the prick back into my brain so I shut him out of my head again as I tie down the tarp. Muzz and me hop back in our trucks and head back to the Century for another load.

Opening hours at
Barney's Twist and Shout

10.08 a.m.

We knock off at ten. The operation is still undercover until Easter starts but until then we're trying to look as much as possible like there's nothing happening. We had a discussion on whether to go for the orange cones or not. They're a beacon for nosey people but they could stop people from looking round the back to see where the real action is happening. All the trucks got cleared out before people started arriving to work at eight thirty and the only sign of trouble is T-Rex covered in a massive-as piece of tarp out the back.

I'm clearing outta there and I'm on the phone. It's still doing its stupid trick of turning off every couple of minutes. I clear out some messages and it behaves itself a bit better while I phone a few contacts who may know someone who knows someone who wants to buy nine hundred chairs. I could even sell more if necessary. I've managed to clear out the bottom floor but there's a whole lot on the top floor that I could take nice and easy if there was a buyer.

I get this other text on my phone too from a number I don't recognize: 'Hey. Alastair Shook here. Any luck with Tom?'

I'd like to switch the thing off now and not reply but I think, Well, what choice do I have?

I've headed out for the most obvious place he'd go to at eleven on any weekday: Barney's Twist and Shout. I hate the place. It's so pathetic, watching the regulars gather outside at ten forty-five. Beer for breakfast, huh? What a way to start the day.

On the other hand I've just finished a working day so if anyone deserves a beer at this time it's me.

I've stayed away from the turps for a good five weeks now. Life without booze and ciggies is driving me up the wall. What've I got left to turn to? Porn? Peanuts? Gum? Shopping? Rescue Remedy? The nicotine patches? I question this whole clean living thing. Where is it leading me? I don't feel very good so why am I trying so hard not to have any fuckin fun?

I head into Barney's and I scan the place. It's a long time since I was last here. It's pretty empty. There's a couple of punters at a table, and a guy at the bar. He turns to face me and I recognize him straight away.

It's Tom. I panic.

I panic. I feel my chest pounding and my breathing tighten. I have to get out of here. I can't be in the same room as him without feeling nausea or a need to smash his face in. I almost fall over getting off my stool and I head straight out of the stinking place, bashing my shoulder against the doorway and down the stairs to outside. I feel the stairs rushing up to meet my feet and I feel the footpath slamming up against my feet and I'm trying not to pass out or anything stupid like that. My feet carry me back to the Dwarf and I fumble with my keys and make it inside and I turn on the ignition and drive around the corner and I feel taken over, completely taken over. I reach into the glove box and I find the Rescue Remedy and I spray the fuck out of the back of my throat over and over again. I use half the bottle in one go. I fumble underneath my seat and I find the paper bag and I breathe into it and try to calm down. I gotta get a grip on myself. I gotta get a grip on myself. Fuck him. Get a grip, Spud. Get a grip.

I find myself staring at the A4 piece of paper with Tom's ugly face on it. I screw it up and throw it under the seat. I find my phone and I struggle to look for the text from Alastair Shook and when I try to phone him it conks out after four rings. I turn the fuckin thing on and when it finally springs to life I find Alastair Shook's number, I phone him and as I listen to the phone ringing I shut my eyes and I make myself think of Kimbo, who to sell the chairs to, where to store them if I can't sell them, logistics, logistics, logistics, anything but Tom, anything but that fuckin prick, he doesn't deserve to be thought about, and when Alastair Shook finally answers I have to have one final spray of Rescue Remedy just so I can speak to him without screaming.

Talk is not cheap

12.26 p.m.

I could definitely do with some sleep now but that's not going to happen because Kimbo and me have an appointment with Brenda. The last thing I need.

I still have a load of urinals in the Dwarf and when I get home I back into the front yard and there's a nice gap of lawn that has been sitting there for an age waiting for Kimbo to get her shit together and build the veggie patch she bangs on about but has never got around to actually doing.

So I think I might as well start unloading, but Kimbo catches me red-handed pulling urinals out of the truck and she's straight out of the house with, 'Just what the fuck do you think you're doing?'

'It's just a temporary—'

'No! No urinals on the front lawn. Understand?'

She's bossing me around like I'm a kid and I've already unloaded all but one of them. I say to her, 'Are you going to help me load them back in?' and she says, 'No,' and I say, 'It'll have to wait then. I'll have them out again tomorrow.'

'Oh, yeah, tomorrow,' she says sarcastically.

Next thing we're both sitting in the front of the Dwarf and she's giving me the silent treatment, looking at her mobile phone every ten seconds because she's all worried about being late for Brenda. I'm aware I got the picture of Tom down on the floor by her feet and I wish I'd screwed it up and put it in my pocket because there's no way I want her nosing her way into my business. She's looking out the window not saying anything and I wish I had fixed the car stereo so I could have something to take the edge off. I see a nicotine patch on her arm and I feel angry at myself for letting her con me into giving up smoking just because she's on a health kick.

There's a short cut into town up Severn Street but it's a steep street and the motor on the Dwarf is struggling to make it to the top of the hill. The engine is overheating. I have to shift down to first gear and the Dwarf roars and I can hear the remaining urinal slide into the back door and Kimbo sighs one of those sighs that's designed to be heard by everyone in the whole fuckin world and there is nothing I would rather do less than spend an hour in a little room with her and Brenda.

Brenda's office is on the third floor of an old building in King Street. The lift is one of those ones that looks like it could hold a maximum load of three underweight midgets. It rocks back and forth as it struggles to make it to the fifth floor. For some reason I tuck my shirt in as the lift doors open and we head to Brenda's door, room 5, next to the office for the deaf. It's locked, so we have to wait in the hallway. I sit down on the ground and Kimbo paces and I say to her, 'I'd rather be anywhere but here,' and Kimbo says, 'Way to go on the positivity front, Spud.'

Eventually we hear a ding from the lift and Brenda, a woman in her early fifties with dyed red hair, comes in, holding on to a pot plant. She apologizes for being two minutes late and Kimbo says, 'No problem,' which is the opposite of what she would say to me in the same situation.

Next thing we're in her little office. Kimbo sits in an armchair so I get the couch to myself and Brenda sits across in a triangle.

'Right. So how are we today?' Brenda asks, and I can already feel my blood starting to boil. Kimbo's whole personality changes when she's talking to Brenda. I can hear it in her chit-chat. Brenda asks me how I'm doing and I say, 'Fine.' I can feel every inch of myself want to run out of the room but I stay rooted to the spot like a naughty boy in detention. I see Brenda look up at her clock and I see a box of tissues in the corner of her room. I bet she gets moist every time one of her clients cries.

'Okay,' she suddenly announces, as if it's time to get down to business. 'Why are we here?'

We. I wish she'd stop saying that.

I can feel this silence while she's waiting for one of us to speak and I can tell you one thing, it sure as hell isn't going to be me. Kimbo starts up, and I can hear sobbing in her voice and I bet Brenda is salivating right now at the prospect of an easy mark.

Kimbo says, 'It's not working any more.'

'What's not working any more?' Brenda says, leaning forward with pretend sympathy.

'This. Us.' And I can't help but laugh at the patheticness of it all.

'Are you referring to the relationship?' Brenda asks. Wow. Very perceptive. No wonder she earns a hundred an hour.

'Yes,' Kimbo whimpers.

'And what about you, Spud? Why are you here?'

'You know . . .'

'No she doesn't know,' Kimbo says.

'It's obvious,' I say.

'What's obvious?' Brenda asks.

'You know. What she said. It's not . . . you know . . .' I say and I can really feel my chest heaving. I just wish they'd leave me fuckin alone.

Brenda can see I don't want to answer the question and Kimbo shoots me a look and I say to her, 'What? What have I done this time?'

'She asked you a question,' Kimbo says, 'and the least you could do is answer it,' and I look at Brenda and she's smiling like one of those fuckin Buddhists or whatever.

'This is relationship counselling, right?' I say.

'Yes it is,' Brenda says, laughing. I don't see what's so funny.

'I don't know why I'm here,' I say. 'I'm here because Kimbo said I had to be here.'

★

Oh, fuck. Brenda's asked us to draw something. Kimbo agrees straight away and I can just picture what she'll draw. She's going to draw a big picture of my face and over the top she'll write 'Disappointment.'

I've been asked to draw a moment from the last time I can remember things being good.

'So what's good?' I ask Brenda.

'I don't know,' she says, smiling at me.

'What do you mean by good? Do you mean—'

'Just think of a time when you felt good about your relationship,' she says.

The last time I felt good? That feels like a distant memory. I'm thinking of us at the Alice Cooper concert. When Alice Cooper was pushing a pram on stage, and he pulled a bloody baby out of that pram, and then he threw the bloody baby into the crowd and Kimbo jumped four feet in the air and she caught it and we were so amped, screaming at each other and at Alice Cooper and I remember thinking, Yeah, you're the girl for me.

I'm not going to draw the bloody baby. It would be a stupid thing to do in front of your relationship counsellor but I have to draw something so I take a crayon and I just draw a circle. I look at the circle and I add in some eyes and a smiley face.

Brenda asks to look at it and she wants me to describe what I've drawn. 'That's Kimbo,' I say and Brenda asks, 'And what were you doing at that moment?' and I say, 'Huh?'

'What's that a picture of?' Kimbo says. 'Me with a smiley face? Is that it?'

'No,' I say. 'I was thinking of the . . . I was thinking of Alice Cooper,' I say, and Brenda jumps on that like I just shat out a golden egg.

'Tell me about Alice Cooper,' she says and then she says, 'Tell Kim about Alice Cooper,' and I look at Kimbo and she looks at me with a look that makes me feel real . . . sad, you know? The way she used to look at me, I mean, I shoulda drawn that.

'We went to an Alice Cooper concert,' I say, and Brenda says to me, 'Say it to Kim.'

98

So I say to Kimbo, 'You know, when we went to see Alice Cooper. That was fun.'

Kimbo looks at me and she looks away.

'Yeah, that was fun, but . . .'

'But what?' Brenda says.

'Yeah, but what?' I say.

'You know,' she says. 'We used to have sex back then.'

'It's not the sex. It's you at the concert when you caught the—' and I taper off and give Kimbo a wink because I don't want to say it out loud.

'The what?' Brenda says.

'Oh,' Kimbo goes. 'The baby. The bloody baby.'

Then Kimbo gives Brenda a full rundown of Alice's act, and I gotta say, the thought of it makes me laugh, both of us are laughing and then when we stop laughing I feel kinda weird, because we haven't been laughing too much lately.

Then, thank fuckin God, Brenda drops the Alice Cooper thing and asks Kimbo to show her drawing, and Kimbo has drawn a picture of us and Lucy having a picnic and I was mucking around with Lucy on the seesaw and giving her a giggle.

Brenda likes it a lot and asks me, 'Is that a good memory for you too?' and I say, 'Sure,' and Brenda says, 'Tell Kim.'

'Tell her what?'

'Tell her that it was a good memory for you.'

And I have to look at Kimbo and say to her, 'That was a good memory for me,' and Kimbo says, 'Once more with feeling?'

And I'm like, 'What?'

'Nothing,' Kimbo goes, and I say, 'I had a good time at the picnic with you and Lucy, okay?'

'When's the last time you had a picnic?' Brenda asks, and Kimbo laughs a sarcastic laugh, and Brenda thinks she's hit the bull's-eye. She claps her hands and says, 'Why don't you have a picnic?'

'Huh?' Kimbo says.

'Have a picnic,' Brenda says. 'This week.'

'I'm busy this week,' I say.

'He's always busy,' Kimbo says, telling me off in front of the counsellor. I knew it was a matter of time before they started ganging up on me.

'You know I can't fit it in this week,' I say to Kimbo. 'Next week.'

'Next week. Next week,' Kimbo says, and I'm like, 'What? What? When do I say that?'

'Only all the fuckin time,' she goes and I say to Brenda, 'See what she's doing? Telling me off. I'm always getting told off.'

Brenda says, 'Tell Kim that.'

I look at Kimbo and she's totally bought into all this fuckin bullshit. What is this? Fuckin Christian camp? Kimbo is giving me this look and I get up out of my chair.

'What are you doing?' Kimbo says. 'Are you going somewhere?' I don't say anything. I just leave the room. I leave the two of them there to have their own counselling session about how shit I am. Well done, Kimbo. You found a new god to waste our money on. As I'm travelling down in the lift I bash the wall, and I wouldn't mind if the fuckin thing collapsed and took me to the bottom like a rocket. When I make it to the Dwarf I have to fight an urge to drive off. I already know I will pay for what I just did.

There's no way I want to stick around so I chuck the keys in the driver's seat. I leave the door unlocked and I catch a bus home.

Let me sleep!

2.11 p.m.

No one could ever accuse Kimbo of being subtle. When Kimbo is in a bad mood she doesn't try to hide it. Right now she knows I need my sleep. She knows I can't afford to be tired at work.

So what does she do? She's cleaning to the Sabbath. I like Black Sabbath. The driving guitars, the shrieking vocals; it's heavy metal's finest hour, before all the stupid haircuts took it over.

Right now I'm in bed and I've tried to draw the curtains but there's this fuckin gap of light that gets into my eyeline and next door I can hear Ozzy Osbourne screaming and Kimbo vacuuming aggressively. She's hammering the crap out of furniture, violently, designed for me to hear the whole fuckin show. I chuck the pillow over my head to try to muffle it out.

I got a lousy two-hour sleep opportunity before Lucy arrives home and it's my watch. Kimbo's got a date with her best friend Janey. I hear her turn up the volume in the middle of 'Megalomania' and it's beyond a joke. So I get out of bed and I go to the lounge and she's not even fuckin in there, and I turn off the stereo.

Ha! It only takes about twenty seconds of me being back in bed before it comes on again, louder. You know that story that was going around about the guy from Nirvana being driven to suicide by his girlfriend? I think Kimbo's trying to push me there. I swear I could flip at any moment. I got no choice but to reach into the second drawer down and fumble around for the sleeping pills. I'm struggling to find them, mixed in among a whole lot of Kimbo's crap: magnesium vitamin pills, headache pills, a lint roller, Voltaren – where are the sleeping pills? – and fuckin Ozzy Osbourne is yelling in the next room. I pull the drawer right out of its sockets and throw the contents on the floor and I see them, the little red ones, and I swallow a couple and shove the fuckin pillow over my head again while I hear a loud clack clack clack sound next door of Kimbo bashing chair legs with the vacuum cleaner.

We have the loudest alarm clock in the world. I usually have the thing set on radio but if I make a mistake it has this screech like a cat being violently murdered. It's three fifteen which means Lucy's probably home from school. I push the sleep button but then I get a wave of guilt so I get up and walk around the house looking for Loose the Goose.

I find her in the back yard. In our back yard it is hard to see any actual, you know, ground. I've got a lot of stuff there and a lot of it has value. I got a lot of wood, which I haven't had the time to get rid of just yet. I need to sort it and de-nail it first. I got about twenty windows stacked next to where the weeds are fighting to find a patch of sun. Next to the aeroplane cockpit and the rusting old Citroën I got a bunch of European steering columns which I know I can get something for. I got a couple of baths which could be good to clean up but at the moment there's a bunch of weeds growing out of. In the bottom corner of our yard is an incomplete octagonal kit-set glasshouse. I only discovered parts missing after I'd put half of it up. I got a big pile of bricks which I figured I could offload at some point, and I got an old stove and a bunch of barbecues we came across when we cleaned out the old G&C warehouse.

I see Lucy riding her old BMX through it like it's an obstacle course. She doesn't wear a helmet and her hair flows behind her like she's a twelve-year-old character from *Easy Rider*. She's going straight to where the windows are stacked so I yell out to her and she pretends not to hear me. 'Hey, Lucy,' I say to her, and she pulls a tight corner near the windows and then pretends to ignore me again.

There's a lot of rusty nails and bits out there but I lost the battle to stop her from playing in the back yard long ago. I figure it's good for her. If she gets a cut from time to time then she'll learn to be more careful. But I do need to clear out some of the obvious hazards. She likes jumping up and down on the corrugated iron and I haven't tied it together yet so it's just asking to end in tears.

'Come inside,' I yell. 'I'll fix you some tucker.'

I've made us a couple of toasted sandwiches. Kimbo has headed out. I like it when it's just me and the Goose. Kimbo thinks I'm way too soft on her, but she's just jealous that we get on so good. That sleeping pill was definitely a mistake because I'm drowsy as I fumble my way around the kitchen. I feel a bit sick and I know I should go back to bed so I say to Lucy, 'You wanna come and watch TV in bed with me?'

Maybe I'm getting too old for night shift. As I lie here looking at Lucy watching TV I feel a bit guilty. It's a cartoon where some robots fly around in a spaceship and have special powers that make them turn into cars. I'm dozing but it's hard to sleep with Lucy fidgeting.

'Dad, watch this bit,' she says, and I try to pretend I'm interested and I watch a cartoon robot zap another cartoon robot.

'Uh-huh,' I say, and I doze off to sleep.

I wish I could control my thoughts, but Tom keeps getting inside my head. I drowsed off to some sleep and I start seeing him, running away from me. He's got this look in his eyes like he finds the whole thing really funny. He's got his stupid old suit on and I can't keep up with him. I stop and watch him run from me and when he sees I'm not chasing he stops and catches his breath, and when I run towards him again he starts running again.

I hear the phone ring and a whole bunch of canned laughter and Lucy has moved on to some crappy sitcom with a loud laugh track and she passes me the phone and I'm still in a daze.

'Hi. It's Alastair Shook.'

'Yeah?' I say to him.

'It's Tom. We couldn't find him.'

'Uh-huh,' I say.

'Do you have any ideas where he might be?'

'I gave you all the places.'

'Look. Could you go out and have another look for him? I'm busy until after eight.'

'I can't do it,' I say to him.

'You can't do it?'

'I'm busy.'

'Look, we really—'

'I'm busy,' I say to him and then he waits and says, 'Okay. Okay. If you get any other ideas—'

'Yeah, sure. If I get a brainwave I'll call you,' I say, and when I hang up I feel all wound up again, like I never got any sleep at all. I mean, on top of everything, I gotta deal with this? No. I won't lift another muscle for him. I'm busy. I've moved on. I wish the whole fuckin world would leave me alone, you know?

Lucy has the ads on turned up real loud and I snap at her, 'Turn it down!' and she says, 'Huh?' 'The mute. Mute it!' and she's looking at me confused and I yell, 'Fuckin mute it, Lucy!' and she runs out and when I mute the TV I'm left with the sound of her crying in the next room.

Thursday

Why did I buy that loaf of bread again?

5 a.m.

We just took the last of the floorboards out of the main cinema. We found some good stuff underneath. I picked up some old pliers that musta belonged to someone who built this place back in the twenties.

Jim's had a week to get out his pluck. This building is such a treasure-trove and there are still a lot of leftovers. Now the workers have twenty-four hours to take whatever they want. It's not quite a free-for-all. There's a hierarchy to this place and I'm next in the line. I got the pick of the pluck so I'm scouring around looking for the best of what's left. I'm leaving some of the plasterwork so that I can pick it out easy with the crane later.

I'm looking up at all the chairs on the top floor. Jim hasn't taken any of them. There are 540 in total. I could pluck them out without too much difficulty, but I don't think I can take on any more chairs. I'll struggle to sell what I've got.

I'm staring up at a plaster roaring gargoyle, high above me, when I have this flashbulb go off in my head of riding in the lift at the HGC Building. It's one of the coolest elevators in town, that one. It's got glass doors so you have a great view of The City as you shoot up to the twenty-third floor.

And yes, I figure that even though Tom doesn't deserve my time of day it should be no sweat to at least check out Thoroughbred this morning just so that even though I don't give a shit, I can say to Alastair Shook I tried. The sooner I find him the sooner I can forget about him again.

I lay down a lot of tarp underneath the gargoyle. I get the ladder up but it's hard to get her steady as we've already stripped the floorboards. I grab a chainsaw and I head up about twenty rungs and she's a bit rocky up here.

I manage to get up to the gargoyle's height. Now I'm closer to it I admire the artistry of the thing. It's a griffin, I think; a strange-looking creature. It has the wings of an eagle but the face of a lion. Its mouth is wide open and it has fierce eyes like it's ready to rip your neck open.

I'm about a metre and a half to the side of it. I saw behind its wings into the base holding him. There's one final part that's hard to reach and I have to swivel my ladder a bit. This is definitely not easy pluck, but it's amazing the risks a guy is willing to take for his own gain. I find myself awkwardly balanced but I'm so close to cutting the little fucker free that I tip the ladder further, check no one's underneath, I yell, 'Clear!' and I go right through the base. The gargoyle hits the tarp nose first. The release from the saw makes the ladder tip almost out of control. I manage to swivel my weight and the ladder swings back and steadies again.

I get down to it and a part of its nose has chipped. The gargoyle stares up at me and I get stuck looking at its snarling eyes, and I feel like I could fuckin kill the cunt, for what he's done to me. The gargoyle looks right through me and I have to get control of my senses to break away from the stare. I wrap it up in some bubble-wrap and chuck it in the barrow.

10.15 a.m.

I'm sitting in the Dwarf opposite where Thoroughbred used to be and I'm cutting up a nicotine patch. Now that I've made it to Stage Two I've worked out that they fleece you by charging as much for Stage Two as they do for Stage One, even though Stage One has one-third more nicotine in it. I've looked carefully at the Stage One patches and there's a join in it. I cut a third out of it and I shove that patch on and I reach over into the glove box and eat some nuts, and I gotta say, nuts are no replacement for smoking. I need to find a better substitute.

I'm too impatient for stakeouts. I've been waiting in the Dwarf for ten minutes already. I see a big neon Z on the other side of the road so I head inside and I order a coffee from a dweeb who asks me, 'What zing would you like, sir?'

'Huh? I want a coffee. Cappuccino,' and the teenage meatbrain has to ask his co-worker what a cappuccino is and I sit by the window and I go through my phone to see if any of my contacts could lead me to someone I can sell nine hundred chairs to.

My mobile phone has now decided to randomly delete everyone in my address book from the letter H to the letter J. I swear, I should never have bought the cheapest phone on the market, but I could never have guessed just how bad it could be. I mean, I wasn't asking for rocket science. I just want my phone to be a phone, but no – that's out of reach for this piece of shit.

I look up from my phone and I get a royal shock when I see Tom, right in front of me, having a coffee and talking to some redhead business-looking-type lady. I fumble around with my phone looking for Alastair Shook's number but it does its usual trick of turning off at the worst possible moment. A guy brings over my coffee and it tastes like they pulled the coffee beans out of a donkey's anus.

I slug it back and while I have to wait five fuckin minutes for the phone to turn on again I have to listen to Tom, working his shtick on the poor woman. He thinks he's charming, but anyone who has ever spent any time with Tom knows the charm will wear off quicker than cheap deodorant.

My phone finally comes on again and just as I'm about to phone Alastair Shook the phone rings and I answer it.

'Hello?'

'Hi there, I hope I've got the right number. I'm Roger Laing. I heard you've got some movie theatre seats.'

Some good news at last. I head out the front door to take the call.

'Yes. Yes,' I say.

'How many you got?'

'Nine hundred. They're reddy-brown leather. Most of them are in good nick. They're from the Century. Know the ones?'

'Can you send me a picture or something?' the voice says and I'm like, 'Yeah, sure, just a second,' and I hunt around for a pen.

'We're re-doing an old theatre up here in Foxtown. You know the Majestic?'

'No. I haven't been up there for—'

'Listen, are there more than that? I got room for about a thousand.'

I'm trying to calculate if it's worth the effort.

'It'll take a bit of effort to get another hundred out.'

'I'll pay for the extras. And for your time pulling them out.'

'Okay,' I say, when, fuck, Tom walks out the door and down the street. I haven't found a pen or anything and I'm multi-tasking and I'm watching where Tom is going and I say to Roger Laing, 'I got a bit of an emergency. Can I phone you back? What's your number?'

He gives me his number and hangs up. I try to scrawl it down but my pen's not working and Tom's got half a block away from me and he's going in the opposite direction from Thoroughbred, down the street.

Now I'm following Tom. He stops in an alley for a cigarette, so I wait out of view. His smoke wafts down the alley. I hang back until he takes off again. He heads around the corner and into a shop.

I follow him in but I don't want him to notice me so I head down a different aisle, waiting to see where he'll go next, where he'll settle.

Next thing he starts coming down my aisle, so I grab the first thing I can find, a loaf of bread, and I head to the counter and make a purchase. My eyes almost pop out when the guy gives me the price. It's gluten-free rice bread. Jesus. Eight bucks for a loaf of bread! There's a lot of money to be made feeding people with gluten intolerance. I'm in the wrong game. Usually I'd cancel my order but I don't want to draw attention to myself and Tom's coming back in my direction so I pay up and head straight outta there.

My phone rings and it's Muzz. He's ready to pick up a load so I head to the Dwarf and as soon as I'm in there I try to phone Alastair Shook but he doesn't answer so I try to write him a text but the phone decides to switch off just when I am about to hit the send button.

Head in the sand

11.02 a.m.

As I park at the Century I keep thinking about the dream I had, me hung by a hook, by the seat of my pants over a river, maybe the Amazon, and the water is cool and it runs through my fingers and my neck and it calms me down. As I hit the motorway Tom comes into my head again. He's running away from me. I change the subject in my head and I picture Kimbo, banging at my shins with a vacuum cleaner. Everyone wants a piece of me.

I am heading into the back of the Dwarf to get some tarp to cover the chairs with, when my mobile phone goes off. I answer it.

'Hi, it's Alastair Shook. You rang?'

'Hi, Alastair. I saw him.'

'Where?'

'Zing on Collins. Then he went to a shop, on the corner of Collins and Hobs—'

And then my phone switches off spontaneously. Stupid fuckin thing. I swear, I'd like attack it with a jackhammer. Or tape it to the edge of the ball and laugh as it smashes into a thousand pieces. Ha!

I head into the hut where the day-shift boys are having their lunch. I say, 'Who wants to help me pull out some chairs?' and I have to flash a bit of cash to get some volunteers.

The lads grab their tools and we head up to the second-floor balcony. It's getting pretty dusty now. When the floorboards came up it released a lot of old, old dust and young Temaia is coughing his ring out. Joey pulls a bottle of whisky from his pocket and Temaia slugs it back. The best way to deal with dust is to drink a lot of whisky. They offer me some and I turn it down. Joey says, 'You need to loosen up, bro.'

The bottom floor is a bomb site. Full of everything we can't sell. Joists, old rotten timber, bits of plaster, bits of rock, while up top everything is still gleaming new apart from a few holes in walls where we took out plaster and fittings.

We have to work fast. Me and Temaia unbolt the chairs with compressors and Joey and a couple of the younger boys bar them up and throw them over the edge below. It's hard yakka but we manage to pluck out 130 chairs in thirty minutes. Jim comes in and he says, 'You found a buyer, huh?' and I give him the fingers-crossed signal and he has a good laugh.

When I get home Lucy is sitting out the front of the house, on the stairs with her back to me. She must be sick or something. 'What's up?' I say to her, and she heads round to the back yard.

I head inside and into the kitchen to fix myself a sandwich before going to bed and Kimbo is sitting at the kitchen table, doing some work on her little laptop computer.

'What's with Lucy?' I ask.

'Why didn't you answer your phone?' she says.

'Huh?'

'Lucy has been sent home early because she cut some girl's hair off.'

'She did what?'

'I just been at the principal's office with her and they're thinking about suspending her, Spud.'

'What? For cutting someone's hair off?'

'Are you going to take this seriously, Spud? You need to talk to Lucy.'

'What am I supposed to say?'

'I don't know.'

'Why don't you talk to her?'

'Oh yeah. Like she listens to me,' Kimbo says.

So I head straight round to the back of the house. Lucy is sitting in the old Citroën. I sit on the bonnet. I don't know what to say. I'm no good at this heart-to-heart stuff.

'What . . . what happened, Lucy?'

Lucy says nothing to me.

'Hey!' I say to her. 'Tell me what happened,' but she keeps her mouth shut.

'Jesus, Lucy,' I say to her. 'Whose hair did you cut off?'

'It was just a stupid pigtail,' she says.

'Why would you do that?' I ask. Lucy gets out of the car and tries to walk away from me. I say, 'Hey, you're not going anywhere,' to her and she stops in her tracks.

'Did someone make you do it? Was it a dare?'

'No,' she says.

'Jesus, Lucy, I'm not a mind reader. Tell me why you did that. Why would you do something like that?'

She shrugs her shoulders, but there are tears in her eyes. I'm getting nothing out of her. I don't know how to do this. No one gave me a parenting manual. How am I supposed to know what to do or say? Kimbo wants me to punish her. And if I don't punish her I'll be told off for being too soft.

'Can I go now?' Lucy asks

'No BMX for a week,' I say, and she picks up a brick and she throws it at the washing line.

'NO BMX FOR TWO WEEKS!' I yell at her and she runs inside the house.

I get inside and Kimbo says, 'I think she needs to see a therapist.'

'Jesus, Kimbo, she's only twelve.'

'Maybe there's something wrong with her.'

'Yeah, maybe we should put her on Prozac. Maybe we should give her a lobotomy,' I say, and Kimbo says, 'I'm just saying—'

'She's not seeing a therapist. She's a kid. Let her be a kid.'

'Yeah, that's right. Pretend nothing is wrong, Spud. That's your way of dealing with everything,' she says. I can't be bothered hearing any more of this crap so I head to the bedroom.

I shut the door, lie on the bed and turn on the television.

Kimbo comes in and stands in front of the television.

'Fuck, Kimbo. Can I just have a few moments of peace?'

'Anything else you want to tell me?' she asks, and she gives me this look that has become more and more familiar over the last couple of months.

'Fuck off, Brenda,' I say.

'Why is there a picture of Tom on the computer?'

I shrug my shoulders.

'Why?' she repeats.

'Why are you snooping on me?'

'I'm not fuckin stupid, Spud. I know when you're hiding something. What's up with Tom?'

'Nothing.'

'Don't bother telling lies, Spud. I already know.'

'You already know what?' I ask, calling her bluff.

'I know you got an email with Tom's picture attached. And I know who sent the email.'

I sigh. 'Tom's in town.'

'Where's he staying?'

'We don't know,' I say.

'What do you mean you don't know? Is he lost?'

'He's not lost. He just doesn't want to be found.'

'And what are you doing about it?'

'I don't have to answer to you. I got it under control,' I say to her, and I push past her into the hallway, where Lucy is standing, watching.

Kimbo follows me, yells, 'What? That's it? That's your answer? Just to leave the room?'

'There's nothing to discuss.'

'If there's nothing to discuss how come you're having panic attacks?'

'They're not panic attacks.'

115

'Oh, sorry. Breathing into a paper bag is normal, is it?'

'Fuck you,' I say. I grab my car keys from the kitchen and she follows me all the way. I head out the front door towards the truck before I say or do anything I'll regret later. Kimbo yells out after me, 'Are you running away, Spud?'

That's the last straw.

I head back in there.

'I'm not paying for any more of your visits to that stupid shrink.'

'Leave Brenda out of it—'

'Leave Tom out of it—'

'Where is he, Spud? Why haven't you said anything?'

'It's none of your business,' I say, and she's like a bulldog on this one.

'Where have you looked?' she's saying.

I see Lucy watching the argument. 'It's none of your business,' I repeat.

'What state is he in?'

'I don't know. I don't care. I don't need you weighing in on this. It's got nothing to do with you,' I say, and I head towards the truck.

'That's right, Spud. Put your head in the sand,' she yells after me, and I say nothing back. There's no point. Every time I say something it's ammo for her to use later.

I climb into the cab of the Dwarf and I start her up and I drive one block to the sea where I park up. I reach into the glove compartment and spray myself with the Rescue Remedy and I try to turn on my mobile phone. Now it won't turn on at all.

Tom comes into my mind again. This time he's waiting at the school crossing, flirting with a mother by the lollipops. I shut him out of my mind by putting on the car radio, talkback radio sport. I take off my top and I jam it into the window, blocking out the sun. I grab my jacket and I scrunch it up into a pillow, and I shut my eyes, I put my hand down my pants and I try my best to block out the world around me.

Chicken

2.47 p.m.

Alastair Shook told me to look in all the places where Tom would go out of routine. I've already been back to 29 Clyde. There was no sign of him. Now I'm heading to Clyde Street Normal School. I want to be there before the bell rings at three. There is nowhere to park on Clyde Street, so I head up around the corner and park in the Hocken Street cul-de-sac.

As I head to the school I can feel my bladder about to burst. I blame the caffeine pills. I'm watching the kids play on the tennis courts and I'm noticing a lot of changes too. There used to be grassy hills by the school hall. Now they've flattened them. There used to be a maypole too. That was taken out years ago.

I'm busting real bad. I'm looking over at the tennis courts and I see the bushes by the dental clinic have grown so I make a beeline for the dental clinic. School's about to come out, so I'd better be quick.

As I'm walking I'm scanning the street for Tom as a few early-bird parents arrive. A woman walks past with a pram and a three-year-old boy runs along jumping over shadows. I used to do that as a kid.

Then I see this figure in the distance.

It's Tom in his crappy brown suit. He's holding on to a big package. I make it to the dental clinic and I'm watching him as he stares at the kids in the playground.

I hunt around in my pockets for my mobile phone and I hold down the on button but the stupid thing still won't turn on. I think my phone may have finally kicked the bucket.

My bladder is having a meltdown so I take a leak in the bushes behind the dental clinic and the stream that comes out of me is powerful, like a fireman's hose. I'm still midstream when Tom bends round the corner, yelling, 'Hey!' at me, and I piss myself. I try to finish off as Tom comes my way, but I still got a lot more to give. I try to stem the flow and pull up my pants but a lot more comes out and I can feel it down my leg as I try to get away from Tom.

Why am I running away? I'm much bigger than him. I know I should face up to him, but I don't want to have to look at his stupid face. I'm sprinting away from him, up the hill, but he's still following me.

I make it round the bend to the cul-de-sac and I climb into the Dwarf. Tom has made it to the cul-de-sac and he blocks off the entrance. He stands right in the middle of the road with his arms stretched wide. And if that's how he wants to play it, then fine. I drive straight at him, waiting for him to jump out the way, but he stands his ground – the stupid fucker must have a death wish. At the last moment I realize he's not going to dive out of the way. I swerve to miss him but I hear the Dwarf clip him. I look behind me and I see him lying in the middle of the road.

I stop the truck and I run to him. I've really wounded him. He's struggling to move. His whole body looks limp. The only signs of life are his narrow little eyes, staring up at me. I don't know if I should shift him. I don't know what to do.

'Hey,' he says to me.

'You okay?' I ask him, and he says, 'Tell Robert Valentine I have his socks. But if he wants them he can come and face me, man to man.'

For the first time I'm starting to feel sorry for him. I want to get him off the road, so I grab his hand to pull him up, then his leg springs up and kicks me in the nuts.

The toe of his boot lands square in my ballsack and I'm doubled over on my knees and I feel . . . just like he used to make me feel when . . . I feel taken over. I feel like I could . . .

'Fuck you, you fuckin arsehole,' I say. I get the fuck away from him because God knows what I'm capable of right now.

I head straight to the Dwarf and I clear out of here, out of this stupid neighbourhood, out of his stupid life. I don't care what happens to him. He can rot on the streets for all I care. He can rot in hell.

Attack on T-Rex

9.52 p.m.

Kimbo's driving me to work. She wants to borrow the Dwarf tonight while I'm working. I asked her what she wants it for and she said she's helping her friend Denise shift a bunch of stuff.

'I think my mobile phone's busted,' I say.

'Maybe it's the battery,' she says.

'It's not the battery. The battery was full.'

'You want me to have a look at it?'

I shrug my shoulders and hand her the phone.

We drive in silence for a bit, before she breaks in with the subject I've been hoping to avoid.

'Any luck finding Tom?'

I shake my head, say nothing. The less she knows, the better.

'You need any help with it?' she asks and I shake my head. 'I'm on top of it,' I say, and she says, 'Yeah, just like you're on top of everything else, right?'

Kimbo drops me off at the Century and Dick is laying sand and gravel down on the side road. He watches me get out of the truck and head towards T-Rex. 'You in the dog box again?' he says.

'How could you tell?'

'You got that pussy-whipped look about you,' he says, and he has a giggle.

'Ha fuckin ha,' I say and he pats me on the back and I head to the crane to get her up and running.

★

I've been warming T-Rex up and watching the guys up on the roof pulling steel off, figuring out where to hit first. I need to drop the ball in the roof and break through the concrete floor there so all the rubbish has somewhere to fall. Then I can start making cuts up the side of the building and knocking the wall in.

As I'm lifting the ball I see a whole lot of steam in front of the lights. I look at the gauges and they're shooting through the roof. I wave to Temaia, give him a signal to halt for a bit.

I climb out to have a look at the damage and I see a big leak, one I haven't seen before, gushing out like a waterfall. I look to the source of it and I swing one of the lights around to look at the front of T-Rex and the water is coming out from the radiator. I look closer at the radiator and there's a big rip right in the middle.

'Fuck!' I yell.

Temaia comes down. The two of us are staring at the rip.

'Looks like a screwdriver, boss,' Temaia says.

Next thing Dick has joined us, and the three of us are staring at the slit in the radiator. Dick's no use at all.

'You been keeping an eye on things? Seen anyone come in or out of the site?' I ask and he shakes his head, but the fact is Dick's getting a bit old in the tooth. He used to be a great worker, a real joker in the pack, but now as he's getting on we shifted him to the easier jobs and he's been nodding off, I know it.

'What's up?' a new voice says. It's Bull.

'Someone's attacked T-Rex,' I say.

'Jim's gonna spew,' Bull says, and I say, 'Tell me something I don't know.'

I'm trying to think who the fuck did this. Someone with a lot of balls and not much sense, I'd say.

'I need to borrow your phone,' I say to Dick.

I'm on the phone to Jim and he says, 'We need the building to be unstable by Monday, Spud. Should I call in another crane?' and I say, 'Nah, it should be fine.'

Bull takes the phone off me and says to Jim, 'Hey, boss, I can get

121

in one of the hydraulics. I can call in a favour from Davo,' and the last thing I need is someone else cutting in on my business so I say to Jim, 'I can fix her. I can fix her. Give me a few hours and I'll have her back up and running.' Bull looks sceptical and I say, 'What? I can get her fixed.'

'All I'm saying is if we act quick we can bring in another machine,' Bull says and my gut takes a dive at the idea. T-Rex is perfect for this job. She's been holding up okay. Sure there's some slopping but couldn't we at least give her the dignity of allowing her to pull down one final decent building?

'Listen, Jim,' I'm saying down the phone. 'I can get her fixed. You know the ball will pull it all down faster than one of the hydraulics. It's here and we should use it,' and Jim says to me, 'This is a tight job, Spud.'

'I know.'

Jim sighs. 'Look, do what you can but if we're not up and running in two hours then I'm getting hold of Davo. I got no room for sentiment here, you understand?'

'Yeah. Of course.'

He insists I give him a call in an hour, for a progress report. I hang up and I look at Bull who seems itchy to consign T-Rex to an early grave and I have to withhold the urge to yell at him, but it's not his fault. He's just doing his job, and I've just gotta stay calm, keep my emotions out of it. I'll keep my cool and I'll get T-Rex back up and running and she can do the job just like she's done a thousand other jobs.

I'm trying to find Arthur Chapman's name in the phone book and my sense of alphabetical order is the first thing to go under pressure. My phone crapping out has shifted from being a small pain in the arse to a full-scale pain in the arse, the type of pain you might feel if you shoved a prickly hedgehog up there. All my numbers are in it. Every fuckin one.

My big fat fingers are struggling with the buttons on Dick's phone. I get hold of Arthur and I say to him, 'It's Spud. I got an emergency down here,' and Arthur says, 'Is someone dying?' and I say, 'Worse than that. It's T-Rex,' and Arthur says, 'Can't help, sorry. I'm watching a movie about aliens.'

'Please, Arthur, I got a busted radiator.'

'I got a full garage,' he says to me. 'Full of all your shit.'

'I'll clear it out.'

'Yeah, I think I heard that one six months ago,' he says, and I say to him, 'Fine, I'll find a new mechanic,' and there's this gap where I can hear some kinda strange howl coming from his TV before he returns with, 'Sorry, that was a good bit. Does it need a replacement?'

'Sure does,' I say, and he says, 'It's your lucky day, I got one sitting in my garage. Oh, hang on, I might not be able to get at it though, because it's sitting behind all your crap.'

I know he's bullshitting me but I'm playing with a pretty bad hand here.

'Okay, I'll clear it out next week.'

'Wrong answer,' he says. 'Clear it out tonight and I may be inclined to do you a favour.'

'Where am I supposed to put it all?'

'Not my problem,' he says and he holds his phone to his TV and I can hear an alien voice say, 'Take him to the chambers for vaporization.' Arthur comes back on, says, 'You clear all that shit out tonight and I'll get your problem fixed. Then we're both happy.'

'Okay,' I say and he says back to me, 'And a bottle of whisky will sweeten the deal.'

'Fuck, shall I get down on my knees and fondle your fuckin balls too?' I say to him and he laughs, says, 'Laphroaig,' and hangs up.

Joey and Temaia and me pull in to Arthur Chapman's garage and Arthur's waiting outside smoking a cigarette. I wind down my window and he says, 'How's quitting going?' and he blows a load in my face. He holds up a remote control and opens up his garage and the radiator is sitting at the front. We help him load it on his ute and he pats me on the back and heads on his way, while Joey

123

and me and Temaia load a truckful of a whole lot of shit I picked up when we pulled down a church one time: loads of timber, stained glass, long bench seats, varnished floorboards and some toilets. Behind that I got a whole lot of stuff I got from the Bell Building four years ago, and behind that is a massive load I picked up from the old Post Office.

Joey gives me shit about it a couple of times. He jokes that I need to get a new sales team, in full knowledge that the sales team is just me, myself and that fuckin idiot I. Even Temaia chimes in at one point when we're pulling out a bunch of neon signs, tables and a sheep's head on a plaque I got when I pulled down the Shamrock Hotel. He says to me, 'I'm surprised you didn't take the fuckin menus,' and Joey says, 'Can I take the sheep home with me? I wouldn't mind playing a joke on my missus,' and the cheeky buggers actually get me laughing, which is a nice change.

I'm laughing less when we're trying to dump it all at the traffic island. Some of the tarp has been ripped off and a lot of the chairs are exposed and copping the brunt of a rainfall. We just get on with it; there's nothing else we can do. Now my pile is filling the entire traffic island. There's a massive drip coming from the overbridge above and it's pouring directly on to a bunch of chairs. There's nowhere to shift them to so I just flag it as collateral damage and try to ignore the rising sensation of doom in my gut.

I get Temaia and Joey to help me shift the stuff I can't cover to the most sheltered spot and we have to stack pretty high in that area. It's like a mountain of chairs here.

When we get back to the truck Joey slugs back a whisky and hands the bottle to me. I stare at it and say, 'No, I gotta stay sharp.' Joey says to me, 'I hate to break it to you, mate, but you lost your sharpness years ago,' and he holds it under my nose but my will-power wins out. I start the motor and as we leave the traffic island I watch another drip fall from the other side of the overbridge on to my mountain of chairs and I find myself praying to a God that I know doesn't exist just to give me a break for once and stop the fuckin rain.

Good Friday

Showdown at the Century

1.14 a.m.

I gotta hand it to him. Arthur knows his stuff. He may be a drunken bastard and he gives me more shit than an elephant with Delhi belly, but he's the one guy in town who knows my machine better than I do. Old mechanics know how to handle old machines. When he shuffles off it'll be another nail in T-Rex's coffin. Apart from getting the radiator in and back up and running while I've been away, he's also tested out the machine and is giving me a full diagnosis.

He tells me to gib up slow and we listen to the screech she makes and he says to me that one of the bushes is wearing. He says if it craps out this weekend he's happy to try to weld something together.

He gets me to slew left and we hear a racket I've become very familiar with but this time the news isn't so good. He reckons that the parts have got so worn from inactivity that it's just a matter of time before she seizes up completely unless I can keep her running every day. He's confirmed what I already knew. I should try to sell her before she craps out, as there might be some remaining value if I get out in time.

I feel sorry for the beast but time has given her a fatal kick in the guts. He reckons if I nurse her right she'll be able to complete this job, and as far as final jobs go, you couldn't wish for better – the Century is a grand old lady. It all seems fitting somehow. We're going to go out in style.

While I've been away the guys have successfully stacked the steel on the roof. I send the young fella Temaia up on the crane. He winches it on and as we bring it to the ground T-Rex groans.

Bringing down the truss goes pretty smoothly. We get it all down in a couple of hours and loaded out on Muzz's truck and that's ten thousand worth of timber shipped out safely. I feel pretty relieved that the old girl is behaving herself.

As we reattach the ball I feel energy coming back and I start to get excited again. Finally, something to look forward to.

Because we lost a couple of hours I have to operate a bit quicker than I usually would, and that involves taking a few more risks. I've brought down buildings in a weekend before. Back in our heyday me and Jim won a lot of business from the other companies because we could bring 'em down faster than anyone else. You can't bring a building down quick without some element of risk, and I've had a couple of near misses. I once watched a huge lump of concrete fall the wrong way and come straight down towards my windscreen. It landed three feet in front of me. Just luck that I didn't get squashed.

We got known for bringing down four storeys at a time. Back in the day we made quite a public show of it and made sure word spread around town, and, sure enough, the council noticed and business started flooding in and Jim took over as the chief bigwig operator in town. I guess the rot set in when we'd brought down so many buildings that business slowed up. Then when the recession hit a whole lot of the construction boys started moving in to our turf and we had to start scrapping for every job. Suddenly it's all about tenders and applications and Jim gets tied up in a shitload of paperwork. I'm glad I don't have to deal with all that. I guess I should be grateful for small mercies. Still, Jim's done all right out of it. Me, I'm losing money faster than I'm making it now, which is why this latest treasure could be a real make or break for me.

I got the ball up in the air now and young Temaia is guiding me in so that I drop it into the auditorium, where the screen used to be. I gib up real slow and track in a little and Temaia gives me the signal to do the first drop. As it drops I can feel the impact through the machine and Temaia gives me the thumbs up and I lift her and drop her three times and I've broken in and we're under way. I chip away at the hole in the roof for the next hour, then I drop the ball through the hole I made and when I hit the first concrete floor I hear the gib gear screech like a Hendrix guitar solo. It's okay. If I keep her moving she'll start to ease up a little and by the time we hit two o'clock I've broken right through the concrete floor of the second storey and I'm building a nice big crater all around it.

I'm attacking the side wall by the road. I'm pretty in the zone. I'm cutting a line up from the hole I made in the wall yesterday. The line will go all the way up to the roof. I'm making good progress too. I feel a lot more at peace while I just get on with my work. T-Rex has limbered up and the ball is swinging freely and apart from the slew noise when I head to the left everything else is sounding like an orchestra in tune with itself. I'm just about to hit a nice cavity four metres up and I'm listening to the sound of brick and it's all running like clockwork.

I'm staring at the next area that I'm planning to hit when I get this flash in my peripheral vision. I look down to where the light is shining and I see this ghost-like figure, some homeless guy standing right underneath where I'm swinging the ball. The figure stops and I catch this white face and then I see him move into the hole I made, and disappear.

Am I seeing things? I wouldn't be surprised given my lack of sleep but that didn't feel like a hallucination. I figure I'm better safe than sorry, so I track back and gib up but the ball doesn't stop swinging straight away. It cracks the edge of the wall and a couple of bricks fall and I track back further and the ball is far enough back now. I leave T-Rex idling. I grab my torch and I whistle to Temaia to let him know I'm heading in.

I'm shining my torch all around the hole I made.

We often get the homeless turning up to our sites and crashing the night. It could be some glue sniffer from the shelter, or maybe I just saw something that wasn't there.

I climb through the hole and over a pile of fresh rubble. The place is full of dust – everywhere I shine my torch dust is swirling in patterns like little insects. I climb over the rubble. I've made it further inside when I hear someone cough. I shine my torch around inside and the room is mostly a mixture of concrete and clumps of brick. The structure inside still looks firm. I can see the moon through the hole I made in the roof. I hear another noise and I shine my torch around the theatre.

'Hey,' I yell, but no one answers.

Then I hear another noise – some debris falling by the stage area at the far wall. I shine the torch in that direction and move towards the sound, when there's another noise from the stage area. I shine up to where the screen used to be and suddenly a torch flicks on and it shines at me; this bright, bright light is shining right into my eyes.

'Is that you, Dick?' I ask, half thinking it's some kind of practical joke.

Still no answer. I shine my torch at whoever is up there. The torchlight flicks off and I see that someone has made it to the second floor.

'Hey!' I yell, and then the torchlight comes on again, shining right at me, and suddenly I sense a stinking presence in the room.

'Tom,' I say. 'Tom, is that you?'

Tom

Thursday

Debacle with the police

4.46 p.m.

I'm trying to stay calm as I climb in the bathroom window of the house. I walk down the hallway, calling out, 'Frank!' I look in his bedroom, but there's no sign of life. I'm starting to get panicky. 'Frank!' I yell, but I hear nothing but a muffled smoke alarm.

I open the hot-water cupboard and I can hear the alarm loud and clear so I bury it under more towels and shut the door but the damned thing is still going off at just a low enough volume to be messing with my mind.

Stay calm, Tom.

I'm in Frank's bedroom now. 'Frank!' I'm yelling, and I know he's punishing me right now. A little hide and seek to get the old man back for past misdemeanours. 'Frank, it's not funny!' I'm yelling. I'm back in Frank's room and I look under his bed, expecting him to jump out at me, but there's nothing there except for some chocolate wrappers and old socks and a whole lot of crumbs.

I head into our bedroom and I avoid eye contact with the dresser and I open up the wardrobe and look behind all Deborah's dresses and under her bed.

'FRANK!' I'm yelling, and I walk around the house looking in the craziest places, cupboards, behind the couch, behind the giant TV, behind curtains, under the living room table. I search everywhere twice. I stop and listen for signs of breathing but all I hear is the alarm in the hot water cupboard. I go back outside and look in every nook and cranny but there's no one in sight.

I look in the basement and I'm calling out to the darkness. 'Frank? Are you in here?'

I'm listening for the sound of breathing, but all I hear are the cicadas outside.

'Because if you are here and you think this is funny . . . This isn't funny, Frank. Come out right now.'

No one answers.

I'm back in the house, and my head feels hot. I'm staring at a phone that sits on the table.

This isn't the time to panic. I light myself a cigarette and I open my wallet and I find the number for Deborah's mobile phone. I'm dreading this phone call, but there's nothing else for it. I dial, and I wait while it rings and I try to compose what I'm going to say. Eventually there is an answer, but it's not Deborah, it's a computer-generated answerphone message, and I say, 'Deborah, it's Tom, I . . . I lost Frank, I was . . . uhhh . . .' and suddenly there's another loud sound, and wouldn't you know it, I've set off another smoke alarm and this one is even louder than the other one. I hang up on Deborah and I take the smoke alarm out and I find the heaviest implement I can, a cast-iron skillet, and I smash the smoke alarm with it. It comes apart in about ten pieces, and mercifully it stops.

I see a telephone book on the bench and I thumb through it and I do the unthinkable, but desperate times call for desperate measures. I phone the police.

While I wait for the police to arrive I search the house again. I'm looking in all the places I've already searched, hoping that this time he'll be there. I try to think of places I haven't thought to look in yet.

I catch myself looking for Frank in the freezer. I mean, what is Frank going to be doing in a freezer? I've immediately assumed the worst when the opposite is probably true. The most likely explanation is a boring one. I was late and Frank got confused and he headed off to a friend's house. I know who his old friends are but I have no idea if he's still hanging around with the same crowd or if there's a new friend I don't know about. Bad father, bad father.

There's a loud knock on the door. At last.

I open up and two uniformed police stand there, a woman and a guy. The woman is clearly in charge – if they weren't in uniform you'd think it was a mother and her teenage son.

'I'm so relieved you're here,' I say. 'Come in.'

I bring them into the kitchen area. I pull out my photograph of the kid. 'His name's Frank. I was a little late to pick him up from school, and I—'

'Just a second, sorry,' says the policewoman, pulling out a little electronic device from her pocket. I go to speak again but she gives me the shh signal while she darts her fingers around the device.

'What's your name, sir?'

It's tempting to go with William McGinty, but I have to put Frank's needs first.

'Tom. Tom Spotswood. I know there should be a simple explanation. Like, he's gone to a friend's house or something—'

She holds out her hand to get me to stop talking while she touches her little computer again.

'Uhhh . . .' she says, and the teenage policeman heads out of the room. 'Uhhh . . .' she says again. 'Are you . . . Is this your—' and suddenly there's another knock on the door.

Frank?

I rush to the door and the policewoman follows me. I take a deep breath, ready to give the kid a big hug, and I open the door, and standing there are two more police – same scenario too – a policewoman and a younger trainee. Wow. This equal opportunity stuff must be taking hold.

The two police at the door clock the policewoman who's with me, and everyone looks confused.

'Hi, I'm Fiona,' says the policewoman at the door.

'Uhhh . . .' says the other policewoman.

'Not again,' says the young olive-skinned cop next to her.

The new policewoman pulls out a little device and touches it in three places, and goes to the first policewoman and says, 'Are you supposed to be here?' and the first policewoman says, 'Well, yeah, but . . .'

They both show their little computers to each other, and I say, 'Please,' and the first policewoman says, 'Just a second,' and I hear a piercing noise getting louder and louder as the other policeman re-emerges with the smoke alarm, saying, 'I can't turn it off. Does anyone have a screwdriver?'

Next thing I'm trying to make everyone cups of tea but I can't find the tea cups. The young cop with the smoke alarm is turning an Allen key around and the noise of the smoke alarm goes lower and slower. Finally he turns it off and there's peace. The other three police are standing in a huddle and I'm trying to eavesdrop on their conversation.

'Stupid palmtop.'

'Who should take it?'

'I can do it.'

'But . . . what does yours say again? Breaking and entering?'

I interject. 'It's my house! Paid for with my money!' but the teenage cop next to me tells me to shhh – which is very disrespect-ful. I say to him, 'How did you get on the force? You're not even old enough to drive,' and he laughs at me.

'Mr Spotswood. We've had a complaint from a neighbour—'

'Never mind that. I need your help with my son—'

'First things first—'

'First things first? My son might have been abducted! First things first—'

'Calm down—'

'Why is no one taking this seriously?'

A policewoman says to the other two, 'I'll handle this, okay?' and the other policewoman says, 'What'll I type into the palmtop?'

'I don't know.'

'I'm not putting in an incomplete.'

'Check the complete box and just write up the details under Notes.'

'How do I do that?'

'Control shift N.'

'Which one's control?'

'The one with the squiggle.'

'Okay,' the policewoman says and two of them leave.

Fiona the policewoman says to me that before she can help me look for my son we have to clarify the house situation. Frankly, I find this approach absurd and upsetting. I'm forced to sit and answer a lot of questions all to do with the house, how long I've owned it for and all those sorts of details. I don't know what kind of bureaucracy would prioritize settling a minor trespassing complaint over such a major thing as a lost child. It makes no sense to me, but Fiona explains that if I just answer her questions she'll then help me with Frank.

There are a lot of questions I can't have a hope of knowing the answers to. I don't know where Deborah keeps her papers in the house about the property, and frankly, I don't want to go snooping any further than I have to.

I'm waiting for her to ask me the dreaded question about Fire Chief but her little computer hasn't alerted her to it yet, and I sure won't be the one to bring her attention to it.

She finally lets up on the whole house thing. She says, 'Now . . . your son. How old is he Tom?'

'Frank is eleven.'

'When did you last see him?

'When he was seven.'

'Why don't you have a more recent photo?'

'I've lost my suitcase. I have lots of photos in that.'

'How old are you Tom?'

'I'm thirty-nine.'

'Okay,' she says, and she taps away on the screen of her little computer.

I decide not to get her offside by questioning her competency. I just tell her the facts. I tell her about the demolition guy and I tell her what class Frank is in and I name all the places where he might have gone.

At one point, I catch her not taking notes. 'Shouldn't you be writing all this down?' I say, and she says, 'I'm taking it in, Tom,' and I'm starting to feel real exasperated, like I'm not being taken seriously.

She takes me by the arm and says to me, 'We're going to take you back to your hotel now. You let us do the police work.'

'What are you going to do? What are you going to do?'

She tries to escort me out of the house and towards the car and I yank myself free.

She says, 'I'll type all the details into my palmtop and every officer in the neighbourhood will know there's a missing eleven-year-old.'

'And?'

'And I'll drive round this neighbourhood myself and search for your son. Come on, Tom. We need to get you home. You must be exhausted.' She grabs my arm and pulls me along. Her teenage helper grabs me by the other arm and they march me outside and into their police car and I refuse to get in, but they push me in anyway. The teenage cop tries to buckle me in to a seat belt. I bite into his arm and Fiona yells, 'TOM! STOP THAT AT ONCE!' She's talking to me like I'm a child.

The teenage cop sits in the passenger seat with Frank's train set on his lap.

I say, 'Can we at least drive around the neighbourhood?' and Fiona gives a firm, 'No, Tom. You need to get some rest.'

'How am I supposed to rest when my son is missing? This is absurd!'

'Let us do the police work, Tom.'

'Oh, and how are you going to find him? You call yourselves police? You couldn't find food at a restaurant.'

The teenage cop turns on the radio to drown me out; loud music with a thudding low beat. It sounds like there's a dance party happening inside the cop car.

The cops are dropping me off at the wrong hotel. I've been liberal with the truth. I've told these two dimwits I'm staying at the Savoy which is five blocks away from the Ascot. Fiona rushes round and opens the door for me and helps me out of the car.

You would think I might have a few leads on how to find my own son, but are they interested? I say to her, 'Look, my son could be *anywhere* out there. I mean, you should have a whole *team* on it.'

'Just let us do our job, Tom.'

'Find my son. Tell everyone on that stupid little radio of yours, there is a missing eleven-year-old. And he answers to the name Frank. Okay? I can give you a list of friends—'

'Just email them to me,' she says, passing me a business card.

'Maybe if you spent more time catching criminals and less time making business cards we might have better law enforcement in this town,' I say, as a parting shot, and the male cop says, 'Shuuut uppp,' like a teenager telling his father where to put it.

Help at the cigarette machine

8.20 p.m.

I have a confession to make. There have been times in my life when I have not thought about Frank as often as I should have. It's a hard thing to explain. The world deals you out some cards, and one of the cards I was dealt was Frank. Other treasures you go out and find, you pursue with a kind of obsession. Exhibit A is Deborah. You lose these and you obsess about them. But with Frank . . .

Don't get me wrong. I have always loved the kid. But I haven't obsessed about him.

Until now.

I've been thinking about all those times I was with Frank when my mind and spirit weren't completely there. I'm picturing this one time – it's typical but it makes me cringe. I'm at a playground with Frank and I just let him do his thing while I read the newspaper and he keeps yelling, 'Dad, look,' and I barely lift my eyes from the newspaper to see what he's doing.

'Oh . . . that's great, Frank.'

He's gone upside down on a slide. I mean, it's laudable, but it doesn't interest me so much. Me – I get a larger thrill from seeing a beautiful woman and imagining her with no clothes on; Frank gets a kick out of going upside down on a slide. We are at different stages in life.

When I find Frank, I swear, it'll be different. I'll engage. I'll really engage. Next time I see Frank I'll ask him so many questions he won't know what's hit him. God, I can feel my insides are shaking . . .

I've made it back to the Ascot and to help me think straight I've ordered a bourbon at the bar and I go to the cigarette machine and try to trick it into giving me a pack of cigarettes. I do everything it tells me. I feed it a ten-dollar note but it doesn't want my ten-dollar note. So I unfold it and try again. I put it in another way and then it beeps at me, like a fridge door that's been left open.

'Need some help with that?' a voice says, and I'm relieved to see a friendly face. Linda smiles and pushes a couple of buttons on the machine and out comes a pack of cigarettes.

'So, where's your son?' she says. I can smell alcohol on her breath.

I down some bourbon and my hands are shaking as I try to pull the cellophane off the cigarettes but the cellophane won't come. Linda slices one of her long nails into the cellophane and pulls out a cigarette for me. She says, 'What just happened, Tom?'

I'm with Linda in the hotel parking lot, in her car. Her back seat is full of fluorescent lights. She's been receiving again. She sips away at the last of a vodka and Campari. 'You want me to drive?' she asks me.

'How many vodkas have you had?' I ask, and she says, 'Three? Four? Five? Who's counting?'

I say, 'Do you mind if I drive?'

The car is not easy to drive. It has all these features I haven't seen before: a little computer with a map on it, distracting digital information on the bottom of the windscreen, intelligent windscreen wipers that detect rain and wipe automatically and an automatic seat belt detection alarm that insistently beeps at me.

As we drive down Elizabeth Street, Linda lights up her cigarette and says, 'You want to wind the windows down?' and I say, 'It's raining out there,' and she says, 'So do you mind?'

She lights two cigarettes, passes one to me and we smoke inside. 'So, you're taking me to the suburbs?' she asks.

★

Our first port of call is Jarrod Mullane's house. I have to admit, I've never liked Jarrod Mullane. Jarrod – when I knew him anyway – was just a seven-year-old, and I know it's a bit immature for an adult to dislike a seven-year-old, but sometimes you meet a kid and you can picture the man they'll go on to become, and I can just tell Jarrod Mullane has a future in real estate.

I pull into Ribble Street and I see a trampoline out the front of their house. Linda says to me, 'You look pale, Tom,' and I say, 'I'll be fine, Linda,' and I wince as I feel a sharp pain in my neck. Linda gives my neck a rub.

'You've got cold hands,' I say.

She rubs them together and goes to work on my neck, and it helps a little.

Linda and I get out of the car. We walk up the path to the Mullanes', and I ring the doorbell.

Inside I can hear laughter – some kind of dinner party. A door opens, and it's Jarrod's father, Scott Mullane. Scott's lost some hair, but he's doing that thing people are doing these days where they shave it so they look like some kind of Eastern guru.

'Hi, Scott,' I say and he stares at me, like he's trying to place me. He looks at Linda – who despite her excellent taste in clothes is struggling with her countenance. Perhaps I should have left her in the car.

'Jesus, Tom?' he says to me. 'It is you, isn't it?'

'Yeah. I've—'

'Jesus Christ. I can't think when it was I last saw you.'

'I've lost Frank. Have you . . . Have you seen him?'

He stares at me a while, and pats me on the shoulder and says, 'Can I get you a drink? Would you like to come in?'

'No thanks. I was thinking Jarrod might have some ideas where he is.'

'Jarrod's in Scotland, with the twins,' he says.

'Really?'

'Yeah, I miss them all, but they seem happy. Uh . . . when you say you lost Frank . . .'

144

'I went to school to pick him up and he wasn't there . . . I was late,' I say, feeling deeply ashamed.

Scott looks me in the eye, and then he gets a call from inside, someone yelling to him. 'It's your turn, Scott!'

'I'm looking in all the obvious places, and—'

'You got a number I can call you on?' he asks and I look to Linda and she writes her number on a piece of paper and hands it to him.

'Okay. If I see anything . . .' he says, and I say, 'I'd appreciate that.'

'You look after yourself, Tom.'

'I'm trying,' I say feebly, and he shoots me a smile of sympathy – the kind of smile that also lets you know he's not going to lift one of his thin muscle-toned arse cheeks to help me out.

Linda has taken me to Herb Lamont's. I don't want to mix Linda up in the finer details of my situation so I ask her to wait for me in the car.

I ring the doorbell and a light comes on. The door opens, and an old woman greets me with a cautious, 'Hello?'

I don't recognize her, but she looks like she was once very beautiful.

'Hi. Uh . . . I'm sorry to distu—'

She looks me in the eye, and says, 'Tom Spotswood? Is that you?'

'Yes,' I say. 'Is Herb in?'

'N-no,' she says.

'I'm sorry to bother you. I've lost my son. You know Frank?'

'Of course.'

'I was hoping he may have come around here,' I say, and she shakes her head and says, 'No. Sorry, Tom. Why did you think he would come over here?'

'Isn't he still kicking around with Lane?'

'I don't think so,' she says.

'Any idea where he might be?' I ask, and the old woman looks confused.

'Lane or Frank?' she asks.

145

'Frank,' I say, and she just looks at me blankly.

'Look. I'm sorry. When will Herb be in?'

She looks at me, like I asked an odd question. 'I'm sorry, Tom. I've got some bad news,' she says.

Next I'm in the kitchen. The old woman is pouring us a whisky each and telling me the grisly details.

'He was driving down Motorway 34, a straight piece of road, broad daylight and he suddenly veered off, hit a tree.'

'What would make him do that?'

'The coroner suspected a heart attack but the car caught fire so his body was . . . he was hard to identify.' She stares into the bottom of her glass. 'For Herb,' she says, and she clinks the glass and we down one in his honour.

'Sorry, I'm in shock,' I say to her, and she leaves me to it for a moment. I'm flummoxed.

She repours my whisky. Jesus. Herb?

'You've been gone a long time, Tom,' she says.

'I'm sorry. I'm really sorry to . . . to hear that,' I say to her, and she shrugs her shoulders as if to say, 'What can you do?'

I'm trying to be tactful. I know Herb must have some details on Robert Valentine that could help me.

'I know this feels like a bad time to ask, I mean, you must still be grieving and everything, but . . .'

'But what?' she says.

'Herb was keeping an eye on something for me. A horse, called Fire Chief. He must have a case file somewhere.'

'I heard the name Fire Chief mentioned about the same time you left town. You certainly left in a hurry,' she says.

'I know,' I say, and I feel a deep sense of shame.

'Don't worry. Herb was very good at only telling me what I needed to know,' the old woman says, with a knowing smile.

I just sit there, not knowing what to say.

'You know what, Tom? I still have a lot of his old files in the basement,' she says. 'You want me to try and dig out some stuff?'

'Yeah, you mind if we do that now?' I ask her, and she looks me in the eyes and I must have the look of a desperate man, because straight away she says, 'Sure, Tom. Now's as good a time as any.'

Next we're downstairs in Herb's basement office where Herb and I used to fraternize without a lot of restraint. He used to keep his alcohol in the third drawer of his old desk. I'd go there for legal advice and I'd leave needing advice on how to put one foot in front of the other.

The old woman is looking in the first of three filing cabinets. 'I'm sorry, Tom,' she says. 'We shifted the filing cabinet and it all fell out and we just shoved it all back in. Everything is out of order here.'

'You mind if I have a little look?' I ask, and she says, 'Sure,' and I start fossicking through a filing cabinet and what is in the files does not correspond with the headings. Everything's out of whack and I'm wading through papers that pretty much all look the same. As I'm doing it I'm wishing I hadn't lost William McGinty's glasses. I'm struggling to concentrate.

I'm frantically searching for a document with the Thoroughbred letterhead on it, but I can't find it. I can't find it. I can't find anything and it all gets a bit much and I tip back for a second . . .

'You okay, Tom?'

'Yeah, maybe I . . . need to sit down for . . .'

Next thing she's got a cold flannel on my face. I don't think I passed out. I'm back up on my feet and at the filing cabinet when the old woman holds my shoulder and says to me, 'I'll tell you what, Tom. I'll keep looking for you, okay?'

Another farce with the police

10.52 p.m.

I figure I should check up on the police to see how they are getting on with their side of the inquiry. I feel nervous heading into the lions' den, but finding Frank is far more important than anything else.

I've gone to the address on Fiona's business card, and I've got Linda waiting in the car, in case I need to leave in a hurry.

The police station is like some kind of sci-fi experiment gone wrong. It looks more like a nightclub than a police station. Glass panels surround the building. Inside is a billboard with a picture of a smiling cop; he looks more like a model who has never spent a day of his life in the police force.

I walk up to the front counter and a homosexual with a headset says to me, 'Welcome to the police. How can I help you?'

'Uhhhh,' I say, 'I . . . Is Fiona here? She's been dealing with me,' and I hand over her business card.

He hands me a giant number thirty-four and tells me to take a seat and I sit down next to other people with numbers.

It's a real mish-mash of low lifes and people in suits and grannies and solo mums and gang members and teenagers with greasy hair.

A policewoman comes up and yells, 'Thirteen.'

Great. Just twenty-one more to go.

'Thirty-four,' a man yells. 'That's me,' I say, and a burly guy takes me to a little desk with a computer screen. 'Tom, is it?' he says.

'That's a good name. I've got an Uncle Tom. Bloody good value, Uncle Tom. I'm Bryan by the way,' and he thrusts out his hand.

'Hi, Bryan.'

'Right, Tom, take a seat.' Bryan looks at his screen. 'Okay, Tom. It's good you came in because it really makes our job so much easier.'

'I wanted to know how you were getting on in finding my son.'

'Well . . . what son is that?'

'You're looking for my son, Frank.'

I show him a photo. 'I have a card . . . this is the police officer who saw me yesterday. Is she here?'

'Says nothing here about a son. That's weird.'

He starts pushing buttons.

'No,' he says to his screen. 'I don't want to update my Firefox. Jesus,' and then he wades through a big mess of menus and boxes that all look a bit incomprehensible to me.

Finally he comes to a file that he starts reading. I try to read over his shoulder but the font is way too small for my peripheral vision.

'Okay. There's nothing about . . . Anyway, Tom. It's so good you came in to see us. I've got some bad news about that house you said was yours last night.'

'Please. I'm not concerned about the house right now.'

'Well, the owner is. Personally I think, well, given the state you're in the owner could show a bit more sympathy, but, you know how people can be. I'm sure we can straighten it out.'

'But I came to ask about Frank—'

'First things first, Tom,' he says, with an irritating smile.

I'm on the verge of blowing my fuse but my smarts tell me it may be better tactically to keep a low profile.

'You're not staying at the Savoy, are you, Tom?'

'Huh?'

'We checked and—'

'This is absurd. Of course I'm at the Savoy.'

'What name are you staying under?'

'Tom Spotswood.'

'Well,' he says, staring at the text on his computer. 'We have checked, Mr Spotswood. Now, it's hard for us to help you with your thing if we don't know where you're staying—'

'My *thing*?'

'Your son. Look, I hate to be a bearer of bad news but . . . It would probably be a good idea if you stay the night with us while we sort this out.'

'Huh?'

'Honestly, our rooms here are excellent. The beds are very comfortable. Like a four-star hotel. I wish I could sleep here but the boss tells me I should do my sleeping at home.'

Was that a joke? Is he trying to joke with me?

I don't like where this is headed so I take advantage of my aching stomach muscles and I let out a gaseous ablution. I make it look like I'm not in control of it and I'm pleased to say it's a real stinker. The guy tries to keep his smiley face but even he can't ignore it.

'I'm sorry. I've got a dicky stomach,' I say. 'Is there a . . .'

'Yes, yes,' he says, trying not to breathe in the toxic fumes.

He points down the corridor.

'I'm sorry. This is very embarrassing,' I say, and I make a real point of getting up slowly and carefully as if I shat myself. It's not a hard act to pull off, as I almost did.

I head down a hallway and instead of going in to the bathroom I keep walking and I take another turn right and I casually walk past the front desk and out of there. It's the oldest trick in the book but I know that I won't find Frank if I'm locked in a room for the night.

I head straight to the car where Linda is waiting. I take off in a hurry.

Linda says, 'How was that? Were they helpful?'

'They're doing everything they can,' I say, and I check the rear-vision mirror and there is no sign of anyone following us.

When we make it back to the Ascot all the reception has gone so we convince the security guard to let us use the photocopier. I pocket a hotel pen and I write a big Missing sign on some A3 with the photo of Frank sitting on the Buffalo Boulders, details of where and when he went missing, and Linda's mobile number underneath.

'Haven't you got a better photo?' Linda says. 'He looks blurry. He's hard to recognize.'

'It's all I've got,' I say, and I stare at Frank sitting on the boulder. Looking at the photo is like listening to a shell. I can hear the waves crashing in and I can hear Deborah yelling at Frank and me to sit closer together.

Me and the security guy haven't a clue how to work the photocopier but Linda sure knows a thing or two. When the first copy of Frank's Missing poster comes out Linda looks at it and decides to change the contrast settings and she makes the picture bigger too. I compliment her on her work, and she tells me she's a jack of not many trades and a master of none. I tell her not to run herself down like that. I don't know how I stumbled upon goodness incarnate, but I can thank my lucky stars I found her.

Next thing Linda is helping me with my magnetic strip. She opens the door of my room for me.

'You should try and get some sleep,' she says, and I laugh at the suggestion and she puts her arms around my neck and rubs my back.

'If you want company I can sleep on the couch here,' she says.

'No. I . . . I should . . . I'll be fine.'

'I'm sorry, I didn't mean to—'

'It's fine.'

'Tom, I'm worried about you.'

I hold up my hand to say I've got it under control, but I know I'm fooling no one.

'I know you can't sleep but you should try,' she says and I tell her I will. I thank her as she heads into her room.

Of course I have no intention of going to sleep. I just don't want Linda to know what I'm up to. I grab my things and I stare at the wrapped train set on my bed. I don't get it. There's a lot that doesn't make sense. Has Robert Valentine taken Frank? Or is Frank hiding from me?

I take a nip of whisky from the shelf above the miniature refrigerator. It's raining, and the raindrops on the window are reflected on to the wall. Looks like the wall is crying.

I look across the road, at the light of the busy convenience store. I head to the bathroom, avoiding the mirror, and I throw water into my face and my hair and I slap myself into action. I fold up a bunch of Missing posters and stuff them in my pockets, and I head out the door.

I've picked up a torch from a 24-hour convenience store. The torch is so bright it lights up a dark street as if there were ten stadium floodlights shining on it. I stare at the light from the torch for a second and my retinas are burned purple with the thing. I flick it off again and I walk down the side streets and I make a beeline for the part of town where the new meets the old.

Good Friday

Showdown at the Century

3.10 a.m.
Threaten someone's family enough and anyone will become a terrorist. Robert Valentine is forcing my hand. He could have played it softly and I would have delivered him the socks he wanted, no problem, but he had to come in hard-ball. I need to send Robert Valentine a message tonight. He's messing with the wrong guy.

I can hear the work going on four blocks before I get there. A booming sound echoes around the buildings as I pass through. The streets are empty as I pass upmarket shop windows where gleaming mannequins display their tits to the world, showing no reaction to the BOOM that is ringing through the city. I head directly for the sound. The road underneath me vibrates as I move past towers of temporary plastic and glass. I arrive at a dilapidated area where a sprinkling of old buildings stand in fear, waiting to be picked off, one by one. I'm getting closer to the source of the sound. Another BOOM and it feels like I'm in the middle of the war zone. Finally I arrive at my target.

I sneak down the side and I see the thug who has been chasing me. Robert Valentine's heavy is sitting in his cab on the side of Regent Street, bashing in the side wall of the Century. I head directly to his machine and every time his ball smashes into the building I put my hands on my ears and brace for impact but I don't particularly care for my personal safety right now. I go directly to where I know he will see me: right in his path, in front of the floodlights, and I spread my arms wide just to make sure my shadow gets cast over the building. The ball swings above my head. I look up at the cab and I see him looking my way. I head for the hole he created and I run inside.

I flick on my torch and all I see in front of me are piles of rubble. The place is unrecognizable. I clamber up over some brick and I dive for cover as I hear another boom of the ball hitting the building and I go in further to where it will be safer but when I have made it over the first pile of rubble all I can see is dust shining all around the torch.

I find the stairwell and race up to the second floor. The ball has stopped pummelling the building. I head out to the balcony. I hear footsteps below and a torchlight comes on. I turn off my torch and I move slowly and stealthily. I creep towards the balcony and I crouch out of sight as I watch my guy come into the building.

I peek over the balcony and I can't see his fat face. All I can see is a torchlight shining around the floor, as he scans the theatre. I want him to get into a more vulnerable position so I wait. When he is halfway across I grab a small piece of concrete and I throw it as far as I can at the wall on the other side to try to coax him in further. It works like a treat. He moves closer to the far wall. I keep my head down as I see his torch beam shining out, and I make sure I get my bearings to where the closest exit is. My position is improving by the second.

'Hey,' he yells and I keep real still and the light shines up in my area and I crawl to a pile of rubble as quiet as I can and when the torchlight shifts again I grab another piece of brick and I throw it at the stage and he shines it there. He moves even further over a pile of rubble into the middle of the floor. I have the advantage now. I shine my torch directly at him. His eyes squint as he looks directly at the bright light.

'Is that you, Dick?' he says, and he sounds nervous.

He shines his torch at me and I drop below the balcony and flick off my torch and I crawl closer to the stairwell. I can see his torchlight searching where I came from. 'Hey!' he yells again, and I stand up and I shine the torch right at him and my torch completely overpowers his. I can see from his eyes that he can't see me, and I can see he's scared.

Then his body position changes and he drops his arms and puffs out his shoulders like a poodle pretending to be a Rottweiler. He looks straight at me and he says, 'Tom. Tom, is that you?'

I shine my torch directly at him. He shields his eyes and stares back.

'Where is my son?' I say.

He stares back at me and yells, 'Who do you think you're speaking to?'

'What?' I say. He drops the hand that was shielding his eyes. 'Who do you think you're speaking to?'

'I don't know you,' I say, and he laughs and says, 'You can say that again.'

I don't get what game he's playing and I don't particularly feel like wasting my time with these stupid games.

'You know where Frank is, don't you?' I ask.

'I don't think Frank wants to see you, Tom,' he says.

'Is he safe?' I ask and he seems to find that funny.

I've had enough. I can see this is much bigger than him.

'I want to talk to Robert Valentine,' I say.

'I don't even know who Robert Valentine is,' he says, laughing at me. I throw a handful of rocks at him and he ducks for cover. He picks one up and throws it back at me.

I yell at him, 'Listen, if you lay one finger on Frank—' and he laughs again, the patronizing prick, and says, 'What? What are you going to do, Tom? Throw rocks at me?'

'Don't fuck with a desperate man,' I say and he fumbles around in his pocket and pulls out a phone. I know who he's dialling. 'Is that Alastair Shook?' I ask.

He says, 'I'm phoning the police.'

I figure it's time to get out of here so I throw a barrage of rocks at him, and when he ducks for cover I flick off my torch and I run for the exit. I make it to the stairwell and I bash my way past some masonry and through a doorway. I feel my way down the wall without my torch on. I race towards the hole in the wall, and I'm out of there quicksmart. I make it across the road and I wait behind a car further down the road.

In a few minutes I hear a siren. A police car stops and my guy heads right over and talks to the policeman.

I'd better make myself scarce. As I run down Regent, through Bond and out Hobson Street I'm thinking whoever Robert Valentine is, whoever Alastair Shook is, whoever the demolition guy is, someone in the puzzle has got a police connection. This goes far further up the food chain than I ever imagined. I hate to think what I've got Frank mixed up in.

I know that whoever is holding him won't want to hurt him. They're just wanting to scare me into giving them what I owe them. One way or another I have to go to the top. Find Robert Valentine so I can get Frank back and safe again. I'm sorry, Frank. I'm sorry I got you mixed up in this.

Desperation in the wee small hours

4.32 a.m.

I'm back in my room, in my hotel dressing gown, and I'm attempting the impossible – sleep. I lie staring at the ceiling, listening to the sound of an air conditioner in the room, listening to the sounds of distant sirens and traffic lights and intermittent traffic and I close my eyes and try to shut my brain off, but instead I see Frank as a cute little six-year-old, lying in bed. I've just got him a hot-water bottle and he's lying wide-eyed in bed like he won't get to sleep in a hurry.

Like father, like son.

'Can't get to sleep?' I say to him and he just stares up at the ceiling.

'Gee, Frank,' I say to him, 'I've got whisky. You want a whisky?' and he giggles, and I show him my glass and he has a sniff and I say to him, 'It's like liquid fire, Frank, but it helps me get to sleep.'

'Is that why you drink so much? So you can get to sleep?'

I sigh and run my hand over the smooth skin of his forehead and as much as I was joking, the joke has turned in on itself and suddenly I'm in confessional with him.

'You think I drink too much, Frank?'

'I don't know. I'm just a kid.'

'Yeah, but you can have an opinion,' I say, and Frank looks up at me and he runs his finger across my chin, against my stubble rolling with the grain, and against the grain.

He says to me, 'When I grow up do you think I'll drink like a fish?'

'Who told you that expression?'

'Mum did.'

'Gee, Frank. I don't know if you . . . I mean . . . I'm not the best role model, maybe you should . . .' and I taper off. Who am I to tell him how he should live his life? I've got no idea how to live mine, so, I say nothing to him, I just look at his cute little ugly face, and I smile.

I sit up and throw a cigarette in my mouth and fumble around for my lighter, when I hear this little voice ask for a cuddle, and I say, 'Of course, Frank. Of course,' and I hug him tight while his fingers roll from the stubble on my chin up a trail to my sideburns. He runs his fingers around the curves of my ears.

Oh God.

I can't face this. I . . .

Please, God, please. A second chance . . .

I can't take it any longer. I've been trying to shut out the tears. I've been in survival mode ever since I lost Frank. Don't surrender to your emotions, Tom, because now more than ever you need to think straight and logical, but I'm dying here. I find myself crying on the inside, like a silent scream, and then the scream stops being silent, my body takes over and I'm shrieking into the ceiling. I'm shrieking and my body is purging and I sound like a washing machine at the end of its cycle.

Next thing I'm at Linda's door. When she opens up I collapse into her, my head in her shoulders. She holds me tight. She pulls up my face and sees that I've been crying. She's stroking my neck. She holds me tight and whispers, 'It's going to be fine, Tom.' She rocks me back and forth. She takes me to her bed and she tucks me in good and tight. She climbs in and cradles me from behind.

She kisses the back of my neck and says, 'Just close your eyes, Tom. You've got to shut out the world for a bit, you know? Give yourself a break,' and I try to breathe deep, and then I sigh, a really big sigh, and Linda says to me, 'That's good, Tom. Sighing's good for you. Give me another sigh.'

Linda is running her fingers through the back of my hair, and it feels nice.

I turn around to face her and I can see she's got some tears too. I don't know why she's crying. Tears of sympathy? Tears of empathy? Tears from a life that's been fucked almost as badly as mine, I don't know, but I catch one of those tears with my lips, and I kiss her, tender, gentle kisses, and I pull back her robe and catch a glint of her collar bone in the streetlights and I kiss her again. She pulls back my robe and climbs on top of me. She whispers in my ear, 'I promise I won't break you,' and she tries to slide herself into me.

I say, 'I like to go on top. I'm kind of old-fashioned in that way,' and there was a day not so long ago when I would have flung her over and taken charge like Humphrey Bogart but I have to wait for her to climb off me and my neck is so sore I can only move a little at a time. I kiss her navel, and I trail light kisses up to her breasts and she sighs, and then up to her neck and I hold her so tight and her face feels different to Deborah's soft smooth face and I start thinking of Deborah. I'm looking into Deborah's eyes as I enter her slowly, and Deborah whispers to me, 'Do you love me, Tom?' and I say, 'You know I do,' and Linda's voice cuts in with, 'Hey, Tom, maybe you should put on a condom,' and I'm staring at Deborah's beautiful eyes that are so full of sorrow and joy. She overwhelms me. I've got her on such a pedestal that when we're close like this I feel like a new person. Linda says, 'Tom, I've got a condom in my bag,' and I'm lost in Deborah's eyes and the tears are flooding from me now. This is more than I can stand. Linda says to me, 'Tom, are you okay?' and I'm shrieking, I can hear my whole body shrieking and I shut my eyes and all I see is Deborah. Deborah, I miss you so much, I miss you so . . .

A phone call for room 834

6.21 a.m.

I wake up to the sound of a phone ringing. I can hear it through the wall, next door in my room. I look at the time.

Pretty early for a phone call . . .

I find my hotel dressing gown at the bottom of Linda's bed.

Next thing I'm outside, struggling with my magnetic strip. I can hear my phone ringing again. I get inside and I make it just in time for whoever it is to hang up.

I look out the window and I see a van has pulled up. Am I being paranoid here? Something isn't right.

I go to the safe and remember the code, Frank's birth date, and I've got the schoolbag of socks out when there is a loud knock.

'Mr McGinty,' a voice says from the other side of the door.

I'm looking out the window. A burly man is down below, waiting by the van, having a cigarette.

No outside fire escape. No exit strategy there.

The door knocks again. 'Tom!'

I pick up a vase. The door is opening. I throw the vase at a man with ginger hair and I charge my way through. I kick my way through a teenage girl in a strange uniform, and I'm out of there. I'm running down the hallway and I run down the stairs two at a time. I have seven more floors to run so every elevator I run past I push the button and now I'm going three stairs at a time until I get to the bottom floor. I sprint outside. I run past the man by the van.

He yells, 'Hey,' to me, and he chases me. I head directly for a big mall.

I'm running through the Grande Arcade. On most days about now this place would be bristling with shopkeepers getting ready for the day, but today is Easter. Every shop is locked and closed so there's nowhere for me to run to hide myself in a crowd. The only person I go past is a cleaner and I manage to slip over on a wet floor. I'm straight on my feet again, running down an escalator that has been switched off for the day.

This place is like a maze. I'm going round in circles on this floor, past a whole series of closed stores, all with their gates down. I stop for a second and I can hear footsteps running some distance behind me.

I head down another escalator that is switched off. Round a corner and I'm in a back corridor. I try a door but it's locked. I try the next door and mercifully it opens. As soon as I'm inside I lock it and instantly some lights flick on in this small room. I look in front of me and I end up staring straight into a mirror, and I feel this big volt of electricity shoot right through me—

I'm lying on a floor.

It's cold against my cheek.

I'm lying on linoleum tiles . . .

I'm in a bathroom.

I'm not sure how much time has passed. One minute? Five minutes? Or has it been longer?

I am careful where to look and where not to look. I follow the tiles to a door.

It's locked. I think I locked myself in here. It's coming back to me. I was being chased . . .

I feel for Frank's backpack. I'm feeling pretty vulnerable carrying all these socks. I'll have to get rid of them. These socks are the only bargaining chip I've got left.

I'm listening outside and I hear nothing.

I think they've gone . . .

163

I sneak out of the bathroom and there's no sign of anyone.

I run up the escalator and hunt for the exit of this goddam maze.

I'm at a payphone. My hotel dressing gown is making it hard to blend in with the general public. I phone the Ascot and I get through to Linda.

I don't trust this payphone so I talk quick. 'Linda, it's me. Tom. Can you bring my clothes to me?'

'Tom!' she says.

'I'll meet you at Zing in an hour.'

'Okay. Tom, what's going on? Who were those people?'

'Did you see them? I was hoping you could tell me.'

'Tom, are you okay?' she says and I see a van drive past. I hang up on Linda and I make a beeline for the green belt.

I'm in the middle of the Mount Elizabeth Bus Tunnel. This tunnel wasn't built for pedestrians. It is supposed to be used by buses only. Of course there are always a few pedestrians, cyclists and cars who try to slip on through. It's a one-way tunnel too, which adds to the challenge.

I can't see a thing in here. I'm gliding my hand along the wall of the tunnel, feeling for the alcove. I look in front of me and a bus has arrived at an inopportune time. I could turn around but I know I'm within a few feet of it. The bus lights are shining in my direction. My heart beats fast as I hear the rumble coming in my direction and I'm relieved when my right hand glides into a hole. I slide in and the bus roars past me.

I feel my way to the back wall of the alcove. I reach up to a concrete ledge, hoping a rat doesn't nibble at my fingers. I take off my bag. I open it up and I'm hit with a whiff of foot odor. One dirty pair of socks has contaminated the whole bag. I stuff a sock in my hotel dressing gown pocket. I shove the bag on top of the ledge. I look back out the alcove and watch another bus coming past. I see the bus driver lit up and looking half asleep as his bus chugs through the tunnel.

A tab at Zing

11.19 a.m.

I arrive at Zing and I'm feeling pretty conspicuous in my dressing gown. I wait in a little alleyway until I see Linda show up. I watch her go inside and come out again for a cigarette. I head across the road, directly to her. When I get to her she looks jittery, shaken up. I swear, my misery is contagious.

I check inside for anyone who looks suspicious. Inside are a couple of women in a cubicle who are clearly checking me out. Then again, who wouldn't check out a guy in the middle of town wearing nothing but a dressing gown? Linda says to me, 'I checked. The coast is clear,' and she hands me my clothes.

I'm in the bathroom getting dressed. My mind is spinning out of control. I don't know if I can keep up with everything that is going on. I seem to be in something much deeper than I could have ever imagined. I should never have come back, but living the rest of my life without Frank wasn't an option.

Another selfish move. If I'd stayed well away I wouldn't have brought all this heat on myself and Frank would be safe right now. Surely they wouldn't hurt him though. Why would they hurt an eleven-year-old boy?

I come back out and Linda is sitting in a cubicle and I sit in with her. I'm scanning throughout Zing and outside too. Everyone is starting to look suspicious to me. I have to calm down the paranoia aspect of this and think straight.

Linda is doing her best to keep me calm. She's bought me a coffee, a croissant and a banana.

'Who were those guys?' I ask her.

'Most of them chased after you but one stayed behind. He wanted to know about you. How long you'd been staying at the Ascot. What your movements were.'

'What did you tell him?'

'I told him you were my neighbour and we'd had a few drinks and . . .'

A trickle of tears slides down her face and she wipes her eyes with the hotel dressing gown.

'Tom. I'm sure Frank's fine,' she says, digging her fingers into my shoulder. 'Jesus,' she says. 'You're just about the nicest person I've met in a long while.'

I know I can't let this develop any further.

'Linda, I can't . . . You don't want to get mixed up with me. I have to do this on my own now. It's got nothing to do with your age—'

'My what?'

'I have a wife.'

'My age?' she says to me.

'I'm sorry. You're a little . . . older than most women I . . . But it's not that. I've got an open mind on that. It's just, I'm . . . this a bad time for me. I can't . . . We . . . I'm hoping to get back together with my wife—'

'It's fine, Tom.'

'What happened last night—'

'I've got no expectations, Tom. It's fine,' she says, but her eyes are saying something very different.

'Honestly, I'm not worth crying about,' I say to her, as she wipes her eyes with a serviette. 'You really think Frank is okay?'

'I know he is, Tom. I know it.'

The look in her eye gives me a chill. Her eyes dart up and I look behind me and suddenly there are four people at my table.

They've sent the full cavalry. Shook's teenage assistant and two big guys – one Polynesian and the other looks like a weightlifter from one of those cold countries where people pull ploughs. The two guys are surrounding me, one on each side, and I try to fight my way free but the guys lean into me and hold me into the table.

Linda says, 'Please be gentle with him,' and I look at her, the one person I thought I could trust.

A guy with a body the shape of an egg and faded ginger hair sits opposite me. He has faux kind eyes and a false smile.

'Alastair Shook?' I say, and he nods.

'Stay calm, Tom. Everything will be fine,' he says.

He takes out my wallet and he opens it up in front of me, and pulls out William McGinty's ID.

'How long have you been carrying this around?' he asks.

I don't answer. He hands me back my wallet.

'Where's my son?' I ask Alastair Shook.

'He's in town. I don't know exactly where he is right now,' he says.

'I don't want to talk to you. No more middle management. I want to talk to Robert Valentine.'

He nods. 'Okay. And what would you like to say to him?'

'I'm willing to come to an arrangement.'

'What arrangement are you willing to come to?' he asks, trying to control the conversation, but there's no way I'll fall for whatever crappy mind-control techniques he's using.

'Who is he? Robert Valentine?' I ask.

'What makes you think I know Robert Valentine?'

'You're working for him.'

'What makes you think I'm working for him?'

'I know you're working for him!'

'How do you know him?' he asks, and he waits patiently while I surmise the best way to play this.

'What do you want?' I ask him.

'I just want to help you out, Tom.'

'Is that why you got your thugs on the job? That's how you help people?'

Alastair Shook raises an eyebrow to the guys next to me and their grip loosens, and I get my arms back.

'I want to help you, Tom,' he says, like he just graduated with a degree from some second-rate psychology correspondence course. 'Do you want me to help you find Robert Valentine?'

He's trying to act like he's on my side, but I'm not buying it. Still, I figure my best chance is to act compliant.

'You'll help me if I come with you, right?' I say.

'Of course,' he says.

I stand up and as we all try to shuffle out of our cubicle I lunge for my coffee and I throw it in the weightlifter's face and try to break free, but Alastair Shook and his teenage assistant manage to stall me until the Polynesian guy wraps his big mitts around me. I bite and I struggle and now my arms are behind my back and I hear Linda scream and Alastair Shook nods and pulls from his hand a little strip of paper – it looks like LSD – and the Polynesian guy tries to pull my jaw open. He holds his hands on my nostrils and I'm forced to take a breath and Shook sticks his finger in my mouth and I can hear myself yell, 'Help!' and I can hear the sounds of the coffee shop become a hush and I catch sight of Linda's guilt-ridden face before everything goes black in my vision.

I can hear voices saying, 'It's okay,' 'Grab his legs,' 'It's okay, Tom,' and I can see Deborah, beautiful Deborah, with such kind eyes, smiling and holding her hand on my cheek, and the voices are saying, 'How's he looking?', 'It's okay, Tom,' 'Everything will be fine,' and 'I can't find his seat belt. Where's the seat belt?'

Now I can see Frank, waiting for me at school. He's excited to see me. We cross the pedestrian crossing together and he's running ahead of me so I run to catch up with him, pretending I can't keep up with him, and he's laughing and we start heading up the rise of Clyde Street and he's going as fast as he can and I up the pace a little and I overtake him, and I run ahead of him. I pass two lamp posts and I'm running hard, thinking he'll find it funny but I can't hear him any more and when I turn around he's crying. He's crying and he's looking at me with these eyes, these hurt eyes like I just did the worst thing in the world and I go back to him and I say, 'What?

What did I do?' He heads off in the opposite direction, back to the school leaving me yelling at him, 'Frank! Frank!'

Now I'm running after him and I catch up with him and he swings his bag like a weapon, slamming it into my leg again and again in front of all the other parents, and I'm saying, 'Calm down, Frank,' but he's not listening. He's just slamming me and screaming. I try to pick him up and he screams in my ear, so I put him down and he runs away again, and this time I let him get far ahead of me. I just let him go.

Spud

Good Friday

Anything from the dessert menu

4.02 a.m.

It doesn't take long for the police to arrive. Two of them: a woman in her thirties and a young buck who looks like he's there to take orders, not give them. The guy is looking around the site with Dick while I talk to the policewoman. She looks too nice to be police, this one.

She's got out her notebook. I've pretty much given her a full description of what happened, and I've showed her where I think he may have run to, when she says to me, 'Can you describe what he looks like?'

I pull out the photo Alastair Shook sent me and she stares at it.

'I'm sorry. I don't understand. You . . . You know him?'

'Unfortunately I do,' I say. 'He's . . . he's a relative of mine.'

'Oh. Okay.'

'He's my father.'

'Your father?'

'Yeah,' I say, and she stops writing in her notebook and stares at the photo of Tom's ugly face, and she looks back at me.

'So . . . okay. Where do you think he's gone?'

'I don't know. He thinks I work for a guy called Robert Valentine.'

'Who's Robert Valentine?'

'I have no idea,' I say to her. 'Look, I need to get back to work. Can we hurry this along?'

'Do you think he could still be in the area?' she asks me.

'He's smarter than that. I don't think so.'

'Any idea where he might be staying?' she asks, and I give her our old home address. 'What other homes has he lived in here?' she asks. I list all the places that I can remember, the places I know he lived in before I was born, but after that there's a big black hole of thirty years in which I have no idea where he's been.

She hands me a business card.

'We'll do what we can to find your father. But you probably have a better idea of where he could be than we do.'

'I gotta work here tonight. I can't leave this job.'

'Okay, so tomorrow morning—'

'Listen, officer. I'd prefer he didn't die on the streets, so I'll help you if I think of anything, but I'm done with him. Alastair Shook is your man,' I say, and I give her his mobile number.

'He could be in a lot of distress,' she says, and I say, 'Good. He's caused everyone else in his life distress. He deserves what he gets.'

She looks at me like I'm a bad human being but she doesn't get it. I bet she was brought up in a nice home with two loving parents who gave a fuck. Me – I've had to do it the hard way. Why should I give a shit about someone who never gave a shit about me? Why should I waste my time on him? I'm stressed enough as it is. She walks around the building to talk to her partner, and I climb back in the cab and nod to Temaia that I'm ready to bash the wall down. I can think of no better way to let off some steam.

5.28 a.m.

I've cut all the way up two sections. In front of me are two straight line cuts all the way up the building, ten metres apart. I have to be careful on this first wall. If I get it wrong the brick could concertina out and I could get a whole heap of brick landing on the street, which could eat up our footpath fee. Still, we're behind schedule so I'm taking some more chances than normal. I'm going in one storey at a time and the top storey comes down nice and easy, falling through the hole I made, making a huge booming sound like thunder.

My mind wanders when I'm doing something repetitive. I'm chipping away at the mid-wall, tapping in section by section, and Tom comes into my brain again. I'm too tired to fight it any more. The time he left for good wasn't the first time. A year earlier, when I was six, Mum kicked him out, probably for sleeping with the next-door neighbour. Not that I knew that at the time. Mum filled in some gaps for me when she thought I was old enough to hear the grisly details.

So I got to spend a weekend with Tom in town. I was a suburban kid, so spending a whole weekend in the heart of The City was exciting. Tom took me to a fancy restaurant but we didn't even have dinner. Tom just ordered from the wine menu and he let me go through the dessert menu and choose anything I wanted.

When I couldn't choose, Tom said to the waiter, 'We'll have them all,' and I ended up with four plates on my table: a chocolate mousse, a steamed pudding, an icecream sundae and a cheesecake. I ate everything except for the cheesecake. Tom put me off that one by saying it was made of cheese that had come straight from a cow they kept in the kitchen.

Tom drank until he could barely walk and he had to rely on me for balance to get back to the hotel room.

I remember the best treat of all, when Tom let me sleep on the vibrating double bed. It was coin operated but Tom had come prepared. He had so much change that I could have vibrated all night if I wanted. We both lay on it and put in coin after coin and it shook so violently that when we'd finished giggling I felt sick and I got a second taste of the steamed pudding in the back of my throat.

Then Tom hit the miniature refrigerator and drank himself to sleep while I operated the remote control and sat up all night watching all the TV shows Mum would never let me see.

It was a real treat, but now I realize it was just straight-out bribery, and I fell for it like any six-year-old would.

As I'm bashing down a big ten-metre-wide chunk of wall I'm trying to think of the name of the place. As a big section falls in front of me it comes to me: the Ascot. I bet Tom is staying at the Ascot.

177

As soon as it's smoko I head to the hut. I pull out Dick's phone and the phone book and I dial the Ascot and when the operator answers I ask, 'Is there a Mr Spotswood staying there?' I can hear the operator tapping keys on a computer before saying, 'I'm sorry. There doesn't appear to be a Mr Spotswood here.'

I'm halfway through my egg sammie when a second wave hits me and I phone the Ascot again. This time I ask for William McGinty, and bingo, suddenly I hear a phone ringing. I don't want to talk to him, so I hang up and I immediately phone the police. They put me on hold so instead I phone Alastair Shook, and tell him where Tom is staying.

After my mother passed away Kimbo handled most of the paper-work. Mum had got a lot of her things in order but there were still a lot of leftover jobs, and one of them was closing down her bank account. When Kimbo looked at the statements she spotted an automatic payment of a hundred dollars a week going into Mum's account that had been active for a long, long time. She got curious who was putting money in and she traced it to a name from up north, William McGinty.

I knew it was him straight away. McGinty was one of his favourite horses back in the day. It won the Ellerslie Cup two years running, it took out the Havelock Stakes and it would have travelled to Japan and raced there if it hadn't developed a lesion on its leg.

I didn't tell Kimbo who it was. I kept it to myself. I knew she'd make a big deal of it. Of course she figured it out herself and tried to snoop further when I told her to close the account. Kimbo said, 'You're kissing goodbye to a hundred dollars a week,' and I said to her, 'I don't want his dirty money.' He thinks he can buy my mother's affections with a hundred bucks a week? He thinks he can buy his way out of all the shitty things he's done but life doesn't work that way.

Turns out Kimbo never closed the account down, but the money stopped coming in half a year later. I took that as a sign that he'd either run out of money or he'd taken it for himself and given up at long last and left us alone. Even better, maybe he'd died and he could leave us all in peace, finally.

But no.

William McGinty has turned up again, after all these years.

A new low with Kimbo

11.06 a.m.

The first wall has been knocked down now. That's the hardest of all the jobs. There's dust everywhere and we're building up a few demolition watchers, including some with video cameras. The protester I saw yesterday now has a sign saying 'Honk For The Century'. Fat load of help she's going to get out of a few horn honks. Would she have had the balls to stick a screwdriver in my radiator? She looks too harmless.

The early morning sunlight is hitting the inside of the theatre for the first time since it was built. You can't make out a stage was there any longer but there's some big pillars still standing and the top floor with half of its seating is still there.

I get a bit nostalgic looking at the place. I saw my first film here. It was about an Australian boy who had a pet pelican, and I had a bit of a blub when the pelican, Mr Percival, came back after the boy thought he'd died.

The morning crew has arrived and Ben's already having a blast in the dozer trying to flatten rubble as he pushes into the building. He rides over a chunk of wooden wall and I hear it all snap like a dozen broken legs.

All the other night-shift guys are heading to the Albert Arms, a little pub that does a cooked breakfast. I'd love to join them but I gotta wait here for Kimbo.

I've borrowed Dick's phone and I call Roger Laing to tell him I'll be needing him to come and get his chairs as soon as possible but he can't do anything about it for a month. Then he says, 'Are there any more?'

'More?' I say. 'Jesus. I got the number you asked for—'

'I'm sorry. I miscalculated. I've got room for at least fifteen hundred chairs. How many are you holding for me?'

'A thousand and thirty.'

'Can you get me any more?'

'I can get you four hundred and ten more chairs, but it'll cost you.'

'I'll take them,' he says. 'I'll take them all.'

'But you need to come and pick them up sooner than a month. I can't sit on this stuff that long,' I say. He says he's a bit stretched but he'll do what he can.

I get off the phone from him and I laugh at the big fuckin mess I'm making.

Finally I see the Dwarf approaching, with Kimbo at the wheel. I get inside and Kimbo pulls a big U-turn.

'How'd your night go?' she asks me and I say, 'We're getting there,' and she says, 'She's a nice building.'

'Yeah, she sure is.'

'I fixed your phone,' Kimbo says, and my phone is sitting on the dashboard.

'You had too many messages. Its memory was full. I deleted everything and it started working again.'

'Cool, thanks,' I say, and she drives silently. Something feels different about her. There's something about her that makes me feel like something has happened.

We're halfway down Lichfield Road when she spits it out.

'I think we should try a trial separation.'

'Huh? What?'

We get stuck at the lights.

'A trial separation? I don't even know what that means.'

'We try not living together, and we see if that makes us happier,' she says, as the lights turn green.

'Fine,' I say, because I can tell she's already decided to do this. I bet Brenda put her up to it.

'I don't want you in the house any more,' she says.

'Whoa! What the fuck?'

'Unless you want me and Lucy to move, but I figure Lucy needs some stability—'

'What are you talking about?'

'I've shifted you out.'

We arrive at an intersection and she points behind us.

'I've shifted your stuff into the truck. You'll sleep better there. I shifted your mattress and I got all your things in there.'

'What? Are you bullshitting me?'

She looks me in the eye. She's not bullshitting.

'Pull over,' I say.

She stops the truck. I get out and open the back.

And I laugh. Jesus fuckin Christ.

Inside Kimbo's been playing interior decorating games. My mattress is there, completely made up with sheets and everything. She's shifted in a tallboy. I open it up and it's full of socks and undies. Next to that is a big black plastic bag. I look inside and my clothes are there. And there's a couple of boxes full of my stuff. My shaver, my toothbrush, my fuckin screwdriver set, some photos. She's left the urinal in here too, at the foot of the bed. Kimbo's twisted finishing touch.

I'm gobsmacked. I sit on the mattress, unable to take it in. Kimbo pops her head in the back door.

'I gotta hand it to you. When you do something you do it properly,' I say, and she says, 'I want you to be comfortable.'

'What about Lucy?' I say, and she says, 'Jesus, Spud. I want you to keep seeing Lucy. I just don't want you in the house any more,' and I just start laughing, laughing at the gall of the whole thing. I never shoulda got hitched up with a wild one. My mother knew she was out of control. Who is this woman?

She looks at me the way Jesus Christ stares at a leper.

'I'll catch a bus home,' she says. 'Lucy is at the Galvins'. I'll be home at about eight. You've got until then to get the last of your stuff.'

'Hold it. What do I say to Lucy?' I say.

'She knows,' Kimbo says, and throws me the keys.

'She knows what?'

'She knows that we aren't getting along at the moment. She knows we're taking space from each other while we decide.'

'While we decide what?' I say, and she looks at me the way a driver looks at a cat they accidentally ran over.

'What are we deciding?' I say again, and she walks away from me, down the street towards a bus stop.

I'm in the shower. I'm looking down at the water beneath me and it's all gone black from the dust of the Century. I'm in shock. I let the water hit my face and I'm thinking, What right does she have to kick me out of my own house? What right does she have to end this marriage? I never had an affair. How come she gets to hold the moral high ground?

She used to be fun. We used to be wild together, in a good way. Her voice used to lift when she saw me. When did that all change?

I mean, I know I'm not the best catch in the universe. But she ain't perfect either. Christ, if she had to go out with herself she'd drive herself nuts in a week.

When she caught the bloody baby at the Alice Cooper concert I really thought I'd met my match. Now I look back at it and I realize my match was a woman screaming, holding on to a prosthetic dead baby. I really should have seen the signs.

I'm back in my new home, the Dwarf. I've parked up directly outside the front gate, just to spite Kimbo. I'm lying on my bed in the truck, and I'm tapping out a rhythm against the wall, a fast rhythm.

I'm looking down at my leg and it's shaking like it's got a mind of its own. I got a lot of energy all of a sudden.

I feel myself taking big breaths. I'm gasping for air, and my mind is racing again. I'm thinking about Lucy, and custody, and lawyers and how Kimbo will be good at all that stuff, I know it, so fuck it, if she wants to be a greedy bitch she can have it all.

My leg starts doing a little dance again and I find myself spelling her name in my head, K – I – M – B – O – K – I – M – fuck it, you can have everything. Whatever you want. You want the clothes on my back, then have them. You want to take Lucy away from me . . .

I'm hearing this new voice inside my head and it's saying cigarettes, cigarettes, have a cigarette have a cigarette, where are they where are they where are they.

I find my jeans crumpled on the floor and I reach into the pockets and I pull out the nicotine patches and I stick a new patch on my chest and I stick a second one on too for good measure.

I bet Kimbo's doing just fine at not smoking. I bet she's replaced it with something real healthy. I bet she's eating some almonds right now and feeling smug.

I'm staring at the foot of the bed, where the television should be, but instead I got a urinal staring back at me. I could do with some television. Just half an hour in front of the television will settle me. I'm staring at the house and I'm thinking about what I promised to myself in the shower, that I'd never set foot in there again until Kimbo apologizes, but I'm thinking, Just a little bit of television could really help right now. I could go watch the telly in the bedroom, just to take my mind off things. Kimbo will never know.

I grab the urinal and I throw it out the back of the truck. I hoist it over the gate so that it sits inside the property. I head for the house and when I get to the front door I realize I forgot to put my pants on, but I don't give a fuck right now. I grab the spare key and I head straight for the bedroom.

I switch on the TV but the volume is up so high that I have to shut it up and I hunt for the remote and I lower the volume and I flick through the channels and I find a channel with a British darts competition and that makes me feel calmer, watching this guy throw a 180. The phone rings and I get jumpy and I get an attack of the guilts and I turn off the TV.

'Hello?' I say.

'That you Spud?'

It's Alastair Shook. He sounds out of breath, like he's been running.

'We lost Tom. We found him and we lost him.'

'Wait. What?'

'We lost him at the Freyberg on-ramp. We don't know where he is. We don't know where he's gone.'

'Look, I'm done with him, okay?' I say.

'Well, we can do with some more help—'

I hang up.

My head is burning up. I head to the bathroom and I splash some water on my face and I stare at the mirror and I see him – in my own face I see him – this ugly, grotesque human being.

I head straight out of the house and I slam the door behind me and when I get back to the Dwarf I sit on my bed and I wish I'd had more balls and come back with the television. I look down at my hand and I see that I'm still holding the remote. And I can't help it. I laugh. I laugh too hard, and the laughing makes me want to cry so I just laugh even harder to shut out the pain.

Hair today, gone tomorrow

2.04 p.m.

I knock on the door of the Galvins'. I'm here to pick up Lucy. I'm not looking forward to seeing Denise. I know for a fact that Denise is the one Kimbo has a good moan to, and guess what moaning topic number one is? I'm sure Denise has helped Kimbo dissect every little aspect of my unfitness to be a father, a lover and a husband. I'm sure Kimbo has spoken in complete detail about every little aspect of our sexless life. When Denise answers the door I can tell she knows all about Kimbo's little plan. I bet the two of them had a great laugh coming up with it over their non-alcoholic cocktails.

'Is Lucy around?' I ask, and Denise says, 'She's out the back.'

I head down the hallway and I can't find her. I hear a toilet flush so I yell, 'Lucy, is that you?' and I hear it flush again.

The door opens and I get a shock when I see her face.

Her hair is short. Where's all her hair gone?

'What the . . .' I say, and Lucy looks like she's about to cry.

'What happened?' I say, and then I see hair all over the bathroom floor of the Galvins'.

'Oh shit,' I say. I close the bathroom door and lock us both in.

'We gotta clean this up,' I say to her, and I look in the toilet bowl and it is completely full of hair.

'Jesus, Lucy!'

I grab some toilet paper and scoop up hair from the Galvins' otherwise spotless toilet.

186

'It's in the bath too,' Lucy says, and I grab a flannel and I wet it and get Lucy to mop up her mess.

I'm scooping hair into wet toilet paper and flushing the toilet again but no matter how much I get rid of there's more hair. There's hair everywhere: in the bath, on the floor, in the basin. The hair's not flushing so there's hair in the toilet bowl. I'm surrounded by hair and I . . .

I feel a bit . . .

'Dad?' Lucy's saying.

I'm trying to breathe. I'm checking my pockets for the Rescue Remedy. I'm opening their medicine cabinet, looking for something to swallow, something to help, but I can't find anything.

From outside the bathroom I hear Denise say, 'Everything all right in there?' and I flush the toilet to mask the sound of me hyperventilating.

'Dad?' Lucy's saying, and I can hear panic in her voice.

I'm opening the bathroom drawers, hunting for a bag. There has to be a bag. I just need a bag but there's no bag.

I see the shower curtain. I pull it back and there's a shower cap and I'm breathing into the shower cap, slow breaths, counting to four breathing in, counting to four breathing out . . .

When I pull myself together I say to her 'I'm okay Goose. Don't tell your Mum about this.'

I take a few more breaths to get calm and I shoot her a wink.

Next thing I'm in the front of the cab with Lucy, driving to the movie theatre. I keep looking at her face whenever we stop at an intersection, and she keeps looking away from me. She hasn't done a great job of cutting her own hair. She's cut whole chunks at the root, so there are a couple of little bald patches on the side.

I don't know what to say to her. It's my fault she's a tomboy. She's on a one-way path to being a lesbian at this rate. I don't know what I'm supposed to think about that. What does she want next? To work on a fuckin building site? Jesus, it makes me want to take up knitting or crochet just to encourage her to find her girly side.

I say to her, 'Your mother and I are going through a rough patch,' and she says, 'I know,' and neither of us say anything else for the rest of the drive.

We get to the movie theatre half an hour before the boys break for lunch. I rev up T-Rex and let her idle and warm up. I get a couple of the boys to pull off the ball and attach some chompers.

I throw Lucy a hard hat and I say to her, 'You wanna look around?' and she nods. We head into what used to be the main circle. A few of the bulldozer boys give Lucy a wave and she waves back, looking a bit self-conscious.

I see a nice path up to the seating area that could be cleared pretty quickly if I can get some of the boys to help me out.

As soon as I hear the machines stop I'm in the shed at smoko flashing the cash for helpers.

Next thing me and Lucy are sitting in the crane, tracking through the hole in the wall. I can see the amazement on Lucy's face as she sees the inside of the place. I chuck a dust mask over her face and we head straight for the seating area. Butterfingers and Joey are up there running air lines, unbolting the chairs and stacking them by the balcony. Me and T-Rex pick them up like a beast picking up a small child. I let Lucy steer the gib and we pull the chairs back. Muzz backs the truck in and we load them up, nice and simple. We get the job done in less than an hour and it feels satisfying having got every last chair out of there.

Apart from one hole the roof is all pretty intact and I see the old stars hanging and I give Temaia a wolf-whistle and he pulls at them and they get caught on the side so I run over and chuck up a ladder and pull the last part free and a big net of stars falls to the ground softly. I give Temaia my keys and he loads the stars into the Dwarf for me.

We're home again, and I've gone to my box of cords and Lucy helps me hook together six extension cords that start from the house and go out the window all the way down the driveway, out on to the road and into the truck. I don't care what Kimbo will say.

I've taken the television. It's only fair. She gets the house and I get the TV.

Me and Lucy have got the stars from the Century outside the truck and we're unravelling them like spaghetti. I get a bit frustrated but Lucy is right into untying the big mess and eventually we have an open net full of lights. I got some gaffer tape and next thing me and Lucy are taping the stars to the insides of the truck all over. We're having a good time doing it too. She gets happy when she's busy. I watch her, hard at work with her short hair and I can see that it doesn't matter how much I want her to act like a girl. She'll be what she wants to be. We got a nice pattern up that creeps along the walls like some kind of electrical vine. I'm about to do the honours and I plug them into the extension cord and they come on.

'Ha,' Lucy says. We lie on my bed and look up at them.

'How bout that,' I say.

They look so pretty up there.

The sound of the TV echoes around the back of the truck but it hasn't stopped me dozing, despite the caffeine pill. I feel spent, and it's a good thing I'm getting some sleep. Trouble is, I get a visitor every time I close my eyes. Tom won't leave me alone now. He's come in to hug me goodnight. He's sitting on the end of my bed.

'Frank, I almost tripped over the cat. Did you hear that?'

I sure heard it. A good cat screech followed by a bump followed by the sound of Tom laughing, and then the familiar stumble into my door.

'Did you know that a cat always lands on its feet,' he's saying to me. I pretend I'm asleep, but he can tell I'm listening. 'You try it some day. Hold a cat upside down, let go and wham, she'll swing around in the air and land on her feet. I wish I could do that.'

Then he gives me a goodnight hug, and I smell mint on his breath. I could always tell when he was sozzled. The mint was the giveaway.

I'd smell mint on his breath when he came to pick me up from school. I'd see red wine stains on his teeth. I'd see his eyes red and bloodshot. I'd see the puffy jaw. We'd have some good times but it never lasted long. He'd always run out of energy and spend the afternoon lying on the couch while I'd be left to play with my toy truck by myself. Way to go, Tom. Way to parent.

As I lie here looking at Lucy watching TV I feel like I'm failing her. I lean over and I pat the back of her head. She had nice hair. Beautiful brown hair that glowed auburn in the sunlight. I'm sad to see it go, but I can't be mad at her. It's her face. She can do what she wants with it. Kimbo might not see it the same way, unfortunately.

Lucy turns around and looks at me and I can smell the bubble-gum on her breath, some ridiculous flavour, berrylicious or some-thing. 'Blow me a bubble,' I say to her, and she chews hard and gets a tiny little bubble that inflates under her nose before it runs out of steam.

'You want a go?' she asks me, holding a packet open. I take a piece of gum and I chew hard and blow a bubble twice as big as hers, and she says to me, 'That's a good one, Dad,' and she climbs on to my back. I'm out of energy so I just lie there and doze off as her elbow digs into my neck and she returns to watching Spongebob What's-his-face on the box.

The place has gone dark and there's no power, no Lucy, nothing, and the whole place is moving. I don't know if I'm asleep or awake but I feel like I'm going backwards. I get jolted forwards again and the back door opens and it's Kimbo.

'You can park in the driveway,' she says. Some olive branch. I bet she got embarrassed about the spectacle I was making on the street.

Kimbo looks as tired as I feel. The list of things I have to do comes flooding back to me and I just want to lie here for the rest of the week.

'Kimbo,' I say, as she closes the door on me again. She opens up and I stare at her silhouette standing there.

'I'm sorry,' I say. 'I've been a shitty husband.'

Kimbo laughs dismissively.

'Kimbo, I . . . I . . .' I'm stumbling. I haven't got the words. 'I'm not coping. I . . . I can't deal with it. I can't . . .'

Kimbo sits at the foot of my mattress. She looks at me, and I can see worry in her face. The light from outside is hitting her skin, making her shoulders glow.

'You know your problem?' she says to me. 'You got this stupid macho thing going on. You think you're a big hard man so you should be able to deal with everything yourself.'

'What's wrong with that?'

'What's wrong with that is it's not working. Look at yourself,' she says.

'I feel like I'm talking to Brenda right now.'

'Well, you're not. You're talking to me. Fuck's sake, Spud. You get a broken arm, what do you do about it?'

'Huh?'

'Do you just walk around with a broken arm or do you do something about it?'

'I go to a doctor.'

'That's right. What if your crane breaks down? Who do you see?'

Jesus, she's on her high horse again.

'You see a mechanic. Jesus, Spud. You got a broken mind. You got a broken heart. You're all broken inside, but do you do anything about it? No, you gotta be a man, don't you? You gotta be the man so you can spend the rest of your life fucked in the head. And if that's what you want—'

'Of course that's not what I want—'

'Then get some fuckin help!'

'I don't know where to get some help!'

'You stupid fuckwit. Help is right in front of you. All you have to do is ask.'

'You want me to grovel, right?'

'Oh yeah, Spud. I really get moist at the idea of you grovelling,' she says and she goes to leave the truck, and I blurt it out.

'I can't get Tom outta my head,' I say.

191

'Good. He should stay in your head until you find him.'

I say nothing. I don't want her knowing about my encounter with Tom yesterday.

'How hard have you looked for him?' she asks.

'Pretty hard.'

'Where have you looked?'

'What is this? An inquisition?'

'Have you looked in your old house?'

'Of course.'

'Where was he last seen?'

'They lost him in the van out at the Freyberg on-ramp.'

'So he'll be in Freyberg?'

'Maybe. I doubt it. That was an hour ago. He's on a mission.'

'What sort of mission?'

Jesus. You open a massive can of worms when Kimbo puts her snout in.

'I got it under control.'

'Clearly you don't. What have you been doing for the last few hours?'

'I got Lucy.'

'And Lucy can't go with you? Jesus, Spud. If we lost a dog you'd be out looking harder than this.'

'Tom's a hell of a lot smarter than a dog.'

'He's an old man.'

'He knows how to look after himself.'

'He must be terrified.'

'Don't ask me to feel sorry for him. I'm happy to find him but don't play the sympathy card.'

There's some blessed silence for a bit. I take a deep breath. I'm just waiting for the next attack, so I get in first.

'Listen. What more could I have done? I got, I got so many, so many things I'm not on top of. I'm in the middle of a big job. I need my sleep.'

'You won't sleep until you find him.'

'I'm dealing with a lot of stuff. I got, I got our marriage falling apart—'

192

'Forget about our marriage right now. Get your fuckin priorities straight.'

'You're my priority.'

She laughs sarcastically. 'Oh, I'm your priority all of a sudden?'

'What? What's weird about that?'

'Spud, how will you feel if he dies out there?'

'I'm comfortable with that.'

'Bullfuckinshit.'

'It's not my fault. We're all responsible for ourselves.'

Kimbo sighs. 'Listen,' she says. 'You might be comfortable about it but I'm not—'

'I got all this other shit to deal with. I got a bunch of chairs sitting on a traffic island. If I don't clear it—'

'That's not life and death, Spud. Your marriage isn't life and death.'

'My job is. I can't fuck up in my job.'

'Fine. Then stick to your job and stick to finding Tom. Let me take care of the rest.'

'You can't . . . how do you know how to—'

'Give me some phone numbers and let me sort it out. What do you think you married? A fuckin stay-at-home mum?'

'No. You have enough on your plate—'

'Jesus, Spud. I don't need you lecturing me about having enough on my plate. How many times do I have to repeat it? Your father is out there on the streets. He needs you.'

'Where was he when I needed him?'

'It doesn't matter.'

'Yes, it does.'

'Fuck Tom. Would you rescue Lucy if the house was on fire?'

'Of course.'

'Okay. A house is on fire and your father is in it. I don't care what kind of cunt he's been to you. You gotta do the right thing and make sure he's safe and you can go back to your fuckin moral high ground after.'

Kimbo is waiting for me to respond. I get this picture in my mind of myself as a boy, sitting in the kitchen with Mum popping prescription pills in front of me, bags under her eyes, not even trying to hide from me how defeated she was when Tom had gone. He left her a wreck. She never got over him. I had to deal with years of her grieving, sometimes hysterical. Somehow I was supposed to know what to do to help her, but I didn't have a clue.

As far as I was concerned, Tom died when he left us. Now he's back and I'm supposed to help him?

But Kimbo's staring at me and I know that I'm a better man than him and even though he doesn't deserve it, I know that she's right. I have to find the fucker.

Hide and seek with Tom

The hide and seek game was his idea. We used to play a lot of games together, but hide and seek was always a favourite for Tom. He would make me close my eyes and he'd spin me around and I'd count to one hundred. When I open my eyes I search all around the house for him. I look in the living room, behind the couch, behind the TV, but no Tom. Next thing I'm in the dining room. I look under the table. I look in the kitchen, behind the fridge. I look in the sunroom behind the old birdcage.

Then I'm in my room and I'm under my bed and in the wardrobe. Same in my mum and dad's room. In the bathroom I punch the shower curtain, but no one is in the shower.

And then I get this terrible feeling that I've looked in all the places I could look. Back to the lounge and behind the couch. No sign. 'Dad?' I call out. I head outside and start looking out there. I search the little area behind the apple tree and can't find him.

I go into the basement and I call out, 'Dad?' and I listen for any breathing. I hear a noise coming from the blackness underneath the house. 'I don't want to play any more,' I say, and I hear a little laugh coming from the blackness inside the basement, so I crawl deep in and there's papers and magazines and tin cans and all sorts of shit, but I can't find him. 'Dad, it's not funny,' I say.

I find myself screaming 'Dad!' I hear a noise upstairs and it's Tom's footsteps. So I crawl back out and I run up the side of the house and look in the gap in the venetian blinds but there's no sign.

I go inside and I say, 'I wanna stop playing now,' and I hear this voice snickering and I follow it to Mum and Dad's bedroom, and I look under the bed again, and this time I see this shape under a blanket and I pull back the cover and Tom yells at me, 'AAAAAAHHHH!' and I scream. He laughs and I run to my bedroom and shut the door. He knocks and tries to come in, but I stand against the door. He says, 'Come on, Frank,' and he forces it open and I hit him with everything I got, I pound my fists into his legs but he just laughs because he thinks he did something really funny.

I scream and punch him some more and he throws his hands in the air and he says, 'I give up,' and I sit on my bed and I cry my eyes out. About half an hour later when I've sworn never to talk to him again the door opens and he throws a whole packet of biscuits on to my bed, saying, 'Macaroons, Frank? Your favourite.' The door closes again and I look at this packet of biscuits he just gave me and even though I hate the man, I eat his biscuits.

When I finally emerge from my room he's in the living room, drinking a glass of whisky and reading the evening newspaper on the La-Z-Boy. He shoots me a wink and says to me, 'That's quite some temper you got, boy. Must've have picked it up from your mother.'

4.52 p.m.

I'm driving the Dwarf and I got a whole lot of pictures of Tom on the seat next to me. I pull up to the Century and the boys are carting out rubble. I made a good mess last night and they look behind schedule. Looks like I may be starting later tonight.

I chuck on my hard hat and I go and speak to some of the day-shift boys. Butterfingers is standing on the side of the truck as they load in rubble to take to the tip. I hand him a photo and I say to him, 'You seen this guy around?'

He says, 'Nah,' and I say to him, 'You see the guy, make sure you get hold of me. It's important.'

I spread the photo round some of the other guys on site and then I head into the hut where Dick and a couple of lads I don't know are on smoko. I hand Dick the photo.

'Seen this guy?' I ask, and he says, 'Everyone's looking for someone at the moment,' and he motions to the fridge which has a poster stuck to it.

I'm blown away when I see the poster. On it is a picture of me, age five, at the Buffalo Boulders, and a phone number underneath.

'Who put this here?' I say.

I phone the number on the poster and a young woman answers.

'Hello?' she says, and I hear a honk, and she says, 'Thank you,' to someone.

'Don't even think about making your move. I bagsed her earlier,' Dick says with a chuckle.

I'm straight out of the hut and walking across the road, and there she is on her mobile phone, the protester, holding up her stupid 'Honk For The Century' sign. She's receiving a lot of honks.

'Where did this come from? Where did you get this?' I say, shoving the picture in her face. The protester looks around for help, and I'm yelling now. 'Where did you get these posters? Is this some kind of joke?'

'No!'

'Did Tom give you these?'

'Yes.'

'Do you know where he is?'

'No. I . . .'

'That's me,' I say.

'What?'

'In the photo. That's me.'

'No. That's . . . I don't understand,' she says.

'Listen,' I say to her. 'Do you know where he is?'

'What are you going to do to him?'

'We'll get him to a safe place. He's a danger to himself.'

'I didn't . . . I . . .' she trails off, trying to put two and two together. 'I thought he was kind of old to have a son that young,' she says, catching up at last.

'Did he say where he was going?'

197

'No. He just asked me to put up a bunch of posters,' she says, before I see another thought hit her. 'He had a rental car,' she says. 'Metallic pink.'

'Make?'

'I don't know. I'm sorry,' she says.

She's looking at the photo on the poster.

'That really you?' she asks.

'Yes,' I say.

'There's a phone number you could try.'

She points me to the phone number on the poster. It's been scrawled on in vivid, next to a number that's been crossed out.

I'm staring at the picture of me and Tom on the Buffalo Boulders. Those boulders were large and round, like a bunch of French giants were playing pétanque and the balls hardened into rocks. They were split down the middle, some of them, and in the cracks I found lots of crabs.

That trip we all went camping, as a family. I got my own tent and Tom would read me stories and then sing me to sleep. His favourite was Zebedee. 'There was a mouse as big as a house, as big as a house and his name was Zebedee,' he'd sing, and my mother would sing along too. Later on I would lie in my tent and listen to the two of them in the next tent, laughing.

I phone the number on the poster and after a few rings a woman answers.

'Is Tom there?' I say. There's a pause and she says, 'What? No. Wait. Who is this?'

'I saw your poster. I think I've found your missing kid.'

'What?' she says. 'I don't understand.'

'I'm Frank,' I say. 'I'm Frank Spotswood. At least I used to be.'

'You used to be?'

'I'm Frank Morell. It's my mother's name.'

'I'm Linda,' she says. 'Is Tom okay?'

'Tom's on the loose again,' I say. 'I was hoping you could help me find him.'

★

I ride the lift to the eighteenth floor on the corner of Grey and Elizabeth. When the doors open I find myself in a big wide-open space with white walls and a blue carpet. I'm almost blinded by the whiteness. I can hear some voices in another part of the building.

I walk past a room stacked full of business chairs piled on top of each other. Blue chairs and purple chairs upside down with their crappy rolling wheels in the air. It's hard to count them because they're stacked poorly, but I'd guess there would be a good fifty there. I could offload those chairs for about fifty each. That's an easy two and a half grand, and I'm being conservative on that figure.

Another room has nothing but a bunch of phone sockets. They could be of value, I guess, to a call centre. All the phones are piled in the corner of a room. If each phone got you ten bucks then there would be about three hundred worth of value there, and they'd be pretty easy to flick off too.

I walk past a reception desk with a long-deceased pot plant sitting on top of it. The leaves have gone brown and they sag limply. This place must have been neglected a bit before the receivers came in. Beside the elevators are a bunch of fluoro lights, stacked carefully, ready to be shipped out. If they work they could be worth, say, twenty each and in front of me there are four, eight, twelve, sixteen, twenty, twenty-four . . . that's 480 dollars worth there. That's worth the effort.

I find Linda talking to a guy in grey overalls. I recognize her straight away. She's the redhead I saw with Tom at that coffee place. She is instructing the guy in overalls on what she wants done with all the partitions that are set up in this rabbit warren. Next to all these ugly blue partitions is a motivational poster that has the word 'Teamwork' on it.

She winds up her meeting and comes my way. She looks at me warily, and shakes my hand.

'Frank?' she says.

'Spud. Everyone knows me as Spud,' I say.

Next thing we're sitting in an abandoned kitchen. Everything has pretty much been stripped. All the shelves have been cleared. There are still a few signs of the old occupants. The fridge is there, with a little handwritten note that says, 'Please label your food'. There's a few cups lying around but the sink is completely full of dead plants. As Linda makes me a cup of tea I explain how Tom got away from Alastair Shook at Freyberg.

She looks shaken from the whole experience. That's what happens to anyone who gets close to Tom, the creep. She says to me, 'I had no idea he was . . . I was completely fooled.'

'Yeah. He has a way with words. He could sell a meat pie to a vegetarian. He's slippery.'

'No, I didn't mean that, but I agree he has a way with words,' Linda says, and she sits down on the floor, leaning against a wall. Her mascara is running and I can see a lot of grey mixed in with her dyed red hair.

'You're really his son?' she asks.

'Sure. Biologically. Whatever.'

She looks at my face and says, 'I can see it.'

'I look a lot like my grandmother on Mum's side.'

'Where is your mother?'

'She passed away four, no, five years ago.'

'Tom doesn't know that.'

'He doesn't know a lot of things.'

She looks at me, into my eyes. 'It's funny to think of you as that kid we were looking for,' she says. 'You know, he was looking forward to seeing you.'

'He's looking forward to seeing a little kid. He doesn't want anything to do with me.'

'He's in a lot of pain,' she says.

'Well, you know, scuse my French but fuck him. Who's not in pain?'

She looks at me like I'm the scum of the earth so I say, 'You reap what you sow. He was a shitty father so if you don't mind I'm quite happy being a shitty son back.'

I'm wound up and I reach over to a nicotine patch to check it is doing its job.

'I'm sorry he duped you with his act,' I say to her. 'I gotta find

200

him. As much as I want to have nothing to do with him I don't want him to die out on the streets. And I don't want him to cause any more trouble. I just want this done with and dealt with.'

'And then what?' she says.

'When it's done he can go back to his life and I can go back to mine.'

'You'll just leave him alone.'

'Yeah, sure. What goes around, comes around,' I say. 'Look, do you have any idea where he might be?'

'I helped him look for . . . for you. We, we looked all through your old neighbourhood. We looked in your old house. We went to a few places there. Your old school friends, but they didn't lead to anything. We went to see his old lawyer—'

'Herb Lamont?' I say.

'Yes. I had to stay in the car for that one.'

Herb Lamont.

Of course. I shoulda thought of that angle earlier.

'He was following you,' she says.

'Yeah, well he found me and now I think he's on the run from me. If he phones you, please call me.'

'He won't come near me any more. He hates me now,' she says, and she starts crying. I feel sorry for her. I grab a kitchen wipe from the sink and I hand it to her.

'He's not worth crying over. Trust me on this one,' I say.

'That's funny,' she says. 'That's exactly what he said.'

I'm back in my old neighbourhood. I head into a place that I used to think was massive when I was a kid, Lane Lamont's house. Lane was a childhood friend of mine. Actually, friend is an exaggeration. We got thrown together a lot. It was Tom's method of parenting. He'd bring me over here and leave me with Lane Lamont while he got plastered with Herb Lamont in Herb's office.

I knock, and I get a scare when Mrs Lamont opens the door. She looks so much older now.

I say to her, 'Hi, Mrs Lamont. I'm Frank Spotswood. Do you remember me?' and her face lights up. 'Of course I do,' she says.

201

She was my first teacher, when I was five years old. I had a little crush on her. She had freckly skin and she liked me a lot.

Now I'm inside at the dinner table and Mrs Lamont is talking to me from the kitchen. I'm looking out the window where Lane and I would run around with a tennis ball. There's a picture of Herb Lamont on the mantelpiece. His blotchy red nose used to scare the shit outta me. I remember Herb coming round for poker nights at our place. I remember as a kid walking into a room full of smoke. I swear, I once walked in there at ten at night and it was like walking into the exhaust fumes of the space shuttle.

Mrs Lamont comes in with a tray that has a coffee plunger, one cup and a glass of milk. She hands me the glass of milk and pours herself a coffee.

'Your father was here just a few nights ago. He was looking for you,' she says.

'Well, I'm looking for him,' I say. 'Got any ideas?'

'Yes I do,' she says. 'Now where did I put it?'

She scans the room. It's weird seeing her look so old. My brain has preserved her perfectly as this beautiful specimen in her twenties. And now there are wrinkle lines all over her face and her neck.

'Ah,' she says, and goes to a shelf and brings me a Manila folder.

'He was looking for this,' she says.

On the front of the file is a sticker that says 'F.C.'.

I flick through it and it looks like a case file. There's an insurance contract for a horse. It's got a few circles drawn around a few bits and bobs. There's a photo in it of a horse bone. And there's a piece of paper, some kind of ownership documentation with Robert Valentine circled, and next to it a scrawl in blue faded ink, and in handwriting, a phone number next to an underlined name that looks familiar.

Walter Nurse.

Why do I know that name? I know that name. I know it.

And then I get it. I don't know what Walter Nurse looks like, but I know his voice well. It was a voice of my childhood.

'Is it okay if I use your phone?' I ask Mrs Lamont.

★

I phone the number, and a man with a gravelly voice answers. 'Hello?' he says.

'Hi. I'm looking for Walter Nurse,' I say.

'Oh, well he's here.'

'Could I speak to him?'

'Uhh . . . that could be difficult,' the man says.

I head to the address Peter Nurse gave me and I knock on the door. The door opens, and Peter Nurse looks just like his father. He invites me inside.

'This is Walter,' he says, and the man in front of me is hard to recognize. He is in a wheelchair and he looks me in the eye, like he's trying to place me.

'He can't speak any more. He can hear you though,' his son says.

It's sad. Can this really be the man Tom is chasing?

'Hi,' I say to Walter Nurse.

'He won't really understand you, I'm sorry,' his son says. 'He picks up on feelings though.'

'Has anyone else come to visit your father lately?' I ask Peter Nurse.

'No,' he says. I show Peter a photo of Tom. 'This is Tom. He's looking for Robert Valentine,' and as I say the name I see a small flicker come from the old man. Peter Nurse looks at the picture. 'Nope, never seen him before. Should I keep an eye out for him?' he says.

'Yeah. He knows your father.'

'Show him the picture,' he says to me and I hold the photo of Tom in front of Walter Nurse. In the picture Tom is standing in his old suit in front of a building with tangerine walls. He's squinting at the camera, looking a little dazed. Walter Nurse looks at the picture of Tom and there's no response.

I try something else. I pull from my pocket another photo of Tom, from when he was younger. Walter Nurse looks at him, lifts his finger, almost pointing, but he loses energy in his arm and it drops again.

'Looks like he knows him,' Peter says, looking at the younger photo.

'You know about the horse Fire Chief? Robert Valentine? Tom Spotswood?' I ask, and Peter Nurse shrugs his shoulders.

'I'm sorry. I can't help you,' he says.

'That's okay,' I say, and I write my number on a piece of paper and ask him to call me if Tom shows up.

I look at Walter Nurse and I say to his son, 'You know, he was one of the big voices of my childhood.'

'Me too,' the man says, and smiles, and Walter Nurse looks out the window with no expression on his face.

Next thing I'm on the phone to Kimbo. She's been in touch with Alastair Shook who is driving around in circles at Codfish Bay. The police are stretched but want us to call them if there are any developments. And Kimbo has phoned all the car rental companies in the Freyberg area, asking about metallic pink cars being rented under Tom Spotswood, William McGinty or whatever other name he's invented for himself. She's waiting to hear back from a bunch of people.

She asks me how I've gone and I say, 'He's looking for Walter Nurse.'

'*The* Walter Nurse?' she says. 'Is he still alive?' she asks.

'Barely,' I say. 'I just been to see him. I don't think he's going to lead us to Tom.'

'But Tom's looking for him.'

'Yes. So he might show up. I don't know what I'm supposed to do. Keep a vigil?'

'Tom would be looking for a young Walter Nurse, right?'

'Uh, maybe. That makes sense.'

'Well, where would Walter Nurse be on a work day? Not at home, right?' she says.

I start laughing.

'You're a genius, Kimbo.'

'I've known that a long time,' she says. 'You've been too thick to notice.'

'I think I know where Tom is,' I say.

Tom

Good Friday

Solved: the case of
the missing case

12.16 p.m.

I can feel movement.

I'm awake but I'm keeping my eyes closed.

I'm not sure how much time has passed.

I'm not in a car. I can feel too much space for that.

I'm in a van and we're moving.

I can feel something on my lap. A familiar weight.

I can feel someone sitting next to me. A big presence, breathing heavily.

I can hear voices in the front and they're talking about mundane things, Easter holidays, the Easter bunny.

I can feel the draught of a window on my neck.

I keep my eyes closed while I feel with my right hand the outline of the thing on my lap. I recognize it. Lethalite. I feel the front of it and I feel the smooth metal latch.

They've given me my case back.

I don't know what to make of this.

I open my right eye a little and we're going through traffic on the outskirts of town. This is the industrial district. We're moving past a bunch of old silos and I can see the rail tracks not far away. I know where we are.

We're about to hit the motorway soon. I keep my eyes shut and continue to play dead and floppy, and I study the inside door of the van.

I scan the van without moving my head. There are three in the front and just the one guy with me in the back, but he's big and he's in between me and the van door. He's distracted, pushing buttons on a tiny little cellphone. Up front Alastair Shook and his guard – a teenage girl – are talking about Easter.

'One time when we were kids we made our own Easter eggs, but they weren't hollow,' the teenage guard is saying to Alastair Shook. 'It was just a big block of chocolate. You couldn't get your teeth in it. You had to suck on the thing.'

Alastair Shook is laughing and we slow down as we approach an overbridge. I sneak a look at the guy next to me. He is completely absorbed in his little phone. I know that there may not be an opportunity as good as this one. With as little movement as I can muster I unhook my belt but I leave it on. I can sense someone in front looking around so I play it real floppy and let some drool fall out of my mouth and I sell it well.

I check for an escape route.

I open my left eye by the smallest possible margin and I study the van door handle. We come to the last red light before we hit the motorway, the van slows down.

We take off again and I have limited time before the van gains speed again.

You can do this, Tom. Now's your chance.

One, two, three . . .

I squeeze the nuts of the thug next to me. He shrieks like a soprano. I'm straight to the door and I pull the latch hard. I swing it open and the van is still moving and when my foot hits the road I struggle to keep balance. I manage to get across a lane of traffic before one of Alastair Shook's crew has a door open. The teenage girl is sprinting across traffic.

I make it past four lanes of traffic and I climb over a barrier and below is a decent drop so I run along a slab of concrete, down and underneath the bridge into the motorway. The cars are streaming past and the teenage girl is chasing me.

I cross another two lanes of traffic and I manage to get up and over a fence and now I'm running on stones and gravel until I make it to the train lines. I run along these and I can see a train coming my way about a mile away and so I cross the tracks and run past some more tracks and into the train station. I move at the same pace as everyone else, to blend into the crowd. I pass through the main courtyard and I make it to the car park.

I know the van will be coming in at any moment. I knock on the window of a guy driving an Audi. He winds his window down and I say to him, 'I've got a flattie. Could I get a lift to a petrol station?' The guy nods, I climb in and I sit low in the passenger seat while the Audi driver makes small talk about where the nearest petrol station is. We take off as I see a few of them emerge by the motorway.

The Audi driver says, 'You okay, bud?' and I nod and I say, 'Are you heading into The City?' and he says, 'Yeah,' and I look in the back seat and there is a kid in a child seat sitting there and I wave to him and I wipe my forehead with my sleeve and the guy says to me, 'You look like a travelling salesman,' and I say, 'Huh?' I look down at the Lethalite case on my lap.

My driver pulls off the road and he drops me at a petrol station and offers to give me a lift back and I say, 'Don't worry about it. I'll phone my wife and she can come to my rescue.' He nods and says, 'Happy Easter,' to me and as I watch him drive away I think of the time I got stranded without petrol and I phoned Deborah and she was with me in a taxi in half an hour, holding a big plastic container of petrol, and smiling at me with those eyes, those eyes that I drowned in, regularly.

I am in the bathroom of the petrol station. I still can't figure out why Alastair Shook and the people in the van took my case. And why would they give it back to me? Is Robert Valentine playing mind games with me?

I keep my eyes away from the mirror and open up the case to see what they've left for me. Everything inside looks familiar.

I find a packet of Doublemint chewing gum, and straight away that makes me realize that I haven't had a drink yet today. That's a small achievement. Perhaps if I have a tipple it might help me think calmer and straighter. I'm pleased to find my trusty old hip-flask in here, and I'm salivating like an arachnid as I screw the rusty cap off and wash some whisky down my throat. I'm very disappointed when there's no sharp bite to it. Alastair Shook has replaced the whisky in my hip-flask with water. Why would he do that? Someone's messing with me. I almost get the feeling they're just doing it for kicks.

I am pleased to see William McGinty's glasses here. When I took on the William McGinty identity I wore these glasses all the time. William McGinty's glasses have real lenses too. When I am pretending to be McGinty my eyesight improves out of sight.

There's my trusty lint remover which has serviced me well over the years. I look down at my suit jacket and, sure enough, lint is attached there like barnacles on a rock.

Under a bunch of receipts I find a few toys. There's one of Frank's favourites, a light blue Citroën with doors that open. One of the few cars he didn't smash up.

There are a lot of underpants in the case, some aftershave and my emergency cigarettes. My old underwater camera is here, as well as a little yellow pouch containing a bunch of photos that I can't bear to look at.

It's good to have it all back, but I don't understand why they handed it all back to me. What have they taken? Who are they?

I don't understand what is going on but I know it goes a lot deeper than the demolition guy or Alastair Shook. There is clearly also a police connection. I've stumbled into the middle of something much bigger than I thought possible. I don't understand what is happening but Robert Valentine clearly has some powerful connections.

I'm renting a car. The photo on William McGinty's driver's licence doesn't look a bit like me, but by wearing his glasses and selling it a little I am able to pass myself off as him.

I find the process of filling out the forms pretty difficult but the woman serving me, Sharon – her name badge isn't straight because of the curve of her breast – is being very helpful. I can feel her flirting with me. She takes me to my car and it glows metallic pink. It's terrifyingly ugly, and quite conspicuous. I say to her, 'Haven't you got anything in a more, you know, faded tone?' and she smiles at me and says, 'You know, with Easter, we don't have a lot left. If you waited until noon I might be able to—'

'That's fine, Sharon,' I say and I smile at her. She reminds me of a girl I lusted after in the old school yard.

The power steering in this car is very powerful. I am snaking badly. I lightly touch the steering wheel and it turns at a ninety-degree angle.

I am driving past the Century. I don't want to run into the demolition guy, so I'm keeping on the outskirts.

I don't know where they are keeping Frank. I don't think they'll be treating him badly. I've got a gut feeling that he is safe and okay. He must be very upset. Even when I find him, he may never forgive me for mixing him up in this.

I'm calling past to see if the demolition guy is there, but the wrecking ball isn't in action. No police today either.

I see Celia with her 'Honk For The Century' sign. I honk, and I wind down my window.

She brightens up when she sees me. 'Hi, Tom.'

'Hi, Celia. It's nice to see a friendly face. Could you do a little favour for me?'

'Sure,' she says.

I dig into my pockets and pull out some Missing posters. They have Linda's number on them. Linda the turncoat.

I look up at the writing on Celia's placard.

'Hey, Celia. You got a marker pen?'

'Yeah,' she says, fumbling about in her backpack. She hands me the pen and says, 'What's up?'

A close encounter with
Eddy Malinga's mother

2.46 p.m.

I must have pushed a bad button accidentally during the drive, because the car has started talking to me.

'It looks like you are leaving The City,' it says.

Obviously it wants me to say something back, but I'm not in the mood for talking to a car so I hunt around for a button to shut it up.

'Where would you like to go to?' it asks me.

'Quiet,' I say.

'Where would you like to go to?' it asks again.

'Off. Turn off.'

'I'm sorry. I don't recognize that address,' it says and I'm looking around for an on/off button but I can't find it.

'Where would you like to go to?' it says.

'Herbert Valley,' I say, 'but I know where I'm going. I don't need your help.'

'Herbert Valley,' it says to me. 'Turn left at the next intersection.'

'I don't want to,' I say to it. 'I know a better way.'

'Turn left at the next intersection,' it repeats.

'No,' I say.

I pass the road it wanted me to turn left at, and the car says, 'Oops. You missed your turn. That's okay. You can turn left at Stedman Street.'

'I know,' I say to the car, and it tells me to turn left and I do what it says, not because it told me to, but because that was where I was going anyway.

At the next red light it tells me I am 'ten kilometres from my destination'. 'Thanks,' I say to it. Not that I needed that information. I know where I'm going. I know this road very well.

I used to do this drive a lot when I was working at Thoroughbred.

It's a beautiful drive. Very scenic. I used to love doing the drive with Deb and Frank. As I go to the top of Blacks Road I'm thinking of how much fun I used to give Frank. I'd put my foot down as we'd go over the hill and try to get us airborne for a half-second. He used to love driving quickly over a hill. It was like driving off a tar seal ramp, launching into space. And then the sudden drop in your guts when you're over the hump and it's all downhill. Frank would always ask me to turn around and do it again, and sometimes we did. I suspect I got as many kicks out of it as he did.

Past Herbert Peak there are a lot of stables dotted throughout the valley, including that of my first port of call, Quinton Ellery.

As I approach Ellery's stables I curse the car for not being a more dowdy colour. Pretty hard to look inconspicuous in this pink jelly bean.

Half a mile before Ellery's stables I pass a big open field and I catch a lucky break. Two horses – a grey gelding and a beautiful chestnut – are galloping together, running freely without a care in the world. It makes my heart lift to see them as they keep pace with my car. I give them a little honk of the horn as a way of tipping my hat to them.

I arrive at Ellery's stables but his name isn't on the gate. I leave my talking car out the front and I open the gate and close it behind me. I head to the little hut out the front and knock on the door but no one answers. There's no one. No horses. No humans. No chickens. Nothing.

I walk up to the main house and I knock on the door but there is no answer. I look inside and it looks like the place has been gutted. The rooms are all empty and I can see that what used to be a plush living room is now an old musty room with a broken window and a mess of old crap no one could ever want inside.

I go to a fence that has become rotten and I look at the field where the horses used to roam, but it's just an empty field of long grass and wild daisies.

I don't know what's happened here, but I can see this place isn't going to lead me to Robert Valentine.

Poor Eddy. I'm picturing him eating his last shawarma. I hope he enjoyed it. I've got a nagging feeling about the food poisoning thing. So easy and clean as a way to finish someone off.

I'm at his front door and I'm expecting his wife Barbara to answer but instead an older woman opens up. It must be his mother or something.

'Hi, miss. I'm Tom, I—'

'Tom,' she says and her face lights up and she gives me a big hug. I don't want to ask her if she's Eddy's mother, just in case I cause offence. But she seems to recognize me.

'I'm really sorry about Eddy,' I say to her, and she says, 'Well, he had a good knock,' and I feel like saying something trite like, 'Only the good die young,' but I keep my mouth shut. 'Sorry, I don't know what to say,' I say.

'I'm okay, Tom,' she says. 'Come in.'

She's making me a cup of tea and she's talking about her last days with Eddy, and the shock of it all. She firmly believes it was the shawarma, and I don't want to indicate something more sinister might have happened.

'I fill my days up pretty good now,' she says. 'It's the nights that are hard.'

'Oh yeah. I relate to that,' I say.

'I miss snuggling him at night,' she says, and I can't help but think that maybe Eddy was closer to his mother than he should've been. I don't really want to enquire further along this line, and I need to keep moving if I'm going to find Frank tonight, so I clear my throat and I say, 'I'm sorry to bother you but . . . well, I loaned

Eddy a book back in the day. It was a book that belonged to my mother. I was hoping I could . . . I could get it back.'

Next thing I'm downstairs and Eddy's mother takes me to his office space.

'I started to clear it out,' she says sadly, 'but I . . . I find it hard to . . . you know.'

'Yeah, that must be very hard,' I say to her.

She takes me to a bookshelf full of books. 'Is it one of these?' she says. 'I've got some more of his books in a box.'

She heads out to look for a box and I take the opportunity to open a few drawers in Eddy's old desk. Under some paperwork in the second drawer I find a handgun. It's a revolver, pretty small. I check the barrel and it's loaded.

'Found it!' I hear Mrs Malinga say, and she comes back in with a box of books and a framed photograph she wants to show me. It's of Eddy and Barbara on their wedding day. He had long hair, like a hippy, but Eddy was no hippy. He was a rascal and a ratbag but the girls loved his long hair. Especially Barbara. Eddy's mother sees me staring at the photo and says, 'That was a happy day,' and she struggles to hold back the tears.

'I have some more photos if you want to look at them. There should be a few of you.'

'I'd love to see them, Mrs Malinga.'

She looks at me sadly but she has a smile.

'I keep them in a box because I don't always feel brave enough to look. But maybe I should bring them back out.'

'I've got a bunch of photos I can't look at,' I say to her, and I think of the undeveloped film from the underwater camera. In a way I am grieving too, except I am grieving for someone who is alive and well. Deborah is already a ghost to me. I know I will never see her look into my eyes with love again.

She opens the box and I flick through Eddy's photos. I'm not here to reminisce. I'm looking for a clue. Whoever Robert Valentine was, Eddy must've known him. Anyone can own a horse in a false name. They could be hiding tax money. They could be with the police. They could be in politics. They could have a reputation to protect.

I look at some photos of Eddy with some of his mates. There he is with Ralph McAllister the jockey, wearing a white and fawn striped shirt. He was a scoundrel who was always on for a way to fiddle the books. But he's too small fry to be Robert Valentine. I see pictures of Eddy with some of the trainers from the Herbert Valley. There's one of the McKenna brothers, I think that's Val with Mythical Lad, a beautiful red stallion who never quite reached his potential on the track but he did sire a couple of local legends, Smooth Sailing and Hot To Trot.

And there's a picture of Quintin Ellery himself, holding on to Noble Pursuit, a stallion who was always up for the job. I run through the idea that Ellery is Robert Valentine. He seemed such a lightweight when I met him, unless he was playing me. It just doesn't feel right. I won't rule it out, but my gut tells me he's not the one.

Ha! A photo of me, whisky in hand, at Eddy's barbecue. I forget what we were celebrating.

Wow. This photo album is a real who's who. Eddy worked with a lot of great trainers. There's Bryan McSkimmin with a trophy silver horse head. He knew how to breed a winner. He worked hard and he won everything that could be won.

There's a great photo of a young Eddy with none other than Walter Nurse. This is from back when Eddy was a jockey. It's funny looking at Eddy as a teenager. The photo is in black and white and Eddy looks so fresh-faced, and next to him Walter Nurse looks distinguished even as a young man, nicely suited up with a pendant on the lapel of his suit jacket, which sits gracefully over a V-necked jersey with a tie tucked in underneath. His hair looks a little like the wind has just won a tough battle against his Brylcreem. His ears stick out and the way he looks at the camera you sense he was really happy to pose next to Eddy. They must've been close. I didn't know that.

Walter Nurse is the best racing commentator of a generation. He's often asked to travel far and wide to call a race, such is his reputation. He called races all around the world, including a real rich event in Abu Dhabi. I didn't know Eddy knew him. There's another photo of Eddy and Walter Nurse having a laugh over a beer. Looks like the person who took the photo just said something incredibly funny because both their faces are red with tears of laughter.

Walter Nurse's reputation has been built on honesty. If you were to think of an adjective to describe him it would be fair. He called so many great races. He shot to national fame when Poetic Princess, a horse from Herbert Valley, won the Japan Cup. His call was broadcast all around the world. He was the doyen. Still is, I imagine, even though I've been out of the racket for a while. And a light bulb flicks off in my head. Could he be Robert Valentine? It fits on a lot of levels. He had to look after his reputation. If he'd got mixed up in any of this it would have brought down his commentating career for sure, and a lot of business interests too.

When a mare comes into season she demonstrates. She will wink and she will pee. And when I say wink, let me put it this way, her eyes aren't doing the winking. I feel very awkward because Eddy Malinga's mother is demonstrating right now. Despite everything that has happened, she is taking every opportunity for me to know she's in the market for some extra-curricular entertainment. She's poured us a couple of whiskies and when she hands me a glass her fingers linger on the inside of my palm. It's embarrassing because she's twice my age. I also feel a bit uncomfortable because I used to flirt with Eddy Malinga's wife back in the day. We came very close to removing clothes at one point. There was some close dancing and one thing could have led to another had I not managed to summon a rare burst of self-control.

I believe in respect for the dead. I know life is short but Eddy's mother should at least show a little more decorum and stop showing me how flexible her body still is at such a ripe age. It's not right.

'There are a lot of photos of Walter Nurse here,' I say.

'Oh yeah. He used to come over a lot. That was before . . .'

219

'Before what?' I ask.

'Oh. I'm not supposed to talk about it.'

Ace in the hole, Tom. Good to see your instincts are still good.

'You're not supposed to talk about what?'

'Tom. Where did you go?'

'Huh?'

'I don't know what you guys had cooked up. But Eddy was real stressed when you left town.'

'Mrs Malinga. I'm sorry to ask you this question. I don't mean to be morbid. I just need to—'

'Spit it out,' she says.

'Did Walter Nurse come to Eddy's funeral?'

'No. Their friendship ended a long time ago.'

'Did the friendship end around about when I left town?'

She smiles. 'Why are you dredging up all that old stuff?'

'I'm just—'

'Walter and Deidre used to come over a lot, for all sorts of occasions, including family meals. Then they stopped coming, all of a sudden. I noticed it. Eddy said they'd had a bit of a flare-up. And yes. It was about the same time you skipped town.'

I don't want to tell her anything else that could get her mixed up in all this, so I just say, 'You know, I'm sad about . . . what went down. Eddy was a good man.'

'You know that's not true, Tom.'

That's a strange thing to say about your son. She moves in real close to me and glides her finger down my cheek, stopping just short of my mouth, and her eyes are flitting. She's demonstrating up a storm. 'You know,' she says, 'I don't get many visitors out here in the country. If you wanted to stay here for the afternoon you could . . . I mean, we could . . .'

Okay, enough is enough. I open the box of books and pick a book, *The Tapestry of the Turf*, that'll do.

'Thank you for the book, Mrs Malinga. I have to be on my way now.' She nods sadly and holds her cheek close to my lips. I kiss her on the cheek and she turns her head and I pull back and say, 'It was nice to see you again.'

As I climb in the front seat of the jelly bean she says, 'It's funny. Time passes but we're still the same people we always were, huh? You haven't changed a whole lot.'

'I'm trying to change, Mrs Malinga,' I say, and I start the engine and drive off as my car says to me, 'Where would you like to go to?'

Fireworks in the bus tunnel

4.52 p.m.

I am glad to see the Herbert Valley Petrol Station still exists. It has kept a lot of its integrity. The petrol pumps look very upmarket but the rest of it looks as I remember it, if a little faded.

There's a phone booth out the front and I head in there and look up a phone book. There's a lot of Nunns, one Nutbeam, a Nutsford, about ten Nuttalls and one Nutter, but no Nurse. He's unlisted, which is unsurprising.

No matter. I'm pretty sure I know where to find him tonight.

I head inside the petrol station. It's got a nice feel to it, this place. Like a miniature supermarket, but it also sells fertilizer, clamps, nails and giant bags of apples.

I'm interested in the newspaper. I open one up at the back but there are a lot of new sections.

I take the newspaper to the counter and a woman called Jill asks what I'm looking for.

I say to Jill, 'They shifted the racing page.'

'It's in Section D. Here,' Jill says, helping me find it.

'Got anything on the Easter Stakes tonight?' I ask her.

'Ha. No. I've got a husband going there tonight and he better arrive home in one piece,' she says, and I'm looking at the times for the first race.

That's good. There's enough time to plan this properly.

★

I'm back in town, approaching the Mount Elizabeth Bus Tunnel. The late afternoon sun makes it hard to see as I drive. I have managed to make the car stop talking to me. I don't know how I did it. I pushed every single button on the car's computer, and one of them did the trick.

The sun is heating up the inside of the car and I can feel the vitamin D or K or whatever rushing into my body and lifting my spirits.

I'm on a path here. I'm not thinking about the worst that could happen any more. It's all positivity and best possible outcomes from here. My glass is half full to the brim.

I'm in the middle of the Mount Elizabeth Bus Tunnel. It's pitch black as I get to the alcove. I have to use my cigarette lighter to put one foot in front of another. I reach high up into the ledge and I am relieved to feel the backpack is still there.

I transfer the socks and Easter eggs into my case. The socks I am wearing are getting pretty damp and smelly so I take them off and I replace them with an unworn pair. Unfortunately all the socks are starting to smell. I stuff a sock in my pocket and I hide my case up on the ledge.

I reach into my other pocket and I pull out Eddy Malinga's gun. I figure this is the best place to test it. If anyone hears a noise they'll just think it's a bus backfiring. I aim it at the black wall opposite me and fire. The noise takes me back in time, and I can hear Deborah, next to me. She has excitement in her voice as I've got a whole lot of fireworks from Thailand. It's the middle of the night and I've got them standing upright in the middle of the tunnel.

'You sure this is safe?' she's asking me.

'This could be very unsafe, which if I'm not mistaken is how you like it,' I say to her, as I feel around my pockets for my lighter.

'I don't mind a bit of danger,' she says to me, all bravado, and I light all the fuses. I run to her and kiss her as the first firework goes off. Her kiss turns into a scream and both of us are sprinting out of there as fast as we can as the fireworks echo throughout the tunnel like gunfire. We make it out alive and we're laughing and we're holding each other tight and I'm kissing her neck and I can hear her like it was yesterday, whispering in my ear, 'I think you're the one for me.'

Tom

Spud

Racing!

8.02 p.m.

TOM

I'm glad to see the Easter Stakes has maintained its status as a premier event. Some traditions manage to survive and prosper, despite the world spinning so fast.

I arrived at the Eddington Trotting Club just before sundown. I'm walking to the gate at the final turn. I always loved this place; it was where I fell in love with racing. My father brought me here when I was a child, and Deb and I brought Frank when he was little. We had a lot of good times here.

SPUD

I'm in the Dwarf and I'm being guided through the car park by a guy in a white coat. He ushers me along to the car park – a large field packed with cars as far as the eye can see.

As I park Lucy comes running up to the Dwarf, Kimbo behind her.

I open the door and Kimbo says, 'We just got here.'

'Okay. Any sign of Alastair Shook?'

'Huh?'

'Uh, a van, a white Daihatsu.'

She shakes her head.

TOM

I'm walking past the old public stand. I can hear Walter Nurse on the loudspeakers echoing all around the ground. There are four speakers so everything he says echoes four times. 'Comes from good stock good stock good stock good stock.' 'Ideal Companion companion companion companion looks unsettled unsettled unsettled unsettled.'

He's warming up the crowd nicely for the big race.

He's a real pro, the scumbag.

SPUD

'What's the plan, Spud?' Kimbo asks me.

'Plan? Jesus, there's no time for planning. The plan is we find Tom.'

'Okay, well, why don't you look for Tom and we'll look for the rental car. Metallic pink, right?'

I look around the car park. It's massive. Half of The City must be here. There's a sea of cars all around us. But still, how many of them can be metallic pink?

'Yes. That's a good plan,' I say. 'I got my phone.'

'How can we tell what a rental will look like?' Lucy asks, as Kimbo hands her a torch.

'It'll kinda look new,' I say.

'New and pink. New and pink,' Lucy is repeating to herself.

'I'll call you if we see him,' Kimbo says.

I head off towards the old public stand.

TOM

A couple of red-coats on white horses canter past me and my ears are ringing from the sound of hooves on the earth.

I feel the sock in my pocket and I feel the gun in my other pocket. I start to feel nervous and my heart starts to race.

SPUD

I phone Alastair Shook as I pass the public stand.

'I'm two minutes away,' he says.

'Okay. See you at the finish line,' I say.

'Huh?'

'The finish line of the race. By the birdcage.'

'Oh. Sure. Right,' he says.

I'm heading straight towards the noise of the crowd . . .

TOM

I make it to the birdcage as the last of the horses parade for the crowd and head to the starters. I look up at the Members Stand. High up, almost as high as the roof, I see the little booth and there he is, Walter Nurse, hiding behind a pair of binoculars.

He still has a full head of hair. He reminds me of the Member of Parliament who ran on Christian values who was sent to prison for kiddy fiddling. Never trust a man who smiles too much and looks too clean.

SPUD

I'm walking to the birdcage. It looks packed down there. I'm scanning faces all the time. There's a lot of old people here. This is one of the few crowds Tom doesn't stand out in.

I walk to the finish line. There's so many faces, all of them strangers moving past me, so I'm looking for wrinkles. And I'm looking for brown suits.

'Excuse me, Spud?' a voice says. 'Alastair. Alastair Shook.'

We walk to the birdcage together. Shook is wearing a pair of binoculars. I wish I'd thought of that.

'You look like your father,' he says to me. I hope that's not true.

'Seen him yet?' I say and he shakes his head.

'He's the slipperiest wanderer I've ever dealt with.'

'Oh, yeah. He's a frickin eel,' I say.

TOM

I head to the front of the Members Stand and I check out the man in the white coat who is vigilantly guarding the door. The man is thin, with a neatly combed crop of grey hair, a triangle nose and brass-rimmed glasses. He's looking closely at everyone's Members passes, even asking a couple of men in tweed suits. Could be a tough mark.

I go up to him, confident.

'Listen, there's an overflow in the bathroom. It's not pretty,' I say. He just looks at me. 'Well,' I say, 'are you going to do something about it? It's a bad look for us.'

He shuffles off to look for bathroom assistance and I go through, up the stairs . . .

SPUD

Alastair Shook is a decent operator. He has a couple of twenty-somethings working for him. He pulls out photos of Tom. He organizes them to look in different areas. He gets one of his team to show the photos to some of the police who are floating around.

'Let me get this straight,' Shook says. 'Walter Nurse is a racing commentator?'

'He *was* one.'

He looks around for the commentator's booth and I point it out to him.

'So that's not Walter Nurse?'

'No, but Tom wouldn't know that. Would he?'

'Jesus. With your father it's hard to tell. He's got a lot going on inside.'

'He sure does,' I say, as I scan the Members Stand for old men in brown suits.

TOM

I get out to the stand. The Easter Stakes is about to run and people are rushing to their seats. I keep checking my pockets obsessively. Sock in the left. Gun in the right. The nerves are kicking in. I need a quick stiff burst of Dutch courage, so I head up to the bar . . .

SPUD

I'm staring up at the Members stand through Alastair Shook's binoculars. I'm scanning the area near the commentary booth, shifting from face to face, scanning for Tom.

So many faces. I don't recognize any, when a flash of brown catches my attention.

He's moving through the crowd like a man on a mission.

Is that him? I think it's him. It's Tom. Someone bumps me and I lose him again. 'He's there, he's there,' I'm saying, pointing.

Shook takes the binoculars and scans where I pointed.

'I'm going to the Members,' I say to him.

'I'll keep an eye on the stand from here,' he says, staring at the commentary booth. 'I'll call you if I see anything.'

'Yeah,' I say, and I get moving.

TOM

I order a Famous Grouse, naked. I knock it back and order another. The Dutch courage they serve here isn't strong enough. In my pocket my fingers are feeling their way around the handgun. It's heavy. I'm feeling my way around the safety catch. Moving it up and down. Just getting my hands familiar, just in case.

Okay.

Que sera sera. Down the hatch. Time to do it.

SPUD

I get to the ground-floor entrance of the Members Stand and there's a couple of white-coats there, an old man and a young woman. The man looks like he has several carrots stuck up his anus, so I go to the woman. 'Hi. I'm not a member, but my father is—'

From the other side of the door the male white-coat comes our way and says, 'What's going on, Sandra?'

'He says he's not a member.'

'Well, he can't come in then,' he says, and I look at him and I'm pleading, 'Please, my father is up there. He has—'

'I can't let you in if you are not a member.'

I don't have time for this, so I just push on through.

TOM

I'm back out on the Members, making my way to the commentary box. I want to get a lie of the land, so I fade into the crowd. I sit next to an old couple, a husband and wife. They both have round brooches with VIP written on them.

I'm staring down at Walter Nurse's commentary box. It's next to the photo-finishers and I can't see any security whatsoever. I look down at the birdcage and I catch sight of a face looking in the opposite direction from the race.

'Excuse me,' I ask a Very Important Person next to me. 'Would you mind if I borrow your binoculars for a moment?'

SPUD

I head through the crowd but the old white-coat keeps following me. 'He's not a member,' he's yelling to the crowd as I push through. I up the pace and get well away from him.

I head up the stairs and through the bar and I get to the stand outside and I'm still being followed.

The Easter Stakes is about to run and there's a real hubbub. I scan how to get to the commentary booth from here. I'm at the wrong end of the stand.

TOM

Walter Nurse announces the horses are lining up at the starting gates. I'm looking down at the birdcage through binoculars. I move the binoculars along from the jockeys and trainers to a fence, and finally I see a mop of ginger hair and eyes like peas, looking up at the far end of the stand.

Alastair Shook's eyeline is well away from me. I try to blend in by talking to the Very Important People next to me. I figure it will make me fade into the crowd.

'What are you backing?' I ask them. He says, 'I've got Power of Taro,' and his Very Important Wife says, 'If it comes in he's buying me a diamond ring,' and the Very Important Husband says, 'Yeah, that's a good one,' and I scan back with my binoculars and Shook is looking almost right at me.

SPUD

My phone buzzes and I answer as I move. It's Kimbo.

'We've found fifteen metallic pink cars.'

'Fifteen?' I say.

'Metallic pink is popular all of a sudden. They all look like rentals.'

'Looked inside them?'

'Yes, I'm looking in one and Lucy is looking at another. I really can't tell—'

'Gotta go,' I say, as I see the white-coat emerge into the stand with three others. The commentator calls the start of the race.

TOM

One of the Very Important People starts yelling for Blossom
Lady. I've adjusted the angle of my binoculars to fade into the
crowd, but I'm watching Alastair Shook out the corner of my eye.

His eyeline has shifted away from me. Time to make my move.
I sneak down to some seats beside the photo-finishers' box . . .

*Racing! The Golden Casino Southern Breeders Easter Stakes is under
way and the favourites have both come out slow. Take the Blame
scrambled away and Power of Taro was slow. Ranfurly's got up off
the gate and Happy Go Lucky skipped at the start. Pantomime's gone
to the lead but he's been joined by Barney Dribble and third Always a
Chance. Ideal Companion's racing a head away fourth and three
wide around the first turn Lordship. Take the Blame's away from the
pegs and into the one one . . .*

SPUD

The race starts and the crowd are less patient with me shuffling
past them. Another white-coat sees me, and starts coming down a
set of stairs.

I'm trying to push past a bunch of knees but there are three
more white-coats coming down the aisle I am emerging from.

No point trying to run from them. Instead I say to them, 'I'm
sorry. It was a misunderstanding,' and I go with them back inside
the Members.

As soon as we're inside I break away again. The white-coats are
all way too old to keep up with me.

TOM

I pull the gun out of my pocket and I calmly walk five paces and open the door of the commentary box. I catch Walter Nurse in full flight. I push the gun to the back of his neck and he suddenly stops commentating—

'Keep calling the race. No funny business,' I say to him.

I keep the gun pressed against him as he resumes his commentary.

They're a half a lap from . . . half a lap from home. Take the Blame and Des Ashcroft are about to be joined by Power of Taro. Last half in fifty-eight. Here he comes, Highland Fling is, is on the move at the thousand-metre mark. Barney Dribble looked to g-give him the shove three and four wide. Ideal Companion was next as a few got checked up trying to get on the back of Highland Fling. Frosted Fruit four out from Thunder Thighs, Pantomime, Always a Chance and Congregate is last of the pack.

SPUD

I'm sprinting up some stairs when I hear the commentary stop. Just for half a second. It starts up again. What was that? It could be a microphone glitch or a failing in the sound system because it starts up again, but I suspect Tom is in the commentary box. I run back through the bar on the south side of the stand.

237

TOM

Beads of sweat run down his neck as he calls the race.

'I'm Tom Spotswood,' I whisper in his ear. 'That name familiar?'

Outside the box I can hear the crowd yelling for their horses, a whole chorus of excited voices. Nurse raises his pitch like a tenor.

Inside the half-mile now. And the leader is the chestnut Power of Taro but he's been joined three wide by Highland Fling. Back to third now goes Barney Dribble and Take the Blame. There are a couple very wide here. They include Ideal Companion and Frosted Fruit, then Lordship, Thunder Thighs, Blossom Lady, Pantomime, Congregate, False Step and Always a Chance.

SPUD

I make it outside and I orientate myself. This time I've popped out at the right end of the Members.

There's no white-coats in sight as I'm scampering down the steps to the commentator's booth. I get a buzz in my pocket. I don't need to answer it. It'll be Alastair Shook, saying you-know-who is you-know-where.

TOM

'That's good. You're doing well,' I say to him. The horses have made it around the bend and they are flying towards us in the final straight as Nurse commentates. The timbre of Nurse's voice lifts to a climax as the horses' heads hit the finish line.

He leaves the microphone and tentatively he looks at me. His face looks different. Has he had plastic surgery?

They run for the silverware. Power of Taro leads. Here comes Highland Fling. They're head to head. He's hit the lead Highland Fling. Jimmy May's going to win another Golden Casino Southern Breeders Easter Stakes. Highland Fling will beat Power of Taro and Barney Dribble. False Step fourth, then Blossom Lady, Take the Blame, Ideal Companion. Next in was Thunder Thighs, Congregate, Pantomime, Always a Chance, Lordship was rough in the last bit, Frosted Fruit, Ranfurly and last in was Happy Go Lucky.

SPUD

The horses are round the final turn and the crowd are screaming, 'Go, Highland Fling!' 'Go, Barney Dribble!' 'Go, you beauty!'

They all rise to their feet and it's like Moses parted the Red Sea. I'm able to run along a row of seats . . .

TOM

He's looking at the gun, and he's shaking. Something about him's not right.

'I don't want to hurt you, so stay calm,' I say, and he nods.

'You recognize me?' I ask him.

He shakes his head.

'Tom Spotswood. Fire Chief,' I say to him.

'Please. I have a wife and two kids,' he says and I take the sock from my pocket.

'I have the rest of your socks, and I can tell you where they are. All you have to do is bring me my son.'

He looks at me. Shakes his head. 'Bring me Frank, you fucker!' I yell at him.

'Please,' he begs.

I'm looking closer at his face.

He looks so different.

It's not him. That's not—

SPUD

I make it to a little white door and I burst it open and inside two guys with giant cameras are snapping away.

Fuck, I've got the wrong room. This is the photo-finishers' room.

'I'm sorry,' I say.

'You're not allowed in here,' one of them says.

'I know. I got the wrong room. I—'

I don't know why I'm trying to explain myself to the photo-finishers. I'm back out of there and I go to the next little office along—

TOM

The door bursts open behind me. I panic. My finger clutches at the trigger and the gun goes off, and there's a loud noise, like a jet plane screaming – it's deafening.

Below me, crouched on the floor, is the demolition guy. I sprint out into the crowd. I make my way through people in the stand. I'm yelling, 'Excuse me,' to clear traffic but I have to push a few to propel myself out in a hurry.

I make it out to the balcony. I'm sprinting down a concrete ramp that leads to the bottom. I'm running so fast I'm losing balance. When I make it to the bottom I crash into a man with a pot belly. 'I'm sorry!' I yell, and I keep running.

SPUD

I spring open the door and there he is, that ugly face that I know so well. He's got a gun!

He fires it. I'm down on my knees and there's a loud noise, like feedback, echoing everywhere. Tom has got away. The noise is deafening. It's coming from the microphone. Tom's shot the microphone!

'Shut it off!' I'm yelling and the commentator reaches for a button and cuts the sound off.

I'm back out to the stand and I'm yelling to the white-coats 'Where'd he go?' and they all jump on me.

'Get off me you idiots!' I'm yelling, and I push the old fools away. I see Tom. He's got well away. He's running to the exit and I'm running after him.

TOM

There are big queues coming out of the old tote building as I sprint through. I look behind me and I've got some distance on the demolition guy but I know there'll be more of them. I make it past the old tote and I'm sprinting for the car park.

I'm running through past the old public stand. I make it to the car park. I see Alastair Shook's van. Is Frank in there? I run and look inside but there's no one in it.

SPUD

I make my way to the balcony and I see him far below, scampering across the asphalt, getting lost in the crowd.

I'm on the phone straight away. I try to phone Kimbo but she's engaged. I phone Shook. 'He's got a gun. He's running past the old tote. I think he's on his way to the car park,' I say, and he says, 'Okay.' I hang up and run down the concrete ramp to the bottom.

TOM

I'm running through to the car park and I can see Alastair Shook now, in the distance, with a couple of his teenagers. This is getting out of hand. I hide behind a car and I plot the shortest and best hidden route to the jelly bean. I'm sprinting behind cars and I'm running to the jelly bean, and . . .

And waiting by the car is . . .

Frank.

Frank!

'Frank!' I'm yelling and I look across and Alastair Shook is coming straight for us.

SPUD

I make my way to the edge of the car park and I can see Alastair Shook and his team running a hundred yards ahead of me. I'm running as fast as I can and I can't see Tom and I'm looking for metallic pink cars . . .

TOM

I grab Frank by the arm and I say, 'Come on, this way.' I open the car and I say to Frank, 'Get in, quick,' and I have to yank him to get him in the jelly bean. I feel the gun fall out of my pocket. I scan a teenager running at us while Shook gets in his van. I'm straight on with the engine and Frank is screaming and I'm yelling, 'Stay calm, Frank!' I almost run over the teenager backing out. Now I'm driving full tilt away from Alastair Shook's van and I'm finding it hard to stay calm with Frank screaming.

SPUD

I make it to the Dwarf. I climb in and start the engine as some police run past me. I see a pink car pull out. He's driving erratically through the car park. He's heading straight for a dead end . . .

TOM

Frank's trying to get out but I manage to push the button that locks all the doors and I'm keeping him calm by singing the song he used to love as a boy, 'There was a mouse as big as a house, as big as a house, as big as a house,' and I see the path ahead is blocked. I swing a U-turn and the van has to do a three-point turn and I'm heading back in the opposite direction and the suspension in this car is making us bounce like we're on a brick trampoline.

Frank is screaming and I'm singing to him, 'There was a mouse as big as a house and his name was Zebedee.' Frank is wrestling with me and I'm speeding away from all of them, only to see that our way has been blocked by a truck.

I recognize the truck. It's the demolition guy. I'm heading straight for it and I'm singing, 'He ate fat cats for dinner and tea, for dinner and tea, for dinner and tea.'

I swerve at the last second but the gap's too small and I barge through but there's no path any more, just a horse truck right in front—

SPUD

Tom's getting away from the van. I drive to the end of the row he's on. I'm blocking off his exit.

I'm sitting in the Dwarf and Tom is coming right at me. He's coming at me and he's got no intention of stopping. I see his face, driving towards me. There's someone else in the car with him.

He's coming at me and he's not slowing down. I turn on the ignition and pull forward. His car veers off to the side and I hear an almighty crash—

TOM

The car has come to a halt and the engine is still running and the car we just crashed through is sounding an alarm. 'Are you okay, Frank?' I say, and he lunges for the unlock button. He's sprinting out of the car and I'm out of my door and the alarm is screaming and I'm screaming, 'Frank!' and he's blocked off by a fence. The people from the van and some police are descending on me and I get hold of Frank and I try to hug him and I say, 'Stay calm, Frank!' and he yells something and I say, 'Stay calm!' and he screams in my ear, 'I'M NOT FRANK! I'M NOT FRANK!!!'

Next I feel my body being pulled and the ground rushes up at me and twists around and now I am looking at the sky and Alastair Shook and his teenage heavies are all over me. There must be six of them. Shook forces his finger into my mouth and slips a trip on my tongue. He says to me, 'You're okay, Tom.'

SPUD

I'm out of the truck and the car has hit a horse truck and has skidded ahead and come to a halt. A car alarm is screaming. A kid races out of the car. It's Lucy! He's got Lucy! And he's running after her now and she's screaming and people are coming in from everywhere, Alastair Shook, the police, and I run as fast as I can to them—

One of the police gets there first. They tackle him to the ground. I see Alastair Shook thrust his hand in Tom's face. Lucy's eyes are red and terrified.

TOM

I'm shrieking. They've done something to Frank to turn him against me. My vision blacks out but I can still hear voices yelling, 'Tom!' 'Tom!' and I can see myself lying on the grass and Frank's next to me. We're lying in the middle of our freshly mown lawn with freshly mown grass all over us and we're both singing, 'His legs were like the trunks of trees, the trunks of trees, the trunks of trees, his legs were like the trunks of trees and his name was Zebedee.'

SPUD

Lucy runs into my arms. 'Are you all right?' I'm asking her. Her eyes are wide and she looks completely shaken. I hold her tight and I watch as Shook and his medics hover over Tom's body like a swarm of wasps. There's confusion everywhere as the police and Alastair Shook are arguing with each other about what to do with him, and in the distance I can see Kimbo running our way and as Tom is shoved on to a stretcher and put into Alastair Shook's van I can feel myself start to hyperventilate. My breath is getting faster and I wish they'd turn the fuckin car alarm off and the only thing that calms me is feeling Lucy's fingernails dig into my back. I pat her on the back of her neck and hold her tight and I say, 'I'm sorry, Lucy. I'm sorry.'

Spud

A bedtime story

9.25 p.m.

I've given statements to the police and filled them in as they try to figure out what to do with Tom, whether to charge him, whether to take him to the station or the psycho-geriatric unit. I feel pretty spacey and I say to them halfway through my interview, 'I don't know if I can deal with any more questions right now.' Kimbo steps in and talks to them instead and Lucy says, 'I want to go home.' I'd love to take her but I got a job to do tonight and I can't let Jim down.

Kimbo comes back from talking to the police and talking to Alastair Shook and says, 'You want to press charges?' and I shrug my shoulders.

'Do you want to see Tom?' she asks, and I say, 'No fuckin way.'

Kimbo has taken Lucy home and I climb into the Dwarf and as I drive past I can see them in the back of the van. They've got the seats down and they're all looking after Tom as if he were a precious flower. I drive outta there, half a k down the road. I pull over and it all comes flooding out. I haven't cried like this since I was a kid. I hope that's the last I ever see of him but as soon as I shut my eyes, there he is again.

I'm seven. I'm lying in bed and I feel this weight at the foot of the bed. I look over at my digital alarm clock and it's two o'clock in the morning and guess who's paying me a visit.

I pretend I'm asleep. I can hear a glug glug glug sound of liquid in a hip-flask. I hear him cough a little, and shuffle, and he says, 'You awake, Frank?' and I shift my head and open one of my eyes and I see his silhouette leaning over me, stooped and breathing heavily.

I feel this hand come down on my hair and I shift a bit and he pulls away and clears his throat and says, 'Okay, bedtime story. I've got a good one for you.'

The weight of him is pushing into where I want to stretch my legs out but Tom wants to talk so that's the way it's gotta be.

'There's this horse,' he starts. 'He's a good horse. A champion horse. A beautiful brown horse with big droopy eyes. The kind of horse you can go right up to and he'll eat grass right off your hand. And apples. This horse loves apples. He loves sweet apples, tart apples, rotten apples, any kind of apple.'

'Granny Smiths?' I ask him.

'Yes, the brown horse loves Granny Smiths most of all. Now, one night the horse is minding his own business. He's trying to sleep in the middle of the night, and his best human friend pats him awake. He says, "Come on, Horsey. Let's go for a midnight stroll and look at the beautiful moon." And the beautiful brown horse is taken for a walk in the moonlight. It's the most beautiful crescent moon he's seen in his life.

'But on this fine moonlit night, the beautiful brown horse gets taken out to a fence in the middle of the paddock, and his best human friend feeds him some delicious apples but the apples make him feel really tired. Different from sleepy tired. You know that feeling when you wake up from sleep and you don't know if you're in a dream or not, and you decide to get up but your body won't let you? You know that feeling, Frank?'

I nod, and he wags his finger in the air. 'I knew you would know that feeling. So anyway, the beautiful brown horse is looking up at a perfect crescent moon when he feels this whack on his leg.'

Tom gives my leg a little whack.

'Just a little sharp whack, and the horse thinks to himself, That's funny, that feeling, and he looks down at his leg and you know what he sees, Frank?'

I say nothing. I just lie silent, listening to him. Tom takes another swig from his hip-flask.

'He sees that his leg is now at a funny angle. He can't feel it but he sees that his leg is at a funny angle and then he sees a big big axe, and the beautiful brown horse watches as his best human friend in the world slams the back of the axe into his leg, and the leg bends even more, and the poor brown horse knows something is wrong. And you know what he does?'

I shake my head, terrified.

'He tries to run away, Frank, but he can't. He can't run away because his legs won't move, His body won't move, just the same way your body doesn't move when you want to get out of bed but you can't. So the beautiful brown horse stares at the moon, and he thinks to himself, Why is life so unfair? Why is life so unfair, Frank? Why, is life so . . . unfair?'

Tom puts his hand in my hair and says, 'Sleep well, Frank. I love you.' He leans over and kisses my cheek and I feel the weight lift from my bed and I watch the silhouette of him walk out of my door. I hear him collapse on to the couch in the living room, and I stare at the dark doorway where he was.

Saturday

It takes balls to wreck buildings

6.14 a.m.

In every job there are good parts and bad parts. This is one of those parts of a job that makes it all worthwhile: pulling down the facade. All the prep work has been done. The cuts are complete. The road has been cleared. My dogman is giving me the thumbs up. The ball is in position. A crowd has gathered with their video cameras. But even with everyone around, it's just three of us: me, T-Rex and the building. And it's my job to see the building gets the end that she deserves.

I used to come here as a kid and I used to love running around the place when the lights had gone down and the ushers weren't looking. Back then would I have ever dreamed that I would be the one to bring her down? Not in a thousand years. But here I am. The best seat in the house.

I'd love to do it in one almighty fall, but I'll have to settle for floor by floor. This top floor is the best. We've taken the signage down and we've taken out the windows but the masonry still looks a picture. When they put her together they took a lot of pride in the old girl, and I intend to take a lot of pride in the way I pull her down.

It seems right that this is T-Rex's last job. She's served me so well, and she deserves to be put to pasture having completed one final act of beauty. I'm watching the ball swing into the oval windows in the facade. A perfect shot and we're crunching through nice and easy, making a larger hole, and as I watch the dust puff out of the masonry I feel a wave of pride and a wave of sadness. T-Rex won't be having any more moments like this, and I don't expect to feel the same doing it with the hydraulics. This is the last time we get to work together and I want to treasure every moment. Ride every hit. The machine is an extension of my body and I feel powerful bringing down the last wall of the theatre, piece by piece, using every part of my tactical brain and my skills, putting on a show for the spectators.

I get flashes of Lucy and flashes of Tom while I'm doing the job but I'm glad that the job requires me to be switched on 100 per cent so I roll them up in a little ball in the back of my mind and I forget about them until I've finished this job.

I feel a bit choked up thinking that this is the last time for me and T-Rex, but now's not the time for that kind of reflection. Just get on with the job, but enjoy it. When I have isolated a massive chunk of the top storey that will all go down in one chunk, I look to the side and I'm happy to see Joey there with his camera. The early morning light is coming in and everything is perfect as I hit her front and centre and I see the front shake; two or three more hits will do it.

I swing and I hear a rumble and the ball cuts part-way through. I nod to Joey to say this next one is the one, and I just sit back and watch the hit.

The ball cannons in and I watch whole top storey teeter and fall in one beautiful wide sheet, and the sound is enormous – it drowns out everything, and T-Rex purrs like a kitten underneath it all. I feel the shake throughout my body – this is better than any orgasm you could hope for; the thrill of the front wall still feels as good as it did on my first time with the ball. I hear a few drunken stragglers cheer as the dust rises and my heart rises and races and then sinks again as I realize that I just witnessed the final conquest of a machine that has done the business for me for almost twenty years.

Smoke bubbles and concrete crumbs

1.38 p.m.

I'm asleep in the back of the Dwarf at home, and I'm dreaming of Tom mowing the lawns. He looks over at me and the cigarette droops from his mouth. I can smell the cigarette.

I open my eyes, and the cigarette smell is still there. I look out at the light coming into the back of the truck, and I see a beautiful silhouette of Kimbo, leaning against the wall by the foot of my bed, smoking a rollie. She looks troubled. I feel so bad that I have brought all this on her. All my shit. All my stupid family history. I've brought it all on her and now she feels the weight of it all.

I know why she wants to leave me. If I was her I would want to leave me.

'Nice way to start the day,' I say to her, and she says, 'I'm giving up giving up.'

She blows a load of smoke out and I watch the patterns the smoke makes as the light from outside hits it.

'Okay. I give up giving up too,' I say and I reach out my hand and she hands it over and lights herself up a new one.

Next thing we're out the back of the house. Kimbo has taken the Dwarf out to get some ciggies. The sun is shining and I've laid out a picnic blanket in the back yard, on the patch where the grass won't grow. I'm cutting onions while Lucy mans the sausages on the barbecue.

'You okay?' I say to her and she nods, but her nod is unconvincing.

'Was that my granddad?' she says.

I would love to lie to her. I've never told her Tom was dead or any lies like that. I just never talked about him. If ever it came up all I said was that he's somewhere a long way away.

I am still trying to understand what happened. He musta scared the shit out of her.

'He wasn't trying to hurt you,' I say, amazed that those words are coming from my own mouth.

'I know that,' she says. 'He's just . . . he's just a bit lost.'

'Yeah. Yeah,' I say, and I throw the onions on the grill.

'Don't worry. He'll never bother you again,' I say.

'Do you have any old photos of him?' she asks me, and I shake my head, even though I know I got some in the bottom of a box somewhere in the garage.

'Mum says he's a drunk.'

'Yes. He sure is that.'

'Mum wants me to see a woman about it.'

'Huh?'

Oh, of course. Brenda. As if Lucy isn't spooked enough already.

'Maybe I'm the one who needs that kind of help,' I say.

Kimbo arrives home with a shopping bag and I can make out several packs of ciggies through the plastic. She tears open the cellophane and lights up.

'Don't take up smoking,' she warns Lucy, who is watching the whole thing.

'I got some bubble mixture,' Lucy says, and she runs into the house.

'When are you working?' Kimbo asks.

'I start at four.'

'I'm a failure,' Kimbo says, puffing away like there's no tomorrow.

'I'm the failure,' I say to her. 'I've dragged you down to my level,' and she says, 'Well, that's true.'

Next thing we've cracked into some emergency beer. I've

dragged them out from a box in the garage and even though they are warm and flat they still taste good. We're already plotting how we can lay our hands on more beer on Easter weekend. I mean, fuck, there's gotta be some fun in this life.

We got the stereo speakers outside and Meatloaf is blaring and Lucy has a whole lot of bubble mixture that Santa musta got her a few years ago. 'Can you blow some smoke bubbles?' she asks, and next thing Kimbo is up on her feet taking a drag and blowing through the little soapy cylinder and a smoky bubble emerges. It pops pretty quick and Kimbo has another go and she blows a big one. The smoke swirls around inside it for about five seconds and when it pops a puff of smoke bursts free and Lucy claps.

My turn next. My first few attempts aren't too flash but then I get a good one up and running. A double-bubble forms and it's a whopper. The weight of the smoke is pulling it down but it lasts a good three seconds before Lucy rushes in and pops it with her finger. I yell, 'Hey!' but Kimbo tells her she's a good girl for looking out for her mother.

9.16 p.m.

Where the Century used to be is now just a huge square block of rubble. Now that the facade is down everyone can see it. We got a lot of people out looking at it all. A few with video cameras, including the protester who will no doubt post it on YouTube or Facebook or whatever. It'll be nice to have a recording of it on the web.

There's a junk pile at the back where a lot of the wood has been chucked, and there's another pile of steel. We won't be able to get to that until we've shipped out a huge amount of rubble.

It's a big day for the bulldozer boys, riding over the top of what they can, squashing it flat. The jackhammer boys are getting a good workout too, breaking down concrete, turning it into crumbs. There's a few boys out hovering to salvage brick but pretty much 95 per cent of what's left is worthless and just needs to get taken to the dump. I've been given all the bigger bits of concrete to smash. I lift stuff off the road, gib it up and drop it from a decent height back on the site in a corner away from the others.

I take my dinner after finishing a bunch of work on the road. I don't leave T-Rex. I just eat in the cab and while I'm eating I'm thinking about Kimbo and how maybe if I see that woman of hers she might give me a bit of a second chance. I'm trying to figure out how we can afford her. As long as the theatre chairs come through I could have a couple of sessions and get fixed up mentally as good as new. Then again, I suppose it would take a year's worth of sessions and I'd still be a useless bastard. It's worth a try if that's what it'll take to get Kimbo on side. I mean, I know there's a lot of other fish in the sea, but I doubt many fish would put up with me. I'm not exactly the best catch in the world.

Dick is a lot wiser than he looks. He said to me at smoko, 'In every marriage there are three bags of shit. There's the shit you make, the shit she makes, and the shit you make together. The trick is to know which pile your shit belongs to.' Following his theory I've brought a lot of shit into our marriage, thanks to my fucked-up family. Not that I'm into the blame game. Fuck that. I can stand on my own two feet and that arsehole can't take the credit for all my fuck-ups, but still. I musta got some bad habits from somewhere. He's given me some of his defective genes.

When I finish my dinner I give Kimbo a bell and she tells me she has two bits of news. The good news is she reckons she's found a yard for us. I can't believe it. She's a fast mover is Kimbo. The bad news is Tom is in Green Acres, and Kimbo is acting all intense that I should go and see him. She's real determined about it. I tell her, 'No way,' and I can hear by her fuckin ten months pregnant pause that I'll pay a price if I don't do what she says, so I follow that up with, 'Let me think about it,' and she says, 'Good, Spud. You have a think about it,' and she hangs up the phone.

Tom

Good Friday

Another trip with Alastair Shook

Deborah is in her bra. A red lace bra. She loves to wear her bra in the bedroom. She knows what it does to me and she loves to tease. She's checking herself in the mirror, trying on one of a dozen dresses she is contemplating wearing while I lie in bed, enjoying the view.

She has a glass of wine in her hand and she's telling me a funny story. She knows how to spin a yarn, does Deborah. She's talking to me and her eyes are rolling while she imitates a work colleague, and she's making me laugh. Then I say something appalling and she mock-reacts. She jumps on top of me and we wrestle. I manage to get on top and she's looking up at me and I feel so . . . *necessary*. For a moment my life has a purpose, a point, and I have to kiss that beautiful face of hers, and as I do she's talking to me, we're talking and kissing at the same time, and there's no place I'd rather be than here.

I'm strapped in the van. A strap is right over me and I can't move a muscle and I can hear voices that I don't recognize and all I see out the window are power lines, moving past me, one after the other. The lines make geometric patterns as they rush past me.

I'm trying to get the lawnmower going. I'm yanking the cord of the two-stroke but she isn't responding. Down at the front door Frank is watching me. I tell him to get me a beer. I light up a cigarette and

Frank comes out with a beer and hands it to me and I wink at him and I pull the cord but nothing happens, and Frank giggles. So I use some more elbow grease. I pull the cord so hard I almost rip it out of the machine and she roars into action like an angry lion and I can smell the petrol and I've worked up a sweat just getting this far and Frank runs around the lawn doing roly-polys and I'm yelling to him to get off the grass and he finds that funny. God knows why but he finds that funny.

I'm on a bus full of old people. We're all travelling to The City and I'm sitting next to an old lady and she's flirting with me and I lead her on a little to give her a cheap thrill. I look out the window and I'm seeing all the new buildings in town, buildings I've never seen before. We're rounding a bend and I can hear some coughing behind us and an old woman is having some kind of attack. She's clutching her chest and the driver stops the bus and goes to her aid. Her face looks bright red like she'll pass out and leave this life for whatever is next in a few moments. I get off the bus.

Me and Frank are heading to the Mountain Peaks coffee shop and Frank sprints away from me and I'm sprinting to keep up with him. I stay right behind his tail and I let him keep a good lead and then I sprint past him for the final block, and I make it to the coffee shop first and his face is red. I say to him, 'You almost beat me that time,' and we head inside and I get him the largest milkshake in town. As I drink my coffee he's blowing bubbles through his straw. He's blowing so many bubbles the milkshake spills out over the edges of the glass.

Everything is black. I can hear voices. 'Is he coming round?' 'His heart rate is high.' 'Turn left here.' 'Where's the Promazine?'
    I can't open my eyes. I can feel the earth around me moving relentlessly. My stomach is churning and my hands are shaking and I can't open my eyes and the noise outside is piercing. I can hear the gears of the van grinding away. I don't know where I am.

Where are they taking me? I try to open my eyes but someone has sewed them shut. 'We need to stabilize him,' someone says. 'Tom! Tom!' I hear someone yelling.

I'm in the movie theatre with Deborah and the movie is about to start and we're looking up at the stars. We're waiting for it, waiting for it and there it is. A shooting star.

'Did you see it?' she says to me.

'I saw it'. I look into her eyes and as the lion roars on the screen it lights up her face and she's stuffing her face with popcorn. I kiss her on the neck and she says, 'Careful, Tom. I may get overexcited.' There's nothing I would like to see more than Deborah overexcited.

I'm in a little room. I don't recognize this place. The walls are a drab light khaki. There's an old man here. He's pacing the floor. He looks over at me. And he starts yelling. 'He's woken up! He's woken up!!' I close my eyes but I can still hear his voice, piercing into my skull. Shut him up! Someone shut him up!

I'm at a dinner table. Deborah is opposite me and she has slackjaw and she's yelling excitably. We have guests. Deborah's yelling, 'Tell them about how you got the scar.'

'No,' I can hear myself saying.

'Come on, tell us,' one of Deb's friends says.

'A fight in a bar,' I say, and they all laugh. 'What?' I'm saying.

'Frank did it,' Deb screams out gleefully. 'It was at the swings and Frank was swinging and Tom was doing his shoelaces and Frank kicked him in the head and almost broke his nose—'

I'm sticking to my story. 'It was a fight in a bar. You should've seen the other guy,' I hear myself saying, and Deborah shrieks, 'The other guy was your son, Tom.'

'I deny everything,' I hear myself say, and there's laughter all around the table.

★

269

I'm lying awake in the khaki room. A phone is ringing, but no one's answering. It just keeps ringing. The noise is screaming at me. Why doesn't someone answer the goddam phone?

We're making love. I'm on top of Deborah and she's moaning and I feel her tighten around me and I lose myself in the moment and I shut my eyes as she moans into my ear. She holds me tight and she breathes into my neck and digs into my back with her nails.

I'm running.

I'm running away from Frank.

I'm running and Frank is behind me.

I'm running and I turn and Frank isn't running any more.

But I keep running. I keep running as fast as I can. Frank is behind me.

I can't look back.

I have to keep running.

They've turned the lights out on me. I can see a silhouette in the next room and I'm yelling, 'WHERE IS HE?'

The silhouette hovers at the window, staring at me.

'WHERE IS HE?' I'm yelling. 'WHAT HAVE YOU DONE WITH HIM?'

A woman rushes in and sits at my side.

'Calm down, Tom,' she says.

'WHERE IS HE, YOU BITCH?' I yell in her face. 'BITCH!'

'TOM!'

'Please,' I beg. 'I'll do anything. What do you want? What do you want?'

Another man comes into the room, a big man, and they try to stuff another acid trip into my mouth. I try to keep my mouth shut, and the woman says, 'We just want to help you, Tom. We just want to take the edge off your distress.'

The man manages to get a finger in my mouth and she slips it on my tongue.

★

I'm at the races and I'm watching the favourite, Majestic Sunset, coming round the bend; five lengths in front of him are Princess Leia and Alberon. I'm yelling, 'Go, girl! Go, girl!' as Majestic Sunset passes both of them and sprints for home and I'm up on my feet, I'm up on my feet and yelling, and as she crosses the finish line I'm yelling, 'Yeah! You beauty!' but when I sit down the seat next to me is empty. The whole stand is empty. I'm the only one watching the race.

Saturday

Brainwashing begins

1.15 p.m.

I open my eyes and there is a man with glasses and a beard standing above me. He's looking at me the way a scientist looks at a bug. He smiles a little. He says to me, 'Hi, Tom.'

'Where's my son?' I ask him.

'Your son is fine,' he says.

'Can I see him?'

The man bites his lip and looks around the room.

'I'm not sure about that, Tom,' he says.

'Why won't you let me see him?'

'We have to find him first.'

'I know where to look—'

'That's okay, Tom,' he says, and he smiles. 'You need to rest. You've been through a lot.'

'I need to—'

I feel the words disappearing as I say them, and then I can feel my thoughts disappearing and I look up at the man with glasses who is smiling at me and nodding.

I wake with the sun shining on my face. In front of me is a window with ugly faded pink curtains. The sun is coming through and lighting up a path of dust. The dust floats in front of my eyes.

I move my arms and I'm surprised to discover I'm not restrained in any way. I look around the room and the walls are the same shade of khaki as before. I'm in a dressing gown but they have folded and ironed my suit and it sits on a table beside the bed.

I'm looking around for signs of other life. Through a window I can see some birds burrowing in a tree. I put on my suit jacket and it feels clean and pressed. I go to a door and I try to open it but it is locked, of course.

My energy is low with all the drugs they've been feeding me. A nip of something sharp would help brighten me up, but right now I just feel groggy.

On the other side of the room from me is an old piano. It looks a bit beat up and not well looked after. I shuffle my way over to the piano stool and I rest my hands on the keys. They feel cold on my fingers. I run my finger along the black keys and they remind me of my mother's piano when I was growing up. That piano was never in tune but she loved to play it anyway, and I loved hearing her play.

I don't want to play a note. It would just alert them that I'm up and about, and they'll come in and drug me some more. Yet I feel myself drawn to the keys. I spread my fingers out and I play a couple of basic chords and I can feel the vibrations throughout my body and it feels good so I play some more chords, and I'm playing an old song I knew well when I was a kid, Beethoven's Moonlight Sonata. I'm no virtuoso but it's a calming, simple song to play and even though I haven't played the piano for so long my fingers seem to know what to do. I hit a bum note here and there but the gist of it is nice, and I remember how Deborah got a piano for our place when a friend was giving one away. A bunch of our neighbours had to help us lift it into the house and then it sat there getting dusty, hardly ever getting played. Every now and then I would tinkle away when I thought no one was around and Deb would show up in her dressing gown and I would stop playing and she'd say, 'Keep playing, it's nice.' She'd rest her hand on my shoulder while I fumbled and bumbled my way through the only four tunes that were in my head. It was always the same four tunes, but it didn't matter to her. She was just happy to see me playing her piano.

★

I'm rattling the door, pounding it hard, but no one is listening. They're ignoring me. They've been ignoring me for an hour now. I slam my hand on the window and finally two guards come in, a male and a female.

'You okay, Tom?' the female guard says.

'Of course I'm not okay. Where's Frank? I want to talk to Frank!'

'Where do you think Frank is?' she asks.

'Huh?' I say, and she repeats the question.

'YOU FUCKIN BITCH!'

'Calm down, Tom.'

'I won't calm down. Just tell me where—'

'Frank is fine. Frank is good,' she says and she gives the other guard a nod and he puts his arms around me, holding me tight while she tries to put her finger in my mouth but I keep my mouth shut and she nods to her guy and I feel a sharp pain in my butt, a needle.

'Don't worry, Tom. We'll look after you. Don't you worry,' she says. My eyes blank out and I can feel my body falling and being caught.

I've been taken into a little room and a man and a woman, both in green uniforms, are looking at some forms. She tells me to get on some scales and they weigh me. They push me against a wall and measure my height. They ask me a whole bunch of questions and they seem very interested in my alcohol intake. They poke a stick in my nose and it beeps loudly. They look at the stick and they type a few numbers into their computer. They take a clamp and they wrap it around my arm and they squeeze it so tight it feels like they are trying to stop the blood flow from getting to my hand. When they release it again there's a big red mark where it was. I won't show them any pain. No way. They dig their fingers into my neck and take my pulse. Surprise, surprise, I'm alive.

Then they tell me to take my clothes off and they make me wear an apron and nothing else and they poke around my butt. If they're looking for Robert Valentine's money they won't find it in there. This is all a part of their torture ritual. Humiliate the subject before you go back to the nice guy act. They run a device around my body, like those things they use in airports, and it makes a few blips and bleeps and they touch their computer screens in all the right places, and they touch me in some of the wrong ones.

Next they're poking around my face. Ear, nose and throat, I know the drill, but they're probing with high-tech equipment. They blind me by shining a bright torch into my eyes and they make me listen to a horrible drone.

These are all the first steps of brainwashing. I've read the books. I know how it works.

Out comes the stethoscope but this one has come directly out of a freezer. They force me to lie down and they poke my gut with their palms. They dig their fingers deep into my kidneys and they patronizingly ask me, 'Are you feeling any pain?' I hide the pain I'm experiencing while they push and probe with everything they've got and I have to clench my teeth not to give them any signs of weakness.

Next they make me walk in a straight line. I know this drill because I almost got done for drink driving a couple of times. They make me close my eyes and touch my nose with my fingers. I use my middle finger so that I'm flipping them the bird as I complete their stupid exercise.

Next the man holds on to my testicles and tells me to turn my head and cough and when I cough he gives them a good squeeze, the sick prick.

Then I'm marched to an X-ray and they pump a thousand megawatts of radiation inside my body. I bet when they're at home after work they get themselves off by staring at the insides of people, these sick scumbags.

The ritual humiliation is not complete without asking me to pee into one bottle and poo into another. I refuse the number twos but I go into a little cubicle and I piss into their little bottle with venom. I'd love to piss in their next cup of tea but I doubt I'll get that opportunity.

Humiliation ritual over, they have the nerve to help me get dressed when I can take perfect care of myself. I kick out at a guard who is trying to help me with my pants. The man tries to tell me off but I look him in the eye and I say to him, 'Your mother must be so disappointed to give birth to such a scumbag.' They push me out of the room and take me back to my blessed isolation chamber.

I'm in a little cell and I'm being interviewed by a man pretending to be a doctor. For all I know he may actually be one. I assume it can't be that expensive to buy off a doctor these days. Behind him there is a policewoman, who is sitting writing notes based on this interview. It would be really great to have the whole set of emergency services. All we need now is a fireman. I'm sure Robert Valentine could wield his influence to get one if he wanted.

The pretend-doctor has a warm smile but I won't fall for that. He is a short man with black-rimmed glasses and a compact little face. His hair is black-grey but the bottom of his beard is jet white. He wears a neatly pressed white shirt and he sports a wedding ring. His greatest flamboyance is a tartan tie, blue and green. If I was feeling convivial I would ask him what his clan was but I have no intention of being convivial.

'Hi, Tom,' he says to me, 'I'm Duncan Crafar.'

His voice is soft and glutenous, like he just ate a loaf of bread. I stare him up and down and he offers me a seat and asks me if I would like a cup of tea.

'Sure,' I say. He offers the policewoman a cup of tea too.

'Are you a doctor?' I ask him.

'Yes I am,' he says.

'You got a certificate?'

'Yes I do. I keep it in my bathroom. My wife thinks I should keep it in my office but given my office is also our living room I don't like it there.'

He's trying to be fresh with me.

'I want to speak to Walter Nurse,' I say.

'Who is Walter Nurse?' he asks, feigning ignorance.

'The racing commentator,' the policewoman says.

'Do you know him?' the so-called doctor asks.

'Do you know him?' I ask back.

'No I don't,' he says with a smile.

'You work for him.'

'Why do you think I work for him?'

'He's behind all of this.'

'He's behind what?' he asks, and a guard comes in and puts a cup of tea in front of me.

'Stop acting like you don't know what's going on,' I say, and he smiles at me. I'd love to wipe that smile off his face.

It's amazing. Only now can I see the full extent of Robert Valentine's operation. I don't understand it yet, but I've clearly stumbled on something bigger than a racing commentator. Maybe Walter Nurse isn't Robert Valentine after all. Maybe it goes higher than that. All the way to the police? Maybe even higher than that. Maybe I've tapped into a political thing. Whatever has happened, I've been caught in the wrong place at the wrong time, and these scumbags are happy to use all available channels to keep me where they want me, out of public view.

'I want Frank,' I say.

'Is Frank your son?' he asks me.

'Yes. Frank is his son,' the policewoman says. The so-called doctor ignores her.

'Where do you think he is?'

'You have him,' I say, and he says, 'We don't have your son, but your son is safe.'

'Where is he?' I ask and he says to me, 'I'm not sure. Where do you think he is? When did you last see him?'

'At the races. You have him,' I say.

'Was he in your car with you?'

'Yes. And you took me away from him.'

'Who did?'

'Your people. Robert Valentine.'

'Who is Robert Valentine?' he asks.

'He's your boss.'

'And you think Walter Nurse is Robert Valentine?' the policewoman says. I don't respond.

'Why did you take a gun to the races Tom?' she asks.

'Am I under arrest? Is that what this is?'

'We're assessing that,' she says.

'You're not under arrest, Tom,' the doctor says.

'So I can go then?'

'No. I'm afraid not.'

'So if I'm not under arrest why are you holding me here?'

'What do you think this place is Tom?' he asks.

I can already tell from his line of questioning that the so-called 'doctor' Duncan Crafar is questioning my sanity. The first part of the brainwashing procedure. I'll have to have my wits about me to go toe to toe with these guys.

'You know what? Fuck you and your mind games,' I say to him. 'Just bring me my son. Bring me my son or bring me Robert Valentine or bring me Alastair Shook.'

'Well, I don't know about Robert Valentine but I promise we'll try and find your son for you. And you'd like to see Alastair Shook?'

Condescending bastard. I throw my cup of tea at him and he yelps as it hits his face and tartan tie. The policewoman restrains me and another guard rushes to his aid, asking, 'Are you all right, Duncan?'

He nods and somehow keeps his poise.

'I'm sorry I upset you, Tom,' he says, and he leaves the room.

Some other guards take me out of the torture chamber, down a long corridor and an old lady is walking towards me. She stops in front of me and she says to me, 'Donald, is that you?'

'Huh?' I say, but they shove me out of her way, and into my little prison cell.

Some more proof that I am not in a hospital. I have been assigned a 'nurse'. You should see this guy. He would dwarf your average bouncer at a nightclub. A big pale white whale of a man. He's probably got the brains of a small bird. I bet his method of fighting is to just sit on top of you and it would be like trying to escape from underneath a crocodile. Ha! A nurse, they call him! That's a good one. Since when do people hire nurses with muscles like that? His arms are bigger than my legs. A nurse!

I look over at him and he looks bored out of his skin. I don't think I'll get him talking. It's better that he stays bored. I survey the room for an exit strategy and there are two doors. I suspect they are locked. I will check them when my 'nurse' isn't watching.

There's a window too, overlooking a small garden with a big fence behind it. Why do they bother with a garden? Do they think I'm fooled by a few carnations? A prison with a garden is still a prison. A cell with a piano is still a cell. I don't know why they bothered putting carpet on the floor. They could have saved some money and gone for concrete. I'd be more comfortable if they treated me honestly and called a spade a spade, a cell a cell.

A place where you will feel more comfortable

5.13 p.m.

I'm in my cell and there is a knock on the door and the guard leaves the room and I hear him talking to someone. Next thing I'm hauled outside, with the guard's arm around my arm. They're escorting me to another van. Robert Valentine must own a whole fleet of vans. There's a new heavy who smiles when he sees me and says, 'Hi, Tom. Remember me?'

No. I don't remember you. And smiles do not fool me. This guy has got a big tattoo on his arm. It looks tribal. He sits with me in the back of the van. The driver is a woman. She smiles to me like I am a four-year-old. She says to me, 'We were worried about you. How are you doing?'

I don't answer. They try to offer me a banana but I refuse.

The van is taking us out of town. We hit the motorway and I look out the windows at the rolling green hills and the farms and the cows trying to stay in tiny patches of shade in the sweltering sun. The van climbs the hills and the landscape becomes yellow as we head north. I know this drive. This is the same drive I went on when I got out of The City in the first place. I thought if I headed away from trouble then trouble wouldn't come find me. Little did I realize that I would create trouble wherever I went.

As we cut through the hills the guard next to me points out the window at a hawk, its wings at full stretch as it catches a thermal, high above a farm. Ahead in the next field we pass a giant irrigation sprinkler on wheels. It's a magnificent thing, flicking and jolting and spraying like it's got a mind of its own.

I can feel the motor vibrations against my neck. The suspension in this van is non-existent. I don't know where they are taking me, or why. I am hoping they are taking me to see Robert Valentine himself. Maybe they have realized they have gone too far in trying to scare me. Maybe they have Frank in a facility up this way. I can feel in my bones that he is okay. But I am starting to distrust my hunches; something I never thought would happen.

I feel the van slow and I open my eyes and see we are in a fifty k zone on the outskirts of Northcote. We skirt off a side road and climb into an area by the train tracks.

My guard is yawning and I'm surveying how easy it would be to spring out of here before they take me to my final destination. Unfortunately they seem to have learned their lessons from last time. In addition to my tight seat belt they have another strap around me which I can't seem to find a buckle for.

We pull in to some big gates. The driver taps a code into a machine and the gates open and then close behind us.

I'm taken through a reception area that is well carpeted and full of flowers. A woman at the front desk smiles to me and they usher me through a set of doors. Now we are in a corridor.

A sign in the corridor says 'Zone 2'. I feel like I have been here before, but I can't place it.

This place has a stench of cleaning product. You know when a place smells too much of cleaning product that it must be masking a much worse smell.

They are taking me down a hallway with patterned grey carpet. Maybe this facility belongs to Robert Valentine. What is this place? Why have they taken Frank away from me? Is Deborah involved in this? Where is Deborah? Maybe if I can get hold of Deborah we can straighten this out.

A sign on the wall says 'The Good Old Days' and has a bunch of photos that are nostalgic. One of the photos is of Queen Elizabeth, a young woman in her twenties.

Why are they keeping me here? It doesn't make sense.

I mean, if this is a ransom, they've got a strange way of going about it. Nobody has made a ransom demand. They don't appear to want my money.

Does all this go back to Fire Chief? If so, it's a massive over-reaction on Robert Valentine's part. I'm finding it hard to comprehend.

This feels like a hotel hallway. We pass rooms with numbers on them, but on the doors are photos of old people with their names. There is a photo of an old woman called Ann and another photo of her with what must be her family. We pass Leonard's room and there is a picture of an old man with his hands out and an expression that looks like he is spaced out. It's cruel to imprison people at this age. We pass Iona's room, which has a picture of a kind-looking woman with a woollen hat on and a warm smile.

We come to a door already labelled 'Tom's room' and a picture of me in my suit. I know this picture well. It was taken fifteen years ago, when I received accreditation as an insurance investigator. I thought I had such a bright future then. Now look at me.

What is this? Am I in police custody? Does anyone know I've been detained? Linda knows, but she's in on it. What did they say to her? Are they paying her? Was she always a spy? Why would someone want to spy on me? What else have I done that would make someone want to spy on me?

I don't get it. I don't get it. I don't get it. I don't get it. I don't get it. I don't get it. I don't get it. I don't get it. I don't get it. I don't get it. I don't get it. I don't get it.

There's a simple explanation, and I'm missing it.

Am I insane? Is this an insane institution? Stay calm, Tom. You're not insane. You are still a rational person. Just—

Just take your time with this.

Take a moment.

★

I am taken into my new cell. Inside is a single bed with a blue bed-spread. There is an oil heater, a chair and a small television. On top of the television is Jethro, my teddy bear I grew up with.

Why would they have that? It's almost like Robert Valentine is trying to make me feel comfortable. Why does he want me to feel comfortable? Is it another part of the brainwashing process?

'Feel like a sleep?' the guard asks me.

'No.'

I look around the room. The walls are sickly tangerine. There is a table and a painting of a three-masted ship arriving at some trop-ical paradise. Next to it is a window where I can see a little garden with a small square hedge that would be the perfect height for a high-jumping midget. Behind it is a tree in full pink blossom. In front of the blossom tree are chrysanthemums. Robert Valentine seems to have a lot of flowers at his facilities. Perhaps Robert Valentine is a millionaire florist.

I say to my guy, 'What is this place?' and he looks to the doorway and standing in the door frame is a man I recognize.

Here he is, the big ginger-headed monster. Alastair Shook's eyes are disproportionately small and his puffy forehead is speckled with freckles. His hair is receding so he keeps it short in the modern style of people who are trying to appear younger than they actually are.

'Tom,' he says to me. 'Do you recognize me?'

'Of course,' I say, but I'm not going to let him run the conversation. 'Where's Frank?'

'Frank is safe, Tom,' he says to me. 'You don't need to worry about Frank.'

'I want to talk to Robert Valentine,' I say.

'Why do you want to talk to him?'

'Don't act innocent on me,' I say. I fix my eyes on him and he looks back and we're having a good old-fashioned stare-down and he looks away first. They may hold the power but at least I can win the small battles.

'Fancy a cup of tea, Tom?' one of his cronies asks.

Obviously the left hand isn't talking to the right hand. Haven't they read the memo? Don't serve Tom hot liquid.

'You'll put something in it.'

'I promise you. We won't put anything in your tea.'

I laugh, because his promise is worth about as much as his terrible haircut.

'Got any pills for me?' I ask him, straight up.

'Well, you need to take some pills to thin your blood—'

'Think I was born yesterday? You'll feed me pills and . . .'

'And what?' he asks.

'You want to convince me I'm crazy.'

'Why would I want to do that?'

'I don't know. I don't know what this place is.'

'You don't recognize it?'

'No.'

'This is your home, Tom.'

He says it with a straight face. I don't know this place. I don't recognize this bed. I don't recognize this room. The only thing I recognize is my old teddy bear.

'These are your clothes,' Shook says to me and he shows me a bunch of suits. My old suits. They're all neatly pressed and laundered.

'I might need that cup of tea,' I say. 'And some cigarettes.'

'No cigarettes, Tom.'

'Oh, you really know how to break a man.'

'I am here to help you. That's the main thing you need to know.'

'You're here to help me?' I say to him.

'Yes. I want you to be comfortable.'

'Where is my son?' I ask him. He tries to keep looking at me but I can see him twitching, squirming. I can see that deep down he is afraid of me.

'Your son is in The City,' he says.

'Where is Deborah?' I ask. 'You got her too?'

'We don't have Deborah and we don't have your son. Your son is okay, Tom. He—'

He stops talking all of a sudden, like he's trying to decide whether to tell me something.

'Say it.'

'Your son says he doesn't want to see you.'

'He doesn't want to see me?'

'That's correct.'

'Ha!' I laugh. 'Is Deborah in on this little ruse?'

'No,' he says.

'Who spoke to my son?'

'I did.'

'I bet you been working on him. What do you call it? Stockholm syndrome? Maybe you're brainwashing him the way you're brainwashing me.'

Alastair Shook shakes his head. 'No, Tom,' he says. 'I'm not trying to brainwash you. I'm on your side.'

'Where is he?'

'He's in The City. He has his own house.'

'He has his own house?' I laugh at him. 'That's a good one. He has his own house? You're fucking with me. You and your pills and your—'

'We just want to help you, Tom.'

'I DON'T WANT YOUR HELP. I WANT MY SON!'

'I'll speak to him again. We'll see,' he says.

A guard comes in. Alastair Shook gives him a raised eyebrow. 'Hey, Tom. Can I get you anything? Some food? A banana?' the guard asks.

'No, I don't want a banana. What is this?' I say.

'Okay. You look tired. We can continue this later,' Alastair Shook says. He gets up and goes to the door. 'Just sing out when you want to have another chat,' he says, and he leaves the room, and the guard stays in the room, picking up a *Woman's Weekly* from the table next to him.

'What are you here for?' I say to him, and he says, 'Behave, Tom,' and returns to reading his magazine.

Another knock on my door. A woman comes in and she smiles when she sees me.

'It's good to see you, Tom.'

She's a woman in her fifties. She's got blonde hair and good skin. She has wrinkles around the eyes and mouth, a sure sign she has been doing a lot of smiling in her life. I know I shouldn't trust that smile. She looks like an older, bustier version of Farrah Fawcett from *Charlie's Angels*.

I don't recognize her. She comes right up to me and gives me a hug. It's nice to be touched by a woman, even if the woman is the enemy.

She's acting like she's met me before. She's very convincing and that distresses me. I have never met her before. I am sure of it. Unless I skipped a memory. When you drink a lot, I guess . . .

No, I've never met her. I've never met her in my life. I've never met her in my life.

Her name is Sarah. Her name-tag is right above her breast. I take my time reading her name-tag. She doesn't seem to mind.

This is an aspect of prison I might be able to cope with.

No.

No. Don't let them use their tricks. Whatever kind of spy she is you must be careful, Tom, not to be suckered in by a beautiful woman. A beautiful woman who is a little past her prime. I've been getting a real taste for those lately. Must be the wisdom they carry. Anyway. Don't get suckered in.

'I'm sorry,' I say. 'Do we know each other? That's not a line, by the way, Sarah?'

'Yes, we know each other, Tom,' she says. It's a good thing I'm a gentleman. If this is a honey-trap I'm already half trapped.

'I don't expect you to remember me,' she says, and I get lost a little in her brainwashing eyes. 'That's okay. A good-looking man like yourself has had to remember a lot of women, I bet.'

I know not to trust her. Still, if this is a charm offensive I'm willing to go along with it for a bit.

'Tom,' she says, looking more serious. 'We've really missed you. You have a lot of friends here.'

'I have friends here?' I ask.

Jesus. I can't have friends here. If I have friends here that would mean they've imprisoned my friends too.

'Yes, and don't worry if you can't remember them either. It doesn't matter.'

Wow. These people are skilled at brainwashing. I look at Sarah and I say, 'Is this a hospital?'

She looks me straight in the eye and says, 'This is a retirement village, Tom.'

That answer makes me feel faint for some reason. I have to sit down for a bit. She offers me a banana and I say, 'No. What is it with you people and bananas?'

'I know you love bananas, Tom.'

Goddammit. How does she know about me and bananas? What kind of spy is she?

'Why are you keeping me in a retirement village?' I ask.

'Why do you think?' she asks me, and I say nothing. I'm waiting for her to answer my question. 'This is where you live, Tom,' she says.

'You're pretending to be a nurse.'

'I'm . . .' and she trails off. 'I work at this place,' she says.

'Are you the cleaner?' I ask her, and she laughs.

'Well, actually, I am. I do a lot of cleaning here. I don't recall it being in the job description.' She smiles and says, 'Do you want to have a look around?'

Instinctively I say, 'No. No, I . . .'

'You okay, Tom? Would you like some water?'

'No—'

'You know these pills you're refusing are good fo—'

'GET OUT!' I yell.

She stands there and nods slowly.

'Okay, well . . . The moment you want some help just sing out. There's a button there you can push, and if I'm on shift I'll come see you as soon as I can. Okay?'

I don't answer her. I just stare at Jethro next to the television. He looks like he's been looked after by someone really well. He used to be in a box in the basement. Have they been under my basement? Just how far does this thing go?

It's late at night. Things are pretty quiet. I'm listening out and all I can hear is the whirring of a fan cooling the room.

It's hard to see anything. I sit up and slip into my clothes as quietly as possible.

I push my way through the door out to a big open hallway. Now I'm in the open area and there are tables and chairs against the walls. There are some lights on, but dimmed. I'm listening out for signs anyone is up. A guard is in the tea room doing a crossword. I sneak past, quiet as a mouse with cotton-wool slippers, and I make it to the lounge area near the doors. I hear a noise and I dive for cover behind a sofa.

I hear a man panting, coming from Zone 1. He's being chased by one of the guards. The other guard gets up to help. They run past me and I sit real still, by the curtains of the window and I have a look outside and all I can see is lit-up gravel and plants in little square lots. There's a door and I try to open it but it is locked shut. I study the lock so I can see what the best tool will be to pick it open, but the noise comes in my direction again.

A bright torchlight shines on a naked old man who looks like he is wearing a big nappy. They corner him and drag him away but he's made some kind of rancid stench. It causes me to cough and one of the guard's ears pricks up. One guard escorts the man with the nappy back to his room.

The other guard shines his torch around, and the gap behind the sofa is too large for me to hide well. I can feel the warmth of the torchlight fix in on me. I face the bright light and the guard holds out his hand and says, 'Hi, Tom. Can't get to sleep?'

I choose not to make a fuss. Not this time. I have to pick my battles. If I appear compliant they won't watch me too hard, so when my real opportunity comes, I can take them by surprise.

He takes me back to my room and I settle in my bed.

'You want a cup of tea, Tom?' the scumbag says to me. Yeah, sure. A cup of cold tea is exactly what I need right now. I say nothing and he tucks me into bed, treating me like a child. A shaft of light from outside shines on to a framed tapestry next to my bed. The tapestry has a picture of a rose on it and Ye Olde writing that says:

> *It's the Songs you Sing*
> *and the Smiles you wear*
> *that make the sun shine everywhere.*

Sunday

The visitor

9.01 a.m.

I wake to a beautiful silhouette at my door. It's Sarah the honey-trap, standing there with her sweet smile, a smile I know I can't trust. Right now I'd happily include her in my lucid dreams in a special guest role. Sarah. Such a nice name. She comes over and sits at the end of the bed. She brings with her a smell, an unexpectedly nice smell of baked bread with cinnamon.

'Would you like a hot-cross bun, Tom?' she says, and she's holding a plate with several hot-cross buns, cut half open, roasting sultanas and a lot of butter and they look delicious.

I refuse to touch them, but the smell is driving me crazy. She takes a hot-cross bun and bites into it. I watch her chew and swallow and I hold my hand out for the same hot-cross bun she has been eating. At least I'm fairly confident they haven't poisoned this one, and boy it tastes good. Makes me want to have another. I mean, what choice do I really have? They are either going to poison me or I will starve to death. Either way achieves the same thing and they smell delicious. I bite into another one and if it is poison it is almost worth it.

'They're nice ones,' Sarah says with a fluttery little wink that gives me an instant morning glory.

'I hear you got up in the night,' she says.

I say nothing back.

'We're having scrambled eggs for breakfast. Do you want to come out and see everyone?'

★

I feel a bit like how I felt on my first day at school. Sarah takes me into a brightly lit room full of a lot of old-aged prisoners. They are sitting at tables, some by themselves, some in groups.

The whole room smells of eggs as guards in blue uniforms hand out plates of scrambled eggs on toast.

An old man comes up to me in a check green shirt. He has a friendly face and he looks like he recognizes me but when he opens his mouth his words are incomprehensible mumbo-jumbo. I smile back to him and nod and that seems to give him comfort and he starts whistling through the gaps in his front teeth and he wanders off again.

'That's Colin,' Sarah says, holding my arm. 'Would you like to sit next to Iona?'

Sarah guides me to a kindly-looking old woman with a beautiful woollen hat on.

'I like your hat,' I say to her. She smiles and stares at me. 'Are you my boy?' Iona says.

'No.' I say. 'I'm Tom.' She smiles and moves some scrambled egg to her mouth, getting most of it, spilling a little on the table.

I hear a loud, violent grunt from behind me. It's a bald man with a backward apron on and really scared-looking eyes. God knows what they've been doing to get him in this state. He grunts again and one of the old ladies barks, 'Shut up, Leonard!' to him. He grunts again and one of the guards goes over to him and pats him on the back gently.

I scan around the room and every person here is old, apart from me, Sarah, and the guards. An old woman is slumped in her chair. She's being spoon-fed some purée by a guard.

Another old man sits staring at the ceiling. I don't know what he sees up there. I look up too, and I can't see anything special. It just looks like a plain white ceiling to me.

Some music is being piped through to make us feel like we are having some kind of 'jolly' experience, and Sarah is singing along while spoon-feeding one of the prisoners. She is singing along with Dionne Warwick: 'What the world needs now, is love, sweet love.'

The man behind me yells again. He makes me jump. It's like he is constantly revisiting a nightmare. 'Shut up!' another prisoner yells and a guard helps him to his feet and ushers him out of the room.

I can't be in this room any more. I get to my feet and head back to where I can find some peace and quiet, in Zone 2.

The drugs they put in the hot-cross bun have hit me hard. It's like I've got narcolepsy all of a sudden. I fell into a deep sleep and when I woke I found myself here, in my prison cell. I go to the door and I try to open it and surprise, surprise, they've locked me in.

'Hey!' I'm yelling.

I bang the door again with everything I've got. I'm pounding the walls and I'm yelling. I swear, I'll smash the fuckin place down if someone doesn't come soon.

I hear a voice from the other side of the room.

'Calm down, Tom. I'm coming in!'

The door unlocks and it is Sarah.

'You locked me in,' I yell at her.

'No, Tom. We don't lock anyone in.'

'It was locked.'

'No. It's just a funny handle. See?'

'I don't want to talk to you,' I yell at her. 'I want Alastair Shook.'

She puts her hand on my shoulder.

'Calm down, Tom.'

'I WANNA SEE SHOOK!' I yell.

'He's doing some other work—'

'I WANNA SEE—'

'Okay. Okay,' she says.

A guard, the big guy with the tattoos, has escorted me into the interview room and we're waiting for Shook. Outside an octogenarian woman is staring in through the window. The guard closes a curtain, shutting her out of sight.

The door opens and in comes Alastair Shook. He is carrying some Manila folders. My files, obviously. 'Hi, Tom,' he says. 'I'm really sorry. I was busy helping someone else.'

He slides back in his chair and I can hear it squeak underneath his fat gut. Squeak, squeak, squeak.

'You wanted to see me?' he says.

His voice has a tone to it. The kind of tone you use when you're trying to hypnotize someone. They're playing the good cop, bad cop game here, but I haven't seen the bad cop yet. It's just a matter of time before they throw me in the room with one of the big boys and they rough me up good.

'You're trying to convince me I'm crazy,' I say to him.

'No,' he says. 'I'm not trying to convince you of anything.'

He's so convincing about not convincing me I can almost buy it. That's how good these people are.

'You okay, Tom?'

'Huh?'

'You seem agitated,' and he taps his hand on the table to imitate what I've been doing. I stare down at the table and I hear this tapping, tapping, tapping, and it's me who's doing it.

'Am I crazy?' I ask him.

'Do you think you're crazy?' he says back to me, in that annoying way that everyone talks to me here.

'No,' I say. 'Well . . . A little but I'm not . . . certifiable,' I say, and he is wearing a crocodile sympathetic smile. 'I've got my quirks,' I say, and he nods his fat head.

'Me too. My wife thinks I've got so many quirks I'm hard to live with.'

A door opens and someone brings us both a plastic cup of water and I can smell the stench of ammonia waft through. I look out the window and an old woman with a zimmer frame and pink track-pants comes into view. She's moving at about a millimetre a minute. A snail could outpace her in a sprint.

'So this is an old folks' home?' I ask.

I watch his little pea-eyes shift from side to side while he decides which lie to tell.

'Yes,' he says.

'Why would you keep me in a place like this?'

'Why do you think?' he bats back at me.

298

'You want me off the streets.'

'Why do you think I want you off the streets?' he says.

'I don't know. I DON'T KNOW. I DON'T KNOW. I DON'T KNOW. I DON'T KNOW—'

'Okay. Stay calm, Tom.'

I don't know what's happening. I don't know what's happening. I don't know what's happening.

'Listen, Tom. I've been looking at your records and we're a bit worried about your heart. You have very high blood pressure.'

I can't believe these guys. They're the ones causing me to have high blood pressure and then they have the nerve to lecture me about it.

'I'm not falling for it. I'm not taking your pills.'

'We want you to be healthy, Tom. Look, I've got a brochure. You can read all about them.'

'I don't want your brainwashing pills!' I yell, and he squirms in his seat again.

'Do you think I'm brainwashing you now?' he asks.

'Of course.'

'What makes you think that?'

I don't answer. He writes on a piece of paper in front of him.

I lean forward in my chair.

'Listen. Can I speak to you without him around?' I say, looking at the guard. Alastair Shook nods and the guard opens the curtain of the window and stands outside, looking in.

'Maybe we can come to an arrangement,' I say to him.

'Oh yes. What sort of arrangement?'

'Well. What do you want?'

'What do I want?' he asks.

'I may have it. I may have what you need.'

'What do you think I need?' he asks, and I look at the window, at the guard staring at us.

I lean in closer to Alastair Shook.

'I'm just saying . . . I have five socks I have no need of.'

He looks at me and blinks. 'Pardon?'

And in that single moment, I realize that Alastair Shook is not part of the inner circle.

'What does he pay you?' I ask him.

'What does who pay me?'

'Valentine. Or Walter Nurse. Or whoever is running this part of the operation. Maybe I can help you out if you do me a little favour.'

'What favour would you like me to do?'

'Either find Frank, or let me out of here.'

'I know where Frank is, and I will ask him to come in again. I promise,' he says, 'but if it's money you're offering me, I don't want it. You can keep your money.'

He puts a banana and a sandwich in front of me. I'm hungry, and it's a good-looking banana. I bet they've injected it with some chemical.

'They're good bananas, Tom,' he says to me. 'Go on. You need your strength.'

'You eat it,' I say to him, and he says, 'Okay,' and he eats half of it, thinking that proves something, but it proves nothing.

'You don't trust me, do you?' he says.

'You're keeping me here, right?'

'Yes. And you don't want to be here.'

'Of course I don't. Jesus!'

'That must be distressing,' he says, and that makes me laugh. I mean, what else can I do but laugh.

'You people are really sick,' I say to him.

'I just want to help you, Tom. I think you're sad about some things that happened in the past.'

'Happened?'

'I'm sorry. I don't understand.'

'Things didn't happen to me. I made them happen. I ruined my life. At least I can take the credit for that. I ruined a lot of people's lives. I ruined Deborah's life. I ruined Frank's life.'

'But you didn't do it on purpose,' he says.

'That doesn't matter. That doesn't come into it.'

'That does make a difference, Tom.'

I don't know what kind of game he's playing. But I know one thing. He's wrong. It doesn't make a difference whether I meant to hurt people or not. I hurt them, regardless of my intentions, and I deserve to pay the price. I just wish Frank didn't have to pay the price as well.

When I sleep Deborah is there with me. She's smiling from the pillow next to me. I keep on opening an eye and I catch her just watching me sleep. I smile to her and I hear a little laugh come out of that beautiful throat of hers, and I run my finger along her eyebrow and lightly touch her eyelid and she's smiling and giggling, and then I hear someone knocking on the door.

It's one of the guards, Marion, with some food.

'You sure you don't want to come out and eat with us, Tom?' she says, and I say nothing.

'I have some good news,' she says to me. 'We've contacted Frank. He's coming in to see you.'

'He's coming here?'

'Yes.'

'When?'

'This afternoon, I think.'

I don't trust these people. They're playing with me. Are they really going to bring Frank to me? And here, of all places? Have they contacted Deborah? Is she a part of this? I have so many questions. I don't understand what is happening.

'When you see Frank,' she says, 'what are you expecting to see?'

'Huh? What kind of question is that?'

'Maybe he'll be different to what you're expecting.'

I say nothing to her. I'm sick of being messed with. I throw my food at the floor. Marion bends down to clean it up and she looks annoyed but I don't care.

There's a window where I can see all the traffic coming and going. I've been checking it constantly. Outside the tattooed guard has a clipboard. He's doing a bit of a roll-call of the oldies by a van. And next to it is a familiar-looking vehicle: a small light-blue truck.

It's the demolition guy.

Has he brought Frank to me?

I race back inside and straight into the main room. I go to a guard and I say, 'Where is he?' but the guard is busy spoon-feeding an old man. I head to Zone 2 and into my room but there's no one waiting for me. I head out into the Quiet Room, and next to that, in the office, I can see them through the window: the demolition guy and some woman talking to Alastair Shook.

I pound on the window. I yell, 'Hey!'

Alastair Shook smiles at me and then goes back to talking to them, completely ignoring me, so I pound again.

'HEY!' I'm yelling and an old man with snow-white hair yells, 'Shut up! This is the Quiet Room!' but I ignore him. I'm pounding on the window and the demolition guy doesn't even look at me, the chickenshit.

'WHERE'S FRANK?' I yell, and the old man comes up to me and he wags his finger like a schoolteacher.

'I can't hear myself think! Sit down!' he says, and inside Alastair Shook closes the venetian blinds and I yell, 'OI!' and the old man next to me says, 'They haven't paid me for weeks, you know? I can't remember the last time I got paid. I work hard all day—'

'You're not working,' I say to him, and he says, 'What are you doing? What are they paying you?' and I pound the window hard and Sarah comes in and puts her arm around me and says, 'Stay calm, Tom. He's here to see you. He'll be with you soon. You just need to calm down,' and she walks me away from there and takes me to my room.

'You okay, Tom?' Sarah asks me.

'I'm fine. Is Frank here?'

She looks at me, like she's not sure what to say. She nods. 'Yes, but . . .'

'But what?'

'He might be different from what you're expecting.'

What are they trying to prepare me for? What have they done? I swear, if they've hurt him, if they've laid a finger on him . . .

'Frank's fine,' she says to me, like she's been reading my mind.

Then she gets a beep on her beeper.

'I have to go, Tom,' she says. 'You wait here, okay? And keep calm. Do you know how to breathe from your diaphragm?'

'Huh? Isn't that a contraceptive?'

'No, your stomach. Breathe from your stomach and keep yourself calm. Will you do that for me?'

I wave my hand in a 'whatever' motion and her beeper beeps again and she's out of there. I look out the window at the carnations and I sit up and try to keep myself calm. Keep calm. Stay nice and calm. Big deep breaths. I'm going to be with Frank soon. Keep breathing, Tom. Everything will be fine. Keep breathing.

Spud

Sunday

The day he ran away

3.39 p.m.

I worked until seven in the morning and my sleeping patterns are completely screwed so I only got a couple of hours' sleep. Kimbo came into the Dwarf to check if I was okay and she stayed with me for an hour or so. She held my hand while my breathing got a bit shallow and she made me a cup of tea and she treated me like a sick person.

I got no time for sickness though. I got no time for any of this, but here I am, driving with Kimbo to Green Acres. I feel half dead and in a different time zone. Kimbo's got me on this St John's Wort stuff which she says will keep me calm but for all I know it's one of those pills that is 99 per cent water. I take them anyway. Hell, I'm taking everything but most of all I'm taking cigarettes and smoking like a ten-pack-a-day man.

We pull in to the old folks' home and park up. Kimbo looks at me and says, 'You okay?' and I can barely find my voice to say, 'Yeah, sure.'

I don't want to go in there. I don't see what it will achieve. Kimbo has banged on to me that it's important that I don't look at Tom as the father who let me down. Instead I should just think of him as a scared old man who needs some help. Easy for her to say.

We head in to reception and we sit in the waiting room and wait for Alastair Shook and Kimbo reads the women's magazines and every part of my body is wanting to run out, get in the Dwarf and leave the place, just leave Kimbo there in the waiting room and she can see Tom if she cares so much about him. But I stay here. I have to face this one. I keep telling myself, 'Take a chill-pill,' and I try thinking of something to relax me so I pick up a magazine and I thumb to the spot where some Hollywood celeb starlet I never heard of has been photographed topless on some private island somewhere when Alastair Shook comes in and says, 'Spud, good to see you.'

As we go through the door into a main area I can feel my breathing quicken. I think I left the Rescue Remedy in the Dwarf.

Shook takes us through a big room full of old people. I don't like being here, so I keep my head down. Kimbo has my arm and she's taking me through, saying, 'You okay, Spud?' and I nod and I look up and I see an old woman holding on to a dummy baby and she tries to get eye contact and I look down at the ground again.

In the middle of the room I see a blonde woman with a group of them. She's reading bingo numbers and helping them with their cards. I feel my breath getting shallower. I'm breaking into a sweat. We make it to a hallway and Shook says, 'Tom's room is down there, but first come into my office for a chat.'

So, we have a little love triangle here: there's me, Kimbo and Alastair Shook in a small room with a computer that looks as old as the piece of shit at our house. Behind Shook is an eye chart and as he speaks I'm running through the test to see how my eyesight is.

Next to the eye chart, behind where Kimbo is sitting, is a window that looks out to a room with a television in it. I watch as an old lady slowly moves past us with little footsteps and it takes her forever just to walk a couple of metres.

Alastair Shook has some forms he wants me to sign.

'We need to give Tom stronger medication for his heart,' he says. 'And we'd like to ease his anxiety levels.'

'Could you ease mine too while you're at it?' I joke, and he hands me a pen and I sign on the dotted line. Shook says he'll stay in contact with us to let us know the medication plan.

'Do what you want with him. I don't care,' I say, but Kimbo says to the doctor, 'We don't want him to be in any more pain than he has to be,' and I laugh. So I'm being spoken for now. That's good. Maybe I don't have to listen then.

'So what's he got? Alzheimer's?' she asks.

'No. On top of some major paranoia, he's suffering from vascular dementia.'

'Vascular dementia,' Kimbo repeats, like she's trying to memorize it for a quiz later.

'I don't have medical records for him. It's most likely that he's had a stroke. He may have had a whole series of smaller strokes. They've caused a blockage and he's not getting enough oxygen to some parts of his brain. Tom's not as advanced as most of our people here. A lot of his brain is perfectly intact. He's pretty sharp in a lot of ways, but some parts of his brain are dying off.'

'Like his memory' Kimbo says.

'Well, that appears to be the case. He thinks he's thirty-nine. He seems to have lost the last thirty or so years of his life.'

There's a loud beep and Alastair Shook pulls out a pager and reads it.

'Poor Tom,' says Kimbo, and I shake my head.

'He's far less fragile than he looks,' I say to them.

Kimbo says to him, 'Can this memory loss be . . . er, you know, what's the word?'

'Retrieved? At this advanced stage I would say it's highly unlikely. Recovery of memory in dementia is extremely rare.'

'How convenient,' I say. 'How convenient for him to forget everything.'

'Jesus. It's not like Tom *chose* this,' Kimbo says to me and I look at her sceptically.

Suddenly there's a loud knock on the window and I jump. It's Tom, watching us from the other side of the window. I feel a real wave hit me, and I look away and Alastair Shook says to us, 'The human brain is capable of anything—' He's interrupted by Tom pounding the window. I'm not going to let him freak me out any more. I'm taking big breaths and Shook goes to the window, says, 'We'll be with you soon, Tom,' and he closes the blinds. There is another knock and I can hear Tom yell, 'OI!' and then there's silence out there.

'Maybe this isn't a good idea,' Kimbo says.

'I want to get this over and done with. It'll be fine,' I say.

'I'll come with you,' Kimbo says and I don't want her to witness me under this kind of pressure so I say, 'I'm okay. It'll be fine,' to her, and Shook's beeper goes off again and he sighs.

'I'm sorry,' he says. 'I have to see one of our nurses.'

He gets out of his seat. 'Tom's room is down the hallway. His photo is on the door,' he says and he shuffles out in a hurry. He pops his head back in.

'One last thing. We try to make sure no one gets upset. It's important you don't say anything to upset him.'

'What if he asks where Spud's mother is?' Kimbo says. 'He's going to get upset if we tell him the truth.'

Shook smiles and says, 'We have a little saying here. "Neither confirm nor deny, nor tell an outright lie." If you think something will upset him, avoid the subject,' and that makes me laugh, because Tom has been avoiding the subject for his whole fuckin life.

I'm walking down the hallway of this place, past what look like hotel rooms. On every door is a picture of an old person and their name.

I have been clear to Kimbo. I said to her, 'I need to do this alone.' I'm dreading arriving at Tom's door. I get to a door with his photo on it. He looks so young in the photo. I knock on his door and I edge into his room and there I see him, this old man, sitting on his bed, staring straight at me.

I don't know what to say to him. I got nothing to say and everything to say.

'Where's Frank?' Tom asks.

I could either laugh or cry and that pulls a laugh out of me, and Tom asks, 'What's funny?' and I look the motherfucker in the eye and I say, 'Nothing. Nothing's funny, Tom.'

'What have you done with Frank?' he says and there's real menace in his voice.

'Don't you recognize me?' I ask him.

'You're pulling down the movie theatre,' he says.

'Don't you recognize me? Beyond that?' I ask, and I look at the guy, and for a second I feel like he can see me; he can see me for the person he let down, badly. But then, just as quickly, that look disappears. He looks at me like I'm some kind of scum he'd rather not deal with, and it makes me feel so . . .

I'm feeling a wave of it . . .

'Who am I?' I'm saying.

I can feel myself getting taken over.

'Who am I?! Who am I?!' I'm saying, and he looks at me with a sneer. Don't let him get to you. Don't let the motherfucker get to you. I can't control myself any more and I'm looking him in the eye and I'm yelling, 'WHO AM I, TOM?'

'HOW SHOULD I KNOW?' he's screaming back.

'YOU NAMED ME!' I'm yelling at him. 'YOU NAMED ME!'

'What are you?' he says. 'Some kind of mental patient?' and I'm losing it, I'm yelling, 'YOU NAMED ME FRANK ARCHIBALD SPOTSWOOD!' and the motherfucker has the nerve to get in my face and grab my collar.

'WHAT HAVE YOU DONE TO MY SON?'

'What have I done?' I'm saying. 'What have you done to me?'

'WHERE'S FRANK?' he says and I look into his eyes.

'I'M HERE, DAD!'

'I don't know you from a bar of soap,' he says. He mumbles some other shit but I can't hear it any more. I got this other noise in my head. This buzzing. The sound of jackhammers to block out his bullshit.

'Listen,' he says, trying to pretend he's being reasonable, after all his bullshit. 'Obviously I've done something that's upset you. But hurting an innocent child—'

'Don't lecture me, Tom. I got no time for your stupid homespun wisdom bullshit,' and now that his nice guy act has failed he's straight back into his true self.

'WHAT HAVE YOU DONE WITH MY SON, YOU FUCK?' he's screaming and I twist the knife in his sewerage-filled heart.

'Oh, I'm keeping him in a cold dark room for the rest of his life,' I say.

Tom slaps me on the top of my head.

This is the real Tom. Never mind all the charisma and all the bullshit. This is how he really thinks of me and I can't contain myself, I can't control it any more, he's ruined my fuckin life, he's ruined everything and he's yelling at me just like he did when I was five, practically spitting in my ear saying, 'How you like that, huh? How you like that?' and here he is, this old man all over the top of me, but I'm no kid any more, so I grab him by the arm and I pull him out of the room. I drag him down the hallway, and now he's getting a taste of his own medicine he doesn't like it. He's trying to get away but he can't bully me any more. I take us straight down the hallway. He's trying to resist me but he's just a weak old man, and I push the prick into a bathroom and he's yelling, 'Help,' like the coward he is.

I take him to the basin and I hold him right up close to the mirror. I can see him looking down so I pull his head back so he's looking straight at the mirror but his eyes are shut and I'm yelling at him, 'Look at yourself, Tom, look at yourself,' and I pull up at his eyebrows and finally the coward opens his eyes and he's finally looking at himself and I see him recognize himself for the first time, and he starts shrieking, he's shrieking at the top of his voice but I don't care. I want him to see the truth. His shrieking gets louder, he's screaming now at the top of his voice, he's screaming so high that I let go of him. What have I done?

Suddenly I see this scared old man screaming for help, screaming so much it scares me and he starts going into a spasm. He's shaking, and falling. I don't want him to die here. He's screaming and Kimbo rushes in and I look around the room and there's a button with 'Nurse' on it and I push it and I'm running my hands in the cold water and patting his face down and Kimbo looks at me with panic in her eyes and I'm washing his face and I don't know what to do any more and as a nurse rushes in I shrink to the wall and they're saying, 'Are you all right, Tom?'

I'm having a full-blown panic attack but of course no one's

asking me if I'm all right; they're all busy helping the frail old man, and I have to get out of here, I have to get out of this place and I run down the hallway. More doctors are coming and a bunch of oldies are following the ruckus and I'm walking as fast as I can to get out of this place. I have to get out of here before I faint. I need a paper bag. I get to the exit door of the main room but I don't remember the code any more. What's the code? I'm panicking now, pulling the door but it won't open and Kimbo's with me now, pushing the buttons, taking me with her, out of the room, outside, and everyone is watching me. I feel like I'm four years old and I run to the truck and Kimbo opens the door for me. She helps me into the passenger's seat and I reach into the glove box and I pull out the paper bag and I'm breathing in and out, in and out, and Kimbo saying, 'It's okay, He's all right,' and I'm yelling, 'Get me out of here. Get me out of this fuckin place!!!' and she starts the engine.

I'm trying to keep up with the bus but the bus gets away from me. I run to the next stop hoping that the bus will stop there and I can get on but when I get to the next stop there is no one waiting and the bus carries straight on in front of me.

I'm looking at the back window of the bus and I can see his hat, the back of his head, but he doesn't even turn around. I watch his head get smaller and smaller as the bus shrinks into the distance.

When I get home my mother is smiling but she has tears in her eyes. She has a new dress on. She gives me a hug. She doesn't say much. All she says is, 'He's gone, Frank. He's gone.' She pulls an apple crumble out of the oven, and she puts a portion in a bowl for me. I don't know why she thinks crumble will fix it all. She goes to her room and she doesn't come out for three days.

Tom

Sunday

Whisky smuggler

4.33 p.m.

I'm on a floor.

A bathroom floor.

I can hear voices.

Someone is standing over my body saying, 'Tom?'

Someone is holding my wrist. Someone has their hand near my mouth. There's a cold flannel on my face.

I can hear another voice saying, 'Tom? Tom?'

I can hear footsteps coming down the hallway. I can hear an old woman's voice saying, 'What's going on?'

My eyes blur into focus and I see faces, so many faces staring down at me.

A guard helps me to my feet and asks me if I'm all right.

'Yeah, yeah,' I say and I feel a hand holding my hand. I release my grip and I run, and I've got them running after me.

I'm running down the hallway to the end of Zone 2, to the door that leads outside and to the fence that keeps us locked in here, and I see the man in his truck.

They're taking Frank away from me. They're taking him away, and I'm seeing little Frank, running away from me at school. I'm chasing him and I'm passing him and I'm running away from him and he's crying.

The truck leaves the prison and I watch it drive away and turn into a little dot and I feel some arms around me.

I feel someone slip something into my mouth and as I blank out all I can see is Frank.

All I can see is his little face, and I can hear myself calling his name to anyone who can hear it. 'Frank!' I'm yelling.

'Frank!'

'Fraaaaaaaaa—'

I've taken their pills. I don't care any more. If they want to feed me pills I'll eat their stupid pills. What difference does it make? Maybe if they're going to keep me there it's in my own interests to be brainwashed by them. It might make life easier, right?

I'm sitting in a semicircle of oldies. Some of them just stare at the ground. A woman starts talking to me. She asks me if I have her marbles.

'No,' I say. 'I haven't got your marbles.'

There's a poor old lady across from me, and she's pissing her pants, and I yell, 'Nurse,' and no one comes. I yell it again and one of the old women says, 'Bessie's wet herself,' and she starts laughing, and the woman next to her gives her a little slap. A man nearby is sniggering. I look at the old lady who has pissed her pants, and she's crying. So I go over to her, and I give her a hug, and I go and find a towel and I put it on her lap and dry her off a little. Don't get me wrong. I won't be helping with number twos, but someone has to show a little compassion in this world, surely.

When Sarah comes over and sees what I have done she says, 'Thank you, Tom. It's good to see you being so helpful.' I wish the guards round here were just plain mean instead of pretending to be nice.

I'm in the Quiet Room. They have a TV on permanent mute. They've switched it to the racing channel thinking that may keep me entertained. But it's not the same when you've got no money invested. I'm staring at the horses running around the track and instead of feeling the thunder of the hooves, the excitement of it all, I just feel flat and depressed.

I hear some footsteps coming my way and the pleasant smell of perfume, and I look up and there she is, Linda the turncoat, with a bunch of flowers, bloodshot eyes and that beautiful mane of red, red hair.

We're in my room and I've closed the door and we're hugging and I've got my hands around her neck and my face pressed to her face. My fingers are sliding down her back and they slip further to her bra-strap and she says, 'Tom,' and I shift my hands up a little and let them rest on her neck.

We hold each other and I can feel her tears coming down her cheek, dripping on to my neck.

I know they've sent her in to work on me, but I feel conflicted. I'm grateful to see her and I'm excited down below too. I press myself against her leg just to let her know what she's doing to me and I know she's turned on too, and maybe, just maybe this is the sort of prison where a man can find a kind of relief he won't find in other places of incarceration. She sits beside me on the bed. I pull her close and kiss her neck and I start to move down to her breasts and just when I'm going crazy with excitement she pulls back and says, 'No, Tom. That's enough.'

I pull away and I stare at her guilt-ridden face. She sits next to me on my bed, and she takes a tissue from her bag.

'I got you a peace offering,' she says, and she pulls a small hip-flask of whisky from her handbag.

'Wow,' I say. 'If you can get that through security you could bring in all sorts of things.'

'What do you want me to bring you?' she says, smiling.

Some kind of weapon so I can get out of this place.'

'What weapon?' she says. 'Lead pipe, a candlestick, a spanner?'

'Hey, your weapons are all from, what's the name of it?'

'Cluedo,' she says, smiling. She undoes the top of the whisky bottle and fills up a cap and offers it to me.

'Are they watching us?' she asks.

I shrug my shoulders. 'There may be a little camera in the TV.'

'Is that why you've got a towel over it?' she says, snorting.

'It's all a comedy to you, is it? This is funny?'

'No, Tom,' she says, and she's crying again. 'I knew I shouldn't 've worn eyeliner today,' she says, wiping her sleeve.

I take the bottle off her and have a second shot. It tastes good.

'Tom, don't go too hard on it or they'll be on to you. If I'm going to smuggle in whisky you need to hide it well.'

'I'm an expert in hiding my own drunkenness,' I assure her, and she takes the bottle back off me and has a shot herself.

'They've got Frank,' I say to her.

'Frank is safe,' she says, trotting out the party line.

'How much did they pay you?' I ask her. She shakes her head.

'Tom. I . . . I'm so sorry.'

'Apology not accepted,' I say, and I'm serious. I'll let her visit me, but I won't give her peace of mind. Not after what she did.

'Can you tell me what's going on?' I ask her.

'You're in a retirement home,' she says.

'And why's that? I'm half the age of the people here.

'You are a very attractive man,' she says. 'You had me fooled.'

'What do you mean by that?'

'Nothing. I mean nothing. I'm here for you, Tom. I'm going to come once a week, if you let me.'

I look at her beautiful green eyes. I'm attracted to the little wrinkle lines around her eyes and mouth. I'd love to lick the lipstick off those lips. Anything to take me away for a moment . . .

I sigh, and she puts her hand on my back, and I put my hand on her knee. She's crying as I slide my hand up her thigh.

'I think that's against the rules.'

'Since when did you give a shit about rules,' I say, and she lets me slide my hand right up her leg. She lets me kiss her neck, before she stands up. 'This is very confusing. I'm finding this very confusing,' she says, and she sits on the empty seat near the bed.

'I need you to get me out of this place,' I say to her, and she says, 'I'm sorry, Tom. I don't think I can do that.'

I turn to face the wall and I say, 'Thanks for visiting. I want to be alone now,' and I wait for her to leave.

Twenty weeks later

Swimming with the turtles

I have to admire the genius of Robert Valentine. If you really want a person to go missing, put them where you already have ample security and you can poison their food. Forget torture camps. There are a hundred legitimized torture camps in every city. They are called retirement villages.

I know they are trying to convince me I am insane. Whatever they are putting in the food is having some effect because I am having the occasional moment of weakness where I am inclined to go along with it. I mean, this place is insane. But if I truly was insane, why wouldn't I be in an insane asylum? The people here are insane, but there are a lot of insane people my own age they could have put me with.

But Robert Valentine is much cleverer than that. No one will ever think to look for me in a retirement village. The only person I get visits from is the turncoat who brought me in here. The outside world has no idea I am here and if they did know they wouldn't give a damn anyway. It's a brilliant, brilliant plan. Keep him here with the old fogeys who are losing their marbles.

Poor old Norma. I think she thinks I'm her husband, by the way she looks at me. Not that I can ever know what she thinks because the conversation always goes the same. She staggers over to me and she starts to say something.

'Do . . .' she says and after one word she's lost for all other words. She is trying to find the words and she can never find them. Sometimes I can't face her but I'm so used to it now that I've started helping her. I give her a hug and I sit her down and she's very quiet sitting next to me while I read the newspaper, not that I spend much time on that. The news is too depressing but there's always sport and there's always the Target.

Poor April. She's taken her top off again and she's breastfeeding a soft toy. The staff just let her do it. Never mind that the rest of us have better things to do than be forced to look at a ninety-year-old woman's breasts. I've learned not to look in so many places, at so many things. This is a place where it pays to keep the blinkers on. I'm thinking of growing some cataracts.

'Tom, you got a visitor,' says Sarah, and Linda comes in looking pleased with herself.

'Did you get it?' I ask her.

She nods and shows me the suitcase in its full Lethalite glory.

'That was some adventure,' she says, handing it to me. 'I had a bus go past me while I was in there. Gave me a cheap thrill.'

I wait until Linda is looking away and I go to work on the combination. When I open the case a pungent odour escapes and stinks out the room. Linda has to open a window. I shouldn't have mixed the worn socks with the clean ones.

I shield the contents from Linda and I count the number of socks and it appears she hasn't opened the case, but I won't know until I count my money later. I pull out my hip-flask and say to it, 'Good to see you again.'

I look at Linda and she smiles and pulls a small bottle of whisky from her bag. I put the towel on top of the TV and I tip out the water from my hip-flask and fill it up with the good stuff and Linda and I both have a swig.

'Oh boy,' I say. I've been waiting for that.

'Take it slow, Tom,' she says, and I say to her, 'You know I don't live in the slow lane,' and she laughs as I take another swig of fiery heaven.

'You know, I know where you can get some harder stuff,' I say to her. 'Sodium pentobarbital. It's a horse tranquilizer. Otherwise known as the purple death. It can kill a horse in fifteen seconds. If you could get me some of that I'd really appreciate it.'

'I'm not getting you the purple death, Tom.'

'Why not? You think I like it here in prison?'

'You seem to like Sarah,' she says.

Damn. I was hoping that wouldn't come up.

'Listen. I won't lie to you. There's a shared attraction–'

'Oh, you really like to share around your attraction,' she jokes. 'Do you really want to be . . . what's the word?'

'Euthanized?' I say.

'Tranquilized?'

'Anaesthetized,' I say. 'And the answer to all three is yes. Yes. Yes.'

'You're not happy here,' she says, and I'm not going to sugar-coat it for her.

'You could always get me out of here,' I say. She squirms in her seat and I drop the subject.

'I wish I could be in Morningtown. I wish I could see the place I grew up in. They won't even let me take van trips here. I want to see my old house, my old school. I want to be near The City. I want to . . . Never mind,' I say, and I sigh.

I open the case again and I see my lint roller. 'Hey!' I say to it and I pull it out and de-lint my suit. I fumble around in there; underneath the underwater camera and a bunch of receipts and marshmallow eggs I see a couple of yellow paper pouches, and I pull them out.

'Are they photographs?' Linda asks. 'Can I see them?'

'No,' I say to her. 'No you can't.'

I'm looking through the photos with Sarah and Alastair Shook. There's a picture of me, age four, standing by the letterbox at our house. I'm holding on to a rolled-up newspaper. I had the job of collecting the newspaper and putting money in the milk bottles. Sometimes I would take a little money and we'd have no milk that day. I was a white-collar criminal at a young age.

'Look at your knees,' Sarah says and in the picture there's lots of puppy fat around my knees.

'I used to watch the cars from there all morning long,' I say to them. 'That was when you could tell the make of a car just by looking at it. Now all the cars look the same.'

'They sure do,' Sarah says and Alastair Shook makes me look at the next photo. It's a photo of me aged five, in a full teapot pose.

'Ha!' I laugh. 'We called this photo Camp Tom. That's because I look so camp,' and Sarah and Alastair Shook laugh.

'I think you look very cute,' she says.

We went to Lake Mackenzie and it was the most beautiful lake you ever saw. It was reflective. You could stare down at the lake and see the mountains and it was like you were looking straight at them.

They show me another picture and I'm a teenager in this one, looking rebellious in my old school uniform. In the next photo I'm an older teenager and I've clearly been at a party because my eyes look glazed and my jaw muscles seem to have slackened and I remember this photo well too – my seventeenth birthday, when I started experimenting with what I could get away with as an adult member of society.

Next Alastair Shook gives me a photo where I'm in my late twenties. A very smart photo taken on a very special day, my wedding night, and Deb and I are hamming it up, dancing on our wedding table. It was a trestle table and everyone thought it would collapse, but we were too twinkle-toed for that. I cried during my vows that day.

The next photo was taken eleven years ago. Deborah took this one. Frank's in his cradle and I'm approaching him with a pair of scissors. A very unfair photo. It betrays the reality of the situation. Frank still had his hospital tag around his ankle; I was just cutting it off while he was asleep. Deb thought that photo was funny and showed it to a lot of people. I was good-humoured about it, even though I knew I was being grossly misrepresented.

Next here's one of me and Deb and Frank, travelling on the train. All three of us used to go on a train out to West Bay. The train ride went through six tunnels. Frank loved it.

'You look a bit grouchy, Tom,' Sarah says.

'That's how I always look in photos,' I say.

Next Alastair Shook opens up the other roll of film, the one I don't like to look at.

He shows me a photo and he says, 'What's this?' and in this one there's a guy who looks like Frank. Is that him? Frank looks a bit like a teenager in this one.

'Where is he? Where is this place?' I say, and I look behind Frank and it definitely is Deb's house. Are they keeping him at the old house?

'What's going on?' I say to Sarah, and she holds my arm.

'What about this photo?' Alastair Shook says to me, and he shows me a picture of . . . of someone who looks a bit like Frank, but he's too old to be Frank. It must be . . . Must be one of Frank's cousins on Deb's side.

'Who is that?' I say to Alastair Shook.

'You don't recognize him?' he says.

'Who's this guy?'

'His name is Frank,' Alastair Shook says to me.

To my knowledge Frank doesn't have a cousin Frank, unless someone has come out of the woodwork that I don't know about. I think they're messing with me. They're definitely messing with me.

Shook shows me a picture of Frank, my Frank, aged about four and in front of Deb's mother's plastic white Christmas tree.

'I recognize that,' I say. 'I hated that Christmas tree at the time,' I say, 'but it's nice seeing it again.'

'How many years ago is that?' Sarah asks.

'I don't know. That's about five or six years old I guess.'

'He looks a lot like you there,' Sarah says.

'I look at him and I see his mother.'

'What about this one?' Alastair Shook says to me, and there's this photo of an old man sitting next to an old couple and they're having a cup of tea. Pretty weirdly they've put it in with my photos.

I shrug my shoulders.

'Who's this a photo of?' they ask me.

'No idea,' I say.

'Have a closer look at his face,' Shook says, pointing at the man.

331

I look closer and whoever he is he looks like he's got the weight of the world on his shoulders.

'He looks a bit like you,' Shook says, and I stare at the guy and say, 'Maybe. I don't really see it,' but it's true that he does look a tiny bit like me.

'Who is this guy? My uncle? Who is he?' I ask, and Sarah says nothing.

Shook says, 'How do you feel when you look at this photo?'

I don't get why they're making me look at this photo.

'I mean, what am I supposed to feel? How do you feel when you look at a photo of someone you don't know?' I say to him, and he writes down some notes in his little notepad.

'What about this one?' Shook says, and the man in the photo looks very like me, except he has grey hair. He looks about fifty or sixty. Shook holds it in between a recent photo of me and that photo of the guy who looks like my uncle and he's asking me to look at all three at once and they're trying to brainwash me. They're trying to brainwash me, right now. I slam my hand on the table.

'WHAT ARE YOU DOING?' I'm yelling.

'Calm down, Tom,' Shook says.

'GET OUT!' I'm yelling. 'GET OUT!' and Sarah tries to rub my back and I shake myself free and I say, 'STOP FUCKING WITH ME! STOP FUCKING WITH ME!' and they put away the photos and they leave and Sarah says to me as she leaves, 'I'll give you a little time to yourself, but just press the button if you want to talk—'

'BITCH!' I'm yelling at her. 'BITCH!'

'It's okay, Tom,' she says. 'I'm on your side,' and I put my hands over my ears because I don't want to hear any more lies today.

It's the middle of the night and I'm counting the socks in the case and they are all there. That either means that Linda couldn't crack the combination lock or that I can trust her. I'm not sure which. My socks are getting pretty smelly in there. I could do with a peg on my nose as I go about my business.

I pull out the underwater camera. It's a funny-looking thing. A lime-green camera inside a see-through plastic case. It was a gift from my father. It has undeveloped photos on it from six years ago. Undeveloped photos from when Deborah and I were still together. We were in Samoa, on holiday. We weren't getting on particularly well but we were on holiday and I was in love with her; I've always been in love with her.

We stayed at a resort where you got to swim with giant turtles. They were huge creatures with massive shells. They came right up to us and we could feed them. I put my head under the water with my snorkel and I took a lot of photos of Deb feeding the turtles and swimming with them. I can't attest to the quality of the photos, I expect everything will be out of focus. I should have developed them at the time, but because the writing was on the wall for our marriage when we broke up I could never bring myself to develop them.

I put the camera next to my bed and I hide my suitcase high up in my wardrobe, shielded by my suits and in the dark. I know nothing is safe here but I think it will be safer there than under my bed. Now that I've got money again I will have to pick a target. I'm sure there is someone here whose loyalty to Robert Valentine could be bought at a reasonable price.

Spud

A new home for the dinosaur

My new mobile phone ring sounds like the music was written by a nineteenth-century composer on acid and then played on one of those little plastic toy synthesizer key rings they sell for five bucks as a Santa stocking filler. It's an awful ring but I'm not brainy enough to figure out how to change it. I see Muzz's name and I look at the clock and I realize I've slept in by about twenty minutes. I pick it up and say sorry to him and he tells me to get my hand off it and he'll be over in ten.

I'm still in a daze. This bed feels more comfy than what I'm used to and I roll over and it looks like I've slept in Kimbo's bed again. That's five times in the last month. She's already headed off. I hope she doesn't have any regrets. I crawl out of there and walk down past Lucy's room. I knock on the door and say, 'We're leaving in ten,' and she charges out of bed like the world will end unless she gets up. It's one of her weird motivational 'getting up' techniques. She's a weird kid. Must take after her mother. I head into the bathroom and I open the medicine cabinet and I stare at a bottle of pills.

I'm cutting the pills in half on the chopping board. Lucy comes in and I scoop them into my hand so I don't have to explain myself. The toast pops and Lucy asks me where she put her shoes. 'I got no idea,' I say and she heads out and looks for them. I take half a pill and eat a piece of toast as a chaser. I'm not sure what effect these little guys will have, but I'm willing to give it a go. I feel weird

337

though, like some kind of mental failure. Then I tell myself to get over it.

I mean, Jesus, I ate a little pill. It's not like I'm walking around with a security blanket, sucking my thumb or anything.

Muzz and me are unloading wood and steel from his truck. Lucy is helping, and she's really surprising me today. She insists on getting on one end of a piece of wood that I'm sure will be way too much for her but she takes it fine. We carry it all the way to its final resting place without a stop or anything. She's getting real strong. Muzz jokes that he'd better treat her real nice from now on, otherwise she'll give him the bash one day. We get through all the wood pretty quick and clear the truck. Muzz hops in and Lucy and me hop in the transporter.

Traffic is quiet on the motorway this morning. Somehow Muzz has ended up in front of our little convoy. The transporter is handling nice but the gears are a little tricky. Lucy is keen for me to pass Muzz's truck so I pull out and overtake him in a passing lane and Lucy winds down her window and shakes her fist at him and Muzz pretends to be annoyed that he has been passed. Those two really set each other off. Gives me a giggle, the way they carry on. I'm waiting for the pill to kick in but so far I don't feel anything. I'm not feeling sleepy, which is good.

We take the turn-off past Brighton, and the final road has a wicked rise and a dip. I'd given Lucy a few fun rides up and over the bump here in the Dwarf. This transporter is too heavy for fun and games though.

Another couple of miles and we're here at the farm. Lucy hops out and opens the farm gate for us and Muzz and me roll our trucks in, taking care not to get stuck in the boggy patch right near the start of the paddock.

Lucy runs in the long grass as we head to the big corrugated-iron shed. The grass is getting so long there it dwarfs her and I watch her run and dive into it. She loves coming out here. I've definitely

338

got a tomboy on my hands. I sneeze as I head towards the shed. Having a yard here has been a great move, but the hay fever is a pisser.

Muzz peels off to the shed and I head to where T-Rex has been grazing. I hop in the old beast and get her motor running. She sounds pretty good. I leave her idling and I head to the shed.

The cicadas are almost drowning out T-Rex. I can't believe the number of them out here. It's a full orchestra of percussion and the sun is intense too. The long grass makes me sneeze again and the smell of the place is starting to become familiar. It's a mixture of manure and fertilizer. I have to admit, I am almost growing to like it.

Lucy is sprinting my way. She's covered in grass, head to toe, and we walk together to the shed.

It's a whopper of a shed. The architecture is very 'do-it-yourself'. The corrugated iron is different shades and colours. It's sturdy, apart from the roof. A lot of the nails have come off up there and the farmer has put rocks on it to weigh it down.

We head past all my outside stuff: thirty toilets, some in mint condition, some needing some work, five baths, four upside down and one that I'm in the process of turning into an outside bath.

We head inside and Kimbo is on the phone. She's talking numbers down the phone line. She's a good poker player is Kimbo. She's raising the stakes and it sounds like they're going for it. She's wearing her reading glasses. I never thought I'd find glasses sexy, but on her they really give me the horn, not that now is the best time for such thoughts. She hangs up and says, 'I just sold two urinals.'

'Really? How much?'

'I gave him them for fifteen hundred,' she says, and I'm impressed. I woulda settled for twelve hundred.

'Nice one,' I say, and I can see she's all pumped from a sale. I like it when she gets the fire in her belly.

'I see you snuck in last night,' she says.

'Musta been sleepwalking,' I say, and she looks to make sure Lucy is well out of earshot before she jokes, 'Sleepwanking more like.'

'Takes two to tango,' I say, and she raises her eyebrow.

'Taken your pills this morning?' she asks.

'Yeah.'

'Feel anything?' she says, with her concerned face.

I shake my head.

'Make sure you eat well today,' she says.

'Yes, Mum,' I say.

'Yes, Boss,' she corrects me, and it's a joke that carries pretty much the truth. I've stopped fighting it and I have to admit, life is a hell of a lot easier when I just let her run things the way she wants to. I still get a lot of time to myself. Brenda said if Kimbo was going to become my boss in work it was important that she wasn't the boss everywhere else too, but I tried that and I'm okay with her being the boss. I make more money this way and I don't have to hold so much crap in my head.

I head past the movie projector and the Nibble Nook to the back of the shed, past Lucy who is already fiddling with the door. I watch her operate the latch. It's quite fiddly but she manages to swing it open. Muzz is standing inside the truck on the other side, ready to get down to business. The sunlight streams into the building and the movie theatre chairs glow bright red.

We've loaded a truckful of chairs. Muzz is roping them in while Lucy and I have one side each of a urinal. I'm carrying most of the weight but she's doing pretty well for her size.

'Men are so lucky,' she says after we've hoisted it up on to the back of the truck.

'Why?' I ask her.

'You get to piss standing up,' she says.

'We're pretty lucky all right,' Muzz says, putting the urinal in place, 'but we have to put up with your nagging.'

'I'm not going to nag anyone,' she says, walking off to pick up the next urinal, and she stands there waiting for me.

'You'll nag,' I say. 'It's in your genes.'

'I'm going to have someone nagging me,' she says, all proud, like being nagged is a badge of honour.

★

We're convoying back into town. I got T-Rex in the back of the transporter. We're taking a small detour at the Shamrock Inn, one of those pretend Irish bars. We knock on the door and no one is answering.

'You sure this is the place?' Muzz says.

'Yeah, definitely.'

'Well, what do we do?'

I phone the boss and ask her. 'Just drop them off at the front door,' Kimbo says.

We drag out the urinals and leave them outside the front door of the pub. They look like they're asking for trouble, just sitting there. If I was a passer-by I would be real tempted to piss in them. Just thinking about it makes me want to spring a leak.

'Maybe we should turn them around,' I say to Muzz. 'We don't want to tempt the public.'

Muzz has a big grin and he helps me pick them up and turn them round, and we leave them there, on the street.

Traffic's not too bad as we head down the motorway. Lucy is having fun on the CB radio, talking to Muzz in the truck in front of us. She's got a whole lot of tomato jokes.

'What's red and invisible?' she says.

'I dunno. What's red and invisible?' Muzz says in a crackly voice on the radio.

'No tomatoes,' Lucy says. 'How do you fix a broken tomato?' she says.

'Dunno,' says Muzz.

'Tomato paste,' Lucy says and follows it up with a big ba-doom-tish.

'Jesus, that's a bad one,' Muzz says.

This is a pretty drive. We're going past Rabbit Island to the left. They have a lot of traffic accidents round here, because the view is so nice people stop looking at the road. I'm looking at the side mirror, at T-Rex on the back. I'm feeling a bit sad about it, truth be known, not that I'll admit it to anyone. It's okay. She's going to a good home.

'Why did the tomato blush?' Lucy says to the radio.

'She saw the salad dressing,' I say. 'I told you that one.'

'Enough jokes already,' Muzz is protesting on the radio.

We have arrived in Foxtown, a sleepy little town basking in the heat. The pace of life is a lot slower here. A few retirees are taking an afternoon stroll, slowly going nowhere. A family walk around in shirts and shorts and a couple of kids ride their bikes on the wrong side of the road, no bike helmets or anything. The main shopping area looks about one block long. Everyone is checking out the trucks like they're the most interesting thing they've ever seen.

It's obvious which building is the Majestic. It's an art deco number. Run-down, but clearly the owners are in the process of sprucing her up. There's a guy up doing some work on an arch window at the top. It looks like a nice place.

A man in his early fifties is sitting out the front. He's got a big goofy smile on his face. He comes out to the truck and shakes my hand. 'Spud, is it? I'm Roger.'

Roger Laing is dressed in practical clothes, but his practical clothes look pretty clean. He hasn't exactly got the hands of a labourer. He looks like a decent sort though.

We open up the back of the truck and he has a big smile that looks like it might set permanently when he sees the chairs. He's got a team of locals, who all come and shake our hands. 'You've brought some help of your own,' he says looking at Lucy, who is staring up at the movie theatre.

The unloading of the chairs runs pretty smoothly. The guys here are good sorts and they're well organized too. We load out of the truck and they take the chairs and once the truck is empty Muzz and me and Lucy head in there and help out. The chairs look like they were born to be in this place. Lucy points out that they've made a mistake with the chairs. They've lined them all up directly in front of each other so if you sat and watched a show and someone tall is in front, you're shit out of luck. They've already started screwing some of them in but Roger Laing says, 'She's right,' and he says to me, 'You've got a young engineer on your hands,' and she does make me feel proud.

The first load of chairs are all in place. They still need to be bolted down but the hard part of the job is done. Roger Laing has beers for everyone and all the workers sit in the chairs and knock a few back. I have to say, it feels good having them here. They look like they were made for this place. I'm looking up at the ceiling and there's a nice ceiling rose that I reckon would be worth about two grand. I joke to Roger Laing if ever this one comes down he knows who to call, and he says he's hoping that will never have to happen, to which I reply, 'Everything comes down, eventually.'

He gives me a little programme of the movies they are planning on playing here. They got some copies of some oldies but goodies, and playing a month from now is one of my old favourites: *Butch Cassidy and the Sundance Kid.* I'm tempted to come up and make a day trip of it.

I'm supposed to be careful about drinking with my new medication, so I just have one. I've been told I'll be a cheap drunk now. Roger pays in cash, I say goodbye to Muzz, and me and Lucy hit the road for Anderson's Quarry.

Lucy is napping in the front. Her feet are pushing against my leg. Kimbo calls in with the plan and she's asking about the meds and if I notice any difference and if I'm driving careful and I don't know whether to thank the meds or whether to thank her but today I'm having a real nice day. I still feel a bit weird about giving the beast a send-off though. Kimbo gets off the phone and Santana comes on the radio and I pump up the volume and drive along to some sonic sounds from a guitar legend. I check T-Rex in the side mirror and she looks kind of stoic, sitting up the back there.

I got Lucy navigating. There's a turn-off from the motorway that cuts through farmland and turns into a windy road heading directly for the coast. I got the window down and I can smell the salt air before I get there. We pull on to a dirt road and after a short drive

343

we see the sea for the first time in a while. A wind has picked up and the ocean is swirling today.

We come over the hill and see the quarry in front of us. A lot of piles of gravel and some good cliffs of granite that have been dug in and hollowed out for quite a few decades by the look of it. We pass a sign that tells us that rocks could fall on us at any moment. No kidding. There's a lot of sheer granite to our right as the road winds closer to the sea. We pass a building with a rock crusher and conveyer belt and a few abandoned trucks, excavators and diggers.

Another couple of ks and we arrive at our destination. A big old green truck full of dirt sits next to a digger. Behind them, a steep grey cliff is waiting to be belted into submission.

We pull out some sandwiches and Lucy and me munch away and look up at the cliffs of granite above us. They go high enough to block out the sun. We finish our sammies and our contact, Guy, isn't here yet so I hop in the cab of T-Rex, start her up and I back her off the truck. I figure Guy will want to see her up and running so I've attached the ball and I track along to the rock face and I leave her running and have a good listen to her.

After clearing through some crap she starts running smoothly, no signs of slopping or anything. I check the ground and there's the two familiar leaks which aren't too bad. Apart from that she sounds like she used to back in her heyday.

We see a dusty old four-wheel drive come over the hill and the new owner, Guy, comes over to the machine and looks up at her and I can see the admiration in his eyes. He's an old-timer. I imagine he'd need a bit of help from some younger ones out here.

I talk him through some of T-Rex's quirks. He thinks she's a beauty too. I show him how to work her. I tell him about the gears sometimes sticking. I show him the leaks that he should keep an eye on. He's worked a machine a bit like this back in the day so it makes it a pretty easy conversation. I show him where the nipples are and I teach him the basics.

He asks to see her up and running and I climb in and I gib up and get side-on to a bit of the quarry he reckons is solid enough. I slowly drop the ball and get her swinging and I punch into a mountain of rock and the whack of it is very different from a building. T-Rex will have to get used to the difference. When I pull down a fifty-year-old building that was built of sturdy stuff I think that's a job, but the cliff face in front of me has been around for a few million years. I have a feeling T-Rex will have a bit of a job on her hands trying to conquer this hunk of rock. It feels good though, slamming the ball into the mountain, one last time for the old team.

I hop out of the cab and I feel like I'm stepping out of one life and heading to another. Guy jumps in the cab and he looks like he knows what he's doing. He works her pretty good, lifts the gib, swings the ball and knocks down a good clump of rock. He gets out of the cab and he gives me cash, the exact amount.

I ask Lucy to stand in front of T-Rex so I can get a photo of the old warhorse in her new home. Guy takes a photo of both of us in front of the beast and I wish I'd worn sunglasses because I feel like I'm on the verge of a blub. I feel pretty embarrassed and nervous that I'll completely lose it but Guy looks sympathetic. I think he's probably been through this before himself.

It's not easy saying bye to a machine. I manage to hold it together good enough not to lose it in front of anyone. As we hop in the transporter I shift the mirror so I don't have to look at the old dinosaur any more and Lucy asks me if I'm all right. I wink at her and tell her I'm 'good as gold'.

Lucy is having another sleep, and I feel a bit like I've lost a leg, not that I'll admit that to anyone. I look over at Lucy, lying on her back, her head resting by the passenger door. I've slept in that position so many times myself. Christ, she's really turning into a chip off the old block. Maybe she does have a future in demolition. I don't know whether to encourage or discourage her. She's a smart one. I just have to let her be herself and she can make her own decisions.

I get to the top of a hill and the sun is starting to set. I got a nice view out in front of me of the great plains. I can hear a funny sound underneath the stereo so I turn the music down for a second, and underneath the hum of the truck I can hear Lucy snoring like a trooper. It's nice to have her with me.

I'm back in town, dropping the transporter off at Muzz's. Kimbo is here, waiting for me in the Dwarf. I pull up next to her and wind down my window and I get the weirdest feeling she looks happy to see me. I'm not used to it. Me and the Goose hop in. I'm waiting for Kimbo to give me a hard time about losing my machine, but she's all nice about it. I try to pretend I don't give a shit but it's a waste of energy – she can see right through me.

Fuck, I feel like a dog died.

Return of the Night Mail

As we arrive home Kimbo spots a car parked on the wrong side of the road, and there's someone drinking in it. We pull into the driveway and I'm feeling pretty whacked, but in a good mood. Lucy races ahead of us to the front door.

'Hey, about last night. You okay with that?' I ask Kimbo.

She looks uncertain. She nods and says, 'Small steps, Spud,' before she's interrupted with a big, 'Spud! Kimbo!' from Lucy.

There's a big parcel on the doormat of the front door, beautifully wrapped, with a ribbon and everything. I don't remember ordering anything. There's no name on it, nothing, but it's wrapped in really nice paper. It's clearly a present.

'Is this from you?' I ask Kimbo and she shakes her head.

We take the thing inside and put it on the kitchen table. 'Can I open it?' Lucy says.

'Sure, but I don't know who it's for,' I say.

Lucy is not a careful unwrapper. She rips in and opens up a big red box, gleaming and new-looking.

'Wow,' she says, and stares at the contents. It's a train set. The Night Mail. Looks immaculate. High-quality workmanship, the full deal.

'Is this from you?' Kimbo asks me, and I shake my head. I'm mystified.

There's a knock on the door.

'Must be Santa Claus,' Kimbo jokes.

'He's a bit early,' I say, and I head to the front of the house. I open the door and it's Linda, the redhead receiver. She looks sheepish.

'I'm sorry. You weren't home so . . .'

'Nice train set.'

'It's from Tom,' she says.

Ha. The ghost of Tom strikes again. Kimbo comes to the door to see what is going on.

'If it's from him I don't want it,' I say to Linda.

'Well, he bought it for you.'

Lucy comes to the front door now, holding on to a little train. I can see that giving it back won't be so easy.

Linda introduces herself to Kimbo.

'You wanna come in for a cup of tea?' Kimbo asks her, without checking if I'm okay with it.

'Actually, I could do with a glass of wine,' Linda says, and she smiles at me.

We got Lucy setting up a train set in the next room. Linda is sitting at the kitchen table, knocking back a wine with Kimbo.

'So . . . where do you fit in?' Kimbo asks her.

'I'm a friend of his father,' Linda says.

'Except that Tom is not actually my father,' I say.

'Well, I don't think that's true, Frank,' Linda says.

'Spud,' I say.

'I like Frank,' Linda says. She's determined to bust my balls on this one. I wish she'd come when Kimbo wasn't here.

'Tom may be my biological father, but apart from that he has no moral claim,' I say.

'He was your father for seven years, right?' Linda says, and Kimbo says, 'That's right.'

'And was he a good father in those years?' Linda asks.

I shrug my shoulders. 'Not really,' I say.

'He wasn't all bad,' Kimbo says. God, they're ganging up on me.

'We had some nice times and some shitty times.'

'Well, the nice times, they're worth something, aren't they?' Linda says.

I don't know this woman but clearly Tom has her wrapped around his bony old finger. She's really fighting in his corner.

'Okay, sure,' I say. 'But you know what? Those years don't count. The ones that count are the ones he wasn't there.'

Lucy comes in from the next room with two pieces of track she's struggling to fit together. Kimbo puts them together for her. 'I've almost got it ready,' Lucy says, heading back to the living room. I can't tell if she's listening to the conversation or not.

Kimbo pipes in, saying, 'Just because Tom wasn't there for you it doesn't mean that you shouldn't be there for him.'

'What am I? Jesus? Do I look like Jesus to you?' I say to Kimbo.

'He's in agony. He's paid his price already,' Kimbo says.

'Kimbo, whose side are you on?'

'It's not about sides, you fuckin dickhead.'

'What is this? Christian hour? Did someone change the frequency to Radio God?'

'You are such a dickhead,' she says to me. 'You know, I'm tired of watching you make bad decisions all because of a big fuckin chip on your shoulder. Here's a bumper sticker for you, Spud. GET OVER IT.'

I just laugh at that one. I head to the fridge to get something stronger than a cup of tea.

'Refill, Linda?' I ask, and she says, 'Sure.'

I fill up her glass and fill one for myself as well.

'I tell you, Linda, this lady gives me more shit than you can imagine. I coulda married one of those types that . . . you know . . . agree with you all the time, but instead I got *this*,' I say, and Linda smiles.

Kimbo hits straight back. 'Oh, and meanwhile I am so lucky to have you, Spud. Jesus.'

She continues on her rant. 'Remember when Lucy spewed on the bed that time when you told her not to eat any more ice cream? You seemed capable of forgiveness then—'

'Of course. She's my daughter.'

'Tom's your father,' Linda says.

'It's different.'

'How is it different?' Kimbo says.

I can't believe these two. 'Jesus Christ. You're comparing an ice-cream vomit incident with Tom upping and leaving me for, for the rest of my life.'

'It's not the rest of your life, you stupid dickhead. You think you got no control of your destiny?'

'Yes. That is what I think.'

'Well, Spud, the fact is I can leave you tomorrow if I want to. Or I can stay with you for another year, and it's not fate. It's my decision. And you can be angry at Tom for the rest of your life, or you could give a little old man a break from the hell he must be living in. The decision hasn't been made for you, Spud. The decision is yours to make.'

It pisses me off when Kimbo uses logic on me.

'The train's ready,' Lucy says.

She opens the door and she's set up a beautiful round circle track. She has the Night Mail all set up. A beautiful red train carries two passenger carriages around the track.

'Wow. It's beautiful,' Linda says, and Lucy is beaming.

'You know who gave you that?' Kimbo says, and Lucy says, 'This lady?' and Kimbo shakes her head and looks at me.

I sigh.

'Sure, whatever,' I say. 'It's from your grandfather.'

'Tom?' Lucy says, and I look at Kimbo and shake my head, and she looks back at me, not giving an inch.

We watch the train go round and round and round the track. Tom has good taste. Lucy loves her train. I won't be able to ungive this gift.

Kimbo starts stirring again. 'Spud, tell Linda about your call from Peter Nurse,' she says.

'Huh?'

'The commentator's son,' she says.

'Oh yeah,' I say to Linda. 'Guess who Robert Valentine is?'

Another twenty weeks later (approximately)

Morningtown Park

We're sitting in Kimbo's new ute outside Morningtown Haven. Dick sold me the ute for four hundred. I got a dodgy warrant as it has a lot of rust but apart from that it handles good. Kimbo prefers not relying on me for transport and it's definitely taken some pressure off us. Lucy is in the back seat harping on about wanting an ice cream. She's fidgety and she needs a run around.

A woman in her fifties comes over and knocks on the window, and Kimbo winds it down.

'I'm Karen Strang,' she says. 'I'm Tom's carer. We're just getting him in the car. We haven't told him he's seeing you.'

'How is he?' Kimbo asks.

'Up and down. He's still pretty sharp but his memory is fading. He gets fuzzy on what happened a week ago, but he still holds all the other stuff pretty strong. He's still looking for the eleven-year-old version of you.'

'Well, he's not going to find him,' I say, and Karen says, 'We think it would be good to take him somewhere familiar. Somewhere with a lot of space. Maybe a park.'

'Let's take him to Morningtown Park,' I say.

Karen smiles. 'Okay. Remember he's pretty fragile.'

'I'll be on best behaviour,' I say, and I mean it this time. I've taken my meds, and I'm learning how to breathe through waves of anxiety. I'm learning to live with myself.

'What if he asks about my mother?' I ask.

'There's no need to cause him distress,' Karen Strang says. 'Just change the subject, or talk about her like you haven't seen her for a while.'

'Neither confirm, nor deny, nor tell an outright lie,' Lucy says from the back seat.

'We'll be out in a tick,' Karen says. 'You drive to the park and we'll follow. And remember, if it gets too much, I'm right here.' She has kind eyes. She smiles, and heads off.

Kimbo asks me if I'm okay, and I nod. I wish I didn't have to do this, but I can deal with it. I can do it.

We're at a familiar spot in Kenmure Avenue when the car behind us pulls over. We pull over too and I watch the back mirror and the car door opens and a big Pacific Island guy helps Tom out of the car. Linda is with him too.

'That's his old house,' I say to Kimbo and Lucy.

We watch Tom go up to his front gate and stare at the place, which looks like it has changed a lot since he was a nipper. He looks sad there. He looks older than last time I saw him, if that is possible. I don't know why but I find myself feeling a little bit sorry for him. It's a weird feeling.

Lucy has the soccer ball out and she's in the mood for a good kick around. We're walking down the hill of Morningtown Park and Lucy passes the ball to me and I boot it high in the air and Lucy goes chasing after it like a greyhound after a rabbit.

Kimbo is looking after me like I'm a little kid.

'I'm proud of you, Spud,' she says to me, holding my hand. It's very unlike her. Touchy-feely is not usually her style, but today she's all over me like a blanket. I'm just concentrating on staying calm, and breathing. If there's one thing I've got out of Brenda, it's breathing through a panicky phase.

'I remember this place,' I say to her. 'Tom and Mum took me here for my fifth birthday.'

'Nice place to come for a birthday,' Kimbo says, and I shrug my shoulders.

'It's a park,' I say, and behind Kimbo, coming towards us are

Tom and Linda. Kimbo kisses me and tells me to stay calm, and that she is close by. And she heads down the hill, into the flat area of the park, to kick the ball with Loose the Goose.

Linda comes my way and says, 'Hi. You okay?'

'Yeah,' I say. 'Don't worry. I'm going to be nice.'

And next he walks my way. He's looking at me suspiciously. He doesn't seem angry this time. I can't help it. I'm getting panicky just seeing him. Breathe, Spud. Count to ten and breathe.

I sit down on the grass and he sits beside me, and it feels weird being next to him. I want to run away. I feel it strong. Just keep still, Spud. I'm fumbling in my pockets for my Rescue Remedy but I left it in the car again. Breathe through it.

'Hey, easy, easy. Are you okay?' Tom says to me.

Wow. Seems late in the piece for him to give a shit. I don't know what to say to him. The fantasies I'm having of running away are getting stronger.

'What's your name, son?' he asks me, and that takes me by surprise. Was that on purpose?

'Spud,' I say.

'Spud. Is that a nickname?' he asks, and I laugh, and say, 'Take a look at my face and guess.'

He looks at me, examining my face. I feel shy for some reason.

'Spud,' he says to me, and he seems warm. I'm relieved about that at least.

'I'm sorry. Have we met?' he asks me.

Tom

Escape from Annie

They've shifted me to a luxury asylum. I had to put in a bribe via Linda. I can really trust her 90 per cent of the time. I know she will betray me the other 10 per cent but the odds with her are better than most people here. I'm not sure how much Linda took for herself. Linda doesn't know about the socks. I told her this place lets me go to the bank from time to time, which is true, but I'm still keeping the socks in my suitcase. I've got the case well hidden, but I'm scared to change the combination. I changed it once and I had to write the combination on the back of a receipt, but unfortunately the receipt was in the suitcase. I couldn't get in there for days.

Anyway, this new prison has its benefits. It should have benefits. It cost me a couple of socks. There is a lot more space here, for starters. My room is a lot bigger. They have a piano in the main room, and they have art classes, a few TV rooms, aerobics with a sexy instructor, and they even operate a bar once a week where we get given a glass of low-alcohol beer.

There's another huge benefit to being imprisoned here: I'm back in The City. And I'm back in my old suburb, Morningtown, where I grew up. I've been on my good behaviour strategy so I'm allowed on van trips and we often get to drive around my old neighbourhood.

But no matter how you dress it up, a prison is a prison. I'm still at a loss to know exactly why I'm here. I have made several requests to management here to see Robert Valentine, but no one even pays attention to my requests any more.

I haven't been complaining so much lately. My good behaviour strategy is slowly winning the guards over. I have been as compliant as a lobotomy patient. I've been eating all their food. If something tastes tainted I leave the table and I spit it out into a rubbish bin so they don't know I'm on to them. My act has been convincing. They think I'm completely reformed. They have no idea that I'm hatching plans the whole while.

I've held out for the right opportunity and today's van trip to the Gryphon Theatre's presentation of *Annie* is exactly the opportunity I have been looking for.

I haven't told Karen Strang I am escaping. Karen is another inmate, the only other one remotely close to my age. I admit I've got a flirty thing happening with her too, but it's at a more intellectual level than the usual women I go for. I can't imagine what Karen did to get thrown in here, because she's so kind. Her attitude is 'If I'm going to be here I'm going to help people worse off than me' and I'm with her on that one, genuinely.

I am sad about that as I could be leaving her in here, but I know she doesn't have the testicles needed for a prison escape. I discussed escaping with her once and she encouraged me not to do it. They have her under their spell, unfortunately.

I have dabbled in musical theatre more than I publicly dare to admit, and I know *Annie* particularly well. I've got an accomplice, old Matthew Grace. I've told him to do a runner when the show has hit the half-hour mark, during the song 'I Think I'm Gonna Like It Here'. They trust old Matthew Grace, and he's told me many times he would like to get out of here. The poor doddery fool won't go very far but he's still got a decent sprint in him. If he can make a getaway it can provide exactly the distraction I need to escape.

In the van they put me in the back and they sit the biggest guard, Fui, right next to me. Fui does my belt up far too tight but I don't complain. I just smile and say 'Thank you Fui', and Fui says 'You're in a good mood today.'

The van arrives at the Gryphon, a theatre on the outskirts of The City. A nice old place, this one. I try to trail in at the back of the

360

group so I can sit near an aisle but instead they usher me into a special seat they have saved for me. They try to pretend they've saved me the 'best seat in the house', being in the centre and everything, but I know exactly what they're up to, placing a guard next to me on one side.

As the lights go down I look along the aisle at old Matthew Grace and he looks back at me. I wink to him and he winks back. He's beautifully placed right at the end of an aisle. I'm figuring that as soon as he makes his run I will vault the seat and climb two rows ahead, where there is no one sitting. From there I can get away and take my chances getting to the exit. I've briefed old Matthew Grace to head down Galloway Street towards town. That way I can run in the opposite direction and even if some of them chase me their numbers will be split badly, especially with some guards having to stay inside to make sure there's not a mass prison breakout.

The curtains open and all the fogeys around me gasp at the set. I hear a bunch of them talking to each other and another bunch telling them to be quiet. There's a bit of a kerfuffle in front of us when Marj Baker kicks Sally in the shins for talking too much, but they settle down, and when the cast sings 'Hard Knock Life' some of the fogeys sing along too. I don't think Annie is the same when you have teenagers playing kids. Still, I do enjoy watching the actress playing Miss Hannigan. She reminds me of Deborah when we first got together. I wouldn't mind chatting to Miss Hannigan after the show and spending some quality time with her. Almost makes me not want to escape.

When 'Tomorrow' is sung Sally gets to her feet and a guard has to restrain Marj from yanking her down again. All the fogeys are singing along now and I join in the chorus. It's a beautiful song and I feel tears coming to my eyes as we all sing it like it was a national anthem. After that I know my escape is only three songs away. During 'We'd Like to Thank You, Herbert Hoover' I look over at my guard who is completely absorbed in the thing, and I see everyone's faces. They all look so peaceful, like a bunch of little kids seeing a show for the first time. I look over at old Matthew Grace and he is entranced by the thing. I hope he doesn't get distracted by the show. I need his A game if I'm going to pull this off. I look over at him and this time he looks back and gives me the thumbs up, a bit too obviously for my liking but it goes unnoticed by everyone else.

When Annie and the other girls in the orphanage are shown the mansion I use my peripheral vision and I can see my guard is distracted by the show. I'm getting real fidgety and excited.

Finally the opening lines to 'I Think I'm Gonna Like It Here' come on, and I look over to old Matthew Grace and he's looking at the song with a face like a virgin having his first orgasm. Jesus! He's gone back to some happy place and he's showing no signs of doing a runner. Idiot! I want to get his attention so I reach into my pocket and I find some chewing gum so I chomp on that and I take it out of my mouth and I hiff it at him. It hits him on the side of the face and he doesn't even notice. I'm hoping maybe he's decided he's enjoying the song so much that he's waiting until the song is finished and then he'll do a runner. The song finishes and I look over at him and still he's watching, like he's been frozen into some permanent state of inner peace. Stupid old coot! He's stuffing up everything!

Two songs later during 'You Won't Be An Orphan For Long' he's dozed off and I officially have to abandon today's great escape. I need to find a better accomplice in this place.

Jesus, I'm frustrated as the lights come on for half-time and I'm still here! We don't even get to stay for the second half as the show is too long for the oldies and I'm watched carefully as they take me back into the van. On the way back one of the old ducks, Cheryl, surprises us when she starts singing 'Do You Hear The People Sing?' Poor old dear thinks she just saw *Les Misérables*. Still, no one minds. She's a fine singer and none of us has heard her say anything for quite a while. It's nice to see her animated and her voice even picks up my mood.

On the way back we pass the beach and I hear Ernie start banging the window of the van furiously. Poor old Ernie has lost all his consonants. All he's got left are vowels and when he sees the beach

he starts thumping the windows and yelling, 'Aaaaaooooiiiieeaii-
ioouueeeeeee!!!'

'Shut him up!' Marj yells, but he's going nuts watching the ocean
out there.

'He wants the water,' I say. 'Let him see the water!' but the van
keeps driving.

'Cruel heartless bastards,' I say, but I'm drowned out by Ernie,
yelling, 'Aaaaeeeaaaeeeaaaaaaaiiiiioooeeeeeee!'

Suddenly the van veers left up on to a sand dune and parks next
to the beach.

'All right, Ernie,' says the driver and Ernie is stamping his feet
with excitement. I hope he doesn't wet himself.

Fui opens the door and helps Ernie out. Ernie takes off in a
straight line for the sea and Fui lets him go, as Ernie runs about as
fast as a paraplegic with his shoelaces tied together.

Suddenly there's a mass exodus on to the beach and Karen
Strang helps some of the oldies get out of the van. Karen Strang
puts the passion in compassion. I wouldn't mind her showing me a
little compassion, even if she is a decade or two older than my
preferred compassionate companion. You spend enough time with
the geriatrics and a forty-year-old starts looking like one of Charlie's
Angels.

They're all out now and Fui sits back in the van with me and
says, 'Sorry, Tom. You have to stay.'

'What! That's not fair!'

'You'll do a runner. You're too quick for me.'

So I have to sit and watch in the van while all the oldies are
walking along the beach.

'Please,' I beg, but he won't budge.

I sit in there and I see Sally getting her feet wet even though she
is wearing her shoes. Because Fui has stayed with me in the van
they don't have enough people out there to keep control of them,
but fortunately Karen Strang lends a hand and helps out.

In the distance I can see Ernie has finally made it to the water
and we can hear him even from the van, running at seagulls and
screaming when his feet are in the water. The ocean never heard so

many vowels in one sentence. 'Ooooeeeiiiiaaiiiiiiaaaeeeeeeeuu-ueeee!!!'

When they get back to the van I can smell the salt on them. There are a lot of dripping trouser legs but everyone seems happy for once. There's a lot of giggling. As we take off I look into Ernie's eyes and they are full of tears.

Convoy to Morningtown Park

Another great advantage of the luxury asylum is that there is a smoking area, and a bunch of us are outside and Robert Valentine's azaleas are doing a lot of passive smoking. I've got Len sitting next to me moaning as he puffs on his ciggy.

'They're stealing my money,' he says. 'They've stolen my house from me too.'

'You think you got problems. They've abducted my son.'

But Len's not listening to me.

'They got my house,' he says. 'They sold my house and they've kept all the money.'

'Yeah, well, what can you do?' I say, and I throw my hands in the air and across from us, Elva, the tiniest little old lady you ever saw, is knitting a pattern that looks quite mangled.

'That's some scarf you got there,' I say.

'It's for my grandson,' she says, smiling to me. I look closer and even though the pattern is going astray I sure hope he appreciates it.

'I've got twenty-seven grandchildren,' she says.

'Your family must be good breeders,' I shoot back and I watch the skilful way she folds needle over needle in an elaborate sequence of movements.

She says, without even looking at me, 'It's very rude to smoke a cigarette in front of a lady and not offer her one.'

I apologize and I hand her a cigarette. Both her hands are busy so I put it in her mouth and she waits while I light it for her.

'Did you know that I have quit smoking fourteen times,' she says, and I see a new arrival in the smoking area, and she looks resplendent today. She must have dyed her hair recently because that red hair looks too good to be true.

'Hi, Tom,' she says to me. 'You excited about your trip?'

'Hi, Linda,' I say, looking at her gorgeous face. 'What trip?'

We're in my room getting my things. My room here is nice and spacious. Linda got me some beautiful furniture. I've got an old mahogany wardrobe and really nice wallpaper. A tasteful shade of faded green. I've got pictures on the wall, including one Linda gave me, a class photo of Frank.

Today Linda has brought me several new books to read. I like having the books around but my attention span is dropping. I make it about ten pages in and then I can't be bothered reading any more. The books combine with the drugs they're putting in my food to bring on an insidious form of narcolepsy. I've been getting tired and I can't keep up with what is happening as well. I'm getting fogged up, and I'm starting to get used to this place. It's all a part of the brainwashing process – it's starting to feel like my brain has already been half washed.

Linda puts the books in my bookcase, next to my atlas and my book of giant insect photos. Linda finds a big red book the size of an encyclopedia beside my Funk & Wagnalls. She opens the front page and smiles.

'This is your life!' she says.

That's right. I never thought I'd make it on to *This Is Your Life* but they've given me a book and everything.

Linda thumbs through the book and gets to a section full of photos of Frank.

I struggle to look at those photos. I love that kid. Frank, I'll find you as soon as I get out of this place. They've been poisoning my food but as soon as I get out of here I'm sure I'll get a little less foggy and I'll find you.

She shows me one of Frank feeding the ducks. He's squinting in the photo. 'Frank takes after my mother unfortunately. He didn't inherit my wife's good looks,' I say.

'He's good-looking,' she says.

'Okay, he's unconventionally good-looking then. Can we compromise on that?' I say, and Linda says to me, 'Well, in that way he takes after his father,' and she shoots me a wink.

'How come it's got a bulldog clip on it?' Linda asks, pointing to a clip that holds the last third of the book shut.

'There are some photos I don't like to look at,' I say. They've put a whole lot of photos in the book that are designed to give me the heebie-jeebies. That's how it works in the luxury asylum. They act all nice but they're always thinking of sneaky ways to undermine me at every turn.

I'm in a convoy.

I'm in the back seat of a car and sitting next to me is Fui. Linda is in the front seat with the driver. On the other side of Fui, also in the back seat, is Karen Strang, who for some reason has also been allowed out for a trip. I'm pleased she's here and there doesn't seem to be any weirdness between her and Linda, which is a relief.

Everyone is making a big deal out of this trip. The car is travelling slowly, the way cars do when they come out of a funeral. The driver is extremely careful about not letting the car in front of us out of our sight. Who is in that car? Robert Valentine?

It's nice driving through my old neighbourhood. 'This is where I grew up,' I say to Linda. 'I bought iced buns from that bakery.'

'I love an iced bun,' she says. 'Pink or white?'

'Both, they did both, but I like a white iced bun.'

'I like pink,' she says.

'You say tomato, I say *tomayto*,' I say, and she laughs and Karen Strang and Fui are smiling too.

We drive past my old house. I ask them to stop the car and they let me get out but Fui comes with me to make sure I don't do a runner. He's got his arm around my arm. I always have to have him on my shoulder. I'm lucky he's a likeable guy.

I say that to Fui. 'You should get me a leash. Seriously. Wouldn't it be nicer for both of us if you just had a leash and I could get ten metres away from you. It's practical.'

He can't tell if I'm joking or not and to be really honest I can't tell any more either.

I feel kind of sad seeing the old house. I can picture running around that front yard when I was little, and it feeling like such a big front yard. I love that big old bushy tree on one side, and the tree that had died years ago but we left it up anyway. And I loved the old oak tree. I did a lot of climbing and dangling upside down from branches in that tree. The house has changed dramatically, but the oak tree looks the same as I remember it.

Linda is next to me now, saying, 'You grew up here?'

'I spent the first eighteen years of my life here.'

'Wow,' she says.

'It makes me sad looking at it. I don't know why.'

'It's your childhood. When I sold my parents' house I completely freaked out,' she says.

'To see it now, you'd never know that there was a blue letterbox here and a green door down there with three white rectangles on the front, and the cat bowl used to sit down there and, and the hedgehog used to eat out of the cat's bowl and . . .'

Oh boy, I don't know. It just makes me feel sad. She rubs her hand into my shoulder and I feel pleased to have a friend in this world.

The car in front of us has stopped too. The driver has gone to talk to them and soon I'm ushered back into our car and we slowly drive by my old school.

'I broke that window!' I say to Linda as we drive past a window that I threw an apple through.

'They've got a big old school bell. I had the job of ringing it and no one realized that I was ringing the bell at 2.58 every day so that all my friends could get off school two minutes early!'

'You're a strange card, Tom,' Linda says, then she adds, 'You're the Ace of Spades,' and she smiles.

'I'm the Jack of Diamonds,' I say, and we head down Mailer Road.

★

We're walking down to Morningtown Park. It hasn't changed a lot. The playground is where it always was – at the top of a long grassy bank. It's a nice place to sit and eat a sandwich. Then there's a basin area where sports games can be held. I played soccer on this field. I was a defender. But I would often go off duty and charge up the field in pursuit of glory. My teacher kept telling me off for not sticking to a pattern. Typical me. And I thought I was such a bright spark! What a young idiot.

'Charisma will only take you so far,' my father used to say to me, and I was so stupid I thought *he* was the one who didn't know what he was talking about! Ha!

Linda's got my ear and she says to me, 'I'm here for you, Tom. If you need my help you just wave to me and I'll come and get you.'

'Okay. What's going on?'

'You have a visitor,' she says. 'I don't know if you'll recognize him. You haven't seen him for a quite a while. I've met him, and he's okay. Honestly.'

'Wow,' I say. 'I feel like I've been driven to a crematorium.'

'No, Tom. Not in the slightest. He's a friend. I promise.'

'And why do I trust you again?' I ask her, and she gives me a hug and whispers in my ear, 'Because I love you, Tom. I love you very much.' She kisses me on the cheek and in front of me a guy is waiting . . .

I recognize him.

It's that guy. The guy from the . . .

The guy who . . .

I know this guy. He . . .

I know him.

I know his face . . .

He looks nervous, like he's having some kind of attack.

'Hey, easy, easy, are you okay?' I say to him.

He laughs and coughs and looks down at the ground.

'What's your name, son?' I ask him.

He shakes his head and laughs again and he looks at me again. He seems really agitated.

'Spud,' he says.

'Spud? Is that a nickname?' I ask, and he says, 'Take a look at my face and guess.' Indeed his face bears an uncanny resemblance to a potato.

'Spud,' I say to myself, trying to track the name. They've brainwashed a lot of information out of me at the luxury asylum, but the name rings a bell.

'I'm sorry,' I say to him. 'Have we met?'

'Really? You don't recognize me?' he asks.

'I . . . your face feels familiar,' I say to him and he looks down at the ground. He's fumbling around with the grass.

'I have a special talent,' I say to him. 'I can forget things if they upset me. My brain has an "erase the painful memory" button.'

'I wish I had that button,' he says. 'But I wouldn't use it, you know? If I could get rid of my memories, I wouldn't get rid of the bad ones. Because without them, the good memories are meaningless, you know?'

I can feel myself nodding.

'You're running with a "life is good and bad" theory here?'

'Something like that. You really don't know who I am?' he asks, and I look at his face, looking for clues to who he is. He feels familiar. I just can't get a fix on it. I'm sure he must be tied up with Robert Valentine. I want to ask him where Frank is, but I choose to wait and see what he has to say.

I fumble in my pockets and pull out a pack of cigarettes, and I shield a small breeze and light up and feel calmer as I drag it in. He looks at me jealously.

'You want one?'

'No. I use patches,' he says and he lifts his shirt sleeve and there is a little patch, like a round bandage.

'Wow,' I say. 'That's a strange way of getting cancer.'

'The idea is it will stop me from getting cancer,' he says.

'So you'll just go and die of something else,' I say, and he laughs as I take a big drag of light relief from the sucker.

'How dare you be funny,' he says. 'I'm mad at you. You're not allowed to be funny.'

'Why are you mad at me? You're mad at me? I'm mad at you.'

'Why are you mad at me?' he says.

'I don't know any more. You did something. I don't know what it was.'

'I grew up,' he says, and I look at him and I laugh.

'Okay,' I say, 'I've grown up too.'

'I find that hard to believe,' he says.

'Wow, you must know me well to say a thing like that.'

'I guess so. I don't know if I know you or not,' he says. 'You're a very confusing person to know.'

'I've made a lot of mistakes,' I say to him. 'I'm sorry if one of my mistakes made things hard for you. I can understand why you would be angry at me if that's what happened. Is that what happened?'

'Yes,' he says.

I look over at Linda and she is watching us. She smiles and gives me a little wave.

Spud clears his throat like he's practised what he is going to say to me. 'When my daughter was eleven months old, I had to look after her in the bassinet,' he says. 'You know, just half an hour looking after her unsupervised. She was crying and I didn't know how to help her, and I had this fantasy.'

'Where's this going?'

'I had this fantasy of running away. Just picking up and running away. But I didn't, Tom. I didn't run away. It was just a fantasy,' he says, and he looks upset.

'Hey,' I say to him. 'I can understand why you feel guilty about that. I've done worse. Believe me. I've done far, far worse,' and I find myself reaching out to this guy, putting my arm around his back.

Down below in the park a mother and a son are running around kicking a soccer ball. The mother is a pretty poor kicker. She completely lacks coordination but she's giving it a good go. The son is skilful though.

'That's not Frank. That's a girl. My daughter,' Spud says.

'Oh? Really? And that's your wife?'

371

'Yeah. She has two left feet.'

'You can say that again.' We both laugh as she runs at a ball, kicks it hard and somehow it goes behind her. That's not easy to do.

Makes me think of the games I used to play with Frank. Oh, gosh. We had some great times but it would sure erupt from time to time. He pretends he's a tough kid, but he's a sensitive sort, is Frank.

'I used to play hide and seek with my son,' I say. 'Only it didn't go so well.'

'What do you mean?' he says.

'He was too good at hiding,' I say and I smile at the guy.

He says to me, 'Maybe you were a lazy seeker.'

I have to laugh at that. That's very good. A lazy seeker.

We look back down at the girl and her mother and Spud says to me, 'You know, I used to play hide and seek with my dad. He'd hunt all around the house for me . . .'

And I can picture myself hunting around the house for Frank. Jesus, I would be looking everywhere. Under the bed, behind the fridge. In the shower behind the shower curtain. In the wardrobe. I could get quite panicky searching. 'I know what that's like,' I say.

The guy continues. 'But after a while he'd just give up. Do something else,' he says, and I'm picturing myself trying to calm down, knowing he'll come back, reading the newspaper in the lounge and waiting for him to come out.

'So here I would be,' Spud is saying, 'in a really good hiding place. And I feel good because I'm not being found . . . but I'm thinking, Why doesn't he look for me harder?'

'Well, maybe your father got into a panic,' I say.

'A panic?'

'Yeah, a panic, you know?'

He looks sceptical so I let it pass. Instead both of us watch mother and daughter below. The little girl skilfully flips the ball up with her foot and then kicks it high in the air and then she tries to catch it. At the last moment she tries to run away from it and it hits her in the shoulder. It's highly comical.

'Funny kid,' I say, as the girl does a great Hollywood dive and lies on the ground giggling at how badly her trick went.

'Yeah, she's a strange one. Like her mother,' Spud says and I have a good giggle. She's a livewire.

'My boy's a strange one too,' I say. 'He's kind of . . . angry.'

'Oh yeah. Why do you think he's angry?'

'I don't know. Maybe it's genetic?' I suggest.

'Are you angry, Tom?' Spud asks, and I have to admit, he's got me there. I've got a lot to be angry about. But anger is hard to sustain, you know? I'm getting too tired for anger.

'I don't know. Yes. No. Sometimes. Who doesn't get angry? I mean, I'm normal. My son is, how do I say this, he's got a chip on his shoulder.'

'Oh yeah,' Spud says. 'My father is one of those guys who looks after himself all the time. He thinks he's – what's the word – charismatic, and he thinks he can make up for any shitty behaviour by pouring on the charm.'

'He sounds full of himself,' I say.

'He is,' Spud says, and he looks like it's really affected him. But he's forgetting that his father is just a human being who's made a lot of mistakes.

'Maybe deep down, underneath it all, your father is . . .'

'He's what?'

'He's . . . he's hiding something.'

'And what would he be hiding?'

'I don't know. I don't know the man. Maybe he loves you and he's just very very bad at showing it.'

A breeze comes up and I can feel myself getting emotional. I look over at where Linda is sitting and she is with Karen Strang and Fui and they all have this Are you okay? face on. Linda starts to come over our way, but I put my hand up to say I'm okay.

I want to sit with this guy for a bit longer. He's fidgeting. Playing with the grass and pulling it up out of the ground. Whole root structures and everything.

'Found your son yet?' he asks me, sounding almost angry.

'No. You know where he is?' I ask him, and he smiles and nods and pulls up a big tuft of grass. The roots are twice the size of the grass.

'You know, you're not the only person who's lost someone,' he says. 'I lost my father when I was seven.'

'That must have been awful,' I say to him and he nods.

'It was,' he says quietly.

'Were you close?' I ask, and he shakes his head and then contradicts himself with a nod.

'I thought we were,' he says.

'I'm sure you were,' I say, trying to comfort him.

'Actually, I think he really didn't give much of a second thought about me.'

'I'm sure he thought about you all the time,' I say, and I look into his eyes, which are filling with tears, like a little kid.

I get into his eyeline and I say to him, 'I know that because, well, my son, I really . . . I didn't used to think about him. I was selfish. I really think there were times when my mind was on other things and I feel bad about that, but now . . . now I think about him all the time,' I say, and he wipes his eyes with his hand.

Then he looks at me, and he says, 'My father walked out on me at school one day.'

I don't like the sound of this story.

'He came to pick me up and . . . and he saw me at the gate and . . . and . . .'

And I'm picturing myself on my final day in The City, when I went to visit Frank at school. I knew I was leaving town, but I had to see him one more time, but I didn't want him to see me, and he saw me, and he ran after me . . .

'I don't want to hear this story,' I say to him, and all I can see is Frank's face brighten when he sees me. He comes towards me and I panic, and I'm running away from him. I'm running away from him and he's chasing after me.

There's a bus ahead and I run and I catch the bus. I go to the back seat and I can see him shrieking on the side of the road and I can't look any more, I can't look and I turn around and I tell myself I'm doing this for the good of everyone. I'm doing everyone a

374

favour by getting out of their lives. I shouldn't have come back and seen him, and I tell myself, 'Don't look back. Don't look back or you'll turn into a block of salt. It's for the best, for everyone. Keep your eyes in front of you and don't look back.'

I've got my hands over my face, trying to block it out, and Spud is next to me.

'My father ran away from me,' he says. 'He ran away and he never returned.'

'Where did he go?'

'You tell me,' he says, and I look into his eyes and I don't know what I can say to him.

'Your father doesn't sound like a nice person,' I say.

'I don't know what he is,' Spud says.

I feel a real need to explain to him, to explain to him why a man could do something so . . . hurtful, but I can't explain it. Instead I find myself fumbling. Fumbling for words . . .

'You know, sometimes people have their reasons . . . Sometimes . . . Sometimes people don't cope, you know? Sometimes when life gets on top of some people . . . they panic and they . . . they want to scream out and say, "I can't do this any more." They want to kill themselves but they don't want to do that to everyone around them so they just . . . they just disappear, you know?'

And I'm picturing Frank as a little kid, sitting on his swing . . .

And I can see him the day we got him back from the hospital, in his little cot, sleeping with his hands in the air . . .

I'm staring at this tiny little face, and I'm shaking my head, whispering to him . . . whispering to him, 'Hey there. Hey there, little friend . . .'

Now Spud and I are both crying. But I feel better that I can share this with him. I don't know why. He doesn't feel like a stranger right now.

I look him in the eye, and I say, 'Please. Tell me honestly. Is Frank okay?'

He thinks about it for a bit, and he says, 'Frank is fine.'

'Everyone says that.'

'Yeah, well, they were lying. Frank wasn't fine. He had a lot of hard shit to get through. But he's fine now. He's . . . he's more at peace with himself now.'

'You sound like a therapist,' I say to him. 'I should know. I've slept with one.'

'Bullshit,' he says, laughing, and I say, 'Really. Really.' And he shakes his head and then he goes very quiet, very still.

I pat his back and he laughs and he wipes his tears away and rubs them into the grass, and he says, 'Your son is . . . he's okay. He's getting on with his life. Living day to day. He's a survivor.'

There's something about the way he says it. I believe him. Frank is okay. Frank is a survivor. It hasn't been easy for him but he's okay now.

I look Spud in the eyes and they are red from crying. He's looks like a big, ugly, beautiful kid.

'You know where Frank is?' I ask him and he nods.

'I want to see him,' I say.

'Maybe one day you will,' he says to me. For some reason that sends a shiver down my spine, and he leans towards me, and kisses me on the forehead.

A good egg

On my way home, Linda and I are both in the back seat. She's got her arm around me. She's rubbing my back. I don't really feel like talking, but I'm okay.

'Tom, I think I know who Robert Valentine is,' she says.

I look at her.

'You were right. The commentator's son, Peter Nurse, has been in touch. His father Walter had a Robert Valentine running around his paddocks. I'd say he had a soft spot for him, because even though he never raced he kept him around the stables anyway. He lived to the age of nine.'

'Wait. Are you telling me Robert Valentine is a horse?' I ask.

Linda looks at me, with a flicker of a smile in her eye.

I'm back in the luxury asylum, in my cell. I'm reaching into the wardrobe into the dark area right at the edge. I pull out my Lethalite case and I put it on the bed.

I open up the suitcase and it stinks to high heaven. The fungus that's living in those socks is getting out of control. I've got some of the odorizer spray they use in the bathrooms here and I give it a good spray but it doesn't help much; just makes me cough a lot.

I count the socks and there are only fifteen now. Still, that's easily enough cash to use for one final bribe to get me out of this place at some point, if I spy a good opportunity.

I reach underneath the lint remover and open up the hip-flask and I'm down to my final drop of whisky. I'll have to ask Linda for a sneaky refill.

I pull out the underwater camera. I'm thinking I might ask Linda to get these damned photos developed. I'm expecting it will just be a bunch of out-of-focus aqua. Maybe if I'm lucky I might get a good look at Deborah's swimsuit or a big turtle. Who knows?

I'm a bit scared to look at them of course, so I might tell Linda, 'If there's something you think I don't want to see, don't show me.'

I'm about to close the case again when I spy something glinting at me. It's the gold wrapping of an Easter egg. I'm worried all these Easter eggs will be tainted by the smell of my socks if I leave them there much longer.

I mean, what the hell am I waiting for?

I'm heading down the hallway and here's old Cheryl, hobbling to her room.

'Happy Easter, Cheryl,' I say to her.

She looks up at me and says, 'Are you my husband?'

'No. I'm the Easter bunny,' I say and I hand her a marshmallow egg and she looks at it and says, 'Oooh.'

Next I've made it into the main room and they're all finishing their poisonous meal and I announce as loud as I can, 'HAPPY EASTER, I'M THE EASTER BUNNY!' and I hop from table to table dropping Easter eggs next to their meals.

A lot of them are shrieking with excitement like a bunch of little kids. I'm dancing around like an aid worker handing out food to starving children. I help old Selma unwrap her marshmallow, and Karen Strang pats me on the back and says, 'You're a good man, Tom,' and I sneak her a kiss on the cheek and I yell, 'HAP-PY EAS-TERRRR!' and I run around the room handing out all the Easter eggs, Easter eggs for everyone. The guards are helping the old fogeys unwrap their eggs and it makes my heart swell to see the joy I have brought everyone, for once.

'You're a good egg,' one of them jokes to me, and I yell, 'I like that. I'm a good egg.' I save the final Easter egg for old Ernie. He's drooling like the Niagara Falls as I open his egg for him, and when he puts the chocolate to his mouth he shrieks a good 'Ooooeeeiiiiaaaiiiiii' and I'm celebrating with him. 'Ooouuueeiiiaaaaiiiii,' I'm singing as he eats his chocolate.

I go to the piano and I thump out one of the only four tunes I know but instead of singing words I'm singing, 'Happy Easter, happy Easter, happy Easter,' and I've got all the oldies singing and clapping with me and then I thump a new tune on the piano and I'm singing, 'For I'm a jolly good fellow, for I'm a jolly good fellow,' and they're all joining in, even the guards, singing, 'and so say all of us, and so say all of us, and soooooo say allllll of usssssss.'

I finish playing and I look back at the scene before me, and there's chocolate dribbling down their chins and it's nice to see everyone jolly. I hope to hell my socks haven't contaminated the chocolate because what an irony that would be, if my act of altruism was to result in an outbreak of food poisoning that finished half of them off. Wouldn't that just be typical!

Ha!

Spud

104 weeks later

The ruthless cull

We have a celebration coming up. Kimbo's family are coming from all over for a gathering, and Kimbo wants to throw a party in the back yard. So I got Lucy and a couple of the boys helping out, carting stuff to a skip.

I've already cleared half the back yard and I chucked in a whole lot of big old truck tyres and filled them with soil and Kimbo has been trying her hand at growing vegetables in them. The silver beet was pretty good, the potatoes were not so good and the rhubarb was a total failure. Both Lucy and I got a small bout of food poisoning from Kimbo's first attempt at a rhubarb crumble. I hope the soil's not full of arsenic. I've been trying to track through in my mind what kind of crap may have been sitting where the veggie patch is growing. I have a feeling I used to have a bunch of old car batteries there. It's better not to think about it.

There is a roped-off area where I've been trying to get some grass growing but the grass isn't interested. The grass seed just sits on top of the mud like a decoration.

I got a big tin drum in the middle that we'll turn into an open fire. Knowing Kimbo's family antics I'll be lucky if the house doesn't burn down.

We're carting out most of the barbecues from the barbecue collection, which is up to twenty-seven! Kimbo is going to sell them on the internet but in the meantime she wants them out of the back yard. I said to her that I didn't like double-handling but she just wants to see the back yard before her family descends. I've kept six barbecues though, as it means we can have a good gathering around and be cooking enough food to keep them all happy.

I'm having to make some tough decisions about what I can sell and what I will never sell. The boys have just finished carting the last of the wood to the truck. Lucy has a wheelbarrow full of fire-wood that she's shifting from the shed to outside. Kimbo has got a buyer for the steering wheel columns, so Muzz is wrapping them up and loading them into his truck.

There's a bunch of big old rocks and masonry that will be a pisser to get rid of. Two big pieces were dropped off by Joey years ago as a joke. The rocks sit in the middle of the back yard like Stonefuckinhenge. They'd take a mammoth effort to shift, so we're going to build a rock garden around them. Besides, Lucy loves clambering up them and doing her superhero impressions from up there. We got an old trampoline next to one of the rocks and Lucy loves doing daredevil jumps from there. I've given up trying to encourage her to be more of a girl.

We got a bunch of old fridge-freezers that are on their way to Muzz's truck, and another bunch of whiteware that Kimbo has told me I will never ever sell so that goes into the skip too. I've chucked most of the bikes in the skip but I've held on to two BMX bikes so Lucy and her mates can hoon around the back yard. I might make her a little track with a few jumps and everything.

The Citroën is rusted so badly it's not worth anything, so that's going. And there's been a lot of debate over the aeroplane cockpit. It's from a little plane and it always sits upside down so it doesn't fill up with water. Lucy wants to keep it at the house. Kimbo wants either to get rid of it or take it to the yard. Muzz had the idea that we could fill it with soil and Kimbo could grow some carrots in it. Kimbo wins the day, of course, and it gets loaded on to Muzz's truck. Lucy can do her Red Baron impressions out at the farm.

I have to do a big clear-out of the basement too. Easier said than done for a hoarder, but I have to be tough. Kimbo has been very clear on the subject. I've been in here for most of the day, pulling out stuff. I got a big box of VHS video tapes that have no value whatsoever but it was fun looking through them and seeing what people taped.

I have to be ruthless, Kimbo keeps telling me. If we can't get fifty bucks for it, it's not worth the effort of selling it. But I find sorting it difficult. An old rusted spade (chuck it), gas bottles (keep), sandpaper (keep), a big old lathe that doesn't work any more (biff), an old toy rabbit (chuck, no, keep), an old chest expander from when I was a teenager (chuck), an old empty filing cabinet (ha, me? Filing? What was I thinking? Chuck), an old ghetto blaster (chuck), a church pulpit (sell), an old still working ECG heart monitor (keep), some traffic lights (a definite keeper), my mother's jewellery box (definite keeper), a box of high-heeled shoes (sell? No, chuck, but don't tell Kimbo), a carved wooden pineapple I got from a trip to Hawaii (chuck), a framed photograph of a snow monkey (chuck), an almost complete collection of the *Encyclopedia Britannica* with a missing L–M volume (chuck), and Tom's old suitcase (chuck, no, keep, no, chuck).

I throw the suitcase into a skip full of crap I have collected over the last twenty years. Tom left me the suitcase in his will.

I feel a bit guilty about throwing it into the skip, so I climb back in and I have a good look at it. It's a green Lethalite case still in okay condition, a bit dusty, sure, but it's a nice case. It has a combination lock. I try a few obvious numbers, the date and month of Tom's birth, the year of Tom's birth, Deb's birthday, before I try the year of my birthday. It opens clean and I'm hit with a stench as bad as rotting fish, as it is full of Tom's old socks. They are rolled up and they smell rancid. I empty them into the skip and I hunt through the other contents. A lint roller (chuck), some gum (chuck), some underpants (chuck), and I come to a bunch of photos.

The photos are hazy and green, and I can see a couple of legs and I can see, what is that? These photos have been taken underwater. What the hell is that a photo of? Is that a turtle?

There's one of my mother. That photo must have been taken a long time ago. I thumb through other photos, most of them just an out-of-focus green haze, before I come to a photo of my mother next to a turtle. She's smiling and she looks young. Younger than me, younger than Kimbo, I don't remember her this young. There's something about the expression on her face. She's looking straight at the camera and she looks wary, but she looks vulnerable too. I stare at her and I can feel her presence somehow.

The next photo is of the two of them, Tom and my mother, or I should say the three of them because there's a turtle's head in the foreground. The photo looks like it was taken by Tom, as his arm is outstretched and it's not aimed that well. Some of Mum's face is out of the photo, but they both are striking a pose, like a couple of young lovers. It's all a bit out of focus but I can see by the way he is holding her that he loved her. I feel a wave of anxiety looking at them this young, but it doesn't grip me like it used to. I can look at the past better now.

I empty out the case and I take it through to the kitchen and I clean it out and scrub it down and I hang it in the dish rack. I'll use it for something. I don't know what.

I take the photo of Mum, Tom and the turtle and I go to my room, I open a drawer that has a little book of photos, and I pop it in there next to a photo of Lucy on her eighth birthday.

And I think, Fuck it, give the photo a frame and I drag one out of the wardrobe and it fits fine. I take the photo to the mantelpiece and sit it there and I take a few steps back and I look at it, trying to figure if it's going to bother me, looking at that photo, day after day.

I turn it around to face the wall.

Lucy comes in and sees me with the photo. 'What are you doing?' she asks.

I laugh. 'I'm trying to decide whether to have this picture facing the room or facing the wall.'

'Why would you put up a picture facing the wall?' she asks, and as always, she's right, so I turn it around to face the room, and now I've got all three of them staring at me: my mother, my father and some turtle.

Acknowledgements

There are a lot of people I need to thank. Thanks to my brother, Robert Sarkies, who had the original idea and has been incredibly supportive throughout the long journey of writing this. And to my partner Nic Marshall and my son Stanley Sarkies, who have both kept me buoyant throughout with their support, love and day-to-day ridiculousness.

Special thanks to those who have read for me and offered up their two valuable cents: Alison Wong, Nick White, Graeme Tuckett, Anna Cameron, Peter Mckenzie, Fiona Elwood, Jan Hide, Dean Hewison, Emily Anderton, Toby Manhire and Crawford Duncan.

Thanks to all those I interviewed who were so generous with their knowledge and time: Warren Trent (especially for letting me raid your photo album), Bull Pepere, Doug Hall, Bernadine Lynch, Crawford Duncan, Jan Hide, Darryl Burrows, Peter Mckenzie, Graham Carthew, Greg Halpin, Kate Pope, Murray Thompson, Paul Harper, Peter Entwistle and Tony Lee.

Thanks to the great listeners I shared the story with in the early stages: Quintin Ellery, Sophie Wooles, Simon Morris, Regan O'Brien, Manu Berry, Amelia Pascoe, Jo Langford, Andy Chappell and Sophie Dingemans.

Special thanks to everyone at John Murray, especially Eleanor Birne, Roland Philipps, Becky Walsh and Morag Lyall. Thanks to Katie Haworth from Penguin NZ (who was an absolute godsend), and my agent Georgia Garrett who has been so generous with her feedback.

Thanks to the following people whose work has inspired this novel: Tom Waits (an incredible influence on me), Naomi Feil, Christine Bryden, Peter Wells, Oliver Sacks, Elmer Wheeler, Robert L Shook, Walter Mosley, Mickey Spillane, Keith Haub, Wayne Brittenden, Peter Falk, Brian Kiteley and Stephen Koch.

From the Department of Miscellaneous Helpfulness: Sean O'Brien, Sandra Burt, John Lake, Chris Kelly, Andy Mosse, Peter and Diane Beatson, Matt Grace, Karen Armitage, the amazing staff at Village at the Park, Michael from Rialto Dunedin, Antonia Wallace, Conrad Coom, Creative New Zealand (9th time lucky), Diane Lowe, John Sheehan, Roy Colbert, Kiri Griffin, Des Coppins, Matt Reid, Phillippa Scott and Peter Marshall for his magnificent method-handwriting.

Lastly to all of my wonderful friends, family and loved ones, especially Moira Halliday, Catherine Sinclair, Mel Johnston, Vicky Pope, Chris Bourke, Meredith Marshall and all the other Marshalls, Christine Sarkies, Jane Cameron, Jo Randerson, Sophie Burbery, Max, Buster, Barney, Walter and Ursula, Jemaine Clement, Stephen Templer, James Milne, Miranda Manasiadis, Hone Kouka, Danny Mulheron, Chris Kunz, Ally Jackson, Anna Mcleod, Simon Wilson, Christine Smith, Kim Acland, Mark Williams, Chris House, Rachel Lister, Rebecca Guppy, Jon Coddington, Gert Verhoog, Willemijn Vermaat, Nick McGowan, Mr Meros, Tao Wells and Mushka.

For more information visit the author's website at
www.duncansarkies.co.nz

392